Grandson of Herod

Iesvs Nazarenvs Rex Ivdaeorvm

Joseph Raymond

Tower Grove Publishing
St. Louis, MO USA

Grandson of Herod

Iesvs Nazarenvs Rex Ivdaeorvm

ISBN-10: 0615681697
ISBN-13: 978-0-615-68169-6

Other Books by Joseph Raymond

Herodian Messiah, Case for Yeshua as Grandson of Herod
(Tower Grove Publishing 2010)

Chicken Farmer, An American Fable
(Fiction 2008)

This novel of historical fiction uses as its premise the theory that Yeshua was the grandson of kings Herod the Great and Mattathias Antigonus. Proposed evidence for that theory can be found in the author's 2010 non-fiction work, *Herodian Messiah*.

The author wishes to thank Peter Fromm for his contribution in proofreading a draft of this work.

About the Author

Joseph Raymond was raised in a devout Roman Catholic family in St. Louis, MO USA and educated in Catholic schools. He received degrees from two Jesuit universities graduating law school in 1986. Thereafter, he served as a Department of Justice lawyer in Washington, DC but later left the practice of law to found an internet company. In 1988, he began a spiritual journey of study and reflection largely focused upon the origins of Christianity. Once started, the journey is never complete. He appeared in *Jesus Conspiracies*, a documentary that aired on the Discovery Channel in 2012.

Family Tree of Herod The Great

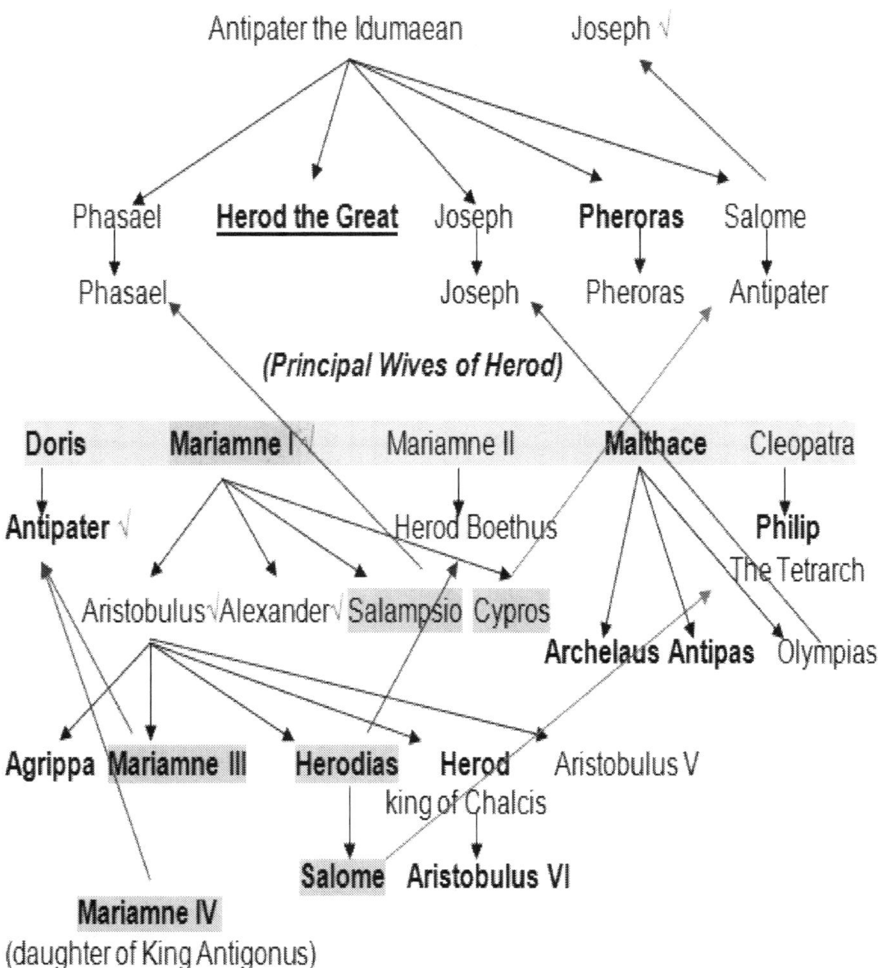

Hasmonean Princess √ Executed by Herod

First marriage of selected Herodian females.

Bold denotes kings / tetrarchs and queens.

Chapter 1

Alexandria, Egypt (67 CE)

Every grandfather harbors a heroic tale to pass along to his grandchildren. Menelaus son of Bathyllus concealed one of the greatest ever told. Time had come for the old man to share his knowledge, as the ranks of persons privy to this secret dwindled yearly.

A knock at the door interrupted the lone household servant from her consuming daily activity—spying on the neighbors. Rhodopis was a middle-aged Egyptian of the lower class, still comely for her age and possessing a sharp wit. Her gaze through the peephole at the front door revealed a familiar figure, the master's grandson. She admitted him into a modest home located just outside the Jewish quarter of the city and pointed toward the courtyard. The grandson, a young man of Greek ancestry mixed with a touch of Jewish blood, called out, "Grandfather, it is Theudas."

Menelaus was 69 years of age and retired to a contemplative life of philosophy. The master of the house tended to his plants oblivious to the presence of his grandson. His skin displayed the weathered look of someone who may have spent years in the fields yet his hands betrayed the former scribe and steward he had been in bygone times. The old man's ancestry held equal parts Greek and Jewish blood although he consciously distanced himself from his Jewish heritage after leaving Israel during the reign of Gaius Caesar, popularly known as Caligula.

Theudas reached the courtyard before Menelaus realized the presence of a visitor. He rose from the dirt and smiled, "And to what occasion do I owe this visit Theudas? I see you rarely these days."

"Oh grandfather, can you not bid me fair greetings? I think you should get out more to enjoy the company of your fellow man."

"So I've become prickly in my old age? That may very well be an accurate assessment but a leopard, especially an aged leopard, does not change its spots. Sit Theudas and I shall have refreshments brought."

Rhodopis hovered on the periphery of the room anticipating her master's request. As with two people long in each other's company, a nod from Menelaus in her direction sent Rhodopis off to retrieve wine cut with water (as it was just past mid-day) to be served with sweet cakes. This was a show for their guest. When alone, master and servant treated each other as equals. Truth be known, Rhodopis was mistress of the house but they reserved knowledge of that fact from his family. Grandfather and grandson sat on benches in the courtyard as Rhodopis served food and drink.

Menelaus, "Your mother tells me you have not yet joined your father's trading house, that you spend your time at the agora listening to oratory and debating points of philosophy."

"No event in life is an accident. Is not my grandfather a philosopher? Perhaps this is my destiny."

"You refer to destiny like a Pythagorean. Have you become one?"

"No grandfather, I am a student of knowledge. It is what brings me here today. Mother has never really told me about our family history in Judea. All she says is that you were a follower of Yeshua the Nazarene before coming to Alexandria and that I should come ask you if I desired more information. So here I am."

Menelaus normally was an animated conversationalist even in his advanced age; however, Theudas noticed his grandfather motionless as if he had turned to marble with a gaze fixed off in the distance. Theudas waited for Menelaus to return to the world of men. Finally Menelaus spoke, "Did you say Yeshua?"

"Yes grandfather, Yeshua. Mother said he was the founder of this Jewish sect called the Nazarenes and that you knew him. His followers call him the Christ and say he was crucified by the Romans in Jerusalem during the reign of Tiberius. I have heard talk of Christ at the agora. His followers have been here in Alexandria for years. Certainly you have heard of him?"

Menelaus again sat lost in his thoughts. Theudas knew his grandfather to be occasionally grumpy but was at a loss why such a harmless question set the old man on edge. Theudas said, "Perhaps mother was mistaken about Yeshua. Maybe you knew another person by the same name. Some say Yeshua the Nazarene is god."

"God?" Menelaus shook his head disappointed to hear such talk. How was it that his grandson raised so thoroughly Greek came to be acquainted with Yeshua in the streets of Alexandria? Those evangelizing in the name of Yeshua must have extended their reach beyond the Jewish quarter of Alexandria in the years since Menelaus lost touch with the Nazarene leadership. He replied, "Yeshua was a king. The Roman prefect of Judea nailed a board to his cross inscribed with the words 'Iesvs Nazarenvs Rex Ivdaeorvm', meaning Yeshua Nazarene King Jews."

Theudas, "Were you there grandfather? Did you see Yeshua on the cross?"

"Yes." Menelaus bowed his head as emotions flooded his being. Theudas patiently waited for his grandfather to continue as he could see the topic of Yeshua deeply affected his grandfather.

Menelaus, "You know I was born in Judea to a Greek father and Jewish mother. We've never discussed it up to now as I consciously left my Jewish heritage behind, embracing my Greek half after moving here to Alexandria. My Greek father was killed before I was born leaving me to be raised in a Jewish household. It was a difficult choice to leave my Jewish roots in the past."

Theudas, "Then we have much to discuss grandfather for I only know the Greek philosopher and sometime gardener who sits with me here today. Your Jewish past is a mystery to me. Does the story of Yeshua also concern my great-grandfather Theudas?"

"Yes, he too followed Yeshua but first a warning. Have you heard that the Jews in Palestine have revolted again?"

"Yes, the reports say the Jews hold the upper-hand against the Romans."

"For now they may but the Romans are nothing if not determined and methodical. And their resources are overwhelming. They'll crush this rebellion no matter how many legions it takes. Any Jewish city opposing them will be leveled. Which means the Temple in Jerusalem, the center of the Jewish universe, will be reduced to rubble."

"How can you be so sure?"

"This is not the first rebellion in Judea against the Romans. The Temple was spared on the prior occasions. This time it will be leveled. And this is not just my opinion. It was that of Yeshua as well. The Jews are destined to lose this war with the kittim. You're too young to remember the horrors committed against the Jews in Alexandria when they resisted desecration of the synagogue by Governor Flaccus."

"This event is known to me but not the particulars. When was this?"

"During the reign of Caligula, the Romans leveled the Alexandrian synagogue to the ground with mass executions in the Jewish quarter. The devastation the Romans shall author in Israel in retribution for this revolt will make the Alexandrian battle under Flaccus look like a picnic."

"Now we're off the subject grandfather. I came to hear of Yeshua but you have wandered off on Caligula and Flaccus."

"The impatience of youth, always in a hurry chasing their tails in circles like dogs."

Menelaus paused taking a long swig of his wine while collecting his thoughts. He continued, "Politics and religion stir the greatest passion in the hearts of men. And for Jews, politics and religion are very much one in the same."

"What about women?"

"What they stir is in the nether regions, not the heart. I am not so old as to have forgotten."

Rhodopis appeared refilling the wine glasses and presenting more cakes. She gave Menelaus a knowing, furtive smirk aware the old goat's nether regions sometime stirred to this day.

Menelaus, "What I shall tell you is private information to be kept within the family. Yeshua the man I knew is already giving way to Yeshua of myth and legend. Zealous people, perhaps ignorant of the true facts, now stake their careers on Yeshua the myth. It may be dangerous to your person if you were to disclose what you are about to hear in the presence of such individuals."

"You seek discretion grandfather. I give my word."

"I should go all the way back to the Hasmonean civil war to tell the full story of Yeshua."

"Please grandfather, must we start with ancient history? Can we not start with the birth of Yeshua?"

"I'll do my best to speed the story along in honor of your limited attention span. Let us begin with Yeshua's father. He was the eldest son of Herod the Great."

The news of Yeshua's connection to Herod startled Theudas, "Yeshua was a Herodian prince?"

"Yes."

"You said he was a king but I am surprised to hear of his relation of Herod."

"Very, very few Nazarenes outside of Israel know this."

"And when the Romans destroy Israel?"

"Then Yeshua the man fades out of memory and we are left with something else."

Theudas nodded his understanding waiting for his grandfather to continue.

Menelaus, "Yeshua's father was Herod's oldest son Antipater, crown prince during the waning years of Herod's reign. Prince Antipater enjoyed strong backing in Rome from Augustus Caesar and the influential men with Caesar's ear. Herod had recently lost status due to a border war against the Nabateans. You know of the Nabateans?"

"A desert people I believe."

"Yes, of the Transjordan region east of Judea. Herod's mother was a Nabatean of high birth."

"Herod attacked his mother's people?"

"He'd trample his own mother in a four-horse chariot if it suited his political ends. But this little war on the Nabateans was not sanctioned by Rome. War between client states is bad for business. It eats up resources that would otherwise go to Rome in the form of taxes or bribes. A client king must do Rome's bidding. And the Romans only sanction war when there is something in it for them. Augustus Caesar punished Herod for his power grab demoting him from 'friend of Rome' to 'subject king' during the twilight of his reign. Augustus Caesar also required Herod to appoint his son Antipater as coregent at this time, meaning the prince wore a king's crown and exercised royal power jointly with Herod. But the Herodian court harbored more intrigue than Mount Olympus. No sooner had Antipater been named coregent than Herod's palace erupted in plots against the designated heir. The surviving wives of Herod schemed constantly to snatch the crown from Antipater's head and place it on the brow of their own offspring. Mix in meddling from Herod's sister, brother, nephews, uncle, cousins, assorted courtiers and you get a sense of the drama. The threat from conspiracies against Antipater grew to such an extent that the newly minted coregent sailed to Rome for extended 'consultations' with Caesar."

Theudas, "It sounds like a Greek tragedy, something by Sophocles or Euripides."

"You're not far off the mark grandson. Antipater harbored a secret from his father the king, a secret that gave Antipater's palace enemies the ammunition they needed to eventually bring him down. I know you are anxious to get to Yeshua's birth but hold still and let me quickly set the table first."

Theudas settled into his seat knowing his grandfather gathered wind for a long oration.

Chapter 2

The story of Yeshua the Nazarene rightly begins with the war waged between his two grandfathers, Hasmonean king Antigonus and Herod the Great. Prior to the Hasmoneans, foreign rulers dominated Israel for four hundred years starting with the Chaldeans. They sacked Jerusalem, destroyed Solomon's Temple, and carried the Davidic royal family off to captivity in Babylon.[1] The Persians arrived next as master over Israel followed by the Greek Seleucids. Although the Hasmoneans succeeded in ousting the Greeks, in the end, their dynasty lasted less than one hundred years when the Romans renewed foreign domination. Nonetheless, Hasmonean rule shone brightly as a time when the Hebrews held sway over the Promised Land. The Hasmoneans (also known as Maccabees) were high-ranking Kohanim priests[2] of the tribe of Levi based in the Judean countryside. They spearheaded a successful war of independence to overthrow Greek Seleucid reign in Israel.[3] The highlight of the revolt came when the Hasmoneans captured Jerusalem then triumphantly cleansed the Temple of corrupting Hellenistic practices and rededicating it to Yahweh.[4] After securing control of Israel, the Hasmonean leaders initially contented themselves with the office of high priest but one

---

[1] Solomon's Temple was destroyed in 586 BCE and the Hasmonean revolt commenced in 167 BCE.

[2] Father to son descendants of the patriarch Aaron who were also called "sons of Aaron".

[3] The Seleucid Empire was founded by generals that served Alexander the Great, who conquered Israel along with the Persian Empire.

[4] This act of the Hasmonean cleansing and rededication of the Temple is celebrated by the present day Jewish feast of Hanukkah.

of their leaders eventually claimed the Jewish throne.[5] Thereafter, Hasmonean kings simultaneously held the office of high priest, the only time this occurred in Jewish history.

Not all Jews rejoiced at the Hasmonean rise to power. In particular, the opposition Pharisees chaffed under Hasmonean rule. In a theocracy such as Israel, religious parties are defacto political parties. The Pharisees launched a Trojan horse in the person of Queen Salome Alexandra into the Hasmonean ranks. She was the sister of the leading Pharisee of the day, Nasi Shetah who served as president of the Grand Sanhedrin. Salome became the wife of two Hasmonean kings, marrying the second after the death of the first. Her second husband, King Alexander Jannai, suffered open Pharisee rebellion against his rule. The Pharisees collaborated with Seleucid king Demetrius III to bring about war. The armies of Demetrius and Jannai collided in battle upon the plain of Shechem in Samaria. King Jannai was outnumbered by the Greek king with 14,000 foot soldiers and 3,000 horse whereas Jannai completely lacked cavalry at Shechem. Great numbers died on both sides during ferocious fighting but the numerical superiority of the Greeks and their Pharisee allies eventually carried the day. Jannai fled the battlefield to nearby mountains with only a remnant of his army still intact. The next day, Demetrius gathered his men for a final assault on the heavily outnumbered Hasmonean forces. Jannai looked to the heavens praying to Yahweh for deliverance and, miraculous, salvation came. The sound of horns blaring carried from beyond the far hills as the sun rose in the east. Then, ghostly figures clad in heavy armor, 6000 strong, appeared out of the early morning fog. The sun glistened off massive bronze shields polished like mirrors. It looked as if an elite Seleucid legion had materialized out of thin air but these soldiers were not Greek. They were the reclusive Hasidim of the Dead Sea and Transjordan region known as the "sons of light". They marched toward the battle lines led by deeply conservative warrior priests of Aaron. Behind the Aaronites strode the Levites followed

---

[5] According to Josephus, Hasmonean Judah Aristobulus I crowned himself king in104 BCE.

by the bulk of the Hasidim soldiers. The Greek king thought the Hasidim had long since gone extinct existing only as legend.

The legend came to life that day near Shechem. The appearance of this Hasidim ghost legion spooked Demetrius and his men. Despite having gravely wounded the army of Jannai, the Greek king retreated in the face of the sons of light and marched his army completely out of Israel. Demetrius never again challenged the rule of King Jannai. With the Hasidim warriors swelling his ranks, Jannai easily defeated the remaining Pharisee warriors who stood alone at Shechem thereby turning sure defeat into victory. In the aftermath, Jannai crucified 800 Pharisees outside the walls of Jerusalem while feasting with his concubines in sight of the dying rabbis.[6] King Jannai was Yeshua's great-great grandfather.[7]

The Pharisee movement persevered despite its crushing rout at the hands of Jannai. Upon his death, Salome Alexandra became queen regent ruling in her own right for nine peaceful years. The Pharisee fortunes reversed during the reign of Queen Salome as she brought them again into power. Salome's eldest son and fellow Pharisee, Hyrcanus II, succeeded the queen upon her death. This did not sit well with Judah Aristobulus II, the purist Sadducean[8] younger brother of Hyrcanus, who challenged his brother's right to the throne sparking a nominal Hasmonean civil war. The true combatants were the Pharisees and purist Sadducees. The Jewish people substantially supported Aristobulus allowing him to depose Hyrcanus as both king and high priest. After being ousted from power, the Pharisees again turned for foreign help. The Romans had recently vanquished remnants of the Seleucid Dynasty in Syria leaving them at the doorstep of Israel and the logical partner for Pharisee ambitions. Consul Pompey Magnus joined forces with the Pharisees, and then captured Jerusalem after a three month siege. However, once an elephant

---

[6] Josephus, Antiquities XIII, Ch. 14.

[7] See *Gospel of Luke* 3:24.

[8] "Purist Sadducee" is a term coined by Prof. Robert Eisenman to refer to the community that wrote the Dead Sea Scrolls. See James the Just in the Habakkuk Pesher by Robert H. Eisenman (Brill 1986) at pages 6-7.

sniffs its nose into the tent, there is no stopping it from gaining mastery over the contents of the tent. The Pharisees invited the Roman elephant into Israel who, thereafter, became the true masters of the country. In essence, the Pharisees became junior partners in the Roman conquest of Israel with the family of Aristobulus II left as the only Jewish nationalist leaders to oppose foreign rule. Pompey allowed Hyrcanus to reclaim the office of high priest (Kohen Gadol) but denied him the title of king. In point of fact, Hyrcanus held no real power in the country outside of ceremonial duties at the Temple as high priest. Pompey placed administrative power over Israel in the hands of Antipater the Idumean, a desert war lord who fought ably beside the Romans. Antipater's son Herod was made governor of Galilee. King Aristobulus, on the other hand, went to Rome as Pompey's prisoner leaving the Jewish nationalist cause in ruin.

All was not yet lost for Jewish nationalists as the Hasmonean ember still flickered. At this time, Julius Caesar and Pompey vied for supremacy of Rome. Caesar crossed the Rubicon capturing Rome, while Pompey and the Roman senate fled in panic to the east. The Jewish leaders picked sides in the Roman civil war, as was the case with all client kingdoms of the Roman Empire. Hyrcanus allied himself with Pompey while Aristobulus, the deposed king, embraced Caesar. An enemy of my enemy is my friend, even for Caesar. He sent Aristobulus back to Israel to reclaim his throne but, before this campaign got underway, agents allied with Antipater the Idumean poisoned the former Hasmonean king. One reaps what he sows for Antipater the Idumean was poisoned by a disgruntled ally not long thereafter. Yet another blow fell upon the family of Aristobulus. The Roman general Scipio captured and beheaded Aristobulus' eldest son, Alexander, in Antioch. Only one son of King Aristobulus remained alive to carry the Hasmonean nationalist torch, Mattathias Antigonus. He was the grandfather of Yeshua.

The Jewish civil war passed to the next generation with Antigonus opposing Herod and his relations for supremacy over the Jewish kingdom. The fight looked one-sided at best. The Romans, titans of the west, stood with Herod's family.

Undaunted, Antigonus forged alliances with anti-Roman rulers in the east–Marion king of Tyre, Fabius governor of Damascus and Ptolemy prince of Chalcis, the last of whom was married to the sister of Antigonus (Alexandra bat Aristobulus). With these allies, Antigonus built an army and confidently rode south into Galilee where his forces at first tasted success. But Herod counter-attacked repulsing Antigonus from the Jewish kingdom. The last Hasmonean nationalist may have lost the battle but he was unbowed. Antigonus licked his wounds and looked east for a more powerful ally—the Parthians, successor of the ancient Persian Empire. Parthia stood as a massive eastern counterweight to Rome. It stretched from the Caucasus Mountain in the north to the Indus River on the Indian subcontinent in the south, from Syria in the west to the Hindu Kush Mountains in the east. Not long after Rome finally vanquished Carthage, Parthia emerged as Rome's principal rival. The state religion of Parthia, Zoroastrianism, was said by some to be even older than Judaism and its priests were known as magi. Parthia embraced Antigonus with open arms and carts full of silver coins but sent him only 500 warriors. Antigonus rebuilt his army and waited for the proper time to strike.

Israel (40 BCE)

A Roman civil war providently bestowed advantage upon Antigonus, perhaps a sign of Yahweh's favor. Marc Antony and Octavian (later Augustus Caesar) engaged in the first round of their eventual struggle to the death. Antony withdrew Roman legions from the east for service in his war with Octavian causing the Roman position in Syria to dissolve into mush. Quintus Labienus, one of Antony's disgruntled generals, defected to the Parthians then led a Parthian invasion into the Roman province of Syria. Labienus mauled the Roman auxiliary forces left behind opening the door for Antigonus to attack the Herodians in Israel. Antigonus rallied Jewish nationalists to his banner and marched into his homeland. Jewish towns threw their gates open to Antigonus as he and his small band of Parthian allies swept over the Jewish kingdom. Antigonus captured his uncle Hyrcanus II outside Jerusalem, then bit his ears off (to disqualify him from ever again serving as high priest). The deposed high priest went into exile in Babylon, deep inside Parthian territory. At this time, Herod's older brother Phasael landed in the prison of Antigonus and elected to kill himself by bashing his head against the stone wall of his cell. Only Herod and his two younger brothers (Pheroras and Joseph) survived this stage of the civil war.

Herod suffered during the year in which Antony and Octavian concluded the Treaty of Brundisium (40 BCE) resulting in a temporary lull in their civil war. By the time Antony and Octavian again clasped hands in friendship, vast stretches of Rome's Syria province and all of Israel had fallen to the Parthians and their allies. Antigonus entered Jerusalem in triumph crowning himself king and appointing himself high priest. The forces of Antigonus chased Herod completely out of Israel. In his haste to flee, Herod left his family behind at the fortress of Masada where Antigonus besieged them. The erstwhile Roman governor of Galilee turned tail making it to safety with only 800 men at his side.

After leaving Israel, Herod first turned east after fleeing the Jewish kingdom seeking assistance from King Malichus of Nabatea who owed Herod large sums of money. Instead of refuge, Malichus turned his back upon Herod rendering him a political refugee. Next, Herod traveled overland west to Egypt for the protection of Cleopatra. Herod reached Egypt on the cusp of winter. The queen strongly urged Herod to stay in Alexandria until spring. Winter crossings of the Mediterranean were hazardous business and rarely attempted. But Herod wouldn't stand for it. He rented a ship and nearly wrecked close to the Island of Rhodes in the Aegean Sea. His ship limped into harbor too badly damaged to continue. Unable to hire another vessel in Rhodes for the winter sail to Rome, Herod commissioned the building of a trireme then outfitted it with men and provisions. The gods smiled upon Herod during his audacious gamble. Early the following year, he landed in Italy at Brundisium and made haste overland to Rome.

Rome (39 BCE)

Upon arrival, Herod found Antony and Octavian still honoring their recent treaty. Antony's first wife Fulvia died the year of the treaty providently clearing the way for Antony to marry Octavian's sister, Octavia. The virile Antony quickly succeeded in getting her with child, yet Antony pined to depart for the east and Cleopatra. He would do so with the first blossoms of spring. Once in the east nestled in the arms of Cleopatra, Antony knew it would only be a matter of time before he and Octavian again squared off in battle for sole possession of the entire Roman Empire. A family marriage had not stopped the inevitable war between Julius Caesar and Pompey Magnus. So it would be with Antony and Octavian. And when that day arrived, Antony needed a reliable and loyal tyrant in command of the resources of the Jewish kingdom. Herod was that man. These two were cut from the same cloth: ambitious, power hungry, killers of men, lovers of women, and commanders of armies. Herod received an audience with Antony promptly upon his arrival in Rome. Antony cut an imposing figure, physically robust with a prominent chin and chiseled features looking more like a common legionnaire or gladiator than the Roman patrician he was. His rough manners were the exact opposite of his collogue, and now brother-in-law, Octavian.

Antony, "Herod, you desert fox. How did you manage to escape Palestine with your head still attached to your shoulders?"

Herod replied, "By the grace of my God, imperator."

"That was a damn foolish act sailing through the Aegean in the dead of winter. I heard you had to build your own trireme in Rhodes because not a single owner would hire his ship out to you."

"This is true imperator but these are desperate times. My family is besieged at a fortress in Judea while my elder brother Phasael is imprisoned in Jerusalem."

"Bad news old friend, received it two days ago. Phasael is dead. Antigonus calls it a suicide."

Herod paused to collect himself. The news came as a shock. His father Antipater had been poisoned three years ago. Now his older brother Phasael was also gone. Only he, Joseph and

Pheroras survived to avenge this latest spilling of their family blood with Herod now head of the clan. Within seconds, Herod shook off the horrible news and changed subjects. "I am not the only one with a death in the family, my condolences on the death of Fulvia."

"You don't strike me as the sentimental type Herod. I guess that makes us two peas in a pod. Fulvia was a magnificent piece of highborn ass but, by the gods, her meddling in my politics nearly got my younger brother killed. Have you heard about this business with Lucius?"

"No, I've received little news these past six months imperator. Every waking moment has been focused on reaching Rome."

"Fulvia goaded Lucius to engage Octavian's legions in battle without coordinating things with me, just stupid. By sounding the war bugle before synchronizing our combined troop strength, she played right into Octavian's hands. He was able to take us on one at a time as opposed to a combined assault. Octavian's defeat of Lucius is what forced me to the treaty table. I'm sick of the entire incident. It was all Fulvia's doing."

Herod, "May we speak privately?"

Antony waived his hand clearing the room of subordinates who hovered on the periphery of the meeting. When they were alone, Antony continued the conversion. "Speak Herod."

"Imperator, you do not sound as if your heart is in this peace treaty."

"That's no secret in Rome. Octavian may be a spindly boy general but he does possess an acute ability to judge people. We both know this matter is not settled."

"Then you shall need friends in the east when the time comes."

Antony smiled for he hated having to explain the obvious. Political negotiations were so much easier when the other party possessed the capability of seeing through the ox manure scattered about allowing for a blunt negotiation of mutual interest. Herod limped into Rome nearly broke. His IOU due from King Malichus was worthless unless Herod rode into Nabatea at the head of an army to collect. Herod needed help but the payback to Antony would be steep.

Antony, "Of course I'll need friends Herod and your family has been my friend and that of Caesar over a long period of time.[9] But here is the rub, I am assembling legions as we speak for an attack against the Parthians but my primary target must be Labienus."

"He's in Cilicia."

"That's what I like about you Herod, you can read a map. My thrust will be north of you. I can't spare any additional troops for Palestine this year."

"But I must free my family. This cannot wait."

"I've seen the balls you carry under that tunic Herod. They are steel. If you had the money, how many men could you raise on short notice from your homeland in Idumea and mercenaries from ports of call along the way?"

Herod replied without hesitation, "10,000."

Antony, "Scattered pockets of Roman troops who were pushed out of Palestine are wintering just to the north of Palestine. I'll give you a Roman commander, ships, and enough money to pay your native troops for three months. Under my authority, scoop up all the stray legionnaires you find in the port cities near Judea then attack Palestine at the location of your choosing. Look for rich cities you can loot or tax to sustain your army. I'll also send a Roman general once you are organized."

Herod, "What about counterattacks from the Parthians?"

"When I strike in Cilicia, it will pin down the Parthian military. They will not be able to reinforce their ally Antigonus. He'll be on his own. My intelligence says Antigonus has limited heavy infantry. I might not be able to send men but there is plenty of armor to be had here in Rome. You shall be well provisioned.

---

[9] Herod received Roman citizenship in 47 BCE from Julius Caesar after he and his father Antipater came to the aid of Caesar during the civil war with Magnus Pompey. Antipater the Idumean started out as a client of Pompey but wisely switched allegiances to Caesar after correctly sensing the tide had turned against Pompey.

Antigonus will group his best troops around Jerusalem opening up targets of opportunity for you in the rest of the kingdom."

Herod sat silently contemplating the boldness of the plan. Antony offered the bare minimum to get him into the field with a mercenary army provisioned for but a few months. Success or failure rested solely upon Herod's ability to secure booty to feed and grow his forces.

Antony, "Why are you thinking about it so long Herod? Do you expect to receive a better offer from Cleopatra?"

Not likely. Cleopatra had designs on controlling Palestine herself. For a small woman, she dreamed large. They both knew Herod possessed no other options.

"I don't need to think. I accept your offer imperator."

"You have not heard what I expect in return yet. What treasure can we expect to capture when Jerusalem falls? I imagine a handsome return on my investment Herod."

Herod thought for a moment before replying. There was only one great treasure in Judea, the Temple treasury at Jerusalem. However, the Jewish people viewed it as sacrosanct to Yahweh. In Herod's view the Temple treasury merely acted as a feeding trough for the Levitical priesthood. Taking the treasury meant angering the people but its riches would cement his relationship with Antony. Herod needed to balance these two competing needs.

"Imperator, there is but one source of wealth in the Jewish kingdom of a scale to interest you, the Temple treasury. No temple outside of Rome and Parthia is as rich. Of course, to maintain goodwill with the Temple priests and the Jewish people we shouldn't take it all. I was thinking they could stomach thirty-percent."

Antony chortled, "Thirty percent? Herod, your penis has gone flaccid on me. Did someone turn you into a eunuch since last we met? Lift up your tunic and let me check to confirm your gonads are in place."

Antony reached underneath the table partially lifting up Herod's tunic to mock his client. Antony continued, "I wouldn't give a floating turd in the Tiber for the worries of Jewish priests about their treasure. Those priests who remain in Jerusalem are collaborators with Antigonus as far as I'm concerned. Slaughter them all if it pleases you but get your hands on the Temple treasury. Is that clear?'

"Yes imperator."

"Oh, and another thing, Antigonus has crowned himself king. Our local man in Palestine must have the same title. Tomorrow the senate will proclaim you king of the Jews."

"King?"

"Come, my colleague Octavian desires to meet you."

****

Not every member of Herod's family was laid up besieged at Masada. He recently traded up by divorcing and exiling his first wife Doris and her son Antipater to Rome upon his betrothal to Hasmonean Princess Mariamne bat Alexander. Doris was an Idumean princess born in Jerusalem, where her royal family resided at the behest of their Hasmonean overlords. The Jewish and Idumean peoples had a long history of enmity between one another but, also, intermarriage. King David and his son Solomon fought wars with the Idumeans nearly wiping out the Idumean royal family. However, there arose a powerful Idumean king named Hadad who was aligned with the Egyptians and gained the upper hand over King Solomon during a protracted war. It resulted in a peace treaty and intermarriage between their royal houses. Solomon married an Idumean princess and sent a minor son to the Idumeans thus infusing the Idumean royal house with King Solomon's bloodline. The Idumean royal family maintained its Davidic bloodline down from the time of Solomon to the days of Herod.[10] King Herod had ten wives in all yet Doris was the only wife exiled to make way for a new bride. Such was the rank

---

[10] 1 *Kings* 11:1 indicates Solomon had an Idumean wife (also called Edomite). It is the author's reasoned inference that a descendent of Solomon was sent to the Idumean royal family in return and that the bloodline of Solomon became prized within the Idumean royal family (in the same fashion as Hasmonean blood became prized within the Herodian clan). This line of reasoning leads to the possibility that Herod's wife Doris descended from King Solomon.

of her royal Davidic bloodline that Hasmonean Mariamne bat Alexander demanded Herod banish Doris.

Although Doris and Antipater were in Rome at the time of Herod's consultation with Antony, Herod never bothered to see them. The new Jewish king had moved up in stature in the world. He gave his first wife and son little thought; however, his new status as an important client king also raised the status of Herod's exiled son. Antipater grew up building friendships among the Roman patrician families and those close to future emperor Augustus. These contacts would play an important role in the political career of the young Herodian prince. Prince Antipater ben Herod was the father of Yeshua the Nazarene.

Jerusalem, Judea (37 BCE)

Antony crushed the Parthians in Cilicia. His general Ventidius, a former mule driver who rose through the ranks in the legions, captured and executed the rogue general Labienus. This strong wind blowing from Anthony's campaign in the north lifted Herod's sails. Fence sitters in Palestine could see the momentum shift to Herod as the possibility of Antigonus receiving reinforcements from Parthia decreased; however, Herodian blood was spilled in the campaign. Herod left his brother Joseph in command of his troops in Judea while he went north to assist Antony. Herod's younger brother attacked Hasmonean forces in Jericho on his own initiative without authority from the king. It was a costly mistake. Antigonus captured and beheaded Joseph in retaliation for the Roman beheading of Antigonus' older brother Alexander. This left Herod and his brother Pheroras as the only sons of Antipater the Idumean still alive. Despite this victory, the war went badly for Antigonus. Each month more Jewish towns defected to Herod's banner or were laid to waste. Still the zealot Jewish nationalists of Judea refused to surrender. Having freed his family from siege at Masada and secured the countryside, Herod finally trained his sights on the Jewish capital in the summer.

Herod had completely reversed his fortunes after resupply from Antony in Rome and a modest infusion of Roman legionnaires two years earlier. Herod's army had grown to 15,000 and he held sway over the entire Jewish kingdom, except Jerusalem. He just didn't have enough men to take the capital resulting in a long siege. After Marc Antony triumphed over the Parthians at Gindarus, he sent two Roman legions south to Herod under General Sossius.[11] The allies now possessed enough man power to destroy the Jewish revolutionaries trapped in Jerusalem.

The Hasmonean dynasty gasped its last breath as Herod's mercenary army tightened its grip on the capital. King Antigonus held out behind the city walls with those loyal to the Hasmonean cause. They prayed for a divine miracle just as the king's ancestor Jannai had done but it never came. No one knows for sure why the Hasidim heavy infantry did not march out of the desert to the aid of Antigonus. The Hasidim were xenophobic so it could be they objected to Antigonus bringing Parthians into his government. The Sons of Light also likely objected to Antigonus taking a concubine of Parthian royal blood, something against their code of conduct for a king although technically allowed by the Torah. Whatever the reason, Hasidim military help failed to arrive at Jerusalem. The Jewish people overwhelmingly supported Antigonus over Herod but the might of Rome could not be denied. Before Jerusalem fell to Herod, Antigonus ordered the royal women and children of his household to flee the city to the Hasmonean stronghold of Fortress Hyrcania under the command of his sister Princess Alexandra. That is, all except one very young infant princess deemed too tender of age to travel into the desert--the king's daughter Mariamne. Antigonus paid a visit to the home of Joseph ben Ellemus, also known as Heli, a chief priest at the Temple and distant Hasmonean relative of the king. A royal bodyguard banged on the door to the palatial residence of Heli but he was not home.

Three nights previously, Heli and his brother Matthias slipped out of Jerusalem to hide in the Judean desert waiting for Herod's army to capture the city. They planned on declaring their support for Herod hoping to save the destruction of their families

---

[11] The Army of Herod the Great by Samuel Rocca (Osprey Publishing, 2009) at page 11.

in the process; however, this left their relatives back in Jerusalem exposed as potential traitors until Herod prevailed. An elderly slave named Eleazar looked through the door slit at the home of Heli to see the king and his retune of guards standing outside the door. This sight paralyzed the slave with fear. Hanan, the chief steward of the household, came to the door having heard the barrage of knocks. He said, "Eleazar, who is at the door?"

The old slave replied, "The king."

Hanan pushed the old slave aside to see for himself. "Say a quick pray to Yahweh, then open the door. We're all dead."

Amidst more banging on the door, the slave said a frantic prayer then opened the lock. The captain of the king's guard burst through the door the moment the bolt was pulled back and grabbed the old slave by the neck.

"Why did you keep the king waiting? I saw you look through the slit then refuse to open the door."

Hanan tried to rescue of Eleazar, who he had known since childhood. "Captain, please forgive this old slave. He is a man of little intellect and froze in awe at the sight of the king. Please forgive the insult."

King Mattathias Antigonus strode through the door wearing a lavish purple cloak with a diadem on his head. Hanan had never been that close to the king and was startled to discover how physically small and delicate he was. Antigonus peered into Hanan's face waiting for the man to pay his respects to royalty. Hanan dropped to a knee and bowed his head to the king. All the servants and slaves who gathered in the vestibule did the same. They dared not speak unless spoken to.

King Antigonus said, "Where is the master of the house?"

Hanan winced fearing the inevitable question. "He is away your highness. Shall I summon his wife, the lady Anna?"

"Yes. Lead me to Heli's study then bring Lady Anna to me."

Behind the king stood a wet nurse holding a baby no more than thirty days old. Antigonus turned to the captain of his guard. "Shimon, you stay here with the child. Send just two men with me to stand guard outside the study. Pull the soldiers off the street into the vestibule of this house. We must keep as low a profile as possible."

Antigonus traveled to the home of priest Heli guarded by a mere squad of twelve soldiers hoping the small number would draw less attention to their movement. Herod's forces held positions outside the city but his spies, and perhaps assassins, were already loose inside the city. Antigonus exposed himself to personal risk for the benefit of his infant daughter.

The king stood inside Heli's study idly poking at expensive scrolls tucked into their cubbyholes. Scattered among the religious texts were Greek plays. Antigonus didn't know his distant cousin Heli on a personal level but was surprised to discover his refined taste in Greek literature. By all rights, the king should round up every member of the family of Heli and execute them. His own spies sniffed out the priest's plan to defect to Herod the day he left the city for the safety of the wilderness. But what were the lives of the family of one priest against the mass carnage that would ensure when Herod breeched the walls of Jerusalem? Antigonus hit upon a plan to turn the defection of Heli into the salvation of his daughter.

Lady Anna, a beautiful and elegant woman around 40 years of age, appeared at the entrance. She uttered the obligatory, "Your highness," and bowed her head.

The king said, "Lady Anna, normally it would be a pleasure to be in your presence but, unfortunately, the purpose for my visit is anything but pleasant."

She immediately replied before the king could elaborate, "My husband has shamed us your highness. I wish to confess his desertion to the desert with the intention of pledging his support for Herod. I beg his highness to grant me a divorce!"

The words took the king by surprise. Surely she knew that Jewish law prevented a woman from seeking a divorce. Was Anna playing the only card available to her to avoid stoning or was she truly devoted to Antigonus? He wasn't sure. The king was more closely related to Anna than to her husband Heli but family relationships didn't guaranty loyalty among Hasmoneans. For example, Herod's new Hasmonean wife was the niece of

Antigonus. The king looked into Anna's eyes seeking the truth within her soul but it lay beyond his grasp.

"Why didn't you come to me sooner cousin? Why wait until I appear at your door for this confession?"

"My husband left orders with the servants and slaves to bar me from leaving this house. I am a prisoner in my own home your highness."

Antigonus smiled inwardly. Had Anna been born a man she would have made a fine rabbi. There was no way for the king to confirm the story as the household staff would back whatever tale their mistress told. As a practical matter, Antigonus had no choice but to trust Anna. The fact that Heli was in the process of defecting to Herod afforded the slimmest of hope that Herod would spare the house of Heli from rape, plunder, and murder when his soldiers finally took the city. Antigonus had no illusions about what would happen to his own immediate family members when Herod gained control of the city. They would be summarily executed. As a king, Antigonus expected that he would be sent to Rome for trial but, by then, his infant daughter Mariamne would be dead. She was too young to travel on horseback out of the city through the tunnels that fed into the Wadi Kidron. Antigonus determined the only way to save little Mariamne was to stash her with a family that Herod was likely to exempt from destruction. The family of Heli fit what he was looking for. Heli and Anna had failed to produce children during their long marriage, to the great shame of both.

The king continued, "I have a favor to ask of you cousin Anna."

"Anything your highness, I am yours to command."

Antigonus walked back to the doorway. He said to the guard, "Bring the wet nurse and the baby."

Awkward silence filed the room until the wet nurse arrived holding an infant. The king continued, "This is my youngest daughter. She's only thirty days old."

The cooing child transfixed Lady Anna. "May I hold her?"

"Of course." The king motioned for the wet nurse, who was very protective of the child, to hand her over.

Anna, "Is this Queen Salina's child?"

"No, she is my child by Princess Artemisia."

Anna attempted but failed to hide her disappointment. Princess Artemisia was the king's Parthian concubine. Jewish law permitted kings to marry eighteen wives but the high priest could have only one wife. As Hasmonean kings also held the office of high priest, they were restricted to one wife but generally possessed a multitude of concubines who were official members of court; however, this practice was disapproved of by the Hasidim. King Antigonus had but one royal concubine, who he took in order to cement his relationship with the Parthian royal family. Lady Anna understood the military and political importance of the king's alliance with Parthia but, as a nationalist, she did not approve of Parthians in the royal family. Nonetheless, the king's command was her law.

Anna asked, "Where is Princess Artemisia your highness?"

"This is why I have come to you cousin Anna. Perhaps the angels had a hand in bringing me here today with Artemisia's baby. All the women of my family and young sons have left the city to link up with the portion of our army trapped outside Jerusalem. I can't tell you where they have sought refuge but, as we speak, they are safe."

"Praise to Yahweh. Then this precious daughter of the king needs a surrogate mother until she can be reunited with Princess Artemisia."

Antigonus, "Will you undertake this service for me cousin Anna?"

Lady Anna didn't hesitate. "I shall care for this child as if she were my own your highness. I have prayed many a night for a child and now the angels answer my prayer, even if the arrangement be temporary."

King Antigonus watched Lady Anna intently for any sign of her true intentions. Would she protect his daughter when the walls of Jerusalem eventually fell to Herod? Doing so would endanger her entire family. The king really had no choice but to trust the wife of a priest who was in the process of defecting to the enemy. His daughter's life was now in Yahweh's hands.

Antigonus continued, "It is extremely important that the identity of my daughter be kept secret. Only you and the wet nurse, who I am leaving with the child, are to know her true identity. This is for your safety as well as the child. Do you understand me?"

Anna, "Yes your highness."

"Herod will execute every member of my family he gets in his grasp. Anyone found to harbor a member of my family also risks execution. Do you accept this assignment knowing the danger?"

"Yes your highness. I pledge my faithfulness to you and to Yahweh."

Antigonus placed a chain around his daughter's neck. On the chain hung a small charm inscribed with small script Anna could not read. She asked, "What does the charm say?"

"It is my priestly name, Matthat, written in ancient Hebrew.[12] Only the oldest Temple priests are capable of reading this script. Keep this chain around my daughter's neck at all times."

"Yes your highness."

Antigonus turned to leave but Anna stopped him.

"Your highness, what is the child's name?"

"How thoughtless of me. Her name is Mariamne."

A popular Hasmonean name but ironic as it was shared with the Hasmonean niece of King Antigonus who recently married his enemy Herod. There wasn't anything left for the king to say to Anna. This was his best dice throw to save his infant daughter. As he left the house of Heli, Antigonus stopped at the vestibule just inside the front door.

He said, "Captain, bring these two men with us." The king pointed to Hanan, the chief steward, and Eleazar, the old slave who had frozen at the door when the king's men knocked. The neighbors surely knew that the king visited the house of Heli, which would excite neighborhood gossip. Antigonus needed to

---

[12] Antigonus minted coins that read "King Antigonus" on one side and "Matthat high priest" on the obverse. See *Luke* 3:24 for the name Matthat in the lineage of Yeshua.

deliver some sort of punishment upon the household of Heli least it appear the priest was a secret double agent still aligned with Antigonus. The king hoped executing Heli's servant and old slave would be enough to cover the ruse.

Anna fell to her knees and gave praise to God after King Antigonus left her home. She got up off the ground taking the baby from her wet nurse and grasped the little treasure in her arms. Anna endured over twenty unhappy and barren years of marriage to Heli not knowing the purpose for her suffering. Now Anna knew why God had kept her alive and brought her to this exact moment in her life. The reason rested in her arms, the last vessel of Antigonus' royal blood, the Hasmonean king and high priest who stood up to the Romans for three glorious years although his defiance would soon cost the king his life. She knew what to do. This little princess would grow up to bear a son who would one day reclaim his grandfather's throne by expelling the Romans from Israel. Anna dedicated her life to the future resurrection of the Hasmonean dynasty through the royal blood of Mariamne bat Antigonus.

Herod's Camp, Mount of Olives, Judea (37 BCE)

Herod, his lieutenants and the Roman command under general Sossius camped on the Mount of Olives affording them a view over the walls into the city. The Temple complex dominated Jerusalem and, more importantly, occupied the center of the entire Jewish universe. It housed not only the manifestation of Yahweh on earth but, also, acted as a colossal money magnet sucking in offerings from pious Jews throughout the known world. In that respect it was unique in the ancient world. Temples to popular gods such as Isis existed at every major city throughout the Roman Empire; however, there was only one temple in the world dedicated to Yahweh. Those wishing to pay homage to Yahweh or seek forgiveness of sins sent their money to this single temple. The Jewish people were nothing if not commercially industrious. Go to any port city or trading center from Babylon in the east all the way to New Carthage (Spain) in the west and there you found Jewish merchants and craftsmen who regularly sent offerings back to the Temple in Jerusalem. The Temple treasury was controlled by the high priest and chief priests who served under him. Antigonus simultaneously held both the offices of king and high priest giving him complete control over the Jewish state and the vast Temple treasury.[13]

Priest Joseph Ellemus (Heli) and his younger brother Matthias (known as Theophilus) walked out of the eastern desert up the slope of the Mount of Olives and into the camp of King Herod not knowing what reception they would receive. Heli was in his early forties with Matthias ten years his junior. Both men dressed in simple robes despite the great wealth they derived from service near the pinnacle of the Temple's priestly hierarchy. The war between Herod and Antigonus had raged for three years and, at the last moment, these two Temple priests were defecting to Herod's winning side. Would he accept their pledge of loyalty or execute them due to their Hasmonean blood? Both were certain they would die if they remained in Jerusalem.

As guards brought the two priests to the commander's tent, Herod engaged Sossius in debate hoping to secure a promise from the Roman general to restrain his troops from thoroughly pillaging the city when they breached the walls. Herod said, "General, I understand we must afford your soldiers an opportunity to plunder but you must also look at things from my point of view. This is a sacred city to the Jewish people, who I hope to rule after this is all done. Your soldiers must leave me an intact kingdom to rule, not a pile of rubble."

Sossius, "And how do you propose rewarding the soldiers for their years of fighting in Syria? It's a soldier's right to plunder after capturing a city, regardless of what temple happens to be located inside its walls."

"I'll pay them out of my own pocket but please restrain your men general."

---

[13] Many scholars believe the Copper Scroll found at Qumran details the hiding places of the Temple treasury. Chris Mitchel of *Christian World News* put the 2009 value of this treasure at $3 billion US. <u>See</u> "The Mystery of the Copper Scroll", cbn.com, September 27, 2009.

An officer entered the command tent and announced the presence of two prisoners, priests from the Temple in Jerusalem.

Sossius, "Priests, I don't give a fart about priests. Lock them up."

But Herod demurred, "General, I beg your indulgence. There are many different ranks of priests in the Jewish religion. Priests grow like mushrooms after a spring rain in the forest; however, if these are high ranking priests then they are to be counted as leaders among the Jewish people and have political value. It would be wise for me to interrogate them and determine their position."

"As you wish Herod." Sossius nodded to the guard who brought the two priests into the command tent.

Herod was then 37 years of age and wore the customary full beard of a Jewish adult male. He addressed the prisoners in Aramaic, his native tongue. Sossius motioned for an aide to interpret as Herod led off the questioning.

Herod, "You two are priests?"

"This is true governor. We are Kohanim."

Herod had been governor of Galilee prior to the outbreak of the revolutionary war. Apparently the priests hadn't heard the news of his promotion by the Romans to king. As Sossius received the translation from his interpreter, he scolded the prisoners in Greek.

Sossius, "His Excellency has been made king by decree of the Roman Senate. You shall address him accordingly. Is that understood?"

The priests did not require a translation. Both responded, "As you wish general."

Sossius, "So you speak Greek then?"

They nodded affirmative. Having scolded the prisoners for not according Herod his proper honorary form of address, Sossius also put up appearances. "Your Excellency, please continue the interrogation in Greek. I never trust these interpreters to get the translation just right. And what is this term 'Kohanim'? I thought they were priests to Yahweh. Is there another Jewish cult?"

"No general. There are grades of priests to Yahweh. First, one must be a father to son descendant of the patriarch Levi to be a priest. The tribe of Levi is dedicated to the priesthood. Aaron was the brother of Moses and, as the high priest appointed by Moses, considered to be the model for all future high priests. For this reason, the high priesthood is reserved for father-to-son descendants of Aaron, who we call Kohanim. They are the highest ranking Levitical priests."

Sossius, "I see. Please continue with your interrogation your Excellency."

Herod, "Give me your names please."

Heli, "I am Joseph ben Ellemus, known as Heli, and this is my younger brother Matthias."

"Are you also of the Hasmonean clan?"

"Yes your Excellency."

Herod's interest in the priests grew with that answer yet the two priests still could not tell whether they were in immediate danger from Herod. He continued the interrogation, "And your ancestors, do you descend from any of the Hasmonean kings?"

Heli replied, "A high priest but not a king. We are the descendants of Yochanan, a son of the righteous Matthias Maccabeus who initiated the revolt against Greek rule. Yochanan Maccabeus served as high priest before his death but was never officially a Jewish king. The Greek king Alexander Balas was said to have placed a purple robe around Yochanan at the king's wedding banquet as a mark of respect but Yochanan never wore the diadem in Jerusalem."

Herod, "What year was this?"

"Yochanan became high priest in the year 160 as reckoned by the Greeks."[14]

Herod rubbed his beard then leaned over to whisper into the ear of Sossius, "High level Hasmonean priests but not technically of royal blood as they are not descendants of a king."

Sossius replied also in a whisper, "They could be useful to us."

---

[14] 1 *Maccabees* 10:21. The year 160 under the Seleucid system was 152 BCE.

Herod nodded in agreement then smiled. Being of common ancestry greatly vexed Herod in his new role as Jewish king. In truth, Herod was not ethnically Jewish but of Arabian blood with a Nabatean mother and Idumean father.[15] And neither of his parents were royals. He married a Hasmonean princess of high royal blood to burnish his credentials as a Jewish king but sat uneasy upon the throne. King David, the most famous of Jewish kings, had also been born a commoner and became king after marrying the daughter of Saul, the prior king. But David was beloved by the Jewish people. Herod was not. The Hasmonean royal family posed a grave threat to his future dynasty. Herod planned on exterminating all Hasmonean royals outside his own family once the walls of the city fell, which surely would cause a backlash among the Jewish people. He needed to keep up appearances by retaining as many high ranking priests as possible who could be trusted to support his administration. Even better would be Hasmonean priests lacking true royal blood. Substantial propaganda value accrued from having Hasmonean priests among his supporters; however, the mere existence of Jewish royal blood in Judea posed a threat to Herod's grasp upon the throne. Therefore, Hasmonean priests who were <u>not</u> of royal blood perfectly fit the king's propaganda needs.

Herod, "Sit down honorable Heli and Matthias. Guard, bring us wine." The two men stood dumbfounded not believing that Herod actually intended for them to sit and drink wine together.

Herod motioned for the priests to sit. "Please, sit my friends. Let me make sure that I correctly understand the nature of your visit to my camp. Do you pledge your allegiance to me as the rightful king of Judea, Samaria, Galilee, and Idumea?"

"Yes your Excellency."

Herod smiled and indicated that the guard should pour out four cups of wine. Herod took the first drink and turned to Sossius. "General, you see what I mean about restraining the

---

[15] Herod was considered Jewish only in the sense that his family was forcibly converted to Judaism before Herod was born. This forced conversion occurred when the Hasmoneans conquered Idumea in the 2nd century BCE.

soldiers when we breach the walls of the city. Here are two high ranking Temple priests who now support me. How many supporters will I have left in the city if we rape their women and plunder their possessions?"

Sossius, "The appearance of these two priests is quite provident. They can create a list of the families most likely to support your kingship and I pledge to do my best to keep soldiers away from those homes."

Herod, "Excellent general, also keep your men away from the Hasmonean palace."

"Why? It contains the best booty."

"General, I will compensate you and your men for the loss of pillage privileges in the Hasmonean palace and the homes of the leading men identified by these priests. If these two were able to sneak out of the city past our blockade, don't you agree that Antigonus has likely transferred some or all of his treasure out of the city?"

Sossius nodded his head in agreement, "I hadn't thought of that your Excellency. You are right."

Herod, "So I must carefully search the palace for treasure and question all the servants and slaves for information. They may have clues as to where Antigonus hid his treasure. I can't conduct a thorough investigation with your men raping and killing everyone in sight."

Heli then volunteered, "King Antigonus sent all his women and young sons out of the city under the command of his sister Princess Alexandra."

Sossius slammed the table with his fist and jumped to his feet, "Jupiter's balls! Tribune Blasius come here at once."

Herod questioned Heli further, "How many days ago?"

Heli replied, "I heard the news four days ago so probably longer."

Sossius, "They could be almost to Petra by now."

Herod didn't think so. "I'm not convinced they are in Nabatea. My mother is Nabatean. I have relations in Petra. King Malchus claims to be neutral in this war so would Antigonus really entrust the care of his family to a man who hasn't declared his friendship? No, they will only be safe in Parthia and would have to cross hostile territory to get there."

Sossius, "So where do you think Antigonus sent his family?"

Herod, "One of the desert fortresses on the eastern edge of the country. I hold Masada so that's out, probably Macherus or Hyrcania."

Sossius sent out one hundred cavalry and a cohort of infantry to scout the eastern edges of the Jewish kingdom looking for the royal Hasmonean refugees who had escaped the blockade of Jerusalem. It didn't take the soldiers long to confirm that Herod had been right. Princess Alexandra was holed up in Fortress Hyrcania with 3000 soldiers and a large contingent of the Jewish royal family. This posed something of a problem for Herod. The Roman legion had orders to move out of Judea to engage the Parthians further north after Jerusalem fell. Making matters worse, the Romans intended on taking 3000 of Herod's best troops with them as auxiliaries for their campaign against the Parthians. Herod's remaining soldiers were tied up pacifying all the major cities of the Jewish kingdom. It would be years before Herod could free up enough man power to overwhelm the stout defensive position of Hyrcania. Antigonus had bet his family's lives on the hope of a Parthian rescue and Herod intended to snuff out that hope as soon as possible. He sent Pheroras, his last remaining brother, to Hyrcania in command of just enough soldiers to blockade Hyrcania but not storm the walls. The strategy was to starve the Hasmoneans out of Hyrcania. Herod could not spare enough soldiers to do more.

Jerusalem, Judea (37 BCE)

In the summer of 37 BCE, the walls of Jerusalem finally fell to Herod and the Romans. Rape and pillage of the city unfolded as expected but Sossius managed to hold back his men from the Hasmonean palace and selected homes of leading priests and rabbis identified by brothers Heli and Matthias as likely supporters of Herod. That left a large swath of the city as fair game for the invading soldiers that came bursting through the walls.

Heli returned to his home inside the city at his first opportunity under the protection of a squad of soldiers Herod assigned to him. Heli banged on his front door but no one answered. "Eleazar, where are you old man? It is the master Heli."

Heli continued banging on the door. "Hanan, surely you must recognize my voice. Pull back the bolt. Don't be frightened. All is safe. These soldiers are here for our protection."

Finally the door opened exposing a young slave whose name Heli couldn't quite remember. The young slave meekly said, "Welcome home master."

"Where are Eleazar and Hanan? Where is my wife?" Heli pushed past the slave into the vestibule.

The young slave trailed behind his master saying, "Eleazar and Hanan were taken by the king shortly after you left the city master. A messenger later told us they were executed. Lady Anna is in her quarters."

Heli, "She was told I am here but waits in her quarters?"

The young slave replied, "Yes master."

Clearly his wife was still upset. She had opposed the defection to Herod as constituting treason against Israel. Heli wondered why she couldn't see that he did what was best for the family. Wasn't she aware that all those who resisted Herod were dead and their homes looted? Had Heli not defected some Roman soldier would be getting intimately acquainted with her private parts that very instant. It was the only option open to preserve the family. Or was she sulking because he ordered her confined to the house while he was gone? Heli entered his wife's quarters expecting to resolve what he thought of as a minor domestic dispute. Instead he found Anna cradling a baby next to a wet nurse who looked like a gladiator with overgrown, milky tits.

Heli, "Anna, is it too much to ask that you come greet your husband at the door when he returns from a long absence?"

Anna, "Lower your voice. The baby has just fallen asleep."

"What is this baby doing here? Whose child is this?"

Anna handed baby Mariamne over to the wet nurse and dismissed her to the next room. It was time for Anna to confront her husband. She was a loyal daughter of Aaron disgraced by her husband who betrayed King Antigonus by kissing the ring of that pig Herod. The king had given Anna a solemn and important mission that she intended to carry out at all costs; however, she could not provide sanctuary for Princess Mariamne without the consent of her husband Heli. She held only one bargaining chip in the negotiation, public shame.

Anna, "You know that our family's honor and my personal honor have been disgraced by your actions in going over to Herod?"

Heli, "All the Jewish people of so-called honor who opposed Herod are now dead. The Roman soldiers standing in the entrance hall of our home would have come here to rape you and our servants had I not done what was necessary. After having their fun, they would have killed us all. Is that what you wanted?"

She replied, "Those who suffer for righteousness sake are upright in the eyes of the Lord."

Heli had enough lecturing from his wife. Jewish women were not taught the Torah so, in his view, whatever little fragments of wisdom they gathered from visits to the Temple or synagogue lacked a full exposure to the word of Yahweh.

"Silence woman. 'Much wealth is in the house of the righteous.'[16] Look about you. Do you not see riches before your eyes? And my relationship with the new king shall lead to even greater wealth. You are my wife and I command your obedience. Return that child to wherever it came from and there shall be no more talk of righteousness from you."

Heli turned to leave but Anna grabbed the sleeve of his cloak. She said, "Our discussion is not yet concluded husband. If that child must leave our house, then I leave as well. Not only that but I shall sit in the outer courtyard of the Temple every day thereafter and shout out your sins to all those with ears to hear until you agree to give me a divorce. Every piece of dirt from our

---

[16] *Proverbs* 15:6.

twenty-two years of marriage will be exposed to the crowd. Do you hear me? That includes the affair with the servant girl and your other vices."

Heli stood mouth agape.

Anna, "So you didn't think I knew. Servants talk Heli and word always gets back to the wife. I know you have designs on the high priesthood. Maybe that is why you are not so sad to see the Hasmonean dynasty destroyed. With the royal family murdered, it opens the way for you and Matthias to rise in office at the Temple. How do you think the words I speak will go over with your colleagues at the Temple?"

Heli, "So you are blackmailing me?"

Anna, "Blackmail is an ugly word husband. You did what you thought was righteous in the eyes of God and now I am doing the same. We'll let God determine who to reward and who to punish for their actions."

"Tell me Anna, who is this child that you are willing to go to such lengths to protect?"

"Her name is Mariamne and you are going to legally adopt her Heli. All you need to know is that her parents are dead. If you agree to these terms then I promise to honor you as an obedient wife. If not, then I shall leave you and destroy your public honor."

Anger rose in the breast of Heli. He very much wished to take a sword and slash his wife's neck right at that instant but she had him boxed in. There really was no alternative for Heli other than to submit to the demands of his wife. Jewish men are known for being strong-willed yet their wives are even stronger.

Heli let his voice rise, "You will submit to me wife!"

Anna replied in a mild tone displaying no emotion, "I shall submit my all to you husband but on one simple condition, adopt Mariamne. She is Hasmonean."

"Hasmonean?" Heli feared the identity of the child. Deep down he knew the secret as there could be no other explanation for Anna's devotion to this child. Heli shut his eyes trying to block out the words he had just heard. He said to Anna, "Lie on the cot and submit to me."

"Do you agree to my terms husband?"

"Yes!" Heli had no choice. His wife could destroy his standing in the priesthood, something that meant everything to Heli.

Anna dropped her tunic and reclined on the cot as instructed. Heli took his wife without satisfaction for he was no longer the master in his own home.

Antony's Headquarters, Antioch (37 BCE)

Herod lacked authority to execute a king as the Romans reserved that privilege to themselves. Thus, the new Jewish king shackled the prior Jewish king Antigonus in chains and carted him off to Marc Antony. The triumvir maintained Antioch as his seat of power in the eastern Roman Empire. Cleopatra remained in Egypt so the legendary courtesan Glaphyra held sway in Antony's bed at this time. The triumvir kept secondary mistresses for the purpose of cheating on his primary mistress. Glaphyra artfully fucked her way into a royal husband through the influence of Antony and her future granddaughter, also named Glaphyra, eventually became Herod's daughter-in-law but all that lay years hence.

Herod transported to Antioch as much gold as he could lay his hands upon after paying off the Roman army under Sossius. This meant ripping gold fixtures off the walls at the Hasmonean palace in Jerusalem and melting them down into coin. The new Jewish king desperately needed to locate the Temple treasury. He ransacked the palaces of Antigonus and the chief priests, tortured members of Antigonus' party yet the treasure location remained a mystery to him. Herod worried like a virgin on her wedding night how Antony would react to his offering. Would the boxes of gold and silver Herod carried to Antioch satisfy the voracious desires of the imperator for spendable coin? Only the gods knew if the taciturn Antony would find his offering acceptable and execute Antigonus.

Guards ushered Herod into the private chambers of Marc Antony, who ignored the vassal king while busying himself with correspondence. Antony's snub of Herod continued for minutes that felt like hours to Herod. He stood patiently and silently waiting to be acknowledged. Antony finally looked up from his papers, "Oh, there you are Herod. I'm glad you are here. Perhaps you can clear up something that my agents have said to me that certainly must be false. They tell me you can't find the Jewish Temple treasure. Reports have it that the Temple contained in excess of six thousand talents in gold and silver!"

Antony pounded his fist on the table three times then got up from his chair circling Herod as the imperator's blood pressure rose. Antony continued, "Sossius reports that your forces had the city of Jerusalem surrounded for months. Is that true Herod?"

Herod, "Yes imperator."

Antony exploded with rage like a beast upon its prey, "Then how in fucking hell did six thousand talents of precious metals disappear from the fucking Temple without your men conspiring to make it disappear?!?! You wouldn't hold out on me, would you Herod? So help me, if I find out you captured the treasure and are hiding it from me, I'll nail you're arse to a cross and personally prod your genitals with hot embers."

Antony cursed like a slave raised in the Subura. Although born a patrician, he squandered his youth cavorting with the Roman underclass thus acquiring their rough manners. Herod didn't tremble with fear nor even wince as Antony circled him while foaming at the mouth. The new Jewish king made it this far in the treacherous world of Middle Eastern politics by keeping his cool no matter the danger. Showing fear to Antony would only compound Herod's problems. "Killing me won't make the gold appear imperator. I've tortured all of Antigonus' men who survived the battle. They all said the same thing as Antigonus himself, the treasure was smuggled out through tunnels leading from the Temple to the Wadi Kidron with instructions that it be hidden. No one left inside Jerusalem when the city fell, including the king himself, knows the hiding place. Torture Antigonus yourself if you like and hear him tell the same story with your own ears."

Antony sat back in his chair. His tone moderated, "Just like that, Antigonus sent six thousand talents out the tunnels with no idea where in Hades it went? Poof, it's gone." Antony gestured with his hand in a dramatic flourish.

"Think of it from his point of view imperator. The only way to safeguard the treasure was to keep knowledge of its location outside of Jerusalem. No secret has ever been safe in Jerusalem."

Antony, "Somebody knows where this fucking treasure is located. String the Jews up by their balls, all the Jews of Judea, string them up by their balls!"

Normally Herod found himself the one whose passions required calming by subordinates yet here he stood in Antioch as the voice of reason against the mania of Marc Antony. All knew Herod possessed the stomach for blood but he dished it out in calculated fashion to further his political ends. Herod, his surviving family members, and his supporters in Israel existed as an extreme minority against the remainder of the Jewish people. He needed Jewish support to stay in power. Randomly torturing large numbers of Judeans in his search for the Temple treasure would only antagonize the populace to stand even more rigidly against his reign than they already were. "Imperator, I have a good idea where we can find individuals who know the hiding place of the treasure, Fortress Hyrcania."

Herod walked over to Antony's map table and leafed through the various maps until he found the one containing the Jewish kingdom. "Here, in Judea near the Dead Sea." Herod pointed to the spot.

Antony, "How can you be so sure?"

"Inside are the last remnants of the Hasmonean army, perhaps as many as 3000 soldiers, and the women of Antigonus' family. They are under the command of Princess Alexandra, older sister of Antigonus and widow of King Ptolemy of Chalcis."

Antony, "Well, what are you waiting for? Breach the walls and find the treasure!"

A typical Roman response thought Herod. Conventional military wisdom held that an assault against a fortified position required three times the troop strength of the defenders. By simple math, Herod needed more than nine thousands soldiers to assault Hyrcania. Herod's military was currently engaged pacifying the Jewish kingdom. Sossius took the cream of the Herodian army north with him to continue the fight against the Parthians. Stripping 9000 soldiers from Herod's already depleted force to assault Hyrcania would surely lead to renewed insurrection in other parts of the Jewish kingdom, such as Galilee. And all the money Herod otherwise might use to buy more mercenaries sat in a wagon train inside the governor's compound at Antioch to be handed over to Antony momentarily. But these were mere details to an elite patrician like Antony. They demanded results and ignored quibbles such as lack of resources. Herod didn't expect a sympathetic ear but felt compelled to defend himself no matter the futility. "I would be happy to breach the walls of Hyrcania tomorrow but that requires the proper resources. I know the imperator has spent substantial time in the east including the Jewish kingdom so you are aware what I'm up against."

"Herod, by Jupiter I never thought I'd see the day the words of a eunuch came out of your mouth." Antony broke into a falsetto voice imitating the high octave sounds of a eunuch. Perhaps the man was a frustrated actor at heart. "Oh imperator, please have pity on me. The Jews are such terrible subjects. How is a king to manage? Woe is me."

Herod ben Antipater was a proud man capable of shouldering only so much abuse before his temper broke. Herod stiffened his back and looked Antony dead in the eye. "You handed me enough money to field an army for three months together with a few thousand legionnaires cobbled together from units shredded by the Parthians, then told me to capture the Jewish kingdom. I did as you asked imperator. During the war, you asked me to bring part of my army north to assist you in your own campaign. I did as you asked and my brother Joseph died at the hands of Antigonus' men while I was at your side."

Herod put his hands on Antony desk and leaned into his face. "The treasure isn't in Jerusalem, Antony. I tore the city apart and it's not there. All the money I have is loaded onto carts sitting inside the walls of your compound here in Antioch. It's all yours Antony, everything I have. Sossius took three thousand of my men north with him when his force left Jerusalem. I need to pacify the entire kingdom and there are barely enough men remaining under my command to accomplish this task."

Antony's mood lightened as his focus shifted to the diminished but not insubstantial treasure Herod delivered to Antioch. Herod and Antony stepped out onto the balcony situated off the imperator's office. From there one had a view of Herod's wagons loaded with gold and silver. Herod said, "Return to me the gold and silver loaded on those carts and I'll buy the men necessary to attack Hyrcania before the heat of summer sets in. It's up to you Antony. Without that money my only option is to besiege Hyrcania and starve them out. God knows how many years that will take."

Another Roman official, one more pompous, may have been offended by Herod's aggressive demeanor but not Antony. He appreciated subordinates who spoke plainly. "How many talents are on those wagons Herod?"

"One hundred talents of gold and two hundred talents of silver. The rest went to Sossius and his men."

Antony walked back into the room and sat down at his desk. He called for wine and waited for the cups to be filled before speaking. He said, "Well you came up short my dear friend. I expected much more out of you but I like the results you obtained in the field. Tax collectors I have. Loyal generals who win battles are hard for a Roman to find in the east. We drink to your victory at Jerusalem."

Herod welcomed the soothing sensation of fine wine as it washed through his veins after the heated confrontation with Antony. The verbal sparring may have been over but Antony had a warning for Herod. "Don't disappoint me again friend. It's the easiest way to become my enemy. You'll find I'm not long on forgiveness."

Antony called for his scribe. "Diomedes, write out a personal promissory note from Herod to me in the amount of six hundred talents."

Herod, "Six hundred talents?"

"You've arrived with about one-third the amount I expected in return for my securing you the Jewish throne. You do agree you shorted me?"

Herod knew his business with Antony this day was not concluded. They still had not discussed the fate of Antigonus and he had no other funds to use as a bribe for the extra favor of executing Antigonus immediately. As luck would have it, fate intervened to help bring about that which Herod desired.

Diomedes interrupted the conversation, "My pardon imperator but there are several hundred, maybe one thousand, leading Jews from Jerusalem and throughout the Syrian province waiting outside for an audience."

Antony, "A thousand? Who are they?"

Diomedes, "Important priests and other citizens."

Herod, "Now you see what I face. Every second Antigonus draws breath he is a danger to me."

Antony further inquired of Diomedes, "What do they want?"

Diomedes, "The return of Antigonus to the Jewish throne. They refuse to accept Herod as their king. If I may be so bold imperator, does it not make sense to export the problem of Antigonus to Rome? He is a king whose trial rightly belongs before the Senate."

Herod objected vehemently to Antony's close advisor and confidant Diomedes, "Imperator, please listen. Did not Pompey Magnus send King Aristobulus back to Rome after he took command of the Jewish kingdom? And what happened with Aristobulus?"

Antony had to admit that Herod had a point, "After Caesar crossed the Rubicon and went to war with Pompey, Caesar released Aristobulus to stir trouble in Palestine."

Herod, "Exactly! The son of Aristobulus is in our hands and the son of Caesar sits in Rome.[17] History will repeat itself when you go to war with Octavian!"

---

[17] Octavian was the great nephew of Julius Caesar but the great man adopted Octavian after the death of his only child Julia.

At that moment the Jewish crowd waiting outside Antony's compound began chanting for the return of their king. These sounds reached the imperator through the window. He walked outside to view the Jewish mob. When they saw Antony, their shouts reached a fever pitch.

Antony turned to Diomedes, "I'm not sending Antigonus to Rome."

Diomedes, "I don't understand imperator. Are you going to try him here in Antioch with all the Jewish protesters present?"

Antony, "Yes. This will send a message to the priests and common people that I mean business. Perhaps those assholes will think twice about refusing to reveal the location of the Temple treasure."

The imperator turned to Herod, "What punishment do you suggest?"

Herod didn't have to think about his reply, "Behead him. Antigonus beheaded my brother Joseph in Jericho. His head comes off!"

Antony, "Yes, I quite agree but we need a public exhibition first. We can't let this miscreant die an easy death with one swift slash of the sword. Diomedes, what is the Roman punishment for insurrection?"

Diomedes humored his master, "We scourge and crucify them."

Antony, "Yes, scourge and crucify. So we shall give this Jewish king a proper Roman sendoff. First scourge and crucify but, before he expires, drag him down from the cross and chop his head off to satisfy our friend Herod's desire to avenge his brother."[18]

Diomedes was shocked at the punishment Antony planned for Antigonus. No Roman consul had crucified a king much less

---

[18] Josephus said Marc Antony beheaded King Antigonus. Antiquities XV 1:2. Cassius Dio gives more detail in his history, "Antigonus he (Marcus Antonius) bound to a cross and flogged--treatment accorded to no other king by the Romans--and subsequently slew him." Dio's Rome XLIX v.22. Reading Dio closely, he tells us Antigonus was flogged, crucified, then executed by another unnamed means. Josephus identifies that other means as beheading.

beheaded one. Diomedes, "But is that legal imperator? Antigonus is a king."

Antony howled, "The Senate declared this piece of shit an enemy of Rome thereby stripping him of the rights of a subject king. Get it arranged Diomedes. I'll try him in my audience chamber this afternoon and execute him before sundown today. Go."

Diomedes, "Yes imperator."

Antony, "Make sure Antigonus is scourged and crucified in sight of the crowd. Let the Jews see what I think of their king. He became a common criminal the day he decided to challenge the authority of Rome." Antony waived his hand dismissing his scribe.

Herod spoke up but in a more deferential tone this time. "Perhaps it would not be wise to further antagonize the passions of the Jewish people imperator. How about letting the men have their fun with Antigonus privately. You and I could go down and enjoy the show while sharing a fine wine."

For better or worse, Antony had a habit of making a decision then sticking with it no matter the rationale presented by subordinates for an alternative course of action. "No, I piss on the Jews. Let them see what happens to insurrectionists. He shall be scourged and crucified in public."

Herod refilled their wine cups and the two drank a toast to the death of Antigonus, the first anointed king of Israel to be scourged and crucified by the Romans but not the last.

Antony's attention returned to the issue of money. "Herod, you must have sources of ready coin. What about selling the high priesthood?"

A headache pounded inside Herod's brain just thinking about the office of high priest. All Jewish mother-in-laws are formidable opponents but one of high royal birth is of an entirely different scale. Herod and his mother-in-law Alexandra bat Hyrcanus circled each other like gladiators angling for position in the coliseum. Princess Alexandra held Herod and his mixed Arabian ancestry in nothing but contempt. Her father Hyrcanus, the former high priest and king, reigned as a weakling allowing others to push him off the throne but Alexandra possessed the will of lioness. She viewed Herod as a necessary evil to her family's destiny to reclaim their rightful place on the Jewish throne. But the first step was the high priesthood, which Alexandra absolutely demanded Herod grant to her son Aristobulus III. She skillfully bargained the office of high priest into the marriage contract between Herod and her daughter Mariamne. However, Aristobulus was then only 16 years of age and Herod naturally expected that he would not be required to name Aristobulus high priest until the boy reached a more appropriate age for the office. No, Alexandra intended to shove her son up Herod's ass no matter the obstacles.

Herod returned his attention to Antony. "My mother-in-law demands I award the office of high priest to her son Aristobulus. The boy is only 16 years of age yet through him she aims on controlling the wealth of the Temple treasury."

Antony frowned at Herod who possessed more excuses than an old house slave. No matter, Antony thought to himself. Cleopatra harbored designs on the Jewish kingdom and Antony lacked the ability to tell his lover and future wife "no". Either Herod delivered the treasure Antony believed was owed to him or Antony would remove cities from Herod's control turning them over to Cleopatra. As Antony saw it, Herod would one day find himself the mayor of Jerusalem unless he soon filled up Antony's coffers with gold and silver.

The trial of King Antigonus lasted but a few minutes as Antigonus refused to speak, nor even look at Marc Antony. This drove the imperator into a rage (which was not difficult to achieve). Antony heckled the prisoner with questions while his soldiers knocked Antigonus about with their fists. The diminutive Jewish king, stripped of his fine garments and bloodied by the soldiers, presented a pitiful sight.

Antony turned to Herod, "He looks like a woman."

"Yes, General Sossius made the same observation." Had Antigonus been a younger man, Herod was certain Antony would have raped the king before crucifying him. Antigonus didn't move his head or otherwise show emotion when Antony issued the death sentence. Roman legionnaires dragged the prisoner out into the courtyard, tied him to a post, and began scourging him in full view of the crowd. This consisted of one hundred lashes with the flagellum, a short whip made of knotted leather thongs with pieces of metal attached at various intervals. This instrument quickly removed the skin. Antigonus' back became a shredded mess of twisted flesh, blood splattering in all directions. The Jewish people stood in silent horror watching their beloved king absorb Roman abuse.

Among the crowd stood ben Eleazar, a young Hasmonean priest and supporter of King Antigonus. Ben Eleazar escaped into the tunnels beneath the Temple just as the Romans breached the walls into the inner courtyard. He knew the king would die but, as the Righteous Teacher taught, life does not end in death. Ben Eleazar pledged to God in heaven that he would secret the remains of King Antigonus out of Roman territory to the east. One day when the evil Romans were driven from the land of Israel, ben Eleazar would return the remains of King Antigonus to the holy city of Jerusalem to await the end of days. So the loyal priest stood quietly during the execution, displaying no emotion as the Romans both tied and nailed Antigonus to the cross. The nails were completely unnecessary to the task as his arms were bound with ropes but the Romans drove nails through sensitive joints in the king's hands merely to amplify his pain. The young priest wept a sigh of relief when King Antigonus became unconscious on the cross after less than an hour. Marc Antony gave the order to haul the king down from the cross and behead him. It was a sloppy process because Antigonus' head hung down at his chest as a sword cleaved his neck. Antony ordered Antigonus' severed head placed on the gate outside his headquarters and the torso thrown into the back streets for the dogs to feed on. Ben Eleazar waited until the small hours of a moonless night to collect the body of his king and, also, recover his head from Antony's gate. More than thirty years elapsed before Herod died and ben Eleazar was able to return King Antigonus' remains to a secret tomb in Jerusalem.[19]

---

[19] The author contends the tomb of King Antigonus was found in 1971 in East Jerusalem. It is known as the Abba Tomb.

Princess Mariamne bat Antigonus and her son Yeshua visited the tomb of King Antigonus just prior to Yeshua's attempted revolution.

Jerusalem, Judea (36 BCE)

History recalls Herod for those he killed but should also remember him as a prolific builder. He rebuilt Solomon's Temple in Jerusalem, lavish palaces at Jerusalem, Caesarea, Masada, and Herodium, and the world's first artificial harbor at Caesarea. And those projects do not even complete the list of major building achievements of King Herod. However, these architectural wonders were still years off in the future during the first full year of Herod's reign. Herod's army labored pacifying the country by stamping out every hint of insurrection throughout the vast Jewish kingdom. Insurrection also struck at Herod from within the walls of his own palace. Every man forced to live with his mother-in-law under the same roof faces a daily challenge to his authority. Princess Alexandra exceeded every known standard for combative mothers-in-law.

What had been a simmering feud erupted into open warfare when Herod initially named Ananelus high priest. The king needed spendable coin in order to consolidate his hold on the kingdom and selling the high priesthood to a qualified Temple priest appeared Herod's easiest avenue to that end, but Herod hadn't factored in the deviousness of Alexandra. First she petitioned Cleopatra for redress of the situation hoping to find a sympathetic ear with the Egyptian queen. However, Cleopatra merely ignored the Hasmonean royal for she had designs on gaining control over Israel, not helping some politically powerless aggrieved Jewish royal to attain priestly office.

Fate dealt Alexandra another chip to play in her war with Herod. Marc Antony's friend Delius toured Judea on a fact finding mission or, put another way, Antony sent Delius to spy on Herod. He arrived looking for any evidence that Herod secreted away the lost Temple treasury. Alexandra seized the opportunity to ingratiate herself and her family to a friend of Antony by inviting him for a private meeting at the Hasmonean mansion in Jerusalem.

She was still a striking beauty then in her mid-forties. Delius came from the equestrian rank of middle citizenship in Rome and possessed the hard features of the cavalry officer he had been. His dark stringy hair, swarthy Mediterranean coloring, broad shoulders, and clean shaven yet prominent chin contrasted with the fair complexion of his Hasmonean hosts. The Hasmonean royals were renowned for their beauty and Queen Mariamne stood as the most beautiful of all her peers. She was petite with blondish hair, green eyes, and delicate features. Her younger brother Aristobulus was equally fair with delicate, perhaps even feminine features. He was yet incapable of growing facial hair. Alexandra greeted Delius in the fashion of a Roman matron as opposed to the custom of her country. The Jewish practice was for men and women to recline for food and / or drink in separate rooms where Roman custom allowed for a certain mixing of the sexes. When her steward announced Delius, Alexandra herself escorted him to a lavishly furnished room near the entrance where her son Aristobulus and Queen Mariamne awaited. After introducing her children, Alexandra invited Delius to recline on a couch with Aristobulus while the women sat in chairs opposite them.

Alexandra, "The sun just now hits mid-day but, if it is not early for you, perhaps wine? We recently received an amphora from Chios, a variety I especially recommend."

Delius, "It is never too early for a soldier to enjoy wine. You have Chios here in Jerusalem? I haven't been able to find a descent wine since I landed in Judea. I'd given up hope to drink anything pleasing until returning to the imperator in Antioch."

Aristobulus said, "I'm sure Antony has a wine cellar fit for a king."

Delius couldn't help but notice Aristobulus' handsome features while reclining next to the young noble. He was certain Antony would be immediately smitten with the future high priest should the two ever meet. The imperator fucked anything appealing with two legs. He didn't much care whether his bed mates had breasts or testes, or both. An awkward silence elapsed as Delius stared at Aristobulus just a tad too long. Delius took a full view of Aristobulus not for his own gratification but in his role as Antony's spy. The boss sent out trusted subordinates such as Delius to fulfill his needs. Antony perpetually needed two things, fresh ass and more money. All his men knew to keep an eye out for both.

Delius, "The answer is yes and no young prince. The imperator has the best wine cellar in the Eastern Roman Empire at the beginning of each month when new shipments arrive. But my old friend manages to exhaust his supplies almost as quickly as the ships make harbor."

Delius turned back to Alexandra to finish responding to her original question. "I would surely enjoy a cup of your wine princess but the palate of a simple soldier is not quite refined enough to fully enjoy Chios. It would be wasted on me. This may be too much to hope for but you wouldn't, per chance, have a Ceretanum from the Iberian coast?"

"Of course we can accommodate you." Alexandra snapped her fingers and the steward appeared. "Judas, open the Ceretanum and bring cups for our guest and for my son." When Alexandra returned her attention to Delius she found him staring at the queen this time. Rather than be offended by the ill manners of Antony's rough subordinate from the middle class, Alexandra saw his desire as an opportunity. She married her daughter to Herod in order to further her political ambitions. Now that Herod had reneged on the agreement to place Aristobulus in the office of high priest, she set her sights higher. Perhaps she could pimp her daughter to Antony and, thereby, completely circumvent the authority of Herod. After making idle conversation for a few minutes while the men enjoyed their wine, Alexandra cut to the chase.

Alexandra, "You know the imperator well, do you not Delius?"

"Yes princess." Delius wasn't quite sure where she was heading with the question but, then again, wasn't totally surprised when Alexandra made her play. In his experience, these eastern types had no qualms about bartering royal flesh for power.

"Do you believe Marc Antony would find the queen attractive?"

Delius quickly checked out of the corner of his eye to see if the queen of his host country blushed at the implied offer carried in her mother's question. Mariamne sat smiling as if they discussed the weather or the latest fashion in Rome. He then said, "Certainly princess. Any man would and the imperator is more man than most, if you get my meaning."

Alexandra, "I do."

"And if I may hazard a further opinion, I believe the imperator would find the young prince equally pleasing to the eye." Delius thought if the old girl was bold enough to try and pimp her married daughter to Antony then she just might be willing to play her son in the same game.

Aristobulus raised his hand as if to protest but Alexandra cut him off. She completely dominated the young prince and was perfectly willing to peddle the sexual favors of her son or daughter to regain the lost family power. "Of course, my son or daughter, whichever he prefers. How might you think it best to raise the matter with the imperator?"

Delius previously bartered for the services of young bed mates for Antony but nothing approaching the directness of this negotiation with Alexandra. The woman held no shame amidst her blind ambition.

Delius, "I suggest portraits be drawn and shipped to the imperator in Antioch."[20]

Alexandra clasped her hands together in excitement. "A most excellent suggestion my friend. The local artists here in Jerusalem won't do at all. Can you recommend anyone?"

"Certainly princess. The imperator commissioned murals for his buildings in Antioch. I am certain we can find a suitable portrait artist among those."

Alexandra, "I can't thank you enough. Please send our well wishes and warmest regards to the imperator."

Three months later, life sized portraits of Aristobulus and Queen Mariamne in the guise of Greek gods arrived in Antioch. Antony immediately went into heat. He desired to fuck them both,

---

[20] *See* Josephus, Antiquities XV 2:6 (26-27).

preferably at the same time. Delius succeeded in talking his old friend out of summoning Herod's wife to Antioch for debauchery, as the act might, you know, weaken an important military alliance, but Antony would not be denied in the case of young Aristobulus. Antony often let his penis administer the Eastern Roman Empire. Not long thereafter, a dispatch from Antony to Herod arrived in Jerusalem summoning young Aristobulus to Antioch. Herod's palace spies previously informed him about the portraits shipped to Antioch so Herod knew exactly why Antony was in such a lather to see Aristobulus in person.

Alexandra had Herod by the balls. If he sent the beautiful young prince to Antioch, he may very well return home the new Jewish king. Herod couldn't risk it. He immediately proclaimed Aristobulus high priest and informed Antony that the boy's priestly duties absolutely required his presence in Jerusalem. He emphasized to Antony that the Jewish people would rebel if their high priest left the country. Alexandra gloated excessively on the day her son took office as high priest, an office held by his grandfather before him. She'd scored a victory against her arch nemesis Herod but those who crossed Herod needed to closely watch their backs. His memory was long, temper short, and he inevitably got even.

Hyrcania, Judea (35 BCE)

Herod's brother Pheroras wasn't a happy man. As one of the only two sons of Antipater the Idumean to survive the war against Antigonus, Pheroras expected to receive a sizable territory to rule within the Jewish kingdom. Judea, Galilee or Samaria? No, Herod retained those territories for himself. The family homeland of Idumea? No, that went to Prince Costobarus (member of the Idumean royal family and future husband of Princess Salome). Pheroras received a rocky scrap of land east of the Jordan called Perea. Herod tried sugarcoating the snub with plans to wrestle control of cities from the neighboring Nabatean kingdom for addition to the territory of Pheroras. King Malichus of Nabatea made himself an enemy of Herod by failing to deliver aid during Herod's darkest hour in 40 BCE for which Herod intended payback. But all Herod's talk of capturing Nabatean cities for the benefit of Pheroras took a back seat to pacifying the Jewish kingdom and breaching the walls of Hyrcania. Herod reigned in splendor from Jerusalem while his younger brother Pheroras toiled away in the field still commanding troops two years after Jerusalem fell. He tired of the daily grind eating dust and longed to enjoy some measure of the fruits of victory.

The worm finally turned for Herod's younger brother during the winter of 35 BCE, the year during which Herod finally freed up enough soldiers to make the final assault upon Hyrcania. Low food supplies sapped the strength of the defenders who put up one last ferocious fight at the point where Herodian forces first breached the walls but the resolve of the remaining Hasmonean army quickly faded as Herodian troops poured through the breech. The rout was on. Pheroras quickly shifted his concerns from securing victory to controlling the rampage of his men who were now inside the fortress. Herod tasked Pheroras with two overriding objectives after the walls of Hyrcania fell: (a) kill all the Hasmonean royals and (b) find the Temple treasure. However, those two objectives clashed as the Hasmoneans inside Hyrcania were the ones who hid the treasure and could be expected to possess knowledge of its location. With any luck, Pheroras hoped to find the entire treasure sitting undisturbed inside the walls of the inner-most citadel of the fortress.

Herodian soldiers surged through the fortress killing any men they encountered and herding the women and boys into a temporary enclosure for interrogation and, ultimately, sexual gratification once the battle concluded.

Pheroras barked a command to his cousin Achiabus, a fellow Idumean, "Cousin, go speak with the captain in charge of prisoners. Tell him I'll have his balls on the platter if the officers spirit away any of the prisoners for their private fun until after interrogations are completed. Tell him his balls, go."

Achiabus ran off to do Pheroras' bidding while the youngest son of Antipater the Idumean waited for his troops to storm the citadel inside Hyrcania. No treasure had been found yet. Pheroras' soldiers began ramming down the massive doors of the citadel as arrows rained down upon the attackers but the end result was never in doubt. To the great disappointment of Pheroras no treasure awaited when he stepped inside the inner-most sanctum of Fortress Hyrcania. Instead a gruesome scene met him in an upper chamber where thirty-two women and boys lay dead with stab wounds to the heart. To all appearances, the dead were the last Hasmonean royals from the family of Antigonus, who now journeyed to the afterlife where their pater familias awaited them.

Pheroras approached the first Herodian centurion he encountered inside the citadel. "Where are the bodies of Princess Alexandra and Queen Salina?" The officer pointed to two finely dressed middle-aged women with fair features and bearing royal markings. They left fine corpses.

Pheroras commanded, "Strip all the dead royal women in this room of jewelry and royal markings, wrap their bodies in lien, and then place them in a burial tomb. If you cannot find a burial tomb nearby, have the soldiers cut one out of the rock. And don't mark the grave. Seal the tomb thickly with stones and rubble."

The officer corps of Herod's army was made up almost entirely of foreign mercenaries, mostly Thracians, Germans, and Gauls. They were proud professional soldiers but the grizzled Gallic centurion demurred at the order. "Governor, we usually burn the bodies of our enemies or leave them for the birds of prey to feast upon."

Perhaps the centurion thought Pheroras had gone soft giving special treatment to an enemy princess and queen but these orders didn't come from Pheroras, they came from Herod. Ruling the Jewish people was no easy task even with the weight of the Roman Empire at your back. Herod worried that his subjects would protest should word get out that the bodies of Princess Alexandra and Queen Salina had been desecrated. The smart play was to give the bodies a proper burial but hide their tomb to deprive Herodian enemies of the propaganda value the bodies may possess.

Pheroras turned and looked his Gallic centurion in the eyes. "I'll make sure to note your dissent in my next dispatch to the king. These orders come directly from him."

The centurion saluted then immediately began carrying out the governor's orders. Two years sucking desert sand, drinking warm wine, waking to the smell of camel dung and this was his reward? Pain emanated from the pit of Pheroras' stomach caused not by disappointment from failing to find the treasure in Hyrcania but, rather, fear in having to relate this news to his older brother Herod. Sure as the sun rose in the east the king would heap abuse on Pheroras' head when he learned the treasure still lay beyond his grasp. Herod had good reason to be desperate for money. The king couldn't abide his upstart brother-in-law, Aristobulus III, in the office of high priest. As feared, the people adored their new Hasmonean high priest. Further, the brat and his mother refused to pay an annual honorarium from the Temple treasury to the king. They basked in popular adulation while hoarding the Temple revenues. This sent the king over the edge. Herod ordered the new high priest drowned in the palace swimming pool at Jericho. One can only push stone cold killers so far. Alexandra bat Hyrcanus (Herod's mother-in-law) didn't understand the boundaries in dealings with a man like Herod and her son paid the ultimate price for it. She vociferously protested to Rome and, also, to Antony at Antioch that her son the high priest had been murdered by Herod. The Jewish king knew it was only a matter of time before Antony summoned him to Antioch, where he would be expected to pay Antony another massive bribe in return for his acquittal on the charge of murder. Herod desperately needed money.

Pheroras shook off concerns about Herod then returned his attention to the job at hand. His men huddled the survivors together as Pheroras walked before them. The trembling of a young slave boy no more than thirteen caught his eye. Pheroras had no appetite for boys although one of the Herodian officers in the room practically burst an erection through his tunic while gawking at the lad. The boy's fear held Pheroras' interest because the boy surely would crack and spill all the information he possessed the first time a fist smashed a blow to his skull.

Pheroras pointed, "That one, yes the boy about to wet himself. Put him in the next room." Pheroras continued his examination of the prisoners when he came upon the beauty of the lot, a young woman in her late teens, fair completion, tall, no fear. The others shifted their feet looking down hoping against hope to somehow disappear into the walls. Not this girl. She looked at Pheroras as if she commanded the room, not him. Only a woman of royal breeding carried herself with such confidence, yet it appeared all the royal women were dead … or were they?

Pheroras growled to one of his aides, "Yochanan, take possession of that young beauty over there. You see the one I'm pointing to?"

"Yes Governor."

"Don't touch a hair on her head. Just hold her right in this room until I return. Is that understood? Not a hair on her head."

Yochanan snapped to attention and saluted Pheroras, who then pulled his cousin Achiabus aside. "Cousin, time to play good cop, bad cop with a young slave in the next room. Got it?"

Achiabus, "Wait, who is the good cop?" A valid question for among the relations of Herod there were only bad and worse.

Pheroras, "Do me a favor cousin and play the heavy. Just stand to one side sharpening your gladius but be careful he doesn't pee on your leg."

Pheroras and Achiabus marched into the next room where the slave boy stood chained to the wall stripped down to a loin cloth. He shivered as evening set in and the temperature dropped. Achiabus unsheathed his short sword letting the metal gleam before the boy's eyes in the fading light.

Pheroras, "What's your name boy?"

"Aristides."

"I assume you are Greek. Were you born a slave?"

"Yes, in Jerusalem. My family served the Hasmonean royal house for generations."

Pheroras wasn't made for the role of good cop. Two questions into the interrogation and he already tired of trying to ingratiate himself to the boy. "Aristides, one of two things can happen to you here in this room today. One, you can truthfully tell us everything you know about where the Temple treasure is hidden or, two, my disagreeable cousin begins cutting off your fingers one by one. After your fingers come your toes. Talk to me Aristides."

The boy looked at Achiabus who now sharpened his sword then back at Pheroras. His mouth became dry as he tried to speak.

Pheroras, "Spit it out boy, what do you know?"

"I … I really know nothing about any treasure. We traveled lightly the day we escaped Jerusalem through the tunnels. I know Princess Alexandra sent provisions to this fortress months ahead of our departure but I really know nothing about any treasure."

Pheroras turned to Achiabus, "You know what cousin, forget the fingers and toes." Pheroras yanked off the boy's loin cloth exposing his genitals. "Just cut this little bastard's balls off. Do it now."

Achiabus took a mock step toward the boy and, as predicted, he peed on Achiabus' leg. Pheroras couldn't help himself from busting into laughter. Achiabus tossed Pheroras his gladius telling his cousin to cut the boy's balls off himself, then left the room to rinse the piss from his leg.

Aristides said, "Noble sir, I don't know anything about a treasure but I did hear a secret about a baby princess."

Those words interested Pheroras who filled a cup with wine from a skin and handed it to the boy to drink. "Apologies for the rough treatment from my men today. After they have their fill of wine, women and boys, they'll be tolerable in the morning."

The slave looked at the wine not sure what to do. A nobleman had never given him wine to drink before and Pheroras did not strike him as the kind type.

"Drink boy!"

The slave drank.

Pheroras continued, "Now back to this baby princess. Whose child might she be, exactly?"

"The king's daughter sir."

Pheroras' interest in the child kicked into overload but he played it calm, feigning limited interest in the girl. "The king's daughter. You mean the daughter of Antigonus?"

The slave took another long pull on the cup of wine. "That's correct sir. She was given to a priest."

Pheroras, "And what priest would that be?"

"A priest in Jerusalem. I don't know his name. I wasn't there when the princess was turned over but I heard from other servants it was in the city."

There were thousands upon thousands of priests in Jerusalem. Pheroras needed to narrow down the list. It was time for the bad cop again. Pheroras wound up and smacked the boy across the face with his leather-gloved hand. "Boy, why did Antigonus place his daughter with this particular priest?"

"All the royal women were leaving for the desert and his baby daughter was too young to travel. The priest is a relative of the king."

Now we're getting somewhere, thought Pheroras. There were a limited number of Hasmonean priests in Jerusalem and most of them were now dead but it left Pheroras with many possibilities to work through.

"But why this priest?"

"They said this priest would not be killed by Herod. He defected to Herod just before the city fell."

Pheroras smiled the smile of the wolf in sheep's clothing. He knew of only two priests fitting the description of the boy's ravings. Heli and his brother Matthias were Hasmonean Temple priests and both defected to Herod mere days before the city fell to Herod. Pheroras knew Herod accepted their pledge of loyalty and not only spared their lives but saw to it that they received high position within the Temple priesthood. One of these two priests had to be his man. With no further use for the boy and desiring to extinguish the secret, Pheroras used the sword handed to him by Achiabus to run the slave through the heart. It was a clean, lethal blow. The prisoner did not suffer.

Pheroras, "An easy death is the best I can offer you boy." On to the next order of business, the girl. Pheroras walked toward the main room of the citadel where the bulk of the high value prisoners were detained when one of his officers stopped him.

A Herodian centurion addressed his commander, "Governor, the men are anxious for their turn with the prisoners." Soldiers were, in many ways, like children. They cry and moan for the treat sitting just beyond their reach.

Pheroras replied, "What information have you received from the interrogations? Where is the treasure?"

"All we know is that before our forces surrounded Jerusalem a large caravan of wagons loaded with something, we don't know what, pulled out of the Temple complex heading toward the Dead Sea."

"That's it? That's all you have centurion? No description of the cargo, no speculation on the final destination?"

"Sorry governor that is all the information we have except one prisoner said priests were leading the convoy."

"Bring me all the priests among the prisoners."

The centurion had more bad news for his commander. "All the priests are dead. They took up arms and mixed themselves in with the Hasmonean soldiers. The defenders died to a man."

Pheroras let fly a stream of expletives upon the centurion knowing the soldier would completely ignore the words like rain rolling off a duck's back. Pheroras hoped the exercise would be cathartic and ease the pain growing in his acidic stomach. No such luck. His stomach churned like wagon wheels on a rocky road, and then he remembered the ravishing servant girl with the pretentious airs. She calmly stood over in the corner with Yochanan, right where Pheroras left her.

Pheroras approached her. "My lady, if I could have the honor of a private interview it would be greatly appreciated." Pheroras meant the pleasantries as sarcasm but she accepted his deferential words with grace replying, "Certainly governor."

She followed him to the same room where Pheroras had recently concluded his "interview" with the slave boy. Soldiers carried the boy's dead, bloodied body past the girl on their way out the door. Pheroras enjoyed the timing assuming the display would unnerve the girl. "Did you know him?"

She replied, "Of course I knew Aristides and his parents as well. We were both born in the palace."

Before Pheroras got out a follow-up question, she took over the conversation. "Governor, there is no need for us to play hide and seek among the date trees. I know what you want."

"And what is that girl?" Pheroras leered at her body to make certain the girl could not miss his intentions.

She continued, "The treasure, it was the first question out of every soldier's mouth when they interviewed the prisoners. But I need something from you before I help you obtain what you desire."

The gall of this servant girl! "You are not in a position to demand anything from me girl. I take that which pleases me. Don't you know who I am?"

"Yes, I know. You are Pheroras ben Antipater, governor of Perea, brother of the king appointed by the Romans." She said the word "Romans" like it brought a foul taste to her mouth practically spitting it out. She continued, "Go ahead and rape me. Get it over with but you'll get nothing from me but limp flesh unless you also give me that which I desire."

The girl's obstinacy aroused Pheroras. Most men went for the demur, submissive types but not Pheroras. He enjoyed feisty women. "What is it that you require of me?"

She replied, "My brother's life. He was captured with me."

"How old?"

"Thirteen."

Pheroras, "All the boys have been passed out to the men already. He's being raped as we speak." Pheroras studied her face to see if she betrayed any sort of fear or anger. Nothing. They might as well have been negotiating the sale of a donkey.

She replied with an even tone, "I know he is being raped but I ask that his life be spared and he be set free in exchange for my help in finding the treasure."

Pheroras scratched his beard not sure what to make of the servant girl with delusions of grandeur. The Herodian soldiers tortured dozens and dozens of prisoners yet none seemed to know anything about any treasure. How could this servant girl know something the other didn't? He posed that question to her.

She replied, "I served the queen."

Pheroras, "Of course you served the queen. Everyone served the queen."

"I am no chambermaid. My mother was consort to the king."

Solomon was said to have had 330 concubines. Hasmonean King Jannai also kept a large retinue of concubines. Given her beauty, Pheroras wondered why Antigonus hadn't made this girl one of his concubines as well. Royal concubines were not prostitutes. They held official position within the king's court as lower ranking members of his extended family.

Pheroras asked, "Who is your father?" Pheroras used the present tense when referring to the father who he took to be some older servant likely still a member of the staff at the former Hasmonean palace, now controlled by Herod.

She replied, "King Aristobulus." King Antigonus was the youngest son of King Aristobulus meaning this girl standing before him was the half-sister of Antigonus.

The words hit Pheroras like a thunderclap. It all made sense now. This girl was truly of royal birth and had been raised alongside the other royal women of Antigonus' household. They found her next to the body of the dead queen because she was a lady in waiting to the queen. Her status as the daughter of a concubine made her a second class royal but, with the extermination of the Hasmonean ruling class by Herod, her status now vaulted up to the top of the heap. Except for the rumored baby princess in Jerusalem, this girl standing before Pheroras was of the most royal Jewish lineage still alive excepting only Queen Mariamne and her mother Alexandra. He continued questioning the girl, "Was your mother Jewish?"

"No, Greek." Having been born to a non-Jewish mother further degraded the status of this royal daughter of a concubine.

"And your name?"

"Alexandra Salome."

"I assume you are named after the former queen."

"Yes, my grandmother."

Hasmonean queen Alexandra Salome reigned as one of only two female monarchs in the history of the Jewish kingdom.[21] Pheroras composed himself trying not to stare at the girl like a star-struck adolescent. He returned his attention to the mission at hand asking, "What information do you have on the treasure? If the information is useful, I give my solemn oath to save your brother."

Alexandra led the governor to the cellar underneath the citadel of Fortress Hyrcania.

Pheroras, "My men have already searched the cellar. There is nothing here."

She ignored him walking to one corner. She began digging with her hands at a floor tile that did not appear to be loose to Pheroras' eyes. She said, "Give me your dagger."

She must be of royal birth, thought Pheroras. What prisoner orders his captor to hand her a dagger? She didn't look sturdy enough to wield it with purpose so Pheroras handed the dagger over to her. She used it to dig out the tile revealing a hole in the floor, out of which she plucked a leather satchel.

She said, "Here, this should help you."

Pheroras opened the satchel finding a large copper scroll inside. He unrolled the scroll revealing what looked like Hebrew inscriptions but Pheroras didn't read Hebrew so he placed it back into the leather satchel. Surely someone in Jerusalem could read the text. "Why do you think this scroll will help me find the treasure?"

Alexandra replied, "The queen showed me the hiding place and told me that if the fortress fell and I survived that I should inform one of King Antigonus' men where to find the copper scroll. I believe it is some sort of treasure map. All the king's men are now dead so I am trading this scroll for my brother's life."

Pheroras kept his word and saved the brother of Alexandra, whose name he later learned was Simon. Coming upon Aristobulus' daughter by a concubine at Hyrcania presented something of a problem. Herod's orders were to exterminate the

---

[21] The other being Athaliah from the ninth century BCE.

family of Antigonus and all those of royal birth. Alexandra was of royal blood yet her mother was not a wife of the king nor even Jewish. The law does not proclaim a child born to the union of a married man and unmarried woman as a mamzer[22], meaning she still possessed high status as the daughter of a Jewish king yet she was subordinate in rank to other royals conceived within wedlock. Further, she was not a descendant of King Antigonus. Pheroras decided to fudge his brother's orders and keep Alexandra for himself.

Pheroras called his trusted aid Yochanan. "Take her to my tent and put a reliable guard at the door. No one is to enter without my permission. Understood?"

Yochanan gave his boss a wink believing he perfectly understood the situation. His general commandeered the best piece of ass for his own private pleasure. The military aide took Alexandra as just another servant girl, albeit an extremely attractive one, and this was the impression Pheroras intended to leave with his men.

Jerusalem, Judea (35 BCE)

Pheroras returned to the capital to deliver the copper scroll to Herod and report upon the destruction of the remnants of the royal family of King Antigonus. After receiving the expected tongue lashing from his older brother for failing to find the Temple treasure, Pheroras paid a visit to Heli. The Hasmonean priest immediately confessed that his wife had accepted the daughter of Antigonus into their home while he was in the desert.

Heli, "The child is in my wife's quarters. Shall I go retrieve her for you?"

Pheroras smiled at Heli's compliant nature. This was a man he could do business with. "No, having the princess safely tucked away in the care of a Temple priest suits my purposes. The two of us shall strike a bargain."

"A bargain?"

---

[22] The Hebrew term that is closest to bastard.

"Not really a bargain in the true sense of the word priest. I shall dictate terms, which you either accept or reject. If you accept, I walk away and we keep this little incident confidential between ourselves. However, if you reject my terms, I shall arrest your entire household and turn them over to Herod this very moment."

"What are the terms?"

Pheroras viewed the princess as a political chip to be stashed for future use. He didn't completely trust his brother Herod so it was the smart play to hold on to all the political leverage that came along. Pheroras appropriated this royal child as his prize of war by striking a deal with the priest—secretly raise Mariamne bat Antigonus in his household as his own daughter, reveal the secret to no one, and make sure she never left Jerusalem under any circumstances. Were Princess Mariamne to escape Jerusalem, it would cost Heli his life. In return, Pheroras promised no harm to the priest or his family. There was one catch--the princess must remain an unmarried virgin until such time as Pheroras selected her husband.

Heli, "Is that all governor?"

"Yes son of Aaron. Do you accept my offer knowing all that I require?"

It was an offer Heli could not refuse.

Chapter 3

Alexandria, Egypt (67 CE)

Rhodopis stood before Menelaus apparently waiting for something.

Menelaus, "Yes Rhodopis."

"Master, it is time for my trip to the agora. I require money."

That struck Menelaus as odd. He controlled their moderate household finances and set out money each day for his servant / mistress to purchase food and other household goods. Not wishing to discuss household business in front of his grandson, Menelaus nodded for Rhodopis to follow him to the kitchen so they could discuss the matter privately.

Menelaus, "Did I fail to set out the daily allowance my dear?"

"No but we have a special guest. I wish to buy goat for the occasion and this requires extra money."

Menelaus suspected Rhodopis was taking advantage of the situation to fulfill her own desire for a rare meal of goat but decided to grant her request. He had become a vegetarian later in life, belatedly adopting the custom of Yeshua and the Nazarenes. Only after embarking upon a contemplative life of reflection while living in Alexandria did Menelaus inexplicably remove meat from his diet. This created an unfair situation for Rhodopis, who happily ate grilled meat as did nearly all Egyptians.

Menelaus said, "I'm not sure Theudas shall stay for the evening meal. A young man his age will want to be off with his friends. But go ahead and purchase goat just in case." He counted extra money and placed it on the table. Rhodopis stood over the table in silent protest looking down at what she considered a paltry sum for the intended purchase.

Menelaus, "There is no need for an entire goat with just one guest. Find two women in the market to share the purchase with."

Rhodopis grudgingly took the money and departed for the market. Frugality, something Yeshua preached, also came to Menelaus later in life. He returned to the inner courtyard and his guest. "Rhodopis goes for goat. Please do us the honor of sharing a bite of food."

How could Theudas say "no" to a grandfather he rarely visited? "Alright grandfather."

"I know you wish to be off with your friends so we shall not keep you late with the meal. Now, where were we in our story?"

"We haven't even discussed the birth of Yeshua! In fact, if I understand what you have said, Yeshua's mother is but a babe in swaddling clothes in Jerusalem with her family having been murdered by Herod and his men."

"You understand correctly. Patience grandson."

Theudas continued his thought, partially to burn off pent up energy from having sat silently for so long. "My goodness grandfather, you have not even reached the Battle of Actium yet. We're in ancient history. But I did enjoy the anecdotes about Antony. What a bugger he was!"

"Actium comes next in the story."

"What about the girl? What happened to her?"

"You mean Princess Mariamne, the mother of Yeshua?"

"No, the beautiful maiden who stood up to that brute Pheroras and saved her brother as the Herodian soldiers raped him. What happened to her?"

Menelaus, "You refer to Alexandra bat Aristobulus, daughter of a king by his concubine."

"Yes, her. You rattled off so many names my mind is spinning."

"She married Pheroras, Herod's brother, and bore him children. She became a powerful force inside Herod's court."

Theudas did not quite believe it. "The daughter of a concubine had high status in Herod's court?"

"Not at first. Queen Mariamne reigned supreme among the Herodian women during her lifetime. But after her death, Alexandra of Perea rose in importance within the Herodian court."

"Death, did Queen Mariamne die in childbirth?"

"We shall arrive at the death of Queen Mariamne right after Actium. You'll hear of it soon enough."

"What about the murder of his brother-in-law the high priest, the one Herod drowned in the swimming pool? Was Herod punished for this act?"

"There was never any doubt of the outcome of the trial of Herod before Antony, only the size of the bribe. However, Cleopatra did goad her husband into stripping Herod of a few cities and transferring them over to her domain."

A knock at the door broke the conversation. With Rhodopis gone, Menelaus became his own door keep. The guest turned out to be the neighbor's wife wishing to borrow some spice whose location in the house Menelaus hadn't a clue, so he turned the neighbor loose in the pantry telling her to root around until she found what she needed. Rhodopis would be furious when she found out her fiefdom had been invaded by the neighbor woman she most despised but Menelaus didn't have the heart to turn the woman away. The old man quickly returned to his seat.

"Where were we grandson, Actium?"

"No, the acquittal of Herod by Antony in the murder of his brother-in-law, the high priest."

"Any other questions before I continue?"

Theudas rubbed his chin trying to summon any loose ends within the portion of the story he had just received. The front door closed as the neighbor lady let herself out without so much as a "thank you."

Menelaus went to lock the door. Upon his return, Theudas was ready with a new question. "The treasure, what happened to the Temple treasure?"

"King Antigonus directed that it be divided and hidden in many locations, whose whereabouts were recorded on a scroll made of copper. The script etched into the copper scroll was in an ancient form of Hebrew known only to a few old and high ranking Temple priests. For many years none would aid Herod in deciphering its text. Even when the text of the copper scroll was deciphered, it took Herod years to fully recover the Temple treasure. This vast wealth stolen from the Temple is what enabled Herod to undertake the massive building projects within the Jewish kingdom."

Theudas, "So Herod did not recover the Temple treasure until after Actium?"

"True, which fact was a huge boon to Herod. Antony knew of the existence of the Temple treasure and expected a sizable cut when it was recovered but died before cashing in. Octavian knew nothing of the lost Temple treasure and Herod left the princeps none the wiser. The Jewish king hoarded the entire treasure as his own."

"Didn't he share any with Pheroras? It was he who obtained the treasure map at Hyrcania."

"No, Pheroras received no portion of the Temple treasure nor was the territory of his governorship increased during Herod's reign."

"I bet that didn't sit too well with Pheroras."

"No, it did not. A quiet, simmering animosity existed between the brothers that only grew with time. Yeshua's father, Prince Antipater, eventually became a close ally of his uncle Pheroras but we're getting ahead of the story. Let us move on to Actium."

Chapter 4

Actium, Greece (31 BCE)

Marc Antony divorced Octavian's sister and married Cleopatra thereby initiating the final war for control of the Roman Empire. It wasn't good enough for Antony to merely insult Octavian. Antony let loose a full-throated roar by declaring Cleopatra's son by Caesar (Caesarian) to be Julius Caesar's sole and lawful heir. That move left no room for reconciliation between the parties and made war inevitable. The decisive battle came at Actium in Greece. Herod backed Antony in the civil war thereby fulfilling prior oaths of loyalty. He offered to provide large numbers of Jewish soldiers and allied mercenaries to Antony for the land battle at Actium; however, blinded by personal ambition, Cleopatra lobbied her husband to reject Herod's offer. Those participating on the winning side in the final battle would expect a share of the spoils. Cleopatra didn't wish to share with Herod. The ever-confident Antony believed he had no need of Herodian troops to crush Octavian on the battlefield, which was the last mistake the mercurial Antony made in life. Nineteen of Antony's legions deserted to Octavian on the eve of the land battle that never came as the remaining troops loyal to Antony were no longer stout enough to battle the augmented forces of Octavian. At sea, Octavian's navy commanded by Agrippa crushed the vast Antonian armada provided by the Egyptian queen. Actium was a devastating and final defeat for both Antony and Cleopatra.

Cleopatra fled the battle by sea back to Egypt. Antony retreated from Actium on land attempting to recruit fresh troops as he moved. He sent entreaties to Herod for help but they fell on deaf ears. The Jewish king knew only one course of action was open to him after Actium—i.e., go to Octavian and pledge his allegiance. Doing so required another risky winter sea voyage on the Aegean Sea to Rhodes.

Island of Rhodes (30 BCE)

Herod sailed for Rhodes to meet his fate leaving the Jewish kingdom in the control of his uncle Joseph. Upon receiving an audience with Octavian Caesar, Herod prostrated himself before the most powerful man on earth. Herod said, "Consul, I have come to pledge my loyalty to you and renounce Marc Antony. As a token of my friendship, I bring 800 talents as a personal gift."

Servants brought in box after box stuffed with Herod's gold placing them at the feet of Julius Caesar's heir.

Octavian said, "Rise old friend. You were a long-time client of Antony so I didn't expect you to desert him when we crossed swords. However, I note your army's absence from the battlefield at Actium. Your absence, Herod, aided me in seeding doubt in the minds of Antony's legion commanders. They wondered why Antony's greatest foreign friend was not in the field with his vast Jewish army at such an important battle. Many of those commanders brought their legions over to my side without a sword being drawn."

Herod began to relax. Caesar held the mistaken belief that Herod refused to bring his army to Actium in support of Antony. The Jewish king never corrected the misunderstanding as it paid huge dividends. Caesar embraced Herod in friendship.

Herod, "I am grateful Caesar benefited from my absence. My relationship with Antony chilled in recent years because of Cleopatra. She had designs on my kingdom. Antony followed that woman blindly."

Octavian, "This I have heard. My ministers inform me that certain of your lands were stripped by Antony and given to Cleopatra after some silly murder trial."

Octavian Caesar (who later renamed himself Augustus with the title princeps, meaning principal man of Rome) returned to Herod the territories Antony previously transferred to Cleopatra plus added two additional cities as a mark of friendship between

Caesar and Herod. It was all Herod could have hoped for and then some. He returned to Jerusalem secure upon his throne.

Jerusalem, Judea (29 BCE)

After his rapprochement with Octavian, Herod finally felt strong enough on the throne to put Queen Mariamne to death. Herod had grown exceedingly attached to his principal wife but he never let personal attachments stand in the way of politics. He harbored jealousy of her royal blood. No matter what Herod accomplished for the Jewish nation, the Jews would forever view him as several cuts below the royal Hasmoneans. One cannot say if Herod hatched his extermination plan from the inception of his reign but time bore out a clear pattern—infuse his family tree with Jewish royal blood then kill off all Hasmoneans other than his own offspring.

The tangled web of intrigue in Herod's court continued to tighten. Herod's sister Salome accused their uncle Joseph (Salome's husband) of bedding Queen Mariamne in Herod's absence at Rhodes. Salome reviled Uncle Joseph, to his great misfortune. She schemed to kill two birds with one stone, goad Herod into executing the two people she hated most at court (her husband and uppity sister-in-law). The king embraced the contrived allegations of his sister as they suited his purposes as well. The Hasmoneans in his family were proving difficult to manage politically, time to kill them. Poor old Uncle Joseph ended up collateral damage in the purge having been at the wrong place at the wrong time. It goes without saying that Herod lacked any sense of familial sentimentality. Herod executed both Queen Mariamne and Uncle Joseph then, in the coming years, also executed his mother-in-law Alexandra and her father Hyrcanus II, the aged former high priest.[23] Herod lured Hyrcanus back to Judea from exile in Babylon for the sole purpose of snuffing out his life. The king had no intention of allowing pure Hasmonean blood to survive for future use by his enemies. He did, however, exhibit

---

[23] Herod's string of Hasmonean executions spanned several years. Aristobulus III (the young high priest) died in 36 BCE, Hyrcanus II in 30 BCE, Mariamne in 29 BCE, and Alexandra in 28 BCE.

one form of macabre remorse at killing his wife Mariamne. The tale goes that Herod preserved Mariamne's body in a vat of honey, which he stored in his personal chambers spawning rumors of necrophilia. Who can say the truth of the matter? Perhaps only in death did Herod gain the degree of control over Mariamne he desired in life.

Ironically, Herod's dead wife was the first cousin of Antigonus' daughter secretly raised by Lady Anna under the protection of the Temple priesthood. The fathers of the two Mariamnes aligned on opposite sides of the bitter Hasmonean civil war, one wing of the family sided with Herod (together with his Roman overlords) and the other with the Parthians who granted greater autonomy to the Jewish nation. In a twist of fate, the winning Hasmonean faction aligned with Herod now all laid in the grave. They were victims of their erstwhile partner, Herod. But his massacre of Hasmoneans did not completely extinguish the Hasmonean flame. Two royal princesses of pure Hasmonean blood survived—Mariamne and Elizabeth (future mothers of Yeshua and Yochanan the Baptizer, respectively). Elizabeth was the great-granddaughter of Hasmonean king Yochanan Hyrcanus II and had also been hidden in Jerusalem with priests at the time Herod seized Jerusalem in 37 BCE.

Herod executed his Hasmonean family members methodically over a number of years. He never acted rashly or with haste in these cases. He allowed accusations to be made, deferred judgment, and later new accusations appeared. Thus, by all appearances, Herod dispensed justice in the cases of his family members after due deliberation and only in response to mounting evidence.

Jerusalem, Judea (25 BCE)

Lady Anna drifted away from her husband Heli the chief priest despite the latter's rise to prominence within the Temple priesthood. She saw Heli's collaboration with Herod as an abomination. Anna devoted herself to Temple duties in the Women's Courtyard practically raising Princess Mariamne there. Daughters of Kohen priests known as "Daughters of Aaron" officiated at the Women's Court taking the honorary title of priestess. Each day Anna and Mariamne went to the Temple where Mariamne assisted her adoptive mother in her duties.

When Princess Mariamne bat Antigonus turned twelve, the Temple priests demanded Anna refrain from bringing her to the Temple each day in light of the fact that the girl's menstruation was due to commence soon. As the chief priests saw it, a pubescent girl constituted a grave risk to defile the Temple. These same priests could slash the jugular of an ox splattering blood in all directions with complete poise but the thought of a newly menstruating teenage girl sent them into utter panic. Later as Princess Mariamne grew into a young woman, the Temple authorities again allowed her to accompany Anna as she performed her duties at the Temple.

Jerusalem, Judea (20 BCE)

At the time Jerusalem fell to Herod, the king's oldest son Antipater was a boy in Rome having been exiled there with his mother Doris. They were thrown aside when Herod married his Hasmonean queen. But Herod recalled Doris and Antipater from exile after the execution of his second wife as she was Herod's only surviving wife of Jewish royal blood. Antipater was now 26 years of age and thoroughly Roman having spent all but the first few years of his life in Rome. Upon their return, Herod restored the positions of Antipater and his mother Doris at his royal court. Thus began the steady march of Herod's eldest son up the succession ladder.

Antipater's mother Doris was born in Jerusalem of Idumean royal blood. King Solomon intermarried with the Idumean royal family as part of an agreement to settle a border war between the two kingdoms in antiquity. On this basis, the Idumean royal family descended from Solomon and this bloodline was the reason Herod chose Doris as his first wife. However, the Idumean royal family also partly descended from the old Egyptian Phaoronic line (pre-Ptolemy Dynasty). In Jewish eyes, Antipater's Idumean royal ancestry was inferior to the Jewish bloodline of his Hasmonean half-brothers (Alexander and Aristobulus). The exalted bloodline of their Hasmonean mother vaulted these two princes ahead of Antipater and his Davidic bloodline. The fact that Antipater was the eldest son did not change this. Bloodline rank trumped seniority in the Jewish palace succession game.

Antipater's dress, hairstyle, and mannerisms were Roman. His primary language was Greek, the lingua franca of the empire. He spoke Aramaic passably but Hebrew not at all. The chief priests referred to Antipater as Herod's Roman son. The king gave Antipater a commission as tribune in his legions upon learning his son desired a career in the military. Herod maintained a Jewish royal army many thousands strong that also served as auxiliaries to the Roman legions of the Syria province. Veteran Roman commanders held the top legate positions in Herod's army but the cream of his soldiers were ethnic Thracian, German and Galatian mercenaries.[24] Herod selected non-Jewish commanders for his army with the hope that they would be devoted solely to him uninfluenced by the political machinations of the Jewish religious sects and palace power struggles. But every general, no matter his country of origin, is one part politician and another part military officer. It goes with the territory. Herod's commanders championed their favorites among his sons; however, Antipater was at the bottom of all lists. The Herodian generals preferred the younger, more malleable sons of Herod over whom they exerted more control. Antipater was of Idumean blood like his father inheriting his father's tenacious spirit.

The young prince and newly minted tribune preferred life in the Hellenized city of Caesarea to the thoroughly Jewish capital of Jerusalem, where the Herodian military kept one cohort of soldiers stationed at Fortress Antonia and another at Herod's sprawling palace complex. During a period when Antipater was posted to Antonia as commander of the garrison, Herod instructed his son to receive religious training at the Temple. Herod told his son, "If you aspire to rule over the Jewish people, then you must study their religion for it is at the center of Jewish life."

---

[24] Antiquities XVII 8:3.

One day Antipater walked past Princess Mariamne on the grounds of the Temple's outer courtyard while he was in the company of his tutor in Jewish religious law. For a brief moment, the eyes of the prince and princess met.

Mariamne turned to her mother and asked, "Who is that man Mother Anna?" Mariamne, then seventeen years of age, was curious of the opposite sex although rarely allowed interaction with boys.

Anna replied, "Does every young girl fall for a soldier?"

"When the soldier is that dashing, yes. What business does a soldier have here at the Temple?"

"That is the king's eldest son, Antipater. He was raised in Rome so his father commands him to learn something of the Jewish religion. Yahweh help us if he ever becomes king."

"But he's quite handsome Mother Anna."

"And cobras are beautiful creatures as well until they inject you with venom. If I have any say in the matter, you shall marry a Kohen priest."

While Mariamne found the appearance of Antipater "dashing", his reaction to her was carnal. Antipater asked his tutor, "Who is that girl rabbi? She is the most beautiful creature I have seen in all Judea."

The rabbi turned around to ascertain to whom the prince referred. Every rabbi is one part match-maker so he took a keen interest in the lady who had drawn the prince's attention. The rabbi replied, "Prince, do you not fear God? We walk on holy ground. Please, is it too much to ask that you have pure thoughts for one hour of the day?"

"Rabbi, don't torture me. Who is she?"

"I see the girl often in the company of the Temple Mother, her daughter I believe."

"And her family?"

"An orphan. She was taken into the home of a chief priest, Joseph ben Ellamus known as Heli."

"I have to meet her."

"That's impossible even for Herod's son. She's dedicated to Yahweh. Young prince, you cannot violate a Temple virgin dedicated to God."

Antipater sprouted the smile of a wolf that knows he'll get his desired meal one day. "Of course not rabbi. I wouldn't dream of such a thing."

The rabbi saw it as part of God's duty to encourage the propagation of the chosen people. He said, "If you are in the market for a wife young prince, I certainly can be of assistance. My niece is a raving beauty."

Antipater already had a wife but, as his father before him, was always in the market another; however, the rabbi possessed the face of a donkey leading Antipater to doubt the rabbi's niece was the beauty he described. The prince took one last look over his shoulder seeking a fleeting glimpse of the most beautiful and royal woman in the Jewish kingdom. He would not see her again for fourteen years. The next meeting would be their wedding day.

Chapter 5

Jerusalem, Judea (7 BCE)

Herod devoted the last years of his reign arranging his place in history by finally stamping out the Hasmonean ghost. Yet again Princess Salome, sister of Herod, acted as his agent in bringing about the necessary pretext of conspiracy allowing Herod to execute Hasmonean members of his family. This time the targets were Herod's own Hasmonean sons, Aristobulus and Alexander. The fact that Aristobulus was Salome's son-in-law and that his execution would leave Salome's daughter a widow was of little concern to the witch of Judea. Ambition trumped familial sentimentality for Salome, as she was very much Herod's sister. These two Hasmonean nephews stood in her way as she schemed for her own son to succeed Herod. Salome didn't need to search to find grounds for her hatred of Aristobulus and Alexander. Princess Glaphyra of Cappadocia, wife of Alexander and granddaughter of Marc Antony's courtesan, degraded all the Herodian women at court save those of Hasmonean blood. She possessed a distinguished royal Greek pedigree and shoved her ancestors up the ass of the other Herodian women at every opportunity. She particularly insulted Herod's wives, save Doris with whom she was on friendly terms, by calling them commoners whom Herod married for their beauty despite their lowly origins. She also bad-mouthed the low birth of Aristobulus' wife Bernice (Salome's daughter) to her face, a charge her husband did not defend her against. This insult sent Salome into a slow boiling rage.

Glaphyra, with red hair and fair skin, was considered a striking beauty in Judea and she knew it. The Greek princess luxuriated in attention from high ranking Herodian males. Even the king spent long periods in conversation with Glaphyra after the evening meal, something the entire court took note of. Salome used Glaphyra's flirtatious nature and conspicuous friendship with Herod as a cudgel to build doubt and jealousy in the heart of her husband Alexander. She whispered in the ears of persons close to Alexander that the aging Herod intended to kill his son and take Glaphyra as his own wife. This seemingly absurd suggestion gained currency in the Herodian court given Herod's propensity for killing members of his family and his obvious infatuation with the redheaded princess. Prince Antipater assisted his aunt Salome in propagating her palace rumors as he stood to gain should his Hasmonean brothers fall from the king's grace.

By this time Salome was an old hand at building the case necessary for Herod to execute a political enemy within the Herodian inner circle. She coerced Herod into killing her first two husbands and provided the pretext he needed to execute Queen Mariamne. Bringing about the execution of Mariamne's two sons was just more of the same, although this time Augustus Caesar would have to approve of the execution. He was not the malleable Roman ruler that Marc Antony had been. It took Salome a number of years to build up sufficient grounds for Augustus to approve the executions of Aristobulus and Alexander but she eventually succeeded.

Salome's whisper campaign made the two Hasmonean princes paranoid about their position in the Jewish kingdom. They stepped up contacts with their friends in high places around the Roman world, including Archelaus, king of Cappadocia and father of Glaphyra. King Archelaus increased his correspondence with Herod pressing for his son-in-law Alexander to be named co-regent. Archelaus sent correspondence to Rome with the same request, news of which made its way back to Herod. The Jewish king very much resented a fellow Roman client-king trying to take control of succession planning in the Jewish kingdom. Salome took this added tension between Herod and his two Hasmonean sons and fanned it. She sowed whispers around the palace that Aristobulus and Alexander were meeting with Jewish opposition parties in a bid to gain their support for one of the brothers succeeding Herod. Salome forged correspondence from the brothers to zealot leaders in Galilee, which naturally landed in the hands of Herod's spy network. The two Hasmonean princes never knew what hit them. Augustus Caesar was said to have remarked when signing their execution order, "I'd rather be Herod's pig than his son."

After the deaths of Aristobulus and Alexander, Herod elevated Antipater to crown prince and coregent. Herod's eldest son now wore a diadem around his head and issued commands under his own authority as ruler. But no son of Herod ever sat comfortably at his father's side.

Jerusalem, Judea (6 BCE)

Pheroras settled in as governor of Perea with his Hasmonean wife Alexandra, the daughter of a Jewish king. Her brother Simon who Pheroras rescued from death the day Hyrcania fell to the Herodians became Pheroras' chief minister. The House of Pheroras cultivated a strong relationship with the Pharisees as had Alexandra's namesake, Queen Salome Alexandra. Herod twice tried to marry his Hasmonean daughters to Pheroras when they came of age but both times Pheroras balked at the match. Herod required Pheroras put away Alexandra as a stipulation to the marriage, an act Pheroras adamantly refused to do despite the massive dowry that accompanied each princess. This strained the relationship between the last two surviving sons of Antipater the Idumean and matters only got worse with time.

The Jews as Roman subjects were required to recite a loyalty oath to Caesar but the Pharisees refused on religious grounds. The number of rabbis who refuse to swear the oath were above six thousand and Herod imposed a fine upon them for their obstinacy, which Alexandra of Perea paid. This greatly pissed off Herod as he desired to imprison the insolent rabbis when they failed to pay the fine. In return, the revolting Pharisees prophesied that God decreed the fall of Herod's government and the Jewish kingdom should come to Alexandra and Pheroras, and to their children.[25] When word of this prophesy reached the ear of Herod he erupted like Mount Vesuvius. The relationship between the last sons of Antipater the Idumean was irretrievably broken from this point forward.

So it came as something of a shock to observers of the Jewish court when Crown Prince Antipater allied himself with his uncle Pheroras, thus putting himself in conflict with his father. They first cemented their friendship with the marriage of Antipater's eldest son to Pheroras' daughter. So it was only natural for the allies to jointly celebrate Antipater's accession to coregent. Well into a long night of drinking the best Falernian wine found in Israel and after their women turned in for the evening, Pheroras put his arm around Antipater drawing him near to whisper into his ear.

Pheroras, "Sire, I have an old secret to share with you."

Antipater replied, "Secret? I was unaware you went in for intrigue uncle."

"I would have long ago died without guile. Mark my words, you'll need the same resourcefulness to make it past middle-age."

"Tell me your tale uncle."

"Thirty years ago, your father and I took Jerusalem from King Antigonus with the aid of Roman troops. Your father bribed Marc Antony to crucify and behead Antigonus while I was sent to Hyrcania to exterminate the remainder of his family."

"These facts are well known to me. I have studied my father's career closely."

"But here is the part you do not know sire, a royal daughter of Antigonus survives to this day."

"A daughter? Impossible."

"A royal daughter recorded in the Temple records as the king's legitimate child. I have been to the Temple and verified this for myself."

---

25 Antiquities XVII 2:4.

"But how can you be so sure this person is in fact the child recorded in the Temple records? Somebody could just be trying to pass her off for their own gain."

"There can be no doubt of her identity on two grounds. First, she has been in the charge of a Temple priestess since she was a baby and the priestess vouches for her identity."

"Interesting and the second reason?"

"You never met Mariamne bat Alexander, your father's dead queen?"

"No uncle, I did not although I heard she was a ravishing beauty."

"That she was. Any daughter of Antigonus would be her first cousin. The woman living with the Temple priestess looks like the ghost of the dead queen, a striking resemblance."

Antipater tried to shake the wine buzz from his brain. A fleeting glimpse long ago of a woman on the Temple grounds came back to him. He replied to his uncle, "I think I saw her once many years ago at the Temple, an orphan girl with an old priestess. Her beauty took the air out of my lungs. Have the years been kind to her?"

"Time has not touched this rose. She retains the beauty of a young woman. I offer her to you in marriage."

Antipater's head swam. He got up from the couch and paced the floor. He knew the implications of taking this woman as wife.

"But my father swore he'd kill off Antigonus' seed. He executed Princess Salome's second husband for sheltering Hasmoneans in Idumea.[26] It would draw me into direct conflict with the king."

"He doesn't have to know. You are now coregent, a king in your own right. Is not a king allowed to marry whomever he wishes?"

"Why can't I just wait for the old buzzard to die and then marry the princess?"

---

[26] Antiquities, XV 7:10 (259-264); see "Sons of Babas" incident leading to execution of Costobarus.

"Perhaps you have not considered the chain of events that shall play out upon your father's death. It will be a boat race west to Rome the minute the door to Herod's tomb closes shut."

"But I am coregent and named as heir in my father's will, what can go wrong?"

"Antipater, my dear nephew. Much time have you spent in Rome yet you fail to see the danger lurking about you. Romans can be bribed. Their law is completely malleable allowing those in power to claim that whatever action they take is in compliance with the law."

Antipater sat back and huddled close to his uncle, "Tell me how the attack will come."

"The Jews hate you. For them, you are a younger, Romanized version of Herod. And they blame you for the death of your Hasmonean brothers."

Light began to dawn within the inebriated mind of Antipater. Pheroras continued, "Next in line for succession after you is Herod Boethus, the grandson of a high priest. Among Herod's surviving sons, he is the favorite of the Jewish people. Here is how it will go down. An 'anybody but Antipater' coalition forms in the palace with that witch Salome serving as the brains and chief organizer. She'll gather around herself disaffected royals and form alliances with the Jewish religious parties. They can be counted on for a timely public riot against you calculated to sway opinion in Rome in favor of Salome's chosen candidate for king. It's very costly for the Romans to send out additional legions to quell local revolts. When rebellion can be circumvented through the administrative expedient of changing subject kings, they do so. A Jewish revolt will be staged and Caesar lobbied by Salome to name her tool the new king."

"Sounds bleak uncle."

"It will be sire. This is why you must bind yourself to the purest Hasmonean blood left on this earth. She is your only hope of raising your stature in the eyes of the Jewish people. You will only be able to effectively rule the Jewish people with a Hasmonean queen at your side. Further, you must get her with child before Herod dies thereby solidifying your place as the next Jewish king."

Antipater thought the matter over. Fathering a child by the daughter of King Antigonus would go a long way to boosting his image with the Jewish people and solidify his hold on the crown against the schemes of his half-brothers. Thus, Antipater saw the wisdom in the plan of uncle Pheroras and, shortly thereafter, secretly married Mariamne bat Antigonus. However, Herod refused to die despite his age and physical decrepitude. That's when Salome the Judean witch unleashed her fifth column campaign against Antipater. She so successfully pressured the crown prince that he was forced to sail for Rome one-year after the marriage to Princess Mariamne. Salome and accomplices accused Antipater of a multitude of nefarious acts but lacked any solid evidence for their accusations. Antipater decided prudence dictated he sail for the safety of Rome; however, Herod refused permission for Antipater's mother to leave the country with him (upon Herod's authority as her husband). Princess Mariamne was still in hiding and Antipater deemed smuggling her out of the country too risky given Herod's spies stalked every corner of the kingdom. For these reasons, Antipater's family remained in Israel while he escaped to Rome despite the fact that he had not yet gotten Mariamne with child.

The coregent expected to be in Rome no more than a few months as Herod appeared at death's doorstep. The city offered splendid options for the pursuit of pleasure to a man with unlimited resources. Using Herod's treasure, Antipater partied with the Roman elite making generous gifts to persons of influence in the court of Augustus. The coregent did his best to put Palestine out of his mind as the months abroad dragged out to a full year. Still Herod lived. Then, reports reached Antipater that his mother Doris had been banished from the palace in Jerusalem. Not a good sign as the standing of mother and son were inextricably linked at court. Next, his father the king started writing letters begging him to return home. The letters carried a warm tone lacking any hint of a breach between the two. But Herod's action of banishing of his mother from the palace spoke otherwise. Was Herod punishing Antipater's mother in an attempt to get the son to return home? And if so, why?

Herod's ploy had its desired effect on the coregent. Concern for the unknown fate of his family back in Judea caused Antipater to leave the capital of the western world sailing east.

Celenderis, Cilicia (4 BCE)[27]

Antipater departed from the Italian port of Tarentum but didn't take a direct route east to Israel. Upon reaching Cyprus, he turned north for the Roman province of Cilicia. As the crew prepared to drop anchor, the coregent looked out from the bridge of his royal ship across the harbor at the fortress city of Celenderis, the best anchorage upon this section of Cilicia. He was 42 years of age, clean-shaven in the Roman style, with flowing dark hair peppered with gray. Antipater dropped anchor in Celenderis for more than provisions. He hoped to gather intelligence on the state of affairs back in Jerusalem before landing at the main Jewish port of Caesarea. His mind pulsed with foreboding while pacing the bridge of his ship. Augustus Caesar urged Antipater to remain in Rome given the inherent danger of being a son of Herod the Great. These thoughts weighed heavily upon Antipater while making the decision whether to return to Judea. With Herod in poor health, Antipater could have opted to ride out his father's waning days in the luxury of Rome or any number of cozy ports of call along the way. But Herod was too obstinate and stubborn to die in a timely manner creating a major dilemma for Antipater.

The coregent interrupted his thoughts to issue a command to the captain, "Actaeon, personally oversee setting of the anchor. I want the sails trimmed and stowed with parade precision. I spy dignitaries on the dock. Make a good showing."

The captain replied, "As you wish your highness."

The Greek captain preferred attending to the affections of his cabin boy rather than the often-mundane duties of commanding a ship. No matter, Antipater comfortably filled the void of command. The Jewish king's eldest son was a forceful and

---

[27] Celenderis is the modern day city of Aydinicik in Turkey.

confident leader yet, at this crucial juncture in his life, Antipater waivered over a decision--wait out Herod's last days safely outside the Jewish kingdom or return home? Given Herod's long history of executing members of his own family (even his own sons), Antipater harbored a legitimate concern for his safety should he return to Palestine. Two lines pulled Antipater's ship inexorably back to Judea. First was news of his mother's banishment from Herod's court. But a stronger line tugged Antipater home, concern for his Hasmonean wife who was the daughter of King Antigonus.

Why not patiently wait outside the kingdom for Herod to die? Many factors swirled in his mind. First, Mariamne's biological clock was short on ticks. The princess was 33 years of age and Antipater was yet to get her with child. Herod was afflicted by a multitude of illnesses but the old buzzard refused death. God only knew how long his father would defy the inevitable. Each day Antipater waited lessened the chance of fathering an heir through the truest of Hasmonean royal blood and, also, increased the chance of Mariamne dying in childbirth. Further, fathering a Hasmonean heir by Mariamne would tighten Antipater's grip on the throne. None of his chief rivals had yet produced an heir via a Hasmonean princess. Lastly, the longer Antipater stayed out of the country, the more alienated he became from the Jewish people and religious parties. Antipater needed to return his hands to the reigns of local government reestablishing his authority over the Jewish bureaucracy. Complicating an already dicey situation was the lurking danger of the wicked witch of Palestine—Princess Salome (his aunt). If Antipater were not personally present in Jerusalem at the death of Herod, sure as the sun rises in the east Salome would seize control of the palace, locate his wife Mariamne, and execute her.

While balancing concern for his personal safety against the safety of his family back in Judea and the machinations of his political enemies at court, one factor in the equation eluded Antipater's grasp. Did Herod know about his marriage to Mariamne bat Antigonus? If Herod knew, then Antipater's life was in danger from his own father.

Jerusalem, Judea (4 BCE)

Herod Romanized the Jewish legions with focus upon strengthening heavy infantry. The Herodian military contained the standard elements of infantry, cavalry, engineering, naval units, et cetera. But there was one unusual element to the Jewish military: a vast, secrete investigative unit charged with domestic spying and counter-espionage named Modiin ule-Tafkidim Meyuhadim (or Intelligence and Special Tasks). Modiin didn't focus on threats from foreign powers. It's greatest concern was keeping an eye on the main Jewish religious parties (the Pharisees, Sadducees, and Essenes), with special emphasis on the emerging subversives of the fourth party, the Zealots.

Zechariah ben Eleazar, a career member of the secret police, was chief of Modiin. Police officials of all nations must keep an eye on the political winds and Zechariah the Modiin spymaster was no different. He apprised the captain of Herod's palace guard of all major developments that came across his desk while striving to avoid the personal attention of Herod or other high ranking royals. To do so was hazardous to one's health.

Zechariah's aide Hanina entered the chief's office and waited to be recognized. The chief said, "Speak."

Hanina replied, "Chief, a servant from the household of Princess Salome, sister of the king, waits outside. He claims to have instructions from the princess to personally deliver a message to you."

Zechariah's stomach turned. Hanina might as well have announced a spitting cobra waited outside his office. In Zechariah's estimation, Princess Salome was the vilest creature to be found in all Israel. She was in the thick of every major palace conspiracy throughout her brother's long reign. Salome was on her third husband, Alexas. He was a high official in the Jewish royal treasury and friend of the king. Her first two husbands had been executed by Herod.

Although the cases against Salome's first two husbands occurred before Zechariah's time as chief, he knew from reading old reports that Modiin allied itself with Salome in both cases. Why? Self-preservation was the answer. She vanquished all foes.

Zechariah prayed political convenience did not require Modiin to again dance with the Herodian witch. Princess Salome's servant entered and handed Zechariah a message. Hanina immediately pestered his boss, "What does it say chief?"

The chief replied, "I am summoned to the chambers of Princess Salome at the palace."

He looked up from the message to address the servant, "Wait in the outer room. You may escort me to the princess momentarily."

Zechariah waited for the royal servant to leave then said to Hanina, "This is very bad."

"You worry too much chief. She probably wants you to spy on her husband or something like that. Women just worry about catching their husbands cheating."

"You're misinformed Hanina. Herodian princesses in general, and Princess Salome in particular, are capable of much more monstrous calamities than finding their husband's wick where it doesn't belong."

"So what do you think this is all about?"

"With Crown Prince Antipater out of the country and the king in poor health, it doesn't take Archimedes to pull the veil back on this mystery. She'll make a play for Antipater's crown."

Hanina's jaw dropped as Zechariah straightened his robes, and then headed out the door to meet with the princess. As he made his way over to the palace, Zechariah's mind raced over Herod's extensive family tree trying to anticipate the angle of Salome's attack. She was sister to the king. Her eldest daughter, Bernice, had four children by Aristobulus, the deceased Hasmonean son of Herod. Bernice's eldest daughter named Mariam[28], later known as Mariam Magdalene, was married to Crown Prince Antipater. Although then only eleven years of age, this Hasmonean princess was in line to become queen when Herod died. Zechariah was stumped. What beef could Salome possibly

---

[28] Mariamne, Mariam, Miriam and Mary are all equivalent names. As Mariamne was an extremely popular Hasmonean name, Mariam is used for Mary Magdalene and Mariamne for the mother of Yeshua to help avoid confusion as each shared the same root Aramaic / Hebrew name.

have with Crown Prince Antipater? Her granddaughter was to become queen. What more could Salome possibly want? Then he remembered a small detail surrounding the arrangements for Salome's last marriage. She desperately wished to marry Syllaeus, the Nabatean prime minister. Herod opposed the match forcefully commanding his sister to marry Alexas (one of Herod's trusted cronies). When Salome appealed to Julia (Caesar's daughter), Julia also rebuffed Salome commenting that she was lucky to get a third husband at all so she should not complain about the choice. Syllaeus tried to grab the Nabatean throne for himself by overthrowing the deceased king's son, Aretas. Having such an ambitious ruler to the east of Judea was against Jewish political interests. Herod commanded Antipater to capture Salome's putative lover and transport Syllaeus to Rome. There Antipater and Aretas jointly accused the Nabatean of insurrection and Caesar executed Syllaeus by having him thrown off the Tarpeian Rock.[29]

God only knew what the witch had on her mind but Zechariah felt in his bones that Salome's latest target was Crown Prince Antipater. And if one judged by her track record, the crown prince would eventually find himself in a world of hurt. Zechariah's feet automatically slipped into military step next to the servant on their walk from his office to Herod's vast palace complex. They passed the old Hasmonean palace before entering Herod's much larger and elegant palace. Salome's servant directed them through back alleys and corridors to arrive at his mistress's chambers by the most surreptitious route possible. Once there Zechariah was made to wait in the time honored manner that one in power utilizes to demonstrate a visitor's lack of importance. The chief inspector knew the drill. He patiently watched a bug crawl across the wall of the princess's anteroom until summoned. Just as he nodded off from boredom with the hint of drool at one corner of his mouth, a servant summoned the chief.

He ushered Zechariah into what appeared to be a private study where the chief unexpectedly found Princess Salome alone. No ministers, stewards, nor ladies in waiting. Just Princess Salome

---

[29] *See* Jewish Wars I 28:6 and Antiquities XVII 1:1.

seated at a table, deep in thought working on correspondence. For a woman whose age Zechariah judged to be around sixty, she displayed amazing vigor popping up out of her chair greeting him as he entered. A broad smile broke across her face. It reminded him of the smile displayed by the best camel traders in Jerusalem.

She said, "Chief Zechariah, how pleased I am to finally have a private audience with you."

He thought it an odd comment, as if she had been the one to journey to his office seeking an audience. Flattery from a Herodian princess? This promised to be heavy so Zechariah put on his guard, "A pleasure to make your acquaintance princess."

Salome continued with the small talk, "But I am sure we have met at one of the king's festivals or some such event."

Herod's festival parties were attended by many thousands of people. Certainly they had both been in attendance but mid-level bureaucrats were not presented to the royal family at such events. She seemed intent on pretending familiarity between the two. The chief played along. "You very well could be correct princess. How may I be of assistance to you?"

"Actually chief, it is I who wish to be of assistance to you. Do you know what this document is?"

She passed a scroll over to Zechariah for inspection. It was a marriage certificate from the Temple archives maintained by the scribes. A quick review of the document revealed nothing unusual to the chief other than the fact that the crown prince apparently had taken a fourth wife. His father Herod married ten women so it seemed only natural that the son would follow the pattern. Zechariah asked, "Where did you get this?"

"That's not the point chief. The point is that Crown Prince Antipater has taken a new wife."

"His father the king has many wives, why should the son be any different?"

"Chief, don't be flippant. Take a close look at the name of the bride—'Mariamne bat Mattatayah'. Look at her age, 33."

"Well, those are common names princess. I'm not sure I can draw any conclusions from them."

She banged her hand down on the table startling the chief. He didn't expect such a powerful smote from a little woman on the back end of life. Salome roared, "Are you blind man? The crown prince already has three young wives. Why on earth would he marry a 33-year-old woman?"

"I can only surmise she is a ravishing beauty of, shall we say, special talents."

"You idiot, kings don't marry whores. And they don't marry old women without some political profit to be gained. No king ever gained politically from marrying the daughter of a commoner. This 'Mariamne bat Mattatayah' has to be a royal."

The light began to come on for Zechariah. Now he could see Salome's line of attack. Crown Prince Antipater had secretly married another royal wife putting her in competition with Salome's granddaughter Mariam to become the next queen. But there was no crime in choosing a new wife. He knew the witch had more to deliver. He said, "I see your point princess. I'll detail a few of my men to get to the bottom of the identity of this Mattatayah."

"Don't bother chief. I've already done your work. He's Mattatayah Antigonus, the last Hasmonean king."

Hearing the words knocked the breath out of Zechariah's lungs. He struggled to speak. "That's not possible. He's been dead for over thirty years. Every member of Antigonus' family was executed. I read the reports myself. We have them in our files."

Princess Salome replied, "Well Modiin fucked up, didn't they! This daughter of Antigonus has been hiding in Jerusalem all these years. Herod will shout like thunder when he finds out."

"I thank you princess for bringing this information to my attention. I shall alert the king at once."

Zechariah got up to leave thinking their business concluded. Salome commanded, "Sit back down chief. You haven't been dismissed."

He was afraid of that. Clearly Princess Salome had some sort of deal in mind.

She said, "His mother Doris--Herod should have killed her years ago-- is a donkey's ass. Antipater has stabbed me in the back for the last time. We worked together to rid the palace of those two insufferable terrors, Aristobulus and Alexander. I kept an open-mind about Antipater after he betrothed my young granddaughter Mariam making her his royal wife but then the ingrate hauled my fiancé Syllaeus to Rome and had him tossed off the Tarpeian Rock."

Her voice broke as she reflected on the death of the singular love of her life, Syllaeus the Nabatean. Together they would have been king and queen of Nabatea with hopes of gaining dominion over additional territories at the death of Herod. But Antipater stomped out the dream on orders from Herod. She couldn't be upset with her brother the king so all her venom fell upon Antipater. "Now the asshole thinks he'll jam it down my throat yet again with this new wife of his. Enough is enough. The claws are out."

Zechariah shuttered in contemplation of the answer but had to ask the question, "What do you have in mind princess?"

"It's time to settle all scores before Herod dies. As the king finds himself physically weak in life, I think he needs my help. Antipater's ally, that snake Pheroras, hid Antigonus' daughter all these years then secretly married her off to Antipater. They're all going down, Antipater, Pheroras, Doris, Alexandra, the lot."

The chief gave the wedding certificate a closer look then brought up a detail that Salome may have missed, "I can see how that sets up nicely for you princess. Your other granddaughter Herodias is married to Prince Herod Boethus, next in line for the throne. But there is the little matter of a signature on this marriage certificate. It's signed by Simon Boethus, the high priest. He's an accomplice to the act. And he's also the grandfather of Prince Herod Boethus. You take down Antipater based on this marriage certificate and it likely brings down the high priest as well. When one pushes a rock down a hill, it smashes into other rocks. No one knows where the chain ends. Herodias' husband may get caught up in the purge that results."

Salome was undeterred by the seeds of doubt Zechariah attempted to sow, "I control the rocks rolling down the hill chief. High priest Simon Boethus is out taking his daughter Mariamne with him. I never cared for the ice princess from Alexandria. But as you say, when Mariamne goes, her son Herod Boethus falls with her. He's married to my granddaughter Herodias but let's not cry over spilled milk. Archelaus moves up to prime heir. I have a deal in place with his mother, Malthace.[30] Upon the death of Antipater, Archelaus will marry my granddaughter Mariam making her his royal wife."

"Death of Antipater?"

"Oh yes chief, no exile for Antipater. He's going to die."

"And what's in it for me?"

"I thought you were a smarter man. If it is within my power to depose one crown prince and replace him with another of my choosing, did it ever occur to you that I might be capable of pulling the same trick with Modiin chiefs?"

Zechariah swallowed hard before responding. "What is it you require from Modiin?"

"One or two small favors. I'll take care of the rest. Here is a vial of Egyptian poison. I wish for it to be planted in the home of . . . ."

Celenderis, Cilicia (4 BCE)

Antipater's thoughts were elsewhere as he descended from his ship into a barge with a retinue of companions and assorted hangers-on for transportation to the dock at Celenderis and the customary exchange of pleasantries with local dignitaries. He couldn't get one thought out of his head--"What if Herod knows about my marriage to Antigonus' daughter?" He traded salutations and polite banter with the local officials and prominent members of the Jewish community present on the dock. The officials invited Antipater to view a local horse race from the governor's box in the hippodrome the following day. Custom required he

---

[30] Another of Herod's wives who bore him Archelaus, Herod Antipas, and Olympias.

accept the offered hospitality. Whatever his status in the Jewish kingdom, in the rest of the Roman Empire Antipater was still accorded the honors of a king. The necessary pleasantries concluded, Antipater turned to the local agent of the Herodian royal family who also appeared on the dock. Any recent correspondence from Palestine would have been forwarded to this man awaiting Antipater's arrival. Antipater inquired, "What do you have for me Ishmael?"

"Two letters your highness. One from your royal father, the king. Another from your son Herod." Ishmael handed both letters over and awaited instructions.

Antipater, "Nothing from my mother or Bathyllus?"

The agent replied, "No your highness. These are the only two pieces of correspondence we received for you. If you care to wait another day or two, perhaps the next ship from the east shall bring the letters you expect."

Antipater accepted the letters and barked, "Dismissed."

My father Bathyllus knew Prince Antipater his entire life. He was the son of a Greek slave owned by Antipater's mother, Doris. Bathyllus and Antipater grew up together in the same household as age mates and were educated side by side. When Antipater rose to power in Herod's kingdom, he freed his friend Bathyllus setting him in charge of his household. Later, my father rose to become Antipater's chief minister and closest confidant. Antipater literally trusted Bathyllus with his life. Yeshua and I, the sons of Antipater and Bathyllus, later shared the same relationship as had our fathers before us.

Acid gushed into the stomach of the crown prince. His mother served as his eyes and ears at court. Bathyllus was his most trusted minister. Highly unusual for both to stay out of touch for a month. With no one from his inner circle back in Jerusalem providing intelligence on the current state of affairs with Herod, Antipater sailed blind toward Palestine. However, Antipater did receive a letter from young Prince Herod, his teenage son who seldom wrote. He was married to the daughter of Pheroras so, perhaps, the letter from his son contained important news of affairs in Jerusalem. He broke the seal and opened the letter.

"Dearest father, if this letter is the first to reach you with the news, my greatest sympathies for our shared loss. Pheroras, my father-in-law, is dead."

Antipater dropped the letter and tore at his clothing in grief. His companions were greatly moved by Antipater's display of emotion. They asked, "What is it your highness?"

"My uncle Pheroras is dead."

"How?"

"The doctors do not know. He was not a young man. Could be natural causes or, my son informs me, the doctors speculate poison."

"Poison? Who would poison Pheroras?"

Antipater knew the answer to the question—Salome perhaps with Herod's authorization. He mourned as much for himself as for Pheroras. His one Herodian ally in a position of power was dead. Antipater now stood alone against his brothers and their mothers. He said to his friends, "I suspect Princess Salome with authorization from my father."

One replied, "The king? You must be joking your highness. Why would the king want his brother dead?"

Even as the question left the mouth of this hanger-on, the group shuddered with foreboding. Herod killed his brother-in-law Aristobulus, his uncle Joseph, his second wife Mariamne, his mother-in-law Alexandra, Mariamne's grandfather Hyrcanus, and his two sons by Mariamne. Fratricide of Pheroras fell well within the bounds of Herod's capabilities. Antipater's mood grew even darker.

Another asked, "Perhaps you are jumping to conclusions your highness. Upon what do you base this suspicion?"

Antipater replied, "Pheroras' wife is the daughter of a Hasmonean king by a concubine. She rules the House of Pheroras with an iron fist and has a network of spies implanted within the staff. If the slaves plotted to kill Pheroras, she would have foiled them. Only a person of great influence could have pulled off the murder of Pheroras."

Another asked, "Maybe Pheroras died of natural causes? Where is the motive for assassinating Pheroras? Would the king kill his brother for refusing marriage to his daughter? Seems a bit harsh."

Antipater, "The timing is just too coincidental. I have a story to tell you boys. This one is best related over wine. Come on."

Antipater and his party retired to the house of the mayor of Celenderis and were given private rooms. While the others enjoyed food and wine, Antipater read the letter from his father. Herod expressed his affection for Antipater and desire for his return home as soon as possible. He intimated that all issues with Antipater's mother Doris would be resolved to Antipater's satisfaction upon the prince's return. The letter contained no hint of anger at Antipater and only briefly touched upon the death of Pheroras with Herod saying he was investigating the matter. Something rotten hung in the wind from Judea. Antipater put down the letter and related to his friends the astonishing tale of Pheroras' discovery of the infant Hasmonean princess stashed with a Kohen priest in Jerusalem and her subsequent marriage to Antipater. The assembled retainers listened with rapt attention.

One friend said, "You could knock us over with a feather your highness. What a coup to secure Antigonus' daughter as wife. She far outranks all other Hasmonean royals at court. Bravo!"

A round of cheers and clanking of cups echoed throughout the chamber. Antipater studied the faces of the men around the room. Those jubilant failed to grasp the gravity of the situation. His gaze fell upon an old childhood friend from Rome, Philip. He was a Jew of the upper merchant class whose parents provided their young, social climbing son with the best tutors available in the city. Philip sat somber as the others reveled.

Antipater called to his old friend, "Philip, join me for a walk in the fresh sea air."

"Certainly your highness."

The crown prince led the way out the door followed by Philip and several armed bodyguards. The others understood they were to remain behind.

The crown prince inquired, "You do not rejoice with the others Philip. Why so?"

"I am troubled your highness."

"Friend, please continue for you speak my mind as well."

"Your highness."

Antipater waived his hand at Philip indicating he should discontinue use of the formalities of office. They had known each other since childhood. Antipater required frank advice from an old friend, not the obsequious babble of hangers-on.

Philip continued, "As you wish Antipater. Your ass is in a tight crack. I believe your intuition is correct. Herod has discovered your secret marriage to the daughter of Antigonus and killed Pheroras in retaliation."

"Thank you. I needed to hear that. What would you do if you were me? Sail back to Rome?"

"That is a question I cannot answer for I am not a king. Sailing back to Rome would be the safest play but, in your absence, Herod or Salome surely kills your Hasmonean wife and maybe even your mother. Continue on to Palestine and I imagine some plot emerges from Salome or another troublemaker in the court. It's not a crime to marry Antigonus' daughter but I'm sure they'll think of something."

Antipater countered, "But as coregent, it's my right to have any case against me heard before Augustus Caesar. That will take time. Herod is not fit to travel. With any luck, he'll die before the case is even heard."

"How important is this wife to you?"

"Without her, I have zero chance of winning over the Jewish people. They'll never forgive me for the deaths of Aristobulus and Alexander, their beloved Hasmonean princes. The king's military opposes me as well, which means Herod Boethus, Archelaus, Antipas, or one of the other contenders for the throne will have an easy time exploiting my weakness. If I keep my arse on the throne a decade under such circumstances it would be a grand achievement."

"A decade as king then a well-funded retirement in Gaul[31] is not a bad thing."

---

[31] Ancient Roman name for France.

But Antipater did not aspire to the smooth path. He eyed lofty goals. The crown prince replied, "My sole ambition in life is to eclipse my father. That man threw my mother and I away like trash to be with his Hasmonean queen. My revenge will be to exceed all his achievements in the history books."

Philip feared this would be Antipater's reply. He didn't try to talk his friend out of his chosen course of action, "Then you need Mariamne, daughter of Antigonus, as your queen. You must continue on to Jerusalem."

"I reached the same conclusion but it's reassuring to hear it from a trusted friend. I have precious few of those in life."

"So you're committed to rolling the bones?"

Antipater replied without hesitation, "And may the gods grant me the Venus Throw!"[32]

Antipater and Philip continued their walk along the dock in silence enjoying the ocean breeze. Neither discussed the situation any further as the die was cast. Antipater's fate was in the hands of the gods and Rome, if any distinction between the two existed.

---

[32] The highest roll in an ancient Roman dice game played with knucklebones. "The Venus Throw" is also the title of a book by Steven Saylor.

Chapter 6

Herod's Palace, Jerusalem (4 BCE)

Princesses Mariamne and Doris, wife and mother of Antipater, entered the royal throne room flanked by armed guards. They were under arrest. Commanding from the dais sat King Herod, ruler of Judea, Samaria, Idumea, Galilee, and, with the death of his brother, Perea. His kingdom exceeded that of the legendary Solomon. This was the first time the daughter of Antigonus and Herod had laid eyes upon one another. Even discounting his age of seventy years, King Herod didn't look good. His left arm moved in an uncontrollable palsy and he suffered severe pain from ulceration of his internal organs. Worst of all, his private member was putrid with infection and infested with worms. Puss ran down his leg oftentimes collecting in pools beneath his chair. The stench disgusted the most faithful of his servants.

Herod did not bother to show any recognition of his wife Doris as he bore no affection for the woman. He stopped having sexual relations with Doris the moment she conceived an heir more than 40 years ago. His eyes riveted upon Princess Mariamne for she possessed a striking resemblance to Herod's second wife, Queen Mariamne bat Alexander, whom he murdered 25 years in the past. Herod grieved her loss even these many years later despite deep-seated political reasons for killing his queen.

It was as if the king gazed upon a reincarnation of his long dead wife. The view transfixed the ailing monarch and infuriating him in the same instant. This princess was not only the first cousin of his dead wife but also the daughter of his mortal enemy, King Antigonus. Pheroras had specific orders to execute all Hasmonean royals. Herod decreed the seed of Antigonus be wiped from the face of the earth but Pheroras got sticky fingers. He pocketed this royal jewel for his own devises. "Supremely stupid Pheroras," thought Herod. In any event, Herod concluded Pheroras forfeited the right to be called "brother" the day he refused his eldest daughter's hand in marriage, a princess dowered by Augustus Caesar himself. The king looked toward the heavens sending silent curses to the ghost of his brother. "You refused my daughter so you could fornicate with the daughter of a manumitted slave. I should have killed you then and there for such an outrageous insult. Your stupidity has landed me in this mess."

No matter, Herod eventually settled all scores. Pheroras lay in the grave while Herod possessed the princess. The king composed himself in preparation for his first interview with the princess. He said, "Daughter of Antigonus, step forward."

Mariamne displayed no fear. She stepped forward and replied, "A pleasure to finally meet you father-in-law. My husband and I were disappointed you could not attend the wedding feast, pressing engagement elsewhere no doubt. We both forgive you for the slight."

The arrogance! Yes, she was her father's daughter. Herod wondered, "Should I just killer her now?" No, he wanted to see the look on Antipater's face as he strides into the throne room only to find his wife and mother under arrest. A smile creased the edges of his lips. Herod gestured with his hand in the direction of his chief minister, Nicolas.[33]

Nicolas announced the charges, "Queen Doris and Princess Mariamne are hereby charged with conspiracy to murder the king together with your prime co-conspirator, Prince Antipater ben Herod. You shall all be tried before Publius Quinctilius Varus, Governor of Syria."

---

[33] Nicolas of Damascus, chief minister to Herod, is a historical figure. After Herod's death, Nicolas served Herod's son Archelaus and, later, moved to Rome where he wrote several works of Jewish history. Josephus extensively used the works of Nicolas in preparing his later Jewish histories. Although Josephus' works survive, we have only fragments from Nicolas.

Doris' face reddened as she listened to the charges. She raged, "That's insane Herod. You're going to execute us just because Antipater married a wife you disapprove of?"

The guards restrained Doris as she tried to charge the dais and pummel the tyrant with her own fists. Salome especially enjoyed this part. She stood with other members of the royal family in an area to the left of the dais. Behind her stood the Modiin chief, Zechariah. As Doris thrashed with the guards, she spied Salome smiling in the gallery.

Doris spit these words at her rival, "You bitch Salome. I know you're behind these pack of lies."

Doris returned her attention to Herod, "The Romans will never stand for this."

Herod, "When have the Romans ever refused me?" The king's smile broadened. He then flicked his wrist indicating that the two prisoners should be led away. The women were locked up pending Antipater's expected arrival from Rome.

The angel of death hovered near Herod despite his indomitable will to continue in life. He congratulated himself on locating the princess before Antipater got her with child. The king knew any son of this couple would eventually be king of the Jews. And it galled Herod to no end thinking of his seed as no more than equal with that of Antigonus in the person of the future king. If this child came to life, the people would see him as Antigonus' grandson whose birth would usher in the return of the Hasmonean royal house. Herod would be consigned to history as a mere usurper who interrupted the Hasmonean dynasty. No, Herod would not stand for it. If the deed required emptying the royal treasury, Herod stood ready to lavishly bribe every Roman official of the entire eastern empire. Herod would see that the seed of Antigonus ended here and now!

Caesarea Maritima, Samaria (4 BCE)

Caesarea, the grandest city in Herod's kingdom outside of Jerusalem, possessed the look of a Roman metropolis--magnificent aqueduct bringing fresh water to the city from Mount Carmel, hippodrome seating 38,000 spectators, amphitheater seating 4500, baths, fountains, and a deep water harbor on the Mediterranean. The port of Caesarea, called Sebastos, contained the first artificial harbor in the world. It equaled the size of Piraeus in Athens with anchorage for 100 ships. Sheltering Sebastos on three sides stood massive artificial breakwaters manufactured with cement that dried underwater. At its entrance from the sea sat a magnificent lighthouse visible for miles out into the Mediterranean. Caesarea was an advanced engineering and architectural wonder.

Antipater never tired of viewing Caesarea from the sea. The sun was but a few hours old in the eastern sky reflecting brilliantly off the white stone of the city walls. It was the crown jewel of Herod's, soon to be Antipater's, kingdom if the old buzzard would just do them all a favor and die. The coregent's ship passed the breakwater and lighthouse entering the harbor as Philip stood at Antipater's side on the bridge.

Antipater, "Strange, no honor guard to meet us. Where are the harbor master and his entourage?"

Philip, "Maybe the watchman at the lighthouse failed to mark us for your royal ship?"

Not even Philip believed those words. The distinctive markings in the sails of a royal Herodian ship could be identified from miles away. They had departed from Sebastos one year ago with great pomp and the full honors due a king. Today, it was as if a private merchant ship of no particular standing just made port. Not a good sign. Antipater and company disembarked onto the dock at the royal birth, still no official welcome. They made their way to the command center of the port guard. Three common legionnaires of the royal army stood on duty. They came to attention at Antipater's approach.

"We'll at least they did not spit on me," he thought.

Antipater addressed the soldiers, "Call your centurion. I wish to speak with him."

The soldiers remained stiff, completely uncomfortable with the situation. Antipater repeated the command, "Are you deaf man? I said call your centurion now."

The soldier replied, "Sorry your highness. We have orders from King Herod that you are to precede directly to the palace in Jerusalem. Horses await you outside the city gate."

A squad of Herodian legionnaires formed up behind Antipater's party. This was not a deferential honor guard. The message from the stance of the troops was clear, Antipater would go to the palace either voluntarily or as a prisoner. The crown prince put his best face on the situation as a show of strength for his friends. He said, "Splendid, I see our military escort has arrived. Gentleman, I know all of us were looking forward to the pleasures of the baths in Caesarea after a sea voyage but it seems my father cannot do without our presence in Jerusalem this evening. How about a nice ride in the country? To the horses men."

It was a long and somber 60-mile ride from Caesarea to Jerusalem. Herod ordered 100 soldiers, under penalty of death, to escort his son to Jerusalem. They were allowed but one stop for food, drink, and a change of horses. The party set a brisk pace exhausting all but Antipater. Despite the bravado, he was a bundle of nervous energy as they entered Jerusalem through the Western gate very near the palace complex. They dismounted upon reaching their destination. Only seven of Antipater's original group of 20 courtiers made the trip with him on horseback from Caesarea. The rest begged off with pleas of pressing business awaiting in Caesarea. So be it, he thought. He would not forget who stayed at his side in his hour of peril. Philip of Rome was one of the seven to accompany Antipater to Jerusalem.

Jerusalem, Judea (4 BCE)

At the entrance to the palace complex beside the ornate Queens Tower, named in honor of Herod's deceased wife Mariamne, Antipater gathered himself in preparation for greeting his father. He threw on his purple cloak and placed the coregent's crown on his head. He nodded for his party to follow and headed through the palace gates but the guards only allowed Antipater to enter. His friends were blocked.

Antipater, "What's going on here? My attendants are to be allowed into the palace."

Philip, "His highness is coregent confirmed by Rome. Orders from the coregent have equal weight to the king. Only Rome has the power to remove his highness from the throne. You're making a huge mistake."

Philip pushed a heavily armed guard to drive home the point. Not exactly a calming gesture in a tense situation. The guards drew swords while stepping back into fighting posture.

"Stand down men," came an order from the captain of the palace guard who appeared on the scene from inside the Temple complex. He quickly diffused the confrontation. He ordered another soldier, "You there, sheath your sword."

The captain addressed Antipater, "My apologies your highness. The order comes from King Herod. Please forgive us. We're caught between a rock and hard place. I beg you as a personal favor to comply with the wishes of your father the king."

Antipater, "I appreciate your candor captain. You disobey the old man and he might boil you in oil."

"Along with my wife and children. Please forgive the insult."

"You are forgiven. Lead the way to the throne room." Antipater tried to save face by "ordering" the captain to lead him to the throne room. The soldiers might have appeared to an uninterested observer to be an honorary escort as opposed to an armed guard with a prisoner under arrest, which was the true state of affairs. If Antipater held out any hope on the ride in from Caesarea that he really was not in trouble, that allusion was blown to bits by the reception at the palace gate. He'd stepped into a massive pile of ox dung.

The palace complex resembled a small city. Herod flattened an entire hill then encased it in stone to serve as the foundation for his colossal palace in Jerusalem. He'd built several others throughout his empire—Jericho, Herodium, Caesarea, and Masada to name but a few. But this palace stood in grandeur above the others. All manner of fountains, bronze statues discharging water, flowers and trees dotted the inside of the

Jerusalem palace compound which had its own internal water source and water distribution system. They reached the throne room whereupon guards flung open the door as a herald announced his arrival shouting, "Prince Antipater."

So they've demoted me from coregent and king, Antipater thought as he heard the reduced introduction he'd just been given. He recognized Publius Quinctilius Varus, Roman governor of Syria, seated on the dais next to his father. Beside Varus stood his lictor displaying a Roman governor's badge of office, the fasces which consisted of an axe bundled with birch rods tied by red ribbon. The fasces symbolize the office holder's authority to dispense punishment. Things were going from bad to worse. The sight of Varus with his fasces gave Antipater a shock. Varus governed from Antioch. What was he doing here? All Antipater could do was put on a brave face. He confidently approached the throne to salute and hug his father as he had done a thousand times before. As Antipater drew near for an embrace, Herod threw out his hands pushing his son away.

Herod said, "Do you mark it Varus? This display of affection is itself evidence of patricide. How heinous of a human is this wretch? To be involved so deeply in a plot to murder his father yet stand here smiling with ease intending to wrap me in a warm embrace. The cold blood of a thief runs in his veins."

Antipater half-expected to be charged with conspiracy to kill his father. What other charge could possibly justify stripping his office? But it stung him to hear the words from his father's lips. Varus, a powerful Roman official, had come to Jerusalem from Antioch for the trial. That fact drove home the point that Herod was serious about pressing forward with the charges.

Antipater responded, "Don't be ridiculous father. As much as it pains me to see you in this state, your heath is poor. Father, you are not long for this earth. The angels are coming for you. Why should I involve myself in a plot of murder when I am already king? It makes no sense. ... Governor Varus, an unexpected pleasure to see you here in Jerusalem on my return from Rome. The emperor sends warm tidings."

Quinctilius Varus merely nodded his head in acknowledgment of Antipater's greeting while maintaining the stone mask of a seasoned Roman legate. His countenance did not betray any indication of his sympathies in the drama unfolding before him.

Herod said to Varus, "The boy is pathological. He deceived me with an intricate and evil web of lies to kill my two sons, Aristobulus and Alexander. He's been nothing but a viper since I recalled him from exile."

Antipater had to smile at his father's use of the term "boy" applied to a 42-year-old prince already with gray hair on his head. So he was dredging up ancient history again. The old man intends to ram Aristobulus and Alexander up my arse, thought Antipater. What a crock of manure! The king's sister Salome gathered all the evidence against those two. She spread the accusations privately in the palace beating the twin drums of rumor and innuendo. Antipater only proclaimed publicly in court what Salome had been gossiping about for months in the back rooms of the palace. Antipater shot his aunt Salome a look. There she stood smug with a small crooked smile at the corner of her mouth. The witch had constructed yet another murder conspiracy for Herod. And her competence at this craft worried the prince. Herod's chief minister Nicolas stepped forward and formally read the charge of conspiracy to murder the king.

Varus then addressed the accused. "Prince Antipater, you have been advised of the charge. Please go now and prepare your defense. I shall hear the evidence tomorrow morning."

Antipater replied, "I have faith in your justice Governor Varus but I was confirmed in my position as coregent by the princeps. Only he holds power over my person. As is my right, I demand trial before Caesar."

"And so you shall have a trial before Augustus Caesar. But your father is too ill for sea travel. All the witnesses are here in Jerusalem. My scribe shall prepare a true and accurate record of all testimony. I'll attest to the evidence and forward it to the princeps along with my recommendation. But your fate rests with Caesar, not me."

"One night Governor Varus? It's not enough time to prepare a defense. I have no idea what the evidence shall be."

Varus pointed to the back of the room. "Consult with your wife and mother. They are familiar with the case."

Antipater turned expecting to see his child wife Mariam Magdalene, daughter of Aristobulus. She would have enjoyed witnessing the comedown Varus gave to Antipater. Instead, there stood Mariamne bat Antigonus, regal, composed, and ravishingly beautiful. While in Rome amusing himself with the charms of female courtesans of that fine metropolis, he'd forgotten just how striking she was. Antipater went and embraced his wife. A brief sense of calm came over his being. He found comfort in her lack of fear. The prince risked all for this woman and, by the gods, she was worth it. Now he knew why he stood on trial for his life. Herod discovered his marriage to Antigonus' daughter and this was his revenge.

Facing the dais, Antipater addressed the room, "As you wish Governor Varus. Till the morrow then."

He left the throne room with his wife and mother. They were taken to a chamber down in the bowels of the palace. Before the guard shut the door, Antipater made a request. "Send in my advocate Philip. He waits at the gate beside the Queens Tower."

"Sorry your highness, orders. No visitors."

"Didn't you hear Governor Varus? I am to prepare my defense for trial tomorrow. Philip is my advocate. I need him to prepare for trial."

The guard hesitated, unsure of himself.

Antipater pushed harder, "Look, do you want me to enter the throne room tomorrow and announce to the king, governor and entire court that you, what's your name?"

"Eleazar."

"That Eleazar the palace guard refused Prince Antipater the means necessary to prepare his defense. Do you want me to announce that? They'll have to give me another day of preparation causing a wasted day in Jerusalem for Governor Varus. He'll be pissed."

The bluff was working as the guard's military demeanor slowly gave way to fear. The crown prince spoke in his command voice, "Do it. Send for Philip of Rome by the Queens Tower. Go man!"

Antipater knew soldiers. Common soldiers were not trained to make decisions. They wanted to be told what to do. Present an air of authority, speak with a commanding voice, and they obey. The guard locked Antipater, Mariamne and Doris into the room and left.

Antipater turned to his mother, "Tell me the information you have on the charges?"

Doris replied, "It started when Pheroras died under mysterious circumstances. Herod tortured the servants but, instead of inquiring about who killed Pheroras, the inquisitors wanted to know about the relationship between Pheroras and yourself."

Antipater, "What does that tell you?"

Mariamne, "That Herod already knew who killed Pheroras so he didn't need to investigate the murder."

Antipater, "Who does the prosecution say are the supposed players in this conspiracy to kill Herod?"

Doris, "You, me, Pheroras, Alexandra (wife of Pheroras), and Mariamne."

She nodded in the direction of Mariamne bat Antigonus to confirm which Mariamne was intended.

Antipater, "Herod charged my wife?"

Doris, "Yes, he intends to kill us all."

Antipater, "That son of a bitch."

Doris, "It gets worse."

Antipater, "How can it get worse?"

Doris, "Herod tortured not just Pheroras' servants but, also, my servants and your servants. He tortured Bathyllus."

It saddened Antipater to learn that his life-long friend and confidant had been tortured. Not only because of the agony his friend endured but, also, it foreboded ill for Antipater's trial. My father Bathyllus knew all Antipater's secrets just as I know the secrets of Yeshua.

Antipater, "So it will be a parade of tortured witnesses tomorrow. Wonderful, I'm sure I'd confess to plotting to kill Caesar if they stuck a hot piece of metal into my genitals. It'll be a farce." He paced nervously around the room trying to figure a plan for extrication from this mess. A knock at the door interrupted Antipater's mad pacing. Philip entered and Antipater motioned his friend to join him in a small anteroom out of hearing of the women.

Philip said, "I have horses ready outside the south gate." He took Antipater over to the window and suggested their escape route. Philip continued, "See that ledge? Jump down there and you have an easy shot to the south gate."

Antipater looked out the window and saw a 15-foot drop to the ledge. He replied, "Are you serious?"

Philip, "It's the only way Antipater. I'm in negotiations with the captain of the palace guard for a bribe to keep the soldiers away from the alley below this window. Wait until just after sundown. I'll meet you at the south gate with horses and an armed escort."

"And we ride off to where?"

Philip was silent. He hadn't planned that far ahead yet. The few available moments had been taken up with the mechanics of springing Antipater from the palace. He weakly offered, "Nabatea?"

"We won't get far at night and road to Petra passes directly in front of two Herodian fortresses. The guards can see for miles eastward from Qumran. We'll be spotted for sure. So we would have to cross the Jordon north of Jericho then head east into the wilderness where Hasidim live. Do you think they are going to welcome Herod's son? In case you have not noticed, I'm not very popular with the Jewish religious parties. They'll piss on me from the ramparts of their walls."

Philip pointed into the next room at Mariamne. "They'll protect her. If we ride into any Jewish village with the daughter of Antigonus, the people will shelter us."

Antipater kicked that idea around in his head. The daughter of Antigonus on the run from Herod and the Romans?

Hell, it might spark a Jewish rebellion. The people might take up arms then and there to defend the princess. With their help, his party just might make it to Nabatea. Antipater had friendly relations with King Aretas of Nabatea. The prince walked back over to the window surveying the long drop to the ledge.

Antipater said, "The women will never survive that drop without injury. My mother, for sure, dies if she tries that jump. We'll never make it to the gate. And getting caught trying to escape will only confirm my guilt for Varus."

"But Varus will convict you tomorrow come what may. The fix is in. Rumors fly around Jerusalem that Herod has paid a massive bribe."

Varus came from a relatively poor patrician family. He arrived in Antioch saddled with heavy debt accrued during his campaign for Roman consul. The governorship of Syria was Varus' opportunity to reverse his family's fortune for generations to come. He was known throughout the province for his willingness to extend his hand for bribes. Any trial before Varus was sure to be rigged. But would Caesar confirm the conviction? Would Herod live long enough for Caesar to rule on the case from Rome?

Neither option looked promising to Antipater. Both attempting to escape and holding fast in Jerusalem to stand trial came with serious risks. Honor dictated Antipater stay and face trial with his mother and wife. He resolved to do just that, come what may. His fate now rested in the hands of the Caesar.

"Philip, I have funds stashed with a banker in Rome."

"A lot of help that is to us here and now."

Antipater grabbed writing supplies and stylist before composing a short letter appointing Philip his financial agent. He then impressed a dab of clay on the parchment with his signet ring. Antipater said, "This will give you access to my funds on deposit in Rome. My agent there knows my handwriting and this seal. I want you to discreetly approach Varus' people and offer a bribe."

Philip, "We'll never outbid Herod for your life."

"I realize that. I'm talking about my wife. What kind of evidence can they have against her? She's been hiding in the Temple most of her life. How will they tie her to the conspiracy?"

"As you wish Antipater but how do I bribe them when I don't have the funds here? I doubt they settle for an IOU."

"Varus or a subordinate must sail to Rome to deliver a report of this trial personally to Caesar. You sail with them and promise the funds will be delivered forthwith on arrival in Rome."

The two old friends embraced, then Philip left. Antipater walked back into the main chamber to join his wife and mother. With so little time before trial and the expected parade of tortured witnesses presenting fabricated testimony, there really was no point to even attempting to put on a case for the defense. His fate was in the hands of the gods and Caesar. Antipater's thoughts migrated from the trial to his wife. "Might as well start working on fathering an heir here and now," he decided. Perhaps something positive comes out of his time in captivity. The fact that Doris shared their room for the evening failed to deter Antipater. He thought, "My mother is too old and hardened of a bird to be embarrassed. And if she's insulted with the deed, to hell with her."

Chapter 7

Alexandria, Egypt (67 CE)

Theudas, "Grandfather, hold on a second."

Menelaus stopped telling the story as thoughts of the last days of Herod's reign flooded his mind. He slowly returned himself to the present. He said, "I thought you wanted me to speed up the story. Now you want to slow down?"

Theudas, "Just a few questions please. Where does your mother come into this story? I thought she was in the employ of Yeshua's mother. Was your mother there in Jerusalem during the trial of Antipater by Governor Varus?"

"Her name was Yohanna[34] and, yes, Princess Mariamne employed my mother in Jerusalem starting two years before Antipater was arrested."

"Now, if I comprehend the situation correctly, your mother was a Jew related to royalty yet she worked as a servant? I'm confused about your mother."

"She came from a family of village Kohen priests in Mod'in, the original home of the Hasmonean clan. Although a member or the Hasmonean clan, her family became acutely poor due to her father having been kicked out of the priesthood for commission of some sort of sin. They stripped him of his priestly stipend also."

Mention of a family scandal peaked Theudas' curiosity. He asked, "What did your grandfather do to get kicked out the priesthood?"

---

[34] Yohanna is a variant of the Hebrew Yehohanah, of which Joanna is the English equivalent.

"I don't know. My mother refused to ever speak of it."

"Oh."

Menelaus continued, "Poverty and the shame of her father's actions led to my mother to hire herself out to Princess Mariamne in Jerusalem. Her prospects for marriage were grim back in her home village. The position of head chamberlain to a royal lady is actually one of importance. She was not a servant in the sense that merchant families such as your own employ servants in the home. In the absence of the princess, my mother held authority to issue orders to the servants in the name of the princess. Others referred to her as 'Lady Yohanna' in honor of her high birth."

"I see. You have a Greek name grandfather so I assume your father was Greek. How did your Jewish mother of high birth come to marry a Greek?"

"Princess Mariamne was in hiding during this period. She and my mother came into contact with very few outsiders. My father Bathyllus was one of the few privileged with access. He served Prince Antipater first as a scribe and later became his chief minister. It was through Antipater that my father was able to strike up a relationship with my mother."

Theudas began to understand how telling the drama of Yeshua uncovered old scars for his grandfather.

Menelaus took the opportunity of momentary silence from his grandson to fill in a few family details. "The marriage of my parents caused a scandal in my mother's family. A Jewish woman only marries through the contract of her father or the ranking male member of the family. My mother broke the rules as no senior male member of her family would sign the contract. It was a legal marriage in Roman eyes but not so in the eyes of the Jews. Under Jewish law, I was born a bastard. My mother's family disowned her at the instant she married my father Bathyllus. It was as if she died. I never saw nor heard from my mother's family despite us both being present in Jerusalem many times during religious feasts."

Theudas, "So your mother was a woman of strong will."

"Yes, she followed the lead of her mistress Mariamne who was the strongest willed woman I have known in life."

"Even more so than Yeshua?"

Menelaus reflected on his former master for a moment before replying. "He was strong of spirit but not necessarily of earthly will in the sense that he desired little in the way of power or wealth. Yeshua actually could have cared less about being king. He pursued the dream of his father and mother out of a sense of family duty. I think he would have been perfectly content to lead the life of a wandering ascetic, dressed in rags, living off the charity of those with whom he shared nuggets of wisdom. This caused occasional tension between mother and son." Menelaus paused before continuing to allow his grandson to ask further questions, should he have any.

Theudas, "One more thing, I still don't understand why Antipater returned to Jerusalem from Rome knowing he likely would face trial there. The risk just seemed too great."

"Easy for us in hindsight to make that judgment. At the time, I am sure he thought his royal position as coregent offered him an aura of protection. As far as he knew, his only crime was marrying the wrong woman and supposed Herod lacked the authority to execute him for that. The authority to execute a royal subject rested with Augustus Caesar, with whom Antipater had a very strong relationship."

"Then Prince Antipater was not executed because Augustus Caesar refused to sentence him to death?"

"You are getting ahead of the story grandson. I shall detail the fate of Prince Antipater shortly."

Theudas still couldn't get his brain around why Antipater ever sailed home given the murderous reputation of Herod. "I understand that Caesar alone held the authority to order the execution of a royal prince from a subject kingdom but his father Herod had a history of killing family members. Antipater knew there was a falling out between them. Why even put your life in jeopardy? A dying man might defy the orders of his superiors before departing this world."

Menelaus smiled at the prescient words from his young grandson. "If the decision involved only his own skin, your course of action is probably the one he takes. Antipater never leaves Rome, Herod eventually dies and Antipater becomes king. But he had his royal wife Princess Mariamne to consider, not merely personal affection for her but, also, the political importance of her bloodline to his ability to rule the Jewish people after Herod's death. The monarchy has long since been dead in Egypt so maybe you don't appreciate the power of the royal bloodline in a game of throne succession. The battle for the Jewish kingdom was expected to be an ongoing contest after Herod's death and Mariamne was the only daughter of a Hasmonean king still alive. Her royal status strengthened Antipater's claim to the throne both in Judea and Rome."

Theudas reflected upon his grandfather's words before replying. "So, this Mariamne was the daughter of a king but Herod also had daughters. Why were they not of equal rank to her?"

"Theudas, you're not thinking like a Jew. Channel that small dose of Jewish blood in your veins. Given the chance, the average Jew defecates on a daughter of Herod. He was an Arabian commoner masquerading as a Jewish king. The Hasmoneans, on the other hand, were priests descended from Aaron and national heroes for their magical victory over the Greeks and Hellenized Jews. Mattathias Maccabee founded a dynasty that returned Israel to Jewish control for the first time in five hundred years. Not only was Mariamne the daughter of a Hasmonean king <u>and</u> high priest, she was free of the taint of Herod's blood. No other woman then alive could make that claim."

Theudas, "So I get the part that the people loved Princess Mariamne for her Hasmonean bloodline but how did that help Antipater?"

"He wanted to be accepted by the Jews. He descended from King David through his mother the Nabatean princess but the Nabatean royal family also traced its roots back to the Pharaohs so his bloodline through his mother was not first-rate Jewish royalty. Antipater was raised in Rome and the Jews hated him for the deaths of his Hasmonean brothers. Without popular support from the Jewish people he would have been a weak ruler with a hoard of brothers and cousins scheming to grab his crown. He wouldn't have survived long on the throne. Antipater was a man of great ambition like his father. He reached for the pantheon unwilling to settle for being a weak Roman vassal. He dreamed large, of pushing the Jewish kingdom to even greater heights than under his father or even King David. He aimed to be the new David. The key to this dream was Princess Mariamne bat Antigonus. The Jewish people held a long tradition of valuing the royal bloodline of the king's wife. We see that going all the way back to King David, then Hasmonean King Jannai, and finally Herod. Thus, the royal status of Antipater's wife conveyed authority upon him in the eyes of the Jewish people. And that position would be cemented by fathering children by his royal Hasmonean wife so that the Jewish people knew his heirs were descendants of King Antigonus, the last rightful Jewish king. Thus, the Jewish people would know that supporting Antipater meant one day a king would come who was the grandson of Antigonus and this, Antipater hoped, would sway them to his side. He risked all for Mariamne."

Nature called upon Theudas's bodily functions. "Give me a second to relieve myself grandfather. I don't want to have to stop your story again until I find out how the plot turns."

"Hah! Get a grip on your bladder grandson. There is much more to tell."

Theudas trundled off to the toilet.

Chapter 8

Jerusalem, Judea (4 BCE)

Antipater awoke with his wife Mariamne huddled close by his side. Amazingly, with all that had transpired the previous day, he'd slept like a rock having passed out the moment he expended himself into his wife. As he returned to the world of the living, warm memories of conjugal relations the previous night were replaced by the horror of the present. Antipater, Mariamne, and Doris silently dressed and, after a miserable breakfast, were summoned to the throne room. The trial was on.

Zechariah ben Eleazar, chief of Modiin, also rose early that day. Following his first meeting with Princess Salome two months ago when she laid out her plans for the destruction of Antipater, Zechariah did what good civil servants do, he covered his ass. The Modiin chief secretly conferred with the captain of Herod's palace guard passing along the entire contents of his exchange with Salome. Zechariah had no qualms with political assassination but he sure as hell wasn't killing a royal until he knew the king authorized it. Word came back that Herod authorized the hit on his brother Pheroras. So Zechariah carried out Salome's scheme, poisoning the king's brother then planting a vile of Egyptian poison in his household. The chief took pride in his work personally attending to the details of this case. The cover story was that Pheroras conspired with Antipater to kill Herod but, somehow, Pheroras accidentally died by the poison intended for Herod. The fantastical nature of the story would be smoothed over by a wagon-train of tortured witnesses from the house of Pheroras, whose testimony confirmed the cover story.

The reputation of Modiin was on the line with high-level eyes scrutinizing every move. Zechariah went the extra mile in framing Antipater with conspiracy to kill his father. He forged correspondence between Antipater and his subordinates back in Palestine planting the evidence on several servants. He also wove Antipater's Idumean uncle, Prince Thendion, into the conspiracy. The chief planted a hoard of damning evidence on Bathyllus--a second deadly Egyptian potion (this one the poison of asps) and the juices of other serpents said to be the fallback option for use in killing Herod should the first poison in the household of Pheroras fail to do the trick.[35] Perhaps it was overkill but Zechariah was determined not to be accused by Salome for lack of effort.

After completing these tasks, Zechariah assisted in torturing the servants of Antipater, Pheroras and Doris. Only he possessed a complete list of all the planted evidence and knew exactly how each piece fit into the master theory of the alleged plot to kill Herod. It was Zechariah who wrote out the confessions signed by each key witness. The king assigned Nicolas of Damascus, his chief minister, the task of presenting the crown's case against Prince Antipater. Zechariah spent long hours laying it all out for Nicolas, one of the most learned men in the kingdom. Nicolas didn't need to be told Antipater was framed. He knew the crown prince's only crime had been to marry the wrong woman. Nicolas, like Zechariah, did as the king desired. After the prisoners took their seats, the king's herald announced the entrance of King Herod and Governor Quinctilius Varus.

Herod commanded, "Get on with it Nicolas. We want to wrap this thing up today."

A host of tortured witnesses paraded to the witness stand proffering their scripted testimony. Pheroras' slaves testified to the alleged machinations between Antipater and Pheroras including their desire to kill Herod. The prosecution next presented Antipater's steward who testified that an agent of Antipater in Egypt secured poison there and transported it to Pheroras in Perea. The first drama of the trial occurred with the appearance in

---

[35] Jewish Wars I 31:1.

the courtroom of Pheroras' widow (Alexandra of Perea). She flung herself out the upper floor of Pheroras' palace when Herod's soldiers arrived to avoid torture but survived the fall with broken bones. Thus, the badly broken yet alive body of Pheroras' wife entered the court room via litter. Nicolas promised Alexandra of Perea that her children would remain unharmed if she testified against Antipater. A mother will do the most horrible act imaginable to save her children. Alexandra clutched a box as she told Governor Varus that Antipater arranged for delivery of the poison to Pheroras from Egypt and that this poison was to be used on Herod.

Varus interrupted her testimony, "You have the poison there in that box?"

Alexandra of Perea, "Yes governor."

Varus gestured for an attendant to get the box from her and bring it to him then commanded, "Herod, send in a condemned prisoner. I wish to conduct an experiment."

Herod complied with the request from Varus promptly producing a prisoner set for execution the next day.

Varus commanded, "Prisoner, drink this."

He handed the prisoner the poison but the prisoner refused to drink it.

Varus urged the man, "Prisoner, you have nothing to lose. If you drink it and die, well, that is your fate in any course. But if you live, King Herod shall commute your sentence allowing you to leave here a free man. It will be up to your god to decide your fate if you drink."

Herod nodded his head affirmatively indicating that he would honor the offer set forth by Varus. Realizing this was his only chance at life, the prisoner grabbed the vile allegedly containing poison and downed its contents in one swift gulp. All eyes fixed on the prisoner who, at first, showed no ill effects from the drink. He turned his head around the room returning the stares. A broad grin broke across his face. The prisoner said to Varus, "Yahweh says I live Governor!"

He began laughing uncontrollably. But the laughter shortly turned to something else. The prisoner gasped for breath as the muscles lining of his lungs constricted. His entire chest felt like it was in the grip of a giant snake. His eyes watered as if sprayed by acid. The prisoner fell to the floor withering in pain, foam seeping from his mouth, and unable to breath.

Varus said to the man, "No prisoner, Rome says you die."

The guards carried the man away just as he expired. Next on the witness stand was my father Bathyllus. A physically robust man before arrest, he limped to the witness chair with great difficulty. When he spoke, Bathyllus' words came out slurred and partially incoherent although he was known to be a felicitous orator. The man in the witness chair that day was a shell of himself. Antipater knew his old friend had been horribly tortured and drugged. My father confirmed all the testimony of the prior witnesses then added a new twist. He produced two libelous letters supposedly written by Antipater for Caesar defaming his brothers Archelaus and Herod Boethus. Bathyllus testified that Antipater intended to do away with his brothers Archelaus and Herod Boethus in the same fashion as he previously destroyed Herod's sons Aristobulus and Alexander. It was a monstrous picture painted by the prosecution.

Why did the prosecution hoe the old field of the deaths of Aristobulus and Alexander? They were raised in the household of Augustus Caesar with the emperor's own children. Caesar was the ultimate audience for the evidence presented. Herod's message to the princeps was clear—this evil viper manipulated me into killing Aristobulus and Alexander who you raised like they were your own children. Antipater must die for his sins.

Nicolas, "Governor Varus, this concludes the king's case against Prince Antipater."

Nicolas took a seat expecting to hear a lengthy defense from Antipater.

Varus, "Call your first witness Prince Antipater."

Antipater strode from his seat to a point directly in front of Varus and Herod, who were seated up on the dais. The accused said, "Honorable governor, father, there is no evidence for me to present other than that which you already have before you. My father has testified how he raised me up to be his prime heir and successor, how he nurtured my advancement in life and protected me against the evil of others. How can I be a patricide against one who has always been my guardian? Further, I am already a king. What would I gain through the murder of my father? There is absolutely no motive for the alleged crime. Now it has been said that I am the subtlest schemer and practiced in the art of deception. Yet when I openly confess love for my father before this court I am called an obvious liar. The evidence points to crude methods that were far from subtle. Which is it father, a subtle schemer or a clumsy butcher? And father, have I not always been fearful of the judgment of God? God knows all things and surely I would not wish to face the judgment of God having conspired to murder my own father. Please be so kind as to name one instance in life where I have not been obedient to your wishes. I was in Rome as your ambassador and returned when you requested. Obviously my enemies fomented hatred against me in the palace during my long absence. They have poisoned you with lies father."

Antipater gave a long, icy stare at his aunt Salome, the Judean witch, before continuing, "I ask Governor Quinctilius Varus to read the letters Caesar sent to my father since I arrived in Rome. I am sure they will reflect how I sang my father's praises before Caesar and all the influential persons of his court within earshot. What does the prosecution have other than testimony from the tortured? Their evidence is completely unreliable. I have the words of Caesar attesting to my love for my father!"

Antipater got down on the ground and prostrated himself before Herod, something he had never before done in life. "If I have offended thee in some way father, I beg your forgiveness. I have only love for you and nothing will change this. God is my witness that I am entirely innocent."

Antipater's speech moved the assembled audience. Several women in the audience wept. Antipater rested his case with this speech putting on no witnesses. Herod and Varus withdrew to an inner chamber where they could privately discuss the case.

Herod said, "Varus, your eyes moistened when the swine got down on his knees spouting venomous lies."

Varus, "Don't mistake compassion for weakness. I'll do what is necessary."

This reiteration from Varus that he stood firm greatly relieved Herod. Antipater must die and Varus was the only man capable of bringing about such an order from Caesar. However Varus did have reservations about the case against the other defendants. He said, "Antipater is guilty but his wife, the daughter of Antigonus, is totally innocent. Her name was barely uttered in the testimony."

"By Jupiter, she's his wife so she must have been in on the conspiracy. It just stands to reason Varus!"

"In Rome, we don't murder every criminal's wife. We are a nation of laws. And you have to be careful of overreaching in presenting your case to Caesar. I'm looking out for your best interests Herod. It will completely undercut the credibility of my recommendation if we claim justification for the execution of Princess Mariamne. Where is the evidence?"

"Do you have any idea how dangerous that woman is? She could single-handedly resurrect the Hasmonean dynasty. You're a general Varus. Wouldn't the Parthians love to back a young Hasmonean prince who was the grandson of Antigonus? The common Jews would go delirious with joy. They would proclaim him messiah. We must stamp out Antigonus' seed. She is too dangerous to let live."

"I can't convict the woman based on her bloodline. She goes free. Death for Antipater, Bathyllus and Thendion."[36]

Herod pushed for more convictions, "And Pheroras' wife dies. I should have killed the tart years ago."

Varus replied, "And Pheroras' wife shall be found guilty. She tried to kill herself when the inquisitors arrived at her door which confirms guilt."

"And Doris."

"No Herod, not Doris."

---

[36] Thendion was an Idumean prince and brother of Doris (thus, Antipater's uncle).

"Quinctilius Varus, you're going soft on me again. She's knee deep in this pile of dung!"

"And an old woman at the end of life with Idumean, Egyptian, and Jewish royal blood. She has friendly relations with Caesar's women in Rome. It'll require much explaining to secure her death sentence and to what gain? Her life is at a close regardless. Exile her Herod."

Herod poured two cups of a prized Setinum wine from Latium, a favorite of Caesar. Knowing that further argument was futile, he handed one cup to Varus. Arguing over the execution of Doris was of no consequence. The execution of her only child, Antipater, would surely kill the old hag.

Herod, "We have a deal then my friend."

The king slapped Varus on the back and smiled. But behind the smile he was uneasy. The daughter of Antigonus was still in their midst and she must be eliminated. Herod believed in keeping his friends close and his enemies closer.[37] Perhaps his nephew Joseph ben Joseph would like a junior wife? He'd stash her with his nephew then kill Mariamne bat Antigonus when the time was right.

---

[37] Poetic license was taken in borrowing this quote from Sun-tzu, the renowned Chinese general.

Chapter 9

Jerusalem, Judea (4 BCE)

There wasn't much for Antipater to do in prison other than pray Herod died. Herod released Antipater's wife Mariamne from jail but kept her under house arrest in the palace. The king exiled his wife Doris and moved Antipater to a cell farther down into the bowels of the palace. There the former crown prince brooded for many months awaiting word from Rome on whether Caesar would confirm the death sentence. No window existed in this cell, thus Antipater had no avenue for escape.

Antipater called for the guard, "Eleazar."

"Yes prince."

"Get the captain of the palace guard. I need to speak with him." A few moments later Eleazar returned with the captain.

Antipater, "Captain, I desire a visit from my wife."

"Sorry prince, the king forbids visitors."

"Not a smart play captain. If Herod dies, I'll be set free and made king. You know it and I know it. Herod's only will on deposit with the Vestal Virgins in Rome states I am to be king on his death. And don't forget I'm on good terms with Caesar. You refuse me this small request and I'll make damn sure you pay when I'm king."

The captain retorted, "Unless you die first."

Antipater shot back, "Cover your bets captain. Caesar might not even sentence me to death. He could opt for exile then, when Herod dies, I return as king. Play it safe."

The longer the captain rolled the issue around in his head, the more Antipater's logic persuaded him. The prisoner just might end up king. Antipater possessed the strongest connections in Rome of all Herod's sons. A betting man would wager Caesar named Antipater king at Herod's death … if the prince survived that long. The captain relented, "Alright, we'll smuggle your wife into your chamber. But she has to be dressed as a common servant. I want her head covered, jewelry removed."

Antipater, "Call on my friend Philip who just returned from Rome. You can trust him to discreetly make the arrangements."

So it was that Prince Antipater resumed conjugal relations with his wife Mariamne while confined in Herod's prison. And it was in this way that Yeshua, known as the Christos, was conceived.

Jericho, Judea (4 BCE)

Time marched on. Summer became winter, which meant Herod moved his court to his winter palace at Jericho. Still no news reached Judea from Rome on Caesar's verdict in the case of Prince Antipater. The king's process of dying accelerated at his winter palace. This spawned rumors throughout Israel of the king's imminent passing.

Trouble brewed in Jerusalem. Governor Varus requested Herod place a Roman eagle on the gate at the entrance to the outer courtyard of the Temple in Jerusalem during his trial of Antipater earlier in the year. Herod attempted to dissuade the Roman Governor of this idea as one likely to offend the priests and rabbis (Jewish law forbade the erecting of images depicting any living creature) but Varus wouldn't listen to reason. So Herod complied ordering a golden eagle placed above the gate farthest away from the inner sanctum of the Temple. With an ailing king away in Jericho and thought to be near death, two ambitious young rabbis, Judas of Sepphoris and Matthias ben Margalus, led a large gang of zealous Jews in tearing down the Roman golden eagle from the Temple gate. Herodian soldiers broke up the mob and arrested forty of the perpetrators but not before the Roman symbol had been smashed to bits. The two leaders, rabbis Judas and Matthias, readily admitted their part in the episode to the authorities. Herod summoned these two prisoners and a large number of leading men from Jerusalem to his palace in Jericho. His guards assembled the group at the amphitheater. Determined to address the crowd even though he could neither walk nor even stand, his slaves carried the king upon a couch placing it on the stage. Herod addressed the prisoners and leading men of Jerusalem from a reclining position on his couch as the two heavily shackled rabbis were brought before the king. Herod said, "You two stand accused of leading a mob that vandalized the temple. How do you respond?"

"Yes, we did it." They both smiled to show their pride in the deed. The prisoners continued, "We follow the commandments given to Moses by God. Whatever punishment you feel is just, we accept it."

Herod inquired, "How can you two be so happy when you are about to be put to death?"

They responded, "Because we shall enjoy greater happiness when we are dead. God rewards those who obey his laws."

If they had shown some sort of remorse perhaps Herod would have condemned them to an easier death; however, they remained defiant to the last. The king was determined that the people respect him until the very moment the angel of death took him. He said, "You are both sentence to be burned alive. I'll be impressed if the smiles remain on your faces while the flames lick at your flesh."

The king nodded to the guards who took the two rabbis a short distance to a spot where a metal stake stuck out of the ground and around which a wooden pyre had been built. A flammable tar substance coated the wood making it highly combustible. The guards chained the rabbis to the stake and lit the wood pyre immediately engulfing them in flames in full view of the assembled crowd and Herod. As the smell of burning human flesh wafted over the crowd, the two rabbis died in silence depriving Herod the pleasure of hearing their screams of agony before passing on to the next world, a journey the king was soon to make.[38]

---

[38] Jewish Wars I 33:1; Antiquities XVII 6:2-3.

Herod appeared too stubborn for death. Any normal human not so desirous of clinging to power would have long since expired. The king's physicians took him east of the Jordan River to the warm springs at Callirrhoe near the Dead Sea in hope of restoring Herod's health; however, treatment in the springs was ineffective. Next, they bathed the dying king in a vessel full of warm oil but, again, Herod experienced no appreciable relief from his symptoms. With little hope of surviving his current illness, a depressed Herod returned to his winter palace at Jericho. One last chapter in the story of the old king's life remained.

A ship from Rome at long last braved a winter passage through the Aegean Sea to arrive in the port of Caesarea carrying correspondence from Augustus to Herod. The princeps confirmed Quinctilius Varus' finding of Antipater's guilt. The sentence of death was approved although Caesar's written order gave Herod the option of sending Antipater into exile. However, separate correspondence from Herod's agents in Rome informed the king that Caesar requested Herod send Antipater into exile. In essence, Caesar split the baby. He officially confirmed the conviction of Antipater upon the charge of patricide and the death sentence but, by private message, told Herod to exile his son instead of executing him. Any "request" made by Caesar to a subject king was in fact a direct command from the emperor. The public ruling allowed Herod to save face but preserved Antipater's life, as Caesar wished. Herod understood a deeper import in the private correspondence: Caesar intended to make Antipater the next Jewish king.

Herod's spirits plummeted immediately upon reading the private correspondence from his Roman agents. Herod had doggedly clung to life these many months for the express purpose of taking his treacherous son Antipater to the grave with him. But Caesar deprived Herod of his dying wish. Feeling faint, he called for an apple and knife as it was his custom to pare the apple himself rather than have the deed performed by servants. Herod took the knife into his hand and, without warning, attempted to thrust the knife into his heart to end the misery. The king would have succeeded had not his first cousin Achiabus stopped Herod's hand from delivering a fatal wound. Achiabus cried out loudly as he struggled with the king to recover the knife.[39] The cries drew the attention of female servants in the vicinity who found Achiabus wrestling Herod for a knife. Naturally, the women themselves shrieked creating even more commotion. Other servants heard the screams coming from the king's chamber and assumed the king had died. Thus began a chain-reaction of wailing in the palace. A cacophony of sobbing reverberated around the upper floors.

Echoes of the screams reached Antipater down in the dungeon underneath the palace. Antipater assumed the crying women meant Herod had died so he looked to heaven and praised the Lord. He called for the guard, "Eleazar get over here. I demand you let me out of this cell at once."

The guard replied, "What is it Prince Antipater?"

"Are you deaf man? Listen to the racket above in the palace. The king is dead. I'm to be proclaimed the new king."

Hearing the lamentation of the women, Eleazar too believed Herod was dead but the guard had no orders to release Antipater. Eleazar paced the corridor for several minutes unsure what to do as the wailing continued. All the while Antipater increased the promised riches he would bestow on Eleazar if he would only free the prince from his cell. Finally, the guard gave in. He broke out a big smile as he opened the cell door. But before the prince could exit the dungeon, the captain of the Herod's palace guard stopped the prince. "Prince, what are you doing out of your cell? I must insist that you return."

Antipater, "Be reasonable captain. The king is dead. Do you not hear the women mourning his passing?"

"I need orders before you can be released. Please understand Prince Antipater. It is a soldier's duty."

Antipater tried to talk his way past the captain, "Joshua, here is your situation. I am coregent confirmed in this office by Augustus Caesar. The king is dead. My father's will on file with the Vestal Virgins in Rome declares I am to be his successor. As

---

[39] Antiquities XVII 7:1.

both coregent and heir, I now give the orders in this kingdom. I hereby order you to release me at once."

The captain hesitated. For all the world it sounded as if the king had died. This prince who stood before the captain could very well become the next king with absolute power over his life. But Joshua needed to be certain for freeing Antipater could also cost him his life should Herod still live. The captain of the guard replied, "I shall this instant send up a man to confirm the death of the king. Please be patient for one moment prince. If King Herod has died, I shall release you."

Joshua motioned for one of his men to go up to the king's chamber and find out whether Herod was alive or dead. Rather than return the prince to his cell, the captain took Antipater to his private room just outside the dungeon and shared a cup of wine with the prince. Order was slowly restored in the king's chambers after the hysterical outburst of the women. Nicolas of Damascus entered the king's chambers finding Herod separated from his knife and once more in command of his senses. The king handed Nicolas both letters from Caesar (i.e., the public and private dispatches), which he read.

Nicolas, "Send Antipater into exile in Gaul your highness. No good comes from crossing Caesar. He'll take it out on your heirs."

Both men's attention turned to the door where one of Herod's bodyguards blocked the entrance of a dungeon guard who struggled to get into the room. The dungeon guard made a racket protesting his need for admittance into the king's chamber upon orders of the captain of the guard. Nicolas stepped to the hallway to see what all the commotion was about.

The dungeon guard said, "Minister, does the king live?"

Nicolas told the man to see for himself gesturing his permission for the guard to stick his head inside the doorway of the chamber. The guard peeked inside seeing Herod sitting upright, alert, and in a pissed off mood.

Guard, "A thousand pardons minister. I was under strict orders to see with my own eyes whether the king lives or had died."

Nicolas, "Why were those orders issued?"

"Only the captain can say for sure minister but we heard the women wailing in the dungeon and Prince Antipater demanded to be set free saying he was still coregent and under the laws of Rome he was the next king."

Nicolas dismissed the guard and returned to Herod. Nicolas said to the king, "Did you hear?"

Herod replied, "No, my hearing is failing me. What did the guard say?"

"The captain in charge of the dungeon nearly set Antipater free thinking you were dead with the women crying and all."

Herod's face got red with anger. With his last remaining strength, the king balled up his fist and slammed it into his hand. Herod resolved to see that his will was done and to hell with Augustus Caesar. He commanded, "This cannot wait another day Nicolas. Antipater will take command of the kingdom at my death unless I act. He'll sit on my throne with that Hasmonean whore as his queen. I'll not stand for it. Execute him at first light! Do you hear me? First light!"

Herod then banged his fist upon the table as hard and as long as his frail body could muster before collapsing in exhaustion onto his couch. Execution of Herodians fell under the jurisdiction of Modiin. Herod didn't want his palace guards feeling comfortable killing members of his family. Two Modiin executioners from Jerusalem had been standing by in Jericho for the express purpose of executing Antipater when authorization arrived from Rome. Nicolas sent a message to Zechariah, chief of Modiin, to come to the palace at first light bringing his men for a "wet job". Modiin created the case against Antipater; now they were to snuff out his life. As Minister Nicolas waited on Modiin, word of Caesar's confirmation of the death sentence raced around the palace setting off wails from various women sympathetic to the crown prince.

The next morning minister Nicolas and the Modiin chief appeared at the door to the palace dungeon. The captain knew Nicolas on sight and was able to surmise the reason for his presence. He opened the dungeon door and led the men to

Antipater's cell without having to be told. As soon as the cell door was open, two huge men pushed past the captain into Antipater's cell without uttering a word. One held Antipater down while the other strangled him. It was over in seconds. Minister Nicolas followed by Chief Zechariah then entered the cell to check on the prisoner lying limp on the floor but Nicolas balked at touching the dead body himself.

Nicolas said, "Touch his chest to see if his heart still beats."

Zechariah did as instructed and said, "Minister, his heart has stopped."

Nicolas replied, "Very good, the other prisoner is further down the corridor. Quickly now."

The assassination committee continued on to the cell of my father Bathyllus repeating the same procedure. So my father and the father of Yeshua died within minutes of each other in the same cell block. After completing the deed, Nicolas pulled Zechariah close by so he could whisper into his ear, "Gather up the bodies and load them onto a cart. Personally stay with the bodies until you receive further instructions from me. I'll send a squad of palace guards down as extra security. The bodies are to be turned over to Princess Mariamne and Lady Yohanna for burial. Have this note delivered to Prince Joseph ben Joseph."

Although not a Jew, Nicolas knew the Jewish religion placed a high importance on the burial ritual. He further knew it would be important to Princess Mariamne, the daughter of a high priest, to comply with Jewish law regarding the burial of her husband. The Torah states that executed criminals are to be buried the same day they die.[40] As a mark of respect for the princess, Nicolas intended to see to it that her wishes for the burial of Antipater were carried out. Perhaps this small gesture would ease the pain in some way. She didn't know it yet but Herod had assigned his nephew Joseph to be her next husband. Jewish custom dictated that a member of Herod's family be present to represent the family at the funeral. Herod had no intention of

---

40 *Deut.* 21:22-23.

going to the burial but gave Nicolas instructions to detail Prince Joseph for the task. Besides, Joseph's presence at the burial killed two birds with one stone—the future couple could meet for the first time. Princess Mariamne was still under house arrest at the palace in Jericho. Minister Nicolas knocked on the door to her suit of rooms trailed by an extremely well dressed, 50 year-old man who was one of the three wealthiest private individuals in all of Palestine. My mother answered the door. Nicolas spoke first, "Minister Nicolas and Prince Joseph to see Princess Mariamne."

Despite the unusual request of Herod's chief minister to meet with Princess Mariamne in her private quarters, Lady Yohanna showed the two gentlemen into the main room, then went to an inner room to announce the arrival of visitors. When Mariamne joined the group in the main room, her beauty knocked the air out of Nicolas' lungs. Radiance flowed from the princess as he'd never witnessed before. Nicolas, the old political pro, stood momentarily flustered by emotion. He completely forgot to introduce Prince Joseph while fixating upon how best to broach a painful subject.

Princess Mariamne broke the silence for him. She said, "I assume you have brought me news minister. I fear by the look on your face that it is not good."

"I'm sorry princess. Your husband Prince Antipater was executed moments ago. Lady Yohanna, your husband Bathyllus has also been executed."

Both women immediate cried out and rent their garments in the rite of K'riah. The words knocked both to the ground like wheat cut with the sickle. The two women tried to comfort each other as best they could. Yeshua and I, though unborn, were there with our mothers in uterus. Our fathers died before laying eyes upon their sons. It was the first of many shared experiences in our lives. Nicolas stepped back from the ladies to let them grieve for a moment. Joseph pulled him aside motioning that the two men should wait outside the door while the ladies composed themselves. After only a few moments, Mariamne emerged from her suite of rooms looking for Nicolas. Now composed, she invited the chief minister and Prince Joseph to come inside once again.

Mariamne, "I'm thankful for your kindness in personally bringing the news to me but I need to know how to retrieve my husband's body for burial."

Nicolas, "I have the bodies of both men on a cart under guard at the palace gate. The soldiers await your instructions for burial."

Nicolas then belatedly remembered his lapse in manners for failing to introduce Joseph, "Princess Mariamne, may I introduce Prince Joseph ben Joseph, nephew of the king." The two appraised each other briefly, like boxers sizing up the opposition.

Mariamne, "Thank you for coming Prince Joseph. Will you be representing my husband's family at the burial?"

He said, "Yes my lady."

Mariamne, "Lady Yohanna and I wish for our husband to be buried in Jerusalem as close as possible to the Mount of Olives."

Nicolas looked at Prince Joseph and, with a nod, requested the prince inform the widows of bad news.

Prince Joseph, "I am sorry Princess Mariamne and Lady Yohanna but the king has denied permission for the deceased to be buried in Jerusalem. Is there another location that suits you?"

Mariamne didn't hesitate with her response, "With my relatives at Hyrcania. Is that a problem?"

Nicolas, "Hyrcania is acceptable my lady. We must get underway at once if we are to travel that distance before sundown."

"One more request. I wish for my kinswoman Mariam bat Aristobulus to join us. She also was wife to Antipater."

It hadn't occurred to Nicolas or Joseph that Princess Mariamne would request the presence of Antipater's eleven-year-old junior wife at the burial; however, given the blood connection, he should have surmised the possibility. Joseph looked at Nicolas who nodded his assent.

Joseph, "As you wish my lady."

Mariamne was determined to be in Hyrcania before the setting sun dipped below the western horizon in accordance with Jewish law. Although her father's burial place was unknown to her, the bones of Mariamne's mother and her aunt (both killed by Pheroras' men captured the fortress) lay in a stone tomb at Hyrcania. Mariamne addressed Joseph, "If you would be so kind as to wait in the hallway for few a moments, we shall prepare ourselves in mourning attire and join you."

The funeral party set off with military escort as quickly as possible for the old Hasmonean fortress of Hyrcania near the Dead Sea. Mariamne and Mariam sat next to each other in the coach but said little on the long ride into the desert. The two were members of the select few living Hasmonean princesses.[41] They were vessels of Jewish royal blood, the "sang réal".[42] It was quite unusual to have two Hasmonean princesses traveling in open country. They were treasures beyond price to the Jewish people so Nicolas took two squads of cavalry with him as escort. Herod had recently named Archelaus his new coregent and heir. The boy was already making an ass of himself. Archelaus demanded both Nicolas and Prince Joseph personally appear before him and beg the favor of additional troops before he released the second squad of cavalry for the trip to Hyrcania. Nicolas had no previous working relationship with the new coregent. He and Herod's senior ministers loathed the idea of breaking in a new king, his hands freshly upon the reins of power. New rulers invariably pulled hard on the reigns merely for the pleasure of seeing their minions dance at the end of a string.

The party rode ten dusty miles south from Herod's palace at Jericho to the old Hasmonean military complex at Qumran, which sat high on a bluff overlooking the Dead Sea with a

---

[41] History mentions five princesses as alive in 4 BCE: Salampsio and Cypros (daughters of Mariamne I); Mariamne bat Aristobulus (called Mariam in this novel), Herodias bat Aristobulus and Mariamne bat Antigonus. As Elizabeth, mother of John the Baptist, is listed as a "kinswoman" of Mariamne bat Antigonus, I heavily suspect she is another Hasmonean princess and have named her as such in our story.

[42] "Sang real" is Spanish for "blood royal". Under one theory, the Holy Grail (san greal in Spanish) was the royal blood of Yeshua' family.

commanding 180 degree view to the north, east, and south. During Herod's reign Qumran was expanded and the fortress converted to a fortified villa rustica. A nearby oasis was farmed for dates and other crops with small manufacturing conducting inside the Qumran complex. Herodian soldiers still watched the roads from the guard tower on the bluff so a messenger was sent by Prince Joseph up to the Qumran tower to identify the traveling party and inform the soldiers of their intended destination. We turned west at Qumran for Fortress Hyrcania, which lay an additional five miles in the distance on the road Jerusalem.

The funeral party pulled into Hyrcania two hours before sunset. There was no time to rest. The first step prior to burial was ritual purification performed by the male members of the deceased's family. Being the only male Herodian in attendance, Prince Joseph personally undertook the task of washing and dressing the body of Antipater. Household slaves washed my father Bathyllus as no male member of his family had been in residence at Jericho. Princess Mariamne, young Mariam, and Lady Yohanna were allowed to observe the process from a distance. The humility shown by this fabulously wealthy Herodian prince using his own hands to wash the dead body of his nephew Antipater, a man to whom he was not particularly close in life and who died a condemned criminal, moved Princess Mariamne. There was no way for Mariamne to know it but Prince Joseph's son, the distinguished Joseph of Arimathea, attended to her son Yeshua at his burial thirty-nine years thereafter.

Antipater ben Herod, former coregent of the Jewish kingdom, was laid to rest in an unmarked stone tomb cut into the base of a cliff in the desert just outside the fortress city of Hyrcania. One accessed the tomb through a steeply sloped shaft of descending steps that led down into a chamber. Inside the chamber, loculi were hewn into each of the rough-cut walls. The entrance to the chamber was sealed with a stone slab. My father was buried nearby in a larger communal tomb stuffed full of bodies. A year or more later, when the flesh had completely fallen away, the bones of Antipater and my father were reburied in stone ossuaries as was the Jewish burial practice of the day. After spending the night in Hyrcania, the party set out on the return trip to Jericho shortly after first light. Mariamne, Mariam, and Yohanna traveled by private coach. Mariamne attempted to thaw the ice between she and her much younger cousin Mariam, who was later to be known as Mariam Magdalene.

Princess Mariamne asked, "Have you given thought to who your next husband might be?"

Although then eleven years of age, it was Mariam's destiny to become a child bride for the second time.

Mariam replied, "Husband? Don't I get a year to grieve?"

"Only thirty days."

"I want to go to Rome to live with my brother Agrippa."

"Yes, every young girl wishes to live in Rome. I highly doubt that will be allowed. Your uncles are surely back in Jericho this instant angling to secure your hand. Archelaus is coregent and heir. He'll win the prize and be your next husband."

"Archelaus, the pimply one?" A look of disgust crossed her face. Mariamne disliked pointing out the realities of the situation to the girl but someone had to enlighten her. Being a princess meant your use as a chess piece in some man's quest for power. It was rare for a royal woman to also find love with her powerful husband.

Mariam said, "What about you? Who will be your next husband?"

"Frankly, I'm shocked Herod didn't execute me along with Prince Antipater. Honestly cousin, my prospects for survival are not good."

The coach came to a halt giving the soldiers a chance to water the horses. Mariam continued, "You're being paranoid." Prince Joseph approached the coach as the ladies spoke. Mariam pointed to Prince Joseph and said, "What about him for a husband?"

The ladies let out a tremendous laugh at the comment shocking Prince Joseph. These were royal women of the priestly tribe of Levi on their first full day of mourning after the death of their husbands. Under Jewish law, it was practically blasphemous for them to laugh. But Prince Joseph was not much for Jewish law.

He said, "Princess Mariamne, might I have a word with you in private?"

Mariam whispered to Mariamne as she left the coach, "Hah, I was right, he will be your next husband."

Mariamne exited the coach. Prince Joseph gestured to a large rock off on the side of the road. He sat down and waited for Mariamne to join him. He said, "Please forgive me for broaching this subject during your period of mourning in such a rustic setting without a male representative of your family present but I much prefer you hear it from my lips first."

Mariamne now knew her young cousin had hit the nail on the head. She asked, "What is it Prince Joseph?"

"The king commands that we be wed."

Mariamne shot back, "How do you feel about that?"

The woman's directness threw him on the defensive. "I'd be happy to serve as your husband, princess. I believe the king shall file the betrothal papers with the Temple authorities the moment your mourning period is over."

Mariamne figured now was as good of time as any to drop a massive rock on Joseph's chest. "I'm pleased with your willingness prince but I think you lack knowledge of complicating factors."

"If you speak of the fact that my father was killed by your father, don't let it trouble you. I'm past that even if my uncle the king is not. It's ancient history. Herod has since killed your father, mother, and husband. What does it profit me to hold these family squabbles against you?"

Joseph's open-mindedness impressed Mariamne but she was about to lay something much heavier on him. "You're a kind man prince but the matter I'm referring to is of more gravity. I'm pregnant with Antipater's child."

"Holy shit" was all Joseph could think. The news literally knocked him off the rock he sat upon. He got up off the ground to walk around trying to catch his breath while his brain wrestled with the enormity of the problem. Antipater's child by Mariamne would be more dangerous than a nest of cobras. Herod and Archelaus would do all in their power to kill that child and most certainly destroy anybody who got in their way. Mariamne was a beautiful woman of the purest Jewish royal blood but it was like drawing a viper to one's breast, exhilarating but deadly. Pacing complete, he returned to sit next to Mariamne.

He said, "Look, here's what we'll do. I'll marry you as the king insists but his health is failing. I'll divorce you quietly a few months later when he is dead and we'll sneak you out of the country. The safest place for you would be Babylon."

Mariamne nodded her agreement with the plan and returned to the coach. She turned to Mariam, "You were right."

The young princess broke out in a big grin satisfied with her foreknowledge. Princess Mariamne stewed over the problem all the way back to Jericho. Her situation was bleak. If she remained unmarried, her pregnancy would eventually show. With no man around and the probable conception date pegged by the doctors to before Antipater's death, it wouldn't take a genius to determine that Antipater was the father. But if she quickly married Joseph, they just might be able to conceal the true paternity by claiming Joseph was the father. But that gamble, if lost, likely would cost Prince Joseph his life. She had no right asking Prince Joseph, father of many children by his wife Olympias, to take such a risk. Joseph would be risking their futures as well as his. Even his proposed course of action, a quick divorce followed by an attempt to smuggle her out of the country, was likewise risky. Serious repercussions would follow if his complicity in the deed was discovered. The more Mariamne thought about it, she fully expected Joseph to turn her in to Herod once they arrived back at the palace. It was the only logical play for him to make. Why would Prince Joseph risk all to save her and a child not of his loins?

For his part, Prince Joseph was shaken by their first private conversation. He'd thought it was a stroke of good fortune when Minister Nicolas approached him relaying King Herod's wish that he wed Mariamne. Joseph always played second spear to his older cousin Phasael in the army of Herod's nephews. Phasael was married to the Princess Salampsio, Herod's oldest Hasmonean daughter. Princess Mariamne's bloodline far outranked Salampsio in Jewish eyes. The marriage would have greatly enhanced Joseph's standing at court and, if he got her with child, possibly vault his children over those of Phasael in the Herodian pecking order. But thoughts of a grand family coup vanished in an instant. Herod undoubtedly would order any baby of Mariamne executed the moment it emerged from the birth canal, if the mother lived that long.

During the long ride back to Jerusalem, Joseph tossed the delicate situation around in his head. Mariamne was a pleasant person and he wished her no ill will but how much risk could he hazard attempting a quiet end to the relationship? Should he rat out Mariamne to Herod? How far along was her pregnancy? Joseph ben Joseph was the shrewdest businessman in the family of Herod, a trader of metals throughout the Roman Empire and importer of raw materials used in Herod's many building projects. Joseph cautiously weighed each decision first gathering as much information as reasonably possible before pulling the trigger on major transactions. He gambled on occasion but his business bets were always calculated moves. He needed more information before making a decision on Mariamne. If her pregnancy was in the early stages, time existed before others became wise to the situation. With any luck, Herod would die soon, problem solved (or so he thought).

Upon arrival back at Herod's palace in Jerusalem, a messenger alerted Prince Joseph to the presence in Jericho of a high level Babylonian delegation escorted by 100 Parthian cavalry. The delegation included a Jewish prince from the House of David who lived in exile in Babylon, a Parthian ambassador and Zoroastrian priest of an order known as the magi. The Parthians backed King Antigonus in the Hasmonean civil war but were expelled from Judea by Herod in the year Marcus Agrippa and Caninius Gallus were consuls of Rome.[43] The Parthian interest in Princess Mariamne went beyond the fact that she was the daughter

[43] 37 BCE.

of a Hasmonean ally. Her mother, a concubine of Antigonus, was a relative of the Parthian king; therefore, Mariamne bat Antigonus was both of Jewish and Parthian royal blood. As such, the political value of her bloodline to the Parthians was beyond measure. Word of Princess Mariamne bat Antigonus's survival reached Babylon two months prior to the death of Antipater. For the Jewish Babylonian exile community, Princess Mariamne was a phoenix rising out of the Hasmonean ashes. She bore the only living blood of the last true Jewish king and high priest. For the Parthians, her royal bloodline presented an opportunity to resurrect a friendly dynasty in Palestine as a bulwark against Roman influence in the region. The Parthian delegation set out with all speed to pay their respects to the venerated princess and check upon her health and safety.

Rumors buzzed around the palace that an elite Parthian cohort of light infantry camped just across the border in Nabatea, apparently with the blessing of King Aretas. Were the Parthians and Nabateans preparing a joint invasion at Herod's death? No one in Judea knew their intentions. Herod required ever increasing levels of opium to dull the pain. After ordering Antipater's execution, Herod ingested a particularly heavy dose of the drug thereafter slipping in and out of consciousness. His family and close advisors could see the final hours of King Herod ben Antipater were at hand.

Handled wrongly, this diplomatic crisis could easily have escalated into war. With Herod on the verge of death and Crown Prince Archelaus too green to manage the crisis, Minister Nicolas stepped into the leadership void making a command decision—Princess Mariamne would meet the visitors but with the following conditions: 1) only the Zoroastrian priests and Jewish nobles in the delegation were to receive an audience, 2) the audience was to be limited to two hours, and 3) the princess would be accompanied by Prince Joseph (her betrothed). Nicolas sent word in Herod's name that the king was outraged by such a large armed contingent arriving at his palace without first seeking an invitation. Further, all Parthian troops were ordered to remain camped outside the city walls. Jewish archers took up positions on the parapets of Jericho's walls within range of the Parthian camp.

The arrival of the Parthians sent young Crown Prince Archelaus into a dither. He paced Herod's private chambers praying his father would awaken and take command of the situation. Why had the Roman official in Damascus given permission for the Parthians to proceed onto Jewish soil? The incompetents should have turned them around back to the east sending the wretches in the directions from whence they came. Archelaus thought, "Uncle Pheroras, you whore! See what trouble your little prize of war costs us? I hope you're rotting in Sheol[44] this very moment." As Archelaus fretted, puss oozed from Herod's loins while he lay unconscious. The king's body had begun the process of decomposition while he still lived.

Prince Joseph was an experienced diplomatic hand having traveled widely on business trips. He'd encountered magi in Babylon so their eastern dress and customers were nothing new to him. Princess Mariamne, on the other hand, led a sheltered existence. The cloistered chapter in her life closed upon her arrest by Herod. This audience marked the beginning of her appearance on the international stage as a princess of stature. Prince Joseph escorted Mariamne into the queen's audience chamber within the Jericho palace, one originally built by the Hasmoneans. Joseph wondered whether Minister Nicolas made the arrangements without consulting the king. For Herod's nephew found it hard to believe the king authorized Mariamne to sit on the queen's throne once occupied by her cousin, Mariamne bat Alexander (the deceased wife of Herod). There wasn't time to check for confirmation as the guests were announced. Prince Josiah, eldest son of the Jewish Exilarch of Babylon, led the Parthian delegation followed by Jewish priests from Babylon, and finally Gaspar, head of the magi in Babylon. All bowed to Princess Mariamne with Joseph seated at her side on the dais.

---

[44] Not all Jews of this period believed in an afterlife and those that did were not uniform in their beliefs on this topic. Sheol was the Jewish underworld where the dead rested, both righteous and wicked. The righteous awaited the resurrection. The wicked existed in eternal torment.

Prince Josiah addressed Mariamne as a queen although she wore no crown. He said, "Your highness, praise be to Yahweh that the daughter of King Mattathias Antigonus lives. If it pleases your highness, Magi Gaspar shall give a traditional blessing of his people."

Mariamne sat regally, unfazed by the strange customs and surroundings. The role of queen resided in her blood. She replied, "I would be most honored to receive the blessing of Magi Gaspar. Please come forward."

Magi Gaspar was born in Jerusalem two years prior to Mariamne. His father, also a magi, served as Zoroastrian liaison to the Jewish high priest prior to the fall of the Hasmonean dynasty. Gaspar escaped Jerusalem with his father shortly before the city fell to the Romans. Because of this connection, his Zoroastrian superiors in the east selected Gaspar for this mission to Judea. Magi Gaspar said, "May we be one with all the righteous, may we be one with all the virtuous. May we be one with the creator Ahura Mazda, the shining Ahura Mazda, the majestic Ahura Mazda. May we be united with all the righteous, with all the virtuous, with all the goodness in the world, with those of bountiful good deeds, with those of fewer sins."[45]

Mariamne responded, "Amen."

All bowed in a moment of silence. Magi Gaspar then gestured for servants to bring in the gifts expected from a visiting foreign delegation to host dignitaries.

Gaspar, "Princess Mariamne, daughter of King Antigonus, the Parthian ambassador was refused permission by King Herod to join our party for this reception. He requests I present these gifts to you in the name of Phraates son of Orodes[46], king of kings, ruler of the east, victor over Marcus Antonius." Gaspar failed to add reference to the blood relation between Phraates and Mariamne as this information was unknown to the Herodians. The Parthians

---

[45] See Afrin of the Six Gahambars, http://www.avesta.org/afrin/afrins.htm.

[46] Phraates IV (ruled from 37–2 BCE) was the Parthian version of Herod the Great. Not only were they contemporaries with long reigns but Phraates murdered his father and brothers seeking to consolidate his grip on the throne.

thought it wise to conceal her relationship to the Parthian royal family.

Servants manhandled a chest chocked full of precious metals, stones, rare spices, and perfumes placing them at the feet of the princess. Mariamne had never before seen with her own eyes such wealth but, wearing the mask of royalty, she exhibited no more than a smile at its presentation. "Please tell his highness, king Phraates, of my gratitude for his fabulous gifts. Unfortunately, as we were not forewarned of your visit and have been engaged in mourning for the death of my husband, Prince Antipater, I'm afraid we have not prepared gifts for the king. Perhaps, in time, we shall find a way to repay his generosity."

Gaspar, "That will not be necessary you highness. The king only wishes your friendship and that of your household."

Prince Josiah, "We all wish to express our condolences on the death of Prince Antipater. It was a cause for great concern among us when we learned of his execution." Josiah gave a look to Joseph, nephew of Herod, not knowing if he was addressing friend or foe.

Mariamne said, "King Herod selected Prince Joseph to be my husband at the conclusion of the mourning period. You may speak to him as you speak to me." Mariamne's vote of confidence before the foreign dignitaries surprised Joseph. Did she truly trust him? Or was this an act of desperation on her part? He had no way of knowing.

Prince Josiah replied, "As you wish your highness. We are concerned for your safety in light of the execution of your husband."

He then turned looking directly into the eyes of Prince Joseph, "Do you recognize that the princess is in danger?"

Joseph said to the visitors, "Of course I do. Her bloodline is a danger to the Herodian dynasty. The question is what can be done about the situation? I see no solution."

Gaspar, "We wish to take the princess with us back to Babylon. She may join the princes of the House of David in exile."

Joseph liked this option. It certainly solved all his problems but would Herod authorize it? Unlikely but it could not hurt to ask. Joseph turned to Mariamne and whispered out of the hearing of the Parthian delegation, "Do you wish to go with these noblemen to Babylon?"

Mariamne also spoke in a whisper, "I wish what is best for my baby. If you cannot protect me here in Judea then I agree to go to Babylon."

Joseph, "I can guaranty nothing princess. As you know, I'm but a private citizen with little influence over the king. He does as he pleases."

Mariamne, "Then ask the king for permission for me to go into exile in Babylon."

Joseph excused himself from the meeting and left the room heading for the king's chambers but was intercepted by Minister Nicolas.

Nicolas, "Where are you going prince?"

Joseph, "To see the king."

"Impossible. His physicians drugged him and he'll be out for hours. In truth, no one knows whether he will ever regain consciousness. What is the problem?"

Joseph was perplexed by the state of affairs. With Herod unconscious, who held power to make a decision in the Jewish kingdom? He said to Nicolas, "Prince Josiah and the Parthians wish to take Princess Mariamne with them to Babylon where she shall remain in exile. I personally agree with the proposal. It removes her bloodline from Judea."

Nicolas replied, "The king will never agree. If he regains his faculties and finds out we let the princess leave the country, you and I are dead men. I mean that Prince Joseph. He will execute us."

Joseph replied, "The Babylonians have troops outside the city gates and are rather insistent. This answer might not go down well with them."

Nicolas, "Don't concern yourself with the Parthian cavalry. One thousand of the king's troops are on the march from Fortress Hyrcania and shall arrive by sundown today but we don't want a confrontation. Tell them you personally guaranty the safety of the princess."

"Me? I don't want anything to do with the Princess. I'm not a politician Nicolas. I build things and make money."

"And who do you think shall award the construction contracts for the next king?"

"Nicolas, you wouldn't."

"Taking the royal building contracts away from you would wound me as I am fond of your wife Princess Olympias; however, politics is a nasty business. I haven't lasted this long in Herod's court without possessing the stomach for doing that which is necessary. Don't test me."

There was no point arguing with Minister Nicolas as his position was well taken. Herod or his successor would punish (even execute) whoever allowed Princess Mariamne to leave Judea. Joseph returned to the audience room where Mariamne and the Parthian delegation waited.

Joseph said, "I am sorry to inform you that the king has denied permission for Princess Mariamne to leave with your party for exile in Babylon. However, I pledge myself as guardian of her safety until the time is right for her to quietly leave the country. I promise to do all in my power to make this happen."

The blunt statement from Joseph pleasantly surprised the visitors. They did not expect a pledge of support from Herod's nephew. Still, they were wary of the Herodian.

Prince Josiah, "We appreciate your pledge of protection Prince Joseph and offer to assist the princess in leaving the country. Is there anything we can do to help?"

Joseph, "There are extenuating circumstances in this matter but I don't think you can help with that issue. I'll cope the best I can and send the princess east when the opportunity presents itself."

Magi Gaspar now addressed Mariamne, "I understand the complication your highness. Your pregnancy is known to me."

The statement from the magi floored Mariamne. She could not comprehend how he attained such knowledge. Did he read minds? "How is that possible? But three people on this earth know of my condition and they have not spoken to you."

Magi Gaspar, "One with sight of the third eye sees. Do not be alarmed."

Joseph was alarmed, very alarmed. Something spooky and magical surrounded this foreign priest. With the Parthians privy to news of the pregnancy, the grand secret had become an international cause célèbre. How long before Herod and Archelaus got wind of Mariamne's child? The walls were closing in on Prince Joseph. He needed to make a decision on what to do with Mariamne much sooner than he imagined.

Babylonian Prince Josiah wasn't sure what to make of Herod's nephew. Mariamne trusted Joseph but what prevented him from reporting every word back to Herod? However, Josiah really had no choice. If they attacked Jericho, Herod would never allow the princess to be captured alive. To save Mariamne, the Parthians needed help from inside the palace. Josiah decided to reach out to Joseph. "If you can get the princess to the gates of the city in the next few days, we will safely conduct her out of Israel. We have a century of cavalry camped outside the city walls backed by a Parthian cohort across the border in Nabatea."

Then addressing Mariamne he said, "Your highness, is this acceptable to you? We offer you sanctuary in Babylon."

Mariamne, "I am under the protection of my fiancé, Prince Joseph. If he grants his permission, then I shall go."

Joseph mulled it over. If she escaped, he could feign no knowledge of the deed. This could solve all his problems. But what if she got caught during an escape attempt from Jericho? Herod would then torture the slaves and Joseph would inevitably be implicated. He'd end up dead like Mariamne's first husband. No, it was too risky of a move at this point, too much attention.

Joseph, "Look, now is not the right time. The Jewish military went on alert the moment your troops appeared in Damascus. Herodian infantry is on the way. I'm sure scouts are watching the Parthian camp night and day. The risk is just too great. When she is my wife, I'll be able to move the princess out of Jerusalem under my own authority. I'm based in Caesarea. From there, it's a much easier proposition smuggling the princess out of the country. I suggest waiting until after Herod's death but before a new king is appointed by Rome. All the claimants to the Jewish throne will depart for Rome after Herod's death and burial. I think this would be a better time to act."

Gaspar said, "If you are based in Caesarea then the simplest plan would be to smuggle princess by ship to Egypt. We have agents in Egypt."

Prince Joseph replied, "Yes, Egypt would be a much easier destination for the handoff when the time comes."

The Parthian delegation conferred amongst themselves briefly. Although hoping to bring the princess out of the country with them in the next few days, the wisdom of Joseph's words left little room for argument. They agreed to wait for the most opportune time. Nothing more was to be done than pray to God that Herod died soon and hope Joseph remained true to his word; however, every Babylonian was born a horse-trader so the negotiations continued.

Prince Josiah, "We accept what you say Prince Joseph but have one counter-demand, break off your engagement to Mariamne and allow her to marry a Hasmonean priest."

This latest twist in the day's proceedings left Joseph with a throbbing headache and dazed. He gathered himself to think through the implications of the Babylonian demand. Herod would never agree to that but would Herod even be alive a week from now? The betrothal contract between himself and Princess Mariamne could not be filed at the Temple in Jerusalem until after the thirty-day mourning period for Antipater ended. Herod was unlikely to last that long. At Herod's death, the Jewish kingdom would go into upheaval over succession. Joseph just might be able to pass off the princess to Parthian agents during the chaos sure to erupt soon after the king's death. But what were the emissaries from Babylon offering? Joseph never gave up something of value without a quid pro quo. What to ask for? Money? Nice but he possessed plenty and, in this case, something more valuable was attainable.

Joseph replied, "I am amenable to your request Prince Josiah; however, I too have a request. The first born daughter from the union of Mariamne and the chosen Hasmonean priest shall be pledge in marriage to one of my sons."

Although Jewish men routinely negotiated such family matters without the input of the female being bartered (including her offspring), Princess Mariamne was not an ordinary Jewish woman. Joseph turned to check her reaction to the proposal.

Mariamne said, "It is my preference to be married to a priest of my family. I thank you Prince Joseph for agreeing to this arrangement and pledge my first-born daughter to your son."

Prince Josiah added, "We accept your terms Prince Joseph ben Joseph."

Business concluded, slaves entered the room with refreshments and the discussion turned to pleasantries. Many toasts followed but, eventually, the Parthian delegation left the palace and not a moment too soon for Joseph. He wasn't sure what, if any, value attached to the promise of Mariamne's first-born daughter as he began to doubt either of them would to live to see the New Year. Their survival, in large measure, was tied to Herod dying before the grand secret of Mariamne's baby leaked out. Unbeknownst to Prince Joseph and Mariamne, a Modiin spy lurked hidden in the curtains of the queen's throne room during her entire audience with the Babylonian delegation. Herod's men now possessed the secret of her pregnancy.

The next morning the king shook off the effects of the narcotics administered by his physicians. After receiving reports from his ministers (including news of the pregnancy), Herod summoned his nephew Joseph to his private chambers as the king was too ill to move. Herod said, "Nephew, come sit beside me and tell me the news."

Joseph had never before been alone with Herod and certainly never been greeted with such informality. Tenderness was not one of Herod's virtues. Joseph said, "It is as you feared sire. The Parthians treat Antigonus' daughter as a queen, the vessel of her father's bloodline. They lavished gifts upon her making clear they stand ready to assist her in any way possible."

Herod previously received a report from his spymaster giving all the details of the meeting with the Parthian dignitaries so he already knew what transpired. The purpose of this discussion with his nephew was to determine whether or not he could trust Joseph going forward. Herod merely replied, "Interesting."

Prince Joseph continued, "And I think it is conceivable they'll attempt to smuggle the princess out of the palace taking her with them to the east."

"How do you think they will attempt it nephew?"

"It's hard to say your highness. I suspect they shall bide their time and spring their plan during the general mourning period at your death. The country shall surely be paralyzed in grief."

"Yes, I've taken steps to ensure the country grieves regardless of how they feel about me."

Herod imprisoned thousands of the leading men of Judea in the hippodrome at Jericho (as the jails of his palace were of insufficient size) with orders to execute these men when he died. Princess Salome pledged to carry out his orders.

Herod, "Now tell me nephew, what are your plans for your new bride? Children?"

"With all that transpired yesterday, I haven't really had the opportunity to contemplate a future with my new wife. My only thought is how to avoid upsetting Olympias." Olympias was Joseph's first wife and daughter of Herod.

Herod, "Any other information you wish to share with me nephew?"

"No your highness."

There was Herod's answer, Prince Joseph could not be trusted. He failed to inform the king about Mariamne's pregnancy.

"Oh, one more thing Joseph. I'm moving Princess Mariamne to Herodium. I don't want to see her at court. She' s creating too big of a stir."

"Herodium?"

"You have a problem with that?"

"No sire. I just assumed that, as she is to be my wife, I could take her to live with me in Caesarea."

"I thought you wanted peace at home with Olympias? Mariamne will be neither seen nor heard from once installed at Herodium."

"Yes sire."

Joseph bowed and left the king's chambers. Herod planned to keep Mariamne under indefinite house arrest in Herodium, his summer palace. At that instant, Joseph forgot any notion of helping her escape the country. Herodium was more a military fortress than a palace. Planning and executing an escape from there was not an undertaking that Joseph was prepared for. Risk taking was not in his nature.

During the king's final days, Herod changed his will one last time. Archelaus was given the lion's share of the kingdom to rule (the territories of Judea, Samaria, and Idumea) and title of "king". Antipas was made second heir bequeathed Galilee and Perea. And Philip was bequeathed Gaulonitis, Trachonitis, and Paneas (to the north of Galilee). The king called these three sons to his bedside as he lay dying. The king's sister Princess Salome was also present.

Herod said with difficulty, "I've divided my kingdom between the three of you to rule. You must work together to preserve the kingdom. There are threats, foreign and domestic, capable of toppling all of you if not on guard. Roman politics is tedious but not too difficult to master. A bribe always works with the Romans. Shower them with gifts and you'll not have trouble. If another Roman civil war comes, send tribute to both sides regardless of which you publicly align yourself with. Governing the Jews is a much more contentious matter. Stand firm with the Temple priesthood and Pharisees of the Sanhedrin class. Only united may the Jews successfully revolt. Play the religious parties against one another. Do not allow them hope for it is a dangerous emotion."

Speaking these few brief words left Herod exhausted. His sons assumed the king had fallen asleep and started to move away from the bed when the king raised his head and motioned for his sons to return.

Herod, "I have more to say. The seed of Antigonus must die. Pure Hasmonean blood is a rallying point uniting the Jews. You must kill Mariamne once Caesar confirms the three of you on your thrones. Do not move against her before then."

Archelaus, "Why should we wait father?"

"The Romans believe only they possess the authority to order the death of royal persons in their subject kingdoms. Second, the Jews would cause a terrible riot in the country if they learned you killed the daughter of Antigonus. Take no controversial action until after Caesar has ruled on my last will and testament. There is one last matter for us to discuss."

Herod's lips became dry and parched. The words were sticking in his throat as he tried to speak. The king's hands trembled uncontrollably as he tried to drink from the water cup by his bed. Archelaus took the cup and gave his father a small drink but Herod collapsed never to regain consciousness. Whatever last message Herod had for his sons died with the king.

Chapter 10

Jericho, Judea (4 BCE)

Herod died in late November five days after he executed Antipater.[47] At that moment, the most senior surviving member of the Herodian dynasty was Princess Salome, the last surviving offspring of Antipater the Idumean. As such, Herod entrusted her with safeguarding his last will. The "witch of Judea" unexpectedly ordered the Jewish prisoners freed from the Jericho hippodrome in violation of the dead king's orders that they be executed. Salome reneged upon a promise made to her dying brother because she hoped to gain favor with the Jewish religious parties to support her quest for increased power in the wake of Herod's death. Next, she assembled the Jewish military on the parade ground at Jericho and announced the king's death to the military. Salome publicly read Herod's will to the soldiers naming Archelaus heir to his throne. In response, the Jewish military hailed Archelaus as king. Then, each unit led by its officers appeared before Archelaus and swore allegiance to the new king. Little consequence attached to this show as only one man on earth possessed the legal authority to name a Jewish king, Augustus Caesar (or so the Romans maintained).

Herodium, Judea (3 BCE)

Archelaus, in his first official act, directed the burial of his father at Herodium. Slaves carried Herod's body on a golden bier,

---

[47] *See* <u>Antiquities</u> XVII 8:1 (191) for the five days reference.

embroidered with precious gems and covered with purple cloth. Archelaus commanded a diadem and gold crown be placed upon his father's head. The deceased's right hand held a scepter. Archelaus marched first in the funeral train followed by Herod's other sons and, behind them, his numerous relations. Next came Herod's elite palace guard followed by the Herodian mercenary army ordered by nationality—Thracians, Germans, and Galatians (in that order). Archelaus took care to make the funeral as ornate and regal as possible.

Princess Mariamne and her household (including Lady Yohanna) began their house arrest at Herodium shortly before the king's burial. The Herodian objective was to keep the princess out of the public eye and, hopefully, out of Jewish collective consciousness. I was born to Lady Yohanna in the royal palace at Herodium three months prior to the birth of Yeshua. Shortly thereafter, Princess Mariamne's belly blossomed and the palace staff at Herodium took notice. One can rightly proclaim Yeshua's birth was a miracle for the ages in light of the powerful forces bent on preventing his conception and, thereafter, destroying him at birth.

Magi Gaspar remained nearby in Petra, the capital of Nabatea, monitoring the situation. The Parthians made repeated inquiries with Prince Joseph through agents in Judea regarding the particulars for smuggling Mariamne out of the country, a venture Joseph previously promised to assist with. But Prince Joseph did little more than promise the Parthians he would contemplate the problem when the dust settled in the wake of Herod's death. Joseph procrastinated while praying that Princess Mariamne and her child vanished into the ether. Mariamne was on her own as far as Prince Joseph was concerned.

Jerusalem, Judea (3 BCE)

Winter

Ships did not travel the Aegean in the dead of winter so there was nothing for Archelaus to do after burying his father until the dawn of spring. The new king-designate settled into his kingdom attempting to make nice with the Jews. Archelaus first appeared publicly at the Temple in Jerusalem shortly after conclusion of the official mourning period for King Herod. The Jewish leaders heaped praise upon young Archelaus hoping to garner favor with him. Although not formally appointed by Rome, Archelaus took over administration of the kingdom at this time including dispensing justice from the king's throne. Initially, he granted requests of the people for release of prisoners and abatement of their taxes. He even sacked the serving high priest appointed by Herod and named, instead, one more agreeable to the Temple priesthood and rabbis. But the amicable relations between Archelaus and the Jewish people were no more than a honeymoon phase. The demands of the Jewish leaders became ever bolder and more forceful.

Jerusalem, Judea (3 BCE)

Beginning of Spring

A meeting of three preeminent former high priests and their sons convened at the home of Heli, now an old Hasmonean Temple priest who had been high priest for one day.[48] He was the adoptive father of Princess Mariamne bat Antigonus. Matthias ben Theophilus, brother of Heli and himself a former high priest, was also present. Matthias was the adopted father of Elizabeth, cousin of Mariamne and mother of Yochanan.[49] Eleazar ben Boethus was the third high priest in attendance. He was the brother-in-law of Matthias ben Theophilus and brother of Simon ben Boethus (the long serving high priest under Herod who also had been Herod's father-in-law). This family wing of the Temple priesthood had been shut out of office when Herod Archelaus stripped Eleazar ben Boethus of the high priesthood giving it to Joshua ben Sie of a competing family. The allied former high priests met to strategize their return to power. The bloodline of Princess Mariamne constituted an important political tool that the brothers intended to

---

[48] High priest Matthias ben Theophilus claimed to be ritually unclean for the Day of Atonement. Thus, a close male relative named Joseph Ellemus stepped in as high priest for just one day. <u>Antiquities</u> XVII 6:4 (166-67).

[49] Yochanan was later to become a popular rabbi known as "Yochanan the Baptizer".

keep within the Theophilus family. They discussed Mariamne's marriage contract with Herodian prince Joseph and concluded it was illegal and, thus, void ab initio (i.e., from its inception). Under their interpretation of Jewish law, the marriage of Mariamne to Prince Joseph never happened. Herod was not a leading male of Mariamne's family; therefore, he had no legal authority to give the princess away in marriage. As her adoptive father, that right fell to Heli. The group decided Heli would draw up a new marriage contract for Princess Mariamne and file it at the Temple on his own authority as a former high priest. The three high priests agreed to jointly confront the chief custodian of Temple records and demand he destroy the marriage contract between Mariamne and Prince Joseph filed by Herod. Any priest even marginally learned in the law would understand immediately that this contract was illegal and, therefore, should never have been accepted for filing. They saw it as an open and shut case.

Now the three chief priests tackled the trickier problem of keeping Mariamne's bloodline within the Theophilus family, who would marry the princess? This was problematic as she was not a virgin, meaning whoever married her disqualified himself from the high priesthood. More importantly, she was then pregnant with another man's child. As fate would have it, the nephew of Lady Anna (also named Joseph) was a Kohen priest and had no interest in the high priesthood. The wife of this now middle aged priest had died and he wished to retire to the desert under a Nazarite vow completely retreating from Jewish society by dedicating himself to God. Priest Joseph's father died years ago during the civil war with Herod leaving the nephew of Lady Anna to be raised in the House of Heli. As such, Heli was his surrogate father and Priest Joseph still addressed him as Abba. The three high priests conferred privately amongst themselves at the head table as their sons and lesser male relatives reclined about the rest of the room waiting for the great men to address them. Heli called his nephew Joseph up to the head table.

Heli said, "I and my fellow high priests have chosen you for a great honor Joseph. You are to take Mariamne bat Antigonus as your wife."

This was the last thing Priest Joseph desired. He was then forty-four years of age and committed to a celibate life of prayer. Joseph tried to avoid accepting his surrogate father's request. He said, "I am not worthy of such a grand honor father. I respectfully decline."

Heli would not be denied. He replied, "This is not a request son. It is a family obligation. You are required to render this service to your family and the priesthood."

"But esteemed high priests, she is not a virgin. As a Kohen priest I cannot marry her."

Matthias ben Theophilus replied, "She is a widow who can legally marry. Of course, this now makes you ineligible for the high priesthood. However, it is my understanding that you have no desire to continue as a Temple priest and plan to retire to the desert under a Nazarite vow."

Joseph, "These are my plans. As you know, the vow requires one to separate oneself from society."

Heli said, "Sorry my son. Your Nazarite vow must wait until later in life. Right now, you have a royal wife to care for."

Joseph, "But she is under arrest in Herodium. How would I go about taking possession of this wife to consummate the marriage?" Priest Joseph presented a valid question for which his father had no answer.

Heli replied, "Let us worry about that problem."

Joseph the Nazarite was dismissed with a wave of Heli's hand. Joseph's concerns were meaningless to the three high priests. Family honor and wealth were all that mattered. Later that evening, Heli's household servants came to Priest Joseph to share gossip regarding his new betrothed—she was pregnant nearing full term. The putative father was Antipater ben Herod. It was one thing for his father to order him to marry a woman previously married. It was quite another to expect him to marry a woman pregnant with another man's baby. And it was beyond unacceptable for a Nazarite monk to be expected to raise a grandson of Herod! Heli had gone too far this time.

Jerusalem, Judea (3 BCE)

Passover

A festive air hung over Jerusalem on the eve of the first Passover after the death of Herod. Although anxious to be off for Rome and secure the Jewish throne from Augustus Caesar, Archelaus relented to the harping of Minister Nicolas to stay in Judea through this important religious holiday and traditional time when Jews revolted against their overlords. So far Archelaus enjoyed amicable relations with the Jewish people; however, Passover stood as his first real test in administering the Jewish kingdom. The bon ami between Archelaus and the Jewish people soon evaporated.

Zealot rabbis from Galilee gathered the people at the Temple near the end of Passover for a public mourning honoring Judas and Matthias, the rabbis burnt alive by Herod for tearing down the golden eagle from the Temple gate. King Herod forbade public displays for these two rabbis at the time of their execution. The Jewish people expressed not only their admiration for these upright men but, also, publicly denounced King Herod. As the assemblage progressed, grumblings were heard against Archelaus as well for not having gone far enough in righting this wrong of his father. Officers of the Herodian army observed the increasingly strident demonstrations inside the Temple outer courtyard from the walls of Fortress Antonia. They were not pleased. Herod's palace guard wore the Herodian crest on their chest and shields. Insults hurled at Herod expressly insulted them as well. Lucius Volumnius, the commanding general of the Herodian military, decided enough was enough. He marched into the palace demanding an audience with Archelaus who was hurriedly wrapping up business intending to depart Jerusalem for Rome in the morning. The ministers tried to keep the general waiting in the anteroom but were unable to do so.

The name Volumnius fit the portly Roman patrician. He was the grandson of Publius Volumnius, a close friend of Marcus Brutus who stood at his side during both the assassination of Julius Caesar and Brutus' own suicide. The younger Volumnius had little hope of a political future at home with the Julian dynasty firmly in control of Rome and the Volumnii indelibly linked to the murder of Julius Caesar. However, he did marry well when selected as husband for the youngest daughter of Gaius Saturninus, the Roman Governor of Syria who immediately preceded Varus. Volumnius served under Saturninus as tribune during his governorship of Syria. When Herod approached Governor Saturninus for his help in securing Caesar's permission to execute his Hasmonean sons, the governor used it as an opportunity to offload his dependent son-in-law upon the Jewish kingdom. Part of the consideration promised Saturinus by Herod, along with mountains of silver and gold, was employment of Volumnius as general of the Jewish army. This allowed General Volumnius to permanently suckle at Herod's tit, so long as the king lived. Herod was now dead; however, Volumnius had the foresight to befriend Archelaus during his teenage years. The general intended to cash in on the influence he built up with Archelaus over the years.

Volumnius made his way through the palace corridors to the king's private office (now occupied by Archelaus). The guards at the door were under the command of Volumnius and, thus, made no move to bar his entrance. Archelaus busily studied several proclamations Minister Nicolas requested he sign before quitting the city. Volumnius loudly marched toward his desk abruptly coming to attention before the new king. The commotion disrupted Archelaus from the business at hand.

The king-designate said, "Ah, General Volumnius. So good of you to wish me well before my departure for Rome but I expected you would ride with us to Caesarea in the morning and see me off at the dock."

"Sire, this is not a social call."

Nicolas interjected himself into the discussion, "General Volumnius is agitated by speeches the Jews are making over at the Temple. I recommend we ignore the Jews for the time being and focus on our trip to Rome and audience with the Emperor."

Archelaus hoped Volumnius would heed the advice of Nicolas. The king-designate inquired, "General?"

The general would have none of it, "More than words have been hurled at my men minister. I sent a captain with 100 men to stand as a show of force at the main entrance to the Temple hoping it would bring about some restraint on the part of the Jews. They stoned my men, bloodied them. Now, your Excellency shall be away from Jerusalem for many months. And, in your absence my men and I must keep order in the country. The Jews are like children sire. When they misbehave, the parents are compelled to put the child in his place or the mischief invariably escalates."

Nicolas, "These are NOT children general. A mob can turn into a very ugly creature. The king gains nothing by retaliating now. If he massacres his own subjects in the Temple, word of it will reach Caesar. The king's enemies will denounce him before Caesar, you can count on it!"

Volumnius found it insufferable that a Greek addressed a Roman patrician in such a manner before a subject king but he bit his tongue. The general had a special relationship with Archelaus that he counted on to carry the day in this palace turf battle. Minister Nicolas spent little time in the company of Archelaus in past years. Their association started in earnest when Archelaus became crown prince only a month prior to the death of Herod. General Volumnius, on the other hand, acted as the new king's personal military tutor. Archelaus rode at the general's side for two years as his student. The teacher-student bond was strong.

Archelaus, "General Volumnius, you do see how important it is for me to depart for Rome while still on good terms with the Jews?"

Volumnius, "Yes sire. But I also know that a king cannot forsake honor and dignity. The Jews are spitting on the grave of King Herod in broad daylight. They get bolder by the minute. And their vile words are not limited to your father. I heard your good name thrown into the mud as well. Remember last year when the rabbis pulled down your father's golden eagle from the Temple and smashed it to bits?"

"How could I forget? It is this incident which has the Jewish people in a lather today."

"I marched my men into the Temple and the mob broke and ran. Only a handful of rabbis stood their ground and they were easily arrested. Your father then burned two of them at the stake. You should follow your father's example sire."

"Minister Nicolas, what say you?"

"The golden eagle incident did not occur during a major festival sire. Today the Temple is jammed with people, many times more than the general confronted last year. Plus there are many thousands more Jews camped outside the city walls in tents waiting for Passover. This is a much more explosive situation."

Volumnius, "Sire, my men demand retribution. Their honor as well as that of your father has been shit upon. They won't stand for it. And they won't respect a king without backbone!" General Volumnius dug his heals into the ground drawing a line in the sand. Essentially, he called the new king a coward. Archelaus was just emerging from his teenage years and not fully prepared to confront powerful men such as Volumnius. Two choices faced the new king, fire his top general or unleash the military on the crowd. He capitulated to the general hoping against hope no one on either side would be killed.

Archelaus said, "Then do what you must general but please restrain the passion of your men. Chastise the Jews but no more."

Nicolas wrung his hands in distress but the young king was beyond his control. As events played out that day, it quickly became apparent General Volumnius had no intention of avoiding violence. He formed up two squads of cavalry (mounted) in light armor near the main entrance to the Temple outer courtyard. Behind the cavalry stood two cohorts of Herodian legionnaires of the royal guard regaled in full armor with weapons at the ready. Minister Nicolas took to the parapets of Fortress Antonia to view the operation. He looked on in confusion at Volumnius parading before his cavalry formation. Why cavalry for crowd control? Why so many soldiers? Approximately 1200 Herodian foot soldiers formed up outside the Temple. Volumnius had come for blood, Jewish blood. With a nod from the general, the cavalry commander took the horsemen outside the city walls toward the tent camp where festivalgoers of lesser means stayed while on holiday in Jerusalem. The city lacked adequate housing for the crush of humanity that descended upon Jerusalem during festival time. The royal cavalry stood as a blocking force keeping those in the tent city from assisting their brethren soon to be under attack in the Temple. After the cavalry got into position and foot soldiers blocked all exits from the Temple, Volumnius nodded to the bugler who sounded, "attack". Two cohorts of legionnaires in heavy armor marched forward in unison, an integrated mass of armor. After realizing the gates were locked and they were trapped, the people drew swords and daggers from their cloaks. They were no match for fully armored legionnaires but the Jews did not perish without a fight. Volumnius exacted his bloody retribution. The royal army of Herod killed every living thing it encountered on the Temple grounds that day, blood flowing like a stream. Not every Jew demonstrating in the Temple that day died as the priests escaped into the inner courtyard before the doors were closed and others obtained deliverance via ladders. Nicolas couldn't even guess at the number killed in the Temple complex. He received a report later in the evening that the royal cavalry themselves killed 3000 outside the city walls. The soldiers inside the Temple complex killed well in excess of that number. It was a true massacre in every sense.[50]

Archelaus left Jerusalem the following morning. Women, faces ashened and dressed in black, wailed from every corner. The new king required 1000 Jewish soldiers arrayed as a screening force to extricate he and his family from his capital city. Archelaus traveled northwest to the port city of Caesarea in Samaria while hordes of Jews streamed the opposite direction toward Jerusalem. The people sensed now was their time for seeking vengeance, not just for Jews killed in the latest incident but for all the outrages perpetrated by the Herodian dynasty from its inception. Archelaus issued orders to his brother Philip, who was to be in charge of Jerusalem and entire the Jewish kingdom in Archelaus' absence, to keep Princess Mariamne bat Antigonus imprisoned at Herodium indefinitely.

Caesarea Maritima, Samaria (3 BCE)

---

[50] Antiquities XVII 9:3 (217-218).

Publius Quinctilius Varus, the governor of the Roman province of Syria who convicted Prince Antipater, traveled to Caesarea to see off young Archelaus on his voyage for Roman. News of the incipient revolt in Jerusalem greeted Varus when he made port. The old Roman general sought out the young monarch on the dock. Archelaus stood by his vessel stamping his feet like a school child. The men loaded all his family's personal baggage brought from the capital unto the flagship as fast as humanly possible but still the new king was not pleased. He wished to fly west before a Jewish storm broke over Palestine.

Varus said, "Your Excellency, I thought I sent word to you that I was coming to Caesarea?" The implication being that the wannabe-subject king should have been dutifully waiting in the Herodian palace at Caesarea for a civilized audience with the Roman governor before departing for Rome. How Varus hated breaking in new kings. This boy would either learn deference to his masters or his reign would be cut very short.

Archelaus replied, "And so you are here as promised. The tide shall turn soon Governor so we're in quite a rush to put out to sea. I hope you understand."

"Why don't you invite me aboard? We can then have a nice chat from your state room until you sail."

"By all means governor."

Varus turned to his chief aide before going aboard the Jewish royal flagship. Also on board was Archelaus' young bride, Princess Mariam bat Aristobulus (later known as Mariam Magdalene). Varus said to his aide, "Maximus find my best Greek scribe and send him to me on the flagship immediately. I want to dictate a status report for Augustus to be delivery by Archelaus."

"Is there time for that Governor? They are preparing to set sail as you can see."

"Have my barge lowered into the water and tell the pilot to take it out of the harbor well past the break water."

"Out into open sea?"

"Yes. I'll stay on the Jewish flagship until they clear the harbor then transfer to the barge."

"With all due respect sir, is that wise? With an outgoing tide the men shall be rowing against the current. They might not make it."

"They will after I tell them that their wives, children, and parents, shall be crucified unless they make the harbor inside an hour."

"Governor, Rome will be outraged when they hear you issued such an order. The pilot of the barge is a Roman citizen. It can't be legal to execute his family for such an offense."

"I know that Maximus but they don't. They'll row like dogs with Hannibal hot on their tail. Don't let it concern you, full tide won't be upon us until well after dark."

Varus successfully made port in his barge and remained in Caesarea after seeing off Archelaus in order to clean up the Jewish revolt touched off by the young Herodian. The governor gathered intelligence on the situation in Jerusalem while waiting on the arrival of another legion from elsewhere in his province before marching on Jerusalem. He was reading a report from the Jewish military commander in Jerusalem, Volumnius, when a knock came at the door. Varus said, "Enter."

His chief aide entered the governor's temporary office in the Herodian palace at Caesarea.

"Yes Maximus."

"Proconsul Gaius Calvisius Sabinus requests an audience."

"What, Sabinus is here in Palestine?"

"Yes governor."

"Keep him waiting out there for awhile, and then send him in. Tell Sabinus I must finish up a dispatch before seeing him."

Gaius Calvisius Sabinus (the younger) had been Roman consul the previous year, with his term only recently concluded.[51] Born of the equestrian rank, the Sabinii owed their political standing in Rome to the exploits of Gaius Calvisius Sabinus (the elder) a legate under Julius Caesar who was later made senator when Caesar became dictator. The elder Sabinus was one of only two senators who attempted to aid Caesar when Brutus, et alia

---

[51] 4 BCE.

assassinated Caesar in the Senate chamber. Also, Sabinus received a triumph in Rome for victories won in Spain. Octavian (later Augustus), upon assuming power, rewarded Sabinus' loyalty to Caesar. Although a man of no particular accomplishment in his own right, Gaius Calvisius Sabinus (the younger) took his father's seat in the Senate and, later, served as consul via appointment by Augustus Caesar.

The sight of Sabinus in Caesarea was an unwelcome one, especially after having just wet nursed a young claimant to the Jewish throne. Every former consul enriches himself in the provinces as proconsul. Varus had done it. Sabinus now appeared in the Jewish kingdom, greed oozing out his eye sockets. Varus objected on two grounds. First, this was his province to exploit. Second, the young proconsul most likely sought a posting to Judea in order to put himself in line to succeed Varus as governor of Syria when his term expired. Varus had already served for three years when the Jewish revolt flared up. Under Augustus, a governor typically served from three to five years. One expected the ambitious Sabinus to lobby Rome to sack Varus and turn the province over to himself; however, Varus has no intention of quitting the rich province of Syria any time soon. Waiting period concluded, Maximus led the proconsul in to see governor Varus.

Sabinus, "Governor Varus, so nice to see a noble Roman face in this barbaric land."

"An unexpected surprise Sabinus. I can't imagine you came to Judea for the fresh air. What is your business?"

Sabinus expected a warmer greeting given his elevated status as proconsul. Varus cut right to the chase without any attempted exchange of pleasantries. Sabinus responded in kind, "Caesar commands me to take charge of Herod's effects pending adjudication of his will."

Varus replied, "Please be so kind as to present me with your formal letter of authority from Caesar."

Sabinus reached into his toga and withdrew Caesar's letter handing it to Varus. Many thoughts raced through Varus' mind as he perused the imperial orders from Caesar. Why did Caesar find it necessary to send an official, a proconsul no less, to safeguard

Herod's riches? Did Caesar not trust Varus to do the job? Had his reputation for taking "gifts" from the locals of his province made its way back to Rome? Or had Sabinus insinuated himself into Judea on his own initiative without any voice of concern from the emperor or his ministers? Varus had no way of knowing at that moment without access to the palace rumor machine back in Rome.

Varus, "Proconsul, your orders make no mention of military command. All legions in Judea shall remain under my command."

Sabinus replied, "Be reasonable Varus, I'm tasked with safeguarding a vast number of palaces and treasuries spread over several nations. Surely such an order implicitly includes authority over Roman or allied troops in Judea."

Varus knew Sabinus possessed only meager military experience never rising above the rank of tribune. Further, no legate under which Sabinus served saw fit to entrust Sabinus with command, not even a temporary one. He was completely unqualified to command a legion during a revolt. When Caesar issued his orders, Rome was then unaware of the Jewish revolt. Varus felt certain that Caesar would deny Sabinus command once the extent of the revolt became known in Rome.

Varus probed further, "What do you know of the Jewish revolt?"

"Revolt, aren't you being a bit dramatic Varus? I understand the situation to be one of unruly festival goers in the capital. The Jews will go home to their farms when their festival ends."

Both men then suspended the charade of pleasantries. Varus laid in to Sabinus, "You're poorly informed Sabinus. This is a major revolt. The rebels have control of the capital. Dissidents are streaming there from all over the Jewish kingdom as we speak. I'm waiting for the arrival of III Gallica here in Palestine from the north then shall march on Jerusalem."

"How long do you expect the campaign to take? Are you going to besiege the city?"

Varus grabbed a map of Jerusalem from the scrolls neatly stacked in a pigeon hole case against one wall and spread the map upon a table so the two men could view it together. He said, "Come Sabinus, let me lay out the situation for you." Sabinus walked over the table feeling like a schoolboy called to the front of the class by the instructor.

Varus pointed to the map, "This is Jerusalem, the Jewish capital. We are in Caesarea 60 miles to the northwest." Varus pointed the approximate location of Caesarea, which extended beyond the scale of the map.

Varus continued his tutorial, "This fortified structure abutting the western city wall of Jerusalem is Herod's palace."

Sabinus interjected, "I can't quite fix the scale of your map. Either Jerusalem is a tiny capital or Herod built a massive palace."

"The later is the case. Herod built on a grand scale as you shall eventually see with your own eyes. Take a tour of Caesarea. It's only a sample of what awaits you in the rest of the kingdom. Herod's auxiliaries are fine troops, Thracian, German and Gallic mercenaries mostly. They have 2000 legionnaires holed up inside the palace. This structure on the far eastern end of the city is the Temple to Yahweh, their sole god. It is the most sacred piece of dirt on the face of the earth for all Jews. We have a sizable Roman fort abutting the north wall of the Temple. The Roman fort is manned by an augmented cohort of 800."

Sabinus, "So we have 2800 allied troops inside the city. How many enemy combatants?"

"Every Jew is a potential enemy combatant. How many zealots are willing to actually stand and fight when we march upon their city? Volumnius, the commander of Herod's army estimates 20,000 Jewish dissidents have taken up arms."

"Then send for more legions."

"Another is on its way from elsewhere in the province in addition to III Gallica plus we have 3000 Herodian auxiliaries based outside of Jerusalem. Waiting is not the prudent course. I intend to hit the rebels with III Gallica and the 3000 Herodian auxiliaries before the scum organize. The other legion will join the fight where needed upon its arrival."

"But is it wise to attack a fortified city without a numerical superiority?"

"They're a mob Sabinus, not an organized fighting force. Herod's palace contains a gate through the western wall of the city. We'll be able to link up with the 2000 Herodian soldiers trapped inside the instant we reach the city. Using Herod's palace as a staging base, we can then simultaneously march upon multiple axes into the heart of Jerusalem. I plan to crush the revolt with one, swift hammer blow before it spreads to other territories. We must contain this rebellion in Judea and kill it. You are welcome to ride with me to Jerusalem to view the operation."

Sabinus didn't much care to be carried to Jerusalem as mere excess baggage by Varus. Such treatment damaged his gravitas as a proconsul. Further, there was nothing in it for himself. If the campaign was successful, all honor flowed to Varus. If unsuccessful, the shit might splatter in many directions. Sabinus determined the prudent move was to keep his distance from the Jerusalem campaign. Sabinus replied, "A very gracious offer governor but I think I shall remain in Caesarea and assemble a team for my assigned task of securing Herod's assets. Please send word to Caesarea when it is safe for me to take up my duties in Jerusalem."

Varus, "Suit yourself proconsul. When the rebels are routed, I'll see if I can't free up a cohort to assist in your mission."

A cohort? 500 men? Proconsuls command armies, not piddling bands. Sabinus decided the situation dictated he raise his own mercenary army, one answerable to his personal commands and pay for it out of Herod's treasury. Such an item would constitute an above-the-line expense that, with creative accounting, the proconsul hoped to bury from detection by auditors once he arrived back in Rome. Sabinus carried with him from Rome a creative Greek bookkeeper who could be counted on to obscure the skim. Further, Sabinus envisioned the recipient of the mercenary supply contract would find it in his heart to pay an honorarium in coin to the proconsul as a sign of goodwill between the parties. In fact, Sabinus would insist on a kickback. Men did not flinch at such proposals in the eastern portion of the Roman

Empire. Their modest brothers in the west may put on a show of being scandalized by what some may call a bribe; however, money talks at both ends of the Mediterranean. Coin under the table was the sine qua non[52] of the Roman economic system.

Jerusalem, Judea (3 BCE)

Once legion III Gallica arrived in Samaria, Varus marched on Jerusalem and rolled up the rebellion in short order. The entire affair lasted sixty days from start to finish. Varus reported his successful mission back to Rome and departed for Antioch, his seat of provincial power. The governor was convinced the rebellion had been extinguished; however, he left III Gallica in Caesarea as a temporary precaution reasoning the presence of a Roman legion and thousands of auxiliary soldiers in one small country would deter any renewal of the revolt during the fast approaching Jewish festival of Pentecost. Nonetheless, what Varus previously extinguished Sabinus flamed anew with amazing speed. The proconsul moved into Jerusalem shortly after Varus vacated. Sabinus possessed neither experience nor training in the complexities of the Jewish religion and its special place in Jewish life. He made two moves immediately upon arriving in Jerusalem that greatly pissed off important constituencies in the Jewish nation. First, he summoned the high priest to the praetorium only to discover that priests refused to enter the praetorium due to the display of graven images on the façade of the structure. What a peculiar people, thought the proconsul.

Sabinus asked his aides, "So tell me, if the high priest refuses to enter the praetorium, where does he propose to meet?"

"Proconsul, he waits in the courtyard outside the praetorium. You may address him from the portico."

Joshua ben Sie had been appointed high priest by Archelaus only three months ago. With his patron out of the country in Rome, ben Sie feared meeting with the politically powerful proconsul. Sabinus stepped to the portico flanked by his

---

52 "Sine qua non" literally translates from Latin as "without which not". It is used in popular English to mean an indispensable element of the object referred to by the phrase.

aides. A holdover minister from Herod's administration gave Sabinus a quick tutorial on how to address the high priest explaining that the high priest was the second most important person in Jewish society behind the king and, in many respects, was regarded as Jewish royalty. He was to be address as "your Excellency" when conducting official duties outside of ceremonial functions at the Temple.

Sabinus said to the high priest, "Your Excellency, I am Gaius Calvisius Sabinus, Roman proconsul on extraordinary assignment here in Judea by the command of Augustus Caesar. My orders are to secure the assets of the Jewish kingdom pending an adjudication of the will of King Herod."

Ben Sie responded, "Welcome to Judea proconsul. How may the Temple priesthood be of assistance to you in this task?" Joshua ben Sie tried to remain stoic waiting for a response that intuition told him would be against the interests of the priesthood.

Sabinus, "So good of you to ask. I understand the Temple treasury is one of the major assets of the country. My accountants must make an inventory of your holdings."

"I'm very sorry proconsul but that's impossible. The holdings of the Temple treasury are dedicated to Yahweh, the one true God. They belong to God and, thus, are themselves holy. We cannot allow foreigners inside the Temple treasury to conduct such an inventory. Now, if you desire that our own scribes prepare such an inventory, I shall happily do so."

Subject people do not dictate terms to a proconsul of Rome. Who did this high priest think he was? Sabinus continued in a more forceful tone, "Perhaps you are not cognizant of the situation. Only months ago, I was consul of Rome, the senior leader of the Roman government behind only the emperor himself. My orders to you in the position of proconsul are to be obeyed as if they came from the emperor himself. There will be no negotiation. Is that clear?"

Joshua ben Sie knelt down on the ground and pulled open his robes to expose his neck. He said, "It is clear proconsul but I answer to Yahweh before Caesar. Strike me down if your law requires it but I must obey the laws of my god."

A dozen other chief priests followed the example of ben Sie and bared their necks for execution. Hundreds of ordinary Jews milled around near the praetorium half-listening to the exchange between the proconsul and high priest. When word spread that the high priest had defied Sabinus, the crowd swelled to thousands and pressed close to the high priest. Many drew daggers from their cloaks ready to attack any Roman who dared raise a hand against the high priest. Sabinus had never seen anything like it.

The Herodian minister whispered in his ear, "Proconsul, we have accountants of the Jewish faith on staff at Herod's palace. They are loyal people whose families have served Herod and the Romans for generations. You can trust them to render an adequate accounting."

Sabinus nodded his head to the minister for providing a bridge out of this predicament. "Rise high priest. I am informed that there are Jewish accountants employed in the palace here in Jerusalem. I propose to deputize them to observe the preparation of the inventory of assets of the Temple to be carried out by your Temple scribes. Our Jewish accountants shall only observe and verify their work. Is this arrangement acceptable to you?"

The high priest got up off the ground showing no physical signs of distress. He truly had been prepared to die. Ben Sie said, "If these scribes of Herod were born in Judea and their names are recorded in the Temple as having been presented to the chief priests by their parents in accordance with Jewish law, then we shall accept them as your witnesses."

Damn these Jews! They negotiated the minutest of details; all proposals were met with counteroffers and every priest was a lawyer. The high priest successfully maneuvered Sabinus into accepting his additional conditions to the compromise. Despite this concession, the ordinary Jews grumbled. Why did Caesar want to know how much gold and silver was in the Temple treasury unless he planned to steal it? This act of Sabinus flared the already deep-seated Jewish suspicion of their Roman masters.

Not one to rest on the laurels won on his first day interacting with the Jewish people in Jerusalem, the proconsul's next move outdid the first with an entirely higher magnitude of stupidity. Sabinus summoned Volumnius, commander of the Jewish military, into his office.

Volumnius greeted Sabinus deferentially, "Proconsul, General Gaius Volumnius reporting as ordered." The general came to attention as a sign of respect for the Roman proconsul. As a patrician, Volumnius expected friendly relations with Sabinus.

Sabinus said, "At ease general. Augustus Caesar has tasked me with safeguarding the assets of King Herod until such time as his last will made adjudicated. The emperor is a busy man so one may reasonably expect it will take some time to complete the business."

General Volumnius merely nodded his head in the affirmative unsure of where the conversation was heading. Sabinus continued, "Which brings us to this revolt business. Varus ordered III Gallica to remain in Judea for an indefinite period to deter the Jews from any unlawful activity. Further, as the Jewish revolt necessitated the presence of III Gallica in this country, the Jewish kingdom shall be responsible for paying its wages and supplying provisions."

Volumnius replied, "As is only fair proconsul."

"Truly said general but I must make the kingdom's accounts balance. This Jewish revolt has interrupted tax revenues at a time when expenses of administration have increased dramatically with the introduction of a legion into the kingdom. You do see my position, don't you Volumnius?"

The general got a bad feeling in the pit of his stomach. Why had the proconsul called him to his office to discuss accounting? The tension in Volumnius' stomach manifested itself in anger. He replied, "Sabinus speak plain. What do these accounting problems have to do with me and my army?"

"There is no money in the budget to pay your men general. They are dismissed from service until such time as Governor Varus removes III Gallica from the province. Of course, you shall stay on the payroll of the kingdom until a new king is selected."[53]

Volumnius couldn't believe what he just heard. The Jewish army, 15,000 strong, had been painstakingly built over the thirty plus year reign of Herod. These were professional, battle tested warriors whose effectiveness far exceeded auxiliaries found elsewhere in the empire. Sabinus was throwing it all in the crapper to save a few talents and balance the books? The general replied, "Jupiter's balls Sabinus. You must be a raving lunatic!"

Sabinus, "Calm down Volumnius. What would you have me do, withhold the annual tribute due the emperor?"

The general's anger boiled over. He charged Sabinus like a rampaging bull toppling his hand-crafted desk made of Phoenician Cedar, which knocked the proconsul to the ground in the process. Before the general could climb over the downed table and get the proconsul's scrawny neck between his fleshy hands, three guards tackled Volumnius. Even then they could barely contain the beefy general. More guards arrived after hearing the shouts of their comrades. They forcefully escorted the general out of the praetorium before Sabinus could bring him up on charges.

Word of the disbandment order spread like wildfire through the Jewish military. The top commanders of the Herodian army rallied around Volumnius on the parade ground outside the praetorium. They were still in shock upon receiving the news. Many had devoted their entire adult lives to serving Herod and Rome. The men asked, "Is it true general? We are turned out into the streets like dogs with no coins in our purse as we go?"

Volumnius replied, "Yes men, it is true."

"What will we do? Is it each man for himself?"

"No, we'll stay together as a fighting force. That jackass Sabinus is too stupid to realize what he has done. The Roman legions only have a skeleton force in Galilee and none in Perea. Those territories will explode with revolt as soon as our units are withdrawn."

---

[53] Josephus records that Herod's army was disbanded after Sabinus took control of Jerusalem and, further, that they fought the Herodians during the rebellion. Antiquities XVII 10:4 (270).

"What is our mission?"

"The Romans have released us from service. The Herodians have wealthy villas littered all over Judea with only slaves guarding them. When the revolt starts and chaos ensues, all Romans legionnaires will be recalled to a few major cities. The countryside will be left wide open. We'll knock over the villas and take our severance pay through spoils."

One of his commanders piped up, "And if we don't, the rebels will anyway."

Volumnius, "Precisely."

Having convinced themselves of the moral justification for their action, the soldiers all nodded their heads in agreement with the plan laid out by their general. They knew it was like Julius Caesar crossing the Rubicon. There was no turning back once they sacked the private villas of Roman citizens; however, Sabinus left them no other option other than turning rogue. Just as Volumnius predicted, localized revolts led by self-appointed messianic figures sprang up throughout the Jewish kingdom in areas thinned of Roman and Herodian troops. The former soldiers of Herod now contributed to the growing violence in the Jewish countryside.

Perea, Transjordan (3 BCE)

Eve of Pentecost

Hasmonean prince Simon of Perea had been Pheroras' chief minister before the latter's assassination by rival Herodians. Simon was the brother of Princess Alexandra (wife of Pheroras) and, also, the boy Pheroras saved from execution some thirty years ago at Fortress Hyrcania. Although of mixed descendent from a Hasmonean king and royal concubine, he assumed the duties of defacto governor of Perea after the death of Pheroras. His sister Alexandra either died from her injuries or was suffocated in her prison cell days after the trial of Antipater. No one knew the exact cause of death. They found her body unceremoniously dumped outside the city walls of Jerusalem having been left for the dogs to scavenge. Alexandra's two sons by Pheroras joined their uncle Simon in declaring war on Rome after the death of Herod. Antipater ben Herod's eldest son who was the husband of

Pheroras' oldest daughter also joined Simon's rebellion. The actions of proconsul Sabinus disbanding the Herodian army left Perea devoid of Roman allied units. In fact, some soldiers formerly of the Herodian military pledged allegiance to Simon.

From Passover forward, Simon occupied Pheroras's fortified palace at Macherus gathering around himself young, nationalistic Jews willing to go to war against Rome in a battle for freedom. The Jewish people hailed Simon of Perea as a son of King Aristobulus despite his mother's status as a Greek concubine and former slave. For the Jewish people of the Transjordan region, Simon of Perea was their messiah sent to them by God to rid their land of the impure Roman filth.

The closest Roman garrison to Macherus was in Jerusalem. The old Hasmonean palace in Jericho sat completely unguarded. Herod confiscated the Jericho palace from the Hasmoneans when he seized the Jewish throne. Jericho was also the location where Herod burned alive two righteous zealot rabbis. Simon aimed to evict the Romans-Herodians from his ancestral home and avenge Herod's execution of the rabbis. As the freedom fighters under Simon lacked the manpower to hold the palace against Roman counterattack, their mission was to loot and burn the palace at Jericho, then retreat into the rugged terrain of Perea.

Caesarea Maritima, Samaria (3 BCE)

Herodian prince Joseph ben Joseph stopped going to the palace at Herodium to see Princess Mariamne bat Antigonus, his second wife. He hunkered down in his opulent dwelling in Caesarea attending to business affairs and the family he fathered with Olympias as if Mariamne and her soon-to-be-born baby didn't exist. When the child came why not claim he was caught unawares? It might work, he thought. Joseph downed another cup of Italian wine while pondering his plan of action. Why not go to Archelaus when he returned from Rome and tell him the truth behind Mariamne's pregnancy? He could truthfully say that he never had sexual relations with Mariamne; therefore, could not be the father of the child. On those grounds, he was entitled to a divorce. To sweeten the deal, Joseph would agree to marry one of

Herod's many daughters by minor wives soon coming of age. What about that corpulent young thing with a face like a donkey that Herod fathered by Phaidra? Certainly the new king must be scratching around the family looking to offload that horse of a sister. In Joseph's mind, humping her mound of flesh was a fair price to pay for extraction from the dangers Princess Mariamne visited upon his family. So it was settled in Joseph's mind. He planned to approach Archelaus the moment the new king returned from Rome to demand an end to his betrothal to Mariamne. The last thing he wanted was to be her legal husband when the baby came. This royal baby would be a lightning rod for political intrigue, if it survived to see the light of day.

In the house of a nobleman, the master's wine cup was bottomless. Each time he drained the cup while lost in thought, an ever-present servant emerged from the shadows to refill it. Prince Joseph lost track of how much wine he drank. No matter, the alcohol would finally allow him a solid night of sleep. He stumbled to his chambers passing out the moment he crashed on the bed. Joseph awoke in the dead of night to find his bed spinning. Too much wine, Joseph thought he would vomit. What was with all the lights? It couldn't be morning already. A glowing figure appeared in his room so brilliant Joseph was unable to glaze directly at it. He trembled. Prince Joseph said, "Who's there?"

The apparition replied, "It is I, Gaspar, magi of Babylon." The glowing figure drew close to Joseph. The prince's eyes adjusted to the light allowing him to look at the figure. Joseph's eyes met the piercing stare of Gaspar. It's an evil spirit, thought Joseph as he involuntarily convulsed in panic. The scare loosened his bladder causing urine to stream down Prince Joseph's leg. Never in life had he been so afraid. Not even Herod moved Joseph to this level of sheer terror.

Gaspar said, "Do not turn Princess Mariamne in to the authorities. You must help her escape from Herodium. She is to leave Judea under the protection of her new husband, Priest Joseph ben Heli. All you must do is get her out of the fortress. Everything has been arranged."

This son of Baal knows my plans, thought Prince Joseph. He reads minds. Prince Joseph trembled barely mustering up the strength to respond. He said, "Herodium is heavily guarded."

Gaspar replied in a calming voice, "Do not worry. Out of darkness comes light. You shall rendezvous at Bethlehem with myself and Priest Joseph ben Heli. There we shall jointly plan the escape of the Princess."

Joseph acquiesced to the demands of the spirit, "As you command magi."

The apparition vanished into thin air as mysteriously as the glowing figure arrived in the prince's chamber. The situation was graver than he had imagined. The noose already looped around Prince Joseph's neck and the hangman prepared to tie the other end of the rope off on a tree. Why had God done this to me? Wasn't I a good husband and father? Didn't I always make sacrifice at the Temple during the holidays? A dangerous journey to an uncertain future awaited him but there was no other option. How could Prince Joseph oppose a spirit? The prince tossed in his bed unable to sleep. Early the next morning he said goodbye to his family not knowing whether he would see them again in this life. Before setting out for Herodium, Prince Joseph stopped at his business headquarters in Caesarea. His eldest son, known as Joseph of Arimathea, was already hard at work. Then age 22, the younger Prince Joseph ably assisted his father in running the vast family business empire. The administrative competence of his eldest son comforted the elder Prince Joseph as he departed for Herodium. He saw it as little more than a suicide mission.

Jerusalem, Judea (3 BCE)

The astral body of Magi Gaspar made one more night visit that evening, this time before Priest Joseph ben Heli. As a devote Jew, Priest Joseph took the apparition of Gaspar to be an angel. He fell to the ground while averted his eyes thinking himself unworthy of gazing upon a vision from God.

Gaspar addressed the priest, "Do not be afraid Joseph. You find favor with the Lord."

So it was an angel, thought Joseph. The being speaks for God.

Gaspar continued, "You are not to divorce Princess Mariamne. I and others shall help you rescue the princess from Herodium. You shall meet us tomorrow in Bethlehem to plan the escape."

How does one decline a command from a visiting angel? Joseph said, "Yes my lord."

Gaspar replied, "I am not an angel Joseph, just a man of God such as yourself."

Priest Joseph did not understand how a man could appear as a spirit. He wondered whether this was an evil spirit?

Gaspar continued, "You shall take the princess into exile in Egypt. Her child is not safe in the Jewish kingdom."

Joseph had no wish to leave his homeland. He asked, "Egypt?"

Gaspar, "You shall depart by sea from the port of Aqaba in Idumea. It is the route out of Israel with the lightest Roman presence. You shall go to Aqaba."

With that, the spirit vanished. Priest Joseph got out of bed to kneel on the cold floor. He prayed with all his might for the Lord to offer him some direction on how to act upon the words of the apparition. Should he go to Bethlehem as the spirit instructed? As he prayed, visions came to him of days long past when a young Mariamne trailed after her mother Anna at the Temple. Priest Joseph recalled how devoted Mariamne had been to serve the Lord in her youth. He took these visions as a sign from God that he should assist the princess in her hour of need. Priest Joseph got off his knees and began preparing for travel to Bethlehem intending to depart the moment the sun broke above the eastern horizon.

Bethlehem, Judea (3 BCE)

Gaspar met both Herodian Prince Joseph and Priest Joseph ben Heli in Bethlehem the following day where the plan of action was hatched. Due to the insurrection in Jerusalem, most of the soldiers normally stationed at Herodium had been moved to reinforce Jerusalem leaving only a skeleton force guarding the king's summer palace. A squad of Parthian light cavalry accompanied Gaspar. They penetrated the Judean border without being spotted by the Jewish or Roman border guards, whose numbers had been reduced during the revolt. But Gaspar judged their presence would draw too much attention as an escort for the princess south to the port of Aqaba. It made more sense for Priest Joseph and the princess to travel lightly in modest dress passing their group off as a traveling merchant accompanied by his wife and a few servants. The Parthians would act as a diversionary force moving east as the princess traveled south. With any luck, the Herodians would chase Gaspar and the Parthians thinking they had the princess. The cover story would be that Parthians kidnapped the princess from Herodium and were taking her to Parthia via Nabatea. Although Mariamne and her child would only find complete sanctuary from the Herodians in Parthia, the route east through Nabatea was currently too dangerous. Nabatea reaffirmed its alliance with Rome at the death of Herod and hoped to gain back control of disputed cities on its northwest border with the Jewish kingdom. King Aretas put the Nabatea military on alert to support the Romans should the Jews revolt. This was why Gaspar chose to feign a move east while Mariamne traveled south. By the time the Herodians discovered the ruse, all hoped the princess would then be safely on a boat bound for Egypt. Neither Prince Joseph nor Priest Joseph knew what to make of the plan, as they were new to this sort of cloak and dagger action; however, they assumed a man such as Gaspar who could turn himself into a spirit possessed some level of talent in the area of subterfuge. Both deferred to Gaspar's judgment.

Herodium, Judea (3 BCE)

Herod's summer palace (Herodium) was more fortress than palace. The king leveled a small, cone shaped mountain to accommodate his palace flanked on its four corners by massive watchtowers. Prince Joseph ben Joseph arrived in Herodium finding a very pregnant Princess Mariamne visited by her cousin Elizabeth, who gave birth months earlier to a son named

Yochanan. Elizabeth was the adoptive daughter of Matthias ben Theophilus, a former high priest and brother of Heli. Priest Matthias gave Elizabeth's hand in marriage to Zechariah, a Kohen priest from a prominent family. With political backing from his new son-in-law and his ancestral credentials as a Hasmonean, Theophilus vaulted into the high priesthood after Herod sacked Simon ben Boethus. The king removed Boethus as high priest for complicity in the secret marriage of Prince Antipater to Antigonus' daughter. Herod hoped the appointment of Theophilus, the first Hasmonean to hold the office in 31 years, would pacify the populace but his term in office was short lived. Herod sacked Matthias ben Theophilus after only one year for the stated reason of failing to control the rabbis who tore down the golden eagle from the gates of the Temple. The unstated reason for Herod's action was that the king became aware that the two Theophilus brothers secretly sheltered relatives of Antigonus after the fall of Jerusalem in 37 BCE.

Elizabeth was the great-granddaughter of Hasmonean king Yochanan Hyrcanus I, a great warrior high priest and ethnarch (but not king). She bore priest Zechariah a son who she named Yochanan after his famous great-grandfather causing consternation among Zechariah's family. Jewish naming convention of the day dictated that the first son be named after the paternal grandfather. Princess Elizabeth demanded her son bear a Hasmonean name and Zechariah acceded to her wishes. Elizabeth's son Yochanan later became a famous rabbi and baptizer living an ascetic life in the Judean desert. I had been born in Herodium a few months prior to this moment. The future rabbi (later known as Yochanan the Baptizer) lay with me in a crib on the far side of the room attended to by my mother, Lady Yohanna, while royal cousins Mariamne and Elizabeth conversed. Elizabeth barely finished relating the briefest of family news when Prince Joseph arrived.

Prince Joseph ben Joseph sized up the situation confronting him upon arrival at Mariamne's quarters at Herodium. Certainly Mariamne confided in her cousin the identity of the father of her baby, meaning yet another party was in on the secret. Why didn't they just have the town herald stand in the middle of the Bethlehem public square and announce Princess Mariamne was soon to give birth to the son of the deceased Herodian crown prince? While pondering this issue, Joseph saw a well-dressed man standing behind Mariamne who threw off an air of authority. Who the hell was he, thought Prince Joseph? Gaspar did not mention any man in the household of Mariamne. Whose side was he on? Joseph needed to get to the bottom of this pronto.

Prince Joseph asked the stranger, "Sir, I don't believe we have met. Are you in the employ of Princess Mariamne?"

Mariamne sensed Prince Joseph's displeasure and tried to calm the situation, "Prince Joseph, this is Philip of Rome. He was a confident and close friend of my deceased husband, Prince Antipater. He offered his services to me then in my time of need and stands ready to assist now. You were away these many months and we had no man in our household."

Philip of Rome said, "My apologies Prince Joseph. I should have obtained permission from you first. My lord Antipater charged me with the protection of Princess Mariamne and I remain bound by this promise."

Joseph began factoring Philip into his plan of action. The circle of conspirators just kept getting wider. At least this Philip looked like he might have trained as a soldier. He wore a Roman sword. Antipater obviously trusted the fellow and he stuck around despite Antipater's execution. Either Philip was a double agent in the employ of the Herodians or one hell of a loyal friend to Antipater. Joseph had to make a snap decision--Philip was either in or out. He looked into the middle-aged man's eyes. They bore back at him with no hint of deception.

"Alright Philip. I am grateful for your past services to Princess Mariamne and shall be glad of your company now as the princess again finds herself in at an hour of peril. This thing may be more than you bargained for so I shall not think ill of you should you wish to back out. The Herodians know the identity of the father of Mariamne's baby. They'll kill the child the moment it is born, perhaps going so far as to execute the princess before the child's birth. We must escape the palace tonight. Herodian soldiers will come for her soon."

Prince Joseph related Gaspar's plans, which startled the group. In the time Mariamne had known Prince Joseph, delay was the hallmark of his decision making style. Fear changes a man.

Prince Joseph continued, "Princess Elizabeth, I'm sorry but you are in danger merely by your presence here with us this day. I think it best if you return to Jerusalem immediately. Do you have male escort? Your husband perhaps?"

Elizabeth, "No, my husband is serving at the Temple presently. I am to join him in Jerusalem. My brother-in-law travels with me and waits in the courtyard."

Prince Joseph, "The less your brother-in-law knows, the safer it is for him and for us. Please rejoin him and leave at once."

Elizabeth, "You have my promise of secrecy." She retrieved Yochanan from the crib across the room. Her cousin Mariamne followed her to the door to exchange their goodbyes.

Philip came to Prince Joseph speaking out of hearing range of the women, "Count me in as part of the escape."

Prince Joseph, "Well, that presents something of a problem."

"How so? I can help you escape."

"The plan is for the princess to travel in disguise as a low level merchant's wife. I know Mariamne will refuse to leave Lady Yohanna and the child Menelaus behind."

"Prince Joseph, please speak plainly. What's your problem?"

"The only way we can fit you into the cover story is if you fill the role of Yohanna's husband."

Philip paused only briefly to respond. He knew what Joseph meant. His performance as Yohanna's husband was not intended as a limited engagement. Prince Joseph was asking Philip to accept responsibility for my mother and me over a lifetime. It was in this fashion that Philip of Rome, friend of Antipater, became my adoptive father. Philip responded, "That is acceptable to me."

Joseph and Philip clasped hands and proceeded with the business of planning their party's escape from Herodium. They had very little time to arrange the matter as the sun was already on its descent in the western sky.

Prince Joseph, "Some more news for you princess, your new husband waits outside the palace walls."

Mariamne, "New husband?"

"Yes, the priests in Jerusalem have ruled our marriage contract to be invalid. They say a leading male of your family must sign the marriage contract and Herod was not a blood relative to you; therefore, his signature on the contract was not legal."

Mariamne, "Who signed the new marriage contract?"

Prince Joseph, "Your adoptive father, High Priest Heli."

Mariamne had no love for Heli. Although Mariamne adored her adoptive mother Anna, Heli treated her as a second-class citizen in his household, more servant than princess. She winced with trepidation at the thought of whom Heli chose as her new husband. "And my new husband?"

Prince Joseph, "His nephew, Priest Joseph."

They were practically raised in the same household although not related to each other by blood. Mariamne stopped to reflect upon the little she remembered of Priest Joseph, a very serious man with a deep love and reverence for God. He retired to the desert after the death of his wife and Mariamne understood he planned on taking a Nazarite vow. The princess was rather surprised to hear that the Nazarite monk was now her husband. Priest Joseph held no ambition in his heart of higher office, completely unlike Heli. Even better, he was Kohen but did Priest Joseph know she was pregnant? Surely Heli would not have married his nephew to her without informing Joseph of her condition. Then again, the deviousness of Heli was not to be underestimated. Princess Mariamne arrived at her decision in seconds, "This match is acceptable to me."

Philip asked Prince Joseph, "Do you know which direction we are to head once out of the palace?"

"Aqaba."

"Aqaba? We're going south, not east?"

Prince Joseph, "It's a long story. A ship awaits you in Aqaba. I shall be handing you off to Priest Joseph once we get outside of Herodium. Magi Gaspar is also expected to join your party but his exact movements are unknown to me."

Just when the men had thought the issue settled between them, Princess Mariamne spoke. "We're not going to Aqaba."

Herodian princesses were notoriously strong willed but Prince Joseph thought of Mariamne as demur, a traditional woman who deferred to her man. He was wrong. He said, "But princess we must trust Magi Gaspar … ."

Mariamne was not in the mood to negotiate, her mind was firm. She cut off Prince Joseph saying, "My son shall be born in Judea and registered at the Temple on the fortieth day in accordance with the law. There shall be no blemish on his record when the time comes for him to claim his kingdom. My son shall sit on the Jewish throne!"

Philip, "The child will never have the chance to take the throne if he dies at the hands of Herod's soldiers as an infant. It is very dangerous for you and the baby in Judea."

These somber words from Philip did not deter Mariamne. She replied, "His life is in the hands of God. No man has the power to alter the will of God."

Prince Joseph and Philip looked at one another realizing they couldn't argue with the will of God. The authorities would surely be hunting for Mariamne in Judea after their escape, should they even make it out of the fortress. Just before sunset, Philip went to the public stables beyond the fortress walls to arrange less auspicious transportation. Both Prince Joseph and Philip owned expensive Arabian horses boarded at the stables. There, Philip exchanged these horses and their ornate accoutrements for several donkeys and a wagon. This prompted numerous questions from the horse trader. The fellow just couldn't understand why a gentleman would exchange such fine horses and gear for a few donkeys and a wagon. The authorities would learn of their escape by morning in any event so there was no use concocting an elaborate cover story for the horse trader. He just left the horse trader scratching his head fairly safe in the expectation that the large profit the trader made on the deal would be expended getting drunk that evening. By morning, his suspicions would be confirmed as Herodium buzzed with news of the escape of Princess Mariamne.

The next step in the escape plan was much more delicate—bribing the night guard stationed at the small servant's entrance on the western edge of the palace. The group needed to slip by the guard without the alarm being raised. With any luck, they'd be well away from the fortress by the time the sun came up. Just after dark, Philip again left Mariamne's quarters in the palace. He approached the guard offering a bribe to desert his post for a short period this evening when Philip gave the sign. The guard thought it was a joke until Philip placed ten gold aurei into his hand. Each gold aureus was worth 100 sestertii. The annual salary of a Roman legionnaire was 900 sestertii; therefore, ten gold aurei equated to in excess of the annual salary of a legionnaire. It was a fantastic sum in the eyes of the guard. It was more coin than the soldier had ever held in his hand at one time. The soldier played the situation cool. He nodded to Philip, slipped the coins into his purse, and then snapped back to attention resuming guard duty as if nothing was amiss.

Philip previously served with Antipater in the military and knew the ways of common soldiers. They were easy to read if one paid attention. Subtlety was not part of the soldier's craft. Philip observed this soldier only pretending to go along with the program. The soldier pocketed the gold aurei but Philip felt in his gut that a double cross was about to occur. Philip walked out of sight then circled back to a spot with a good view of the soldier's duty station. Sure enough, the soldier left his post checking to see if Philip had gone. Thinking the coast clear, he took several steps in the direction of the palace guard headquarters before being intercepted. Philip placed his hand over the soldier's mouth, then a quick thrust of a dagger into the small of the back puncturing vital inner organs. The guard slumped to the ground. Philip took no chance of the soldier sounding the alarm with his last breather by striking a final deathblow running through the man's heart. Philip said, "Sorry friend, I really wish we could have come to a financial arrangement but you forced my hand."

He dragged the body into the bushes, retrieved the ten gold aurei from the man's purse, and then bolted back to Mariamne's chambers. There was no time to spare. An officer making rounds would find the body at some point that evening. They had to flee at once. Philip was out of breath when he arrived back at Mariamne's chambers and reported the situation to Prince Joseph.

Philip said, "Our schedule just got accelerated."

Prince Joseph noticed blood on Philip's clothing. "What happened?"

"The guard tried to double cross me so I ran him through."

"You killed the guard?"

Philip nodded in the affirmative. Joseph called across the room to Princess Mariamne and my mother, "Women, grab what you can. We leave immediately."

The ladies came to join the conversation with the men. Mariamne asked, "Why the rush? What's going on?"

A sense of melancholy unexpectedly descended on Prince Joseph. He spent the better part of the last nine months feverishly searching for a way to end his marriage to Mariamne and, now that it was just about drawn to a close, he was sad. The very pregnant princess radiated beauty. He looked at her now in the soft light coming for the chamber lamps realizing that the two may never set eyes on one another again. His heart skipped a beat and, for a fleeting second, he thought about reneging on his promise to the Parthians and keep Princess Mariamne as his wife.

Philip stepped in to respond to Mariamne's question, "I had trouble with the guard. We must leave now before the alarm is sounded."

Both women saw blood on Philip's cloak. Neither panicked though realized the situation desperate. When one's life is in dire peril, he or she discovers the bare essentials in life--loved ones, the clothes on your back, a few coins in your purse, water and food for a few days. As the party slipped out the servant's entrance of the palace, Mariamne let out a shriek upon seeing the body of the guard stashed in the bushes. Prince Joseph grabbed her mouth but feared the damage was already done. The emotions of a first-time mother late in her term were a fragile thing.

Mariamne knew Philip had stabbed a guard but the unexpected sight of the dead soldier brought a flood of images of the body of her dead husband Antipater back to Mariamne. She went through 34 years of life as a sequestered maiden only to find herself riding turbulent waves in short succession—marriage to a king, conception of her first child, execution of her husband, remarriage, and now running into the night for both her own life and that of her unborn child. She began to weep. My mother Yohanna, with me clutched in her arms, tried to comfort Mariamne as best she could.

Prince Joseph realized the situation required firmness. He grabbed Mariamne by the arm and said, "Princess, we must keep moving." She muffled sobs as the party made its way to the stables. A boy arranged for by Philip stood guard over the wagon that was already hitched up to two donkeys.

Prince Joseph pulled Philip aside, "May Yahweh bless you and keep you safe. Priest Joseph waits to join you just outside the town."

Philip, "I was hoping you would come with us prince. Why don't you join us?"

Any thought Prince Joseph harbored of stealing away in the night with Princess Mariamne vanished the instant he saw the body of the dead soldier laying in the bushes. Prince Joseph ben Joseph owned a luxurious home in Caesarea, had loving children, and a royal wife in Olympias who was demanding yet tolerable when compared against Herod's remaining brood of daughters. Olympias was the full sister of Herod Archelaus and Antipas. As such, Prince Joseph expected to continue receiving valuable building contracts awarded to his company during Herod's reign. Princess Mariamne bat Antigonus was the most dangerous political commodity in Judea. Prince Joseph replied to Philip, "I wish you God's protection my friend but I have a family back in Caesarea that awaits me."

Philip, "How will you avoid implication in our escape?"

Joseph knew the answer but was squeamish about getting on with it. "I need your help with that problem my friend. First, crack me on the head with your fist. Make sure it leaves a mark."

Philip understood Joseph's plan and did as requested by delivering a blow to Joseph's forehead just above the eye. The raised stitching of Philip's leather glove left indentation marks across the prince's face. Joseph hadn't been struck with such force in his entire life. The blow nearly knocked him unconscious. He recovered to say, "Now for the dangerous part. I need you to cut with me your gladius, just a superficial wound but deep enough to draw blood. Please tell me you are skilled in its use."

Philip, "We should do this in a fleshy area away from tendons. How about the flesh of my upper leg?"

"Wherever you think is best."

Prince Joseph looked away not wishing to view his own flesh being lacerated. He barely felt the strike so sharp was Philip's blade. Joseph turned to see blood oozing over his tunic, a sight that startled him.

Philip, "You are fine prince. It's only a flesh wound that any physician can easily bind for you. Sneak back into Mariamne's quarters and lie on the floor pretending to be unconscious. When the guards find you, tell them we struggled and I knocked you unconscious."

Prince Joseph stood motionless staring at his wound transfixed by the sight of his own blood, something he had never witnessed before in life. Philip gave him a shove setting the prince limping back into the fortress.

Road to Bethlehem, Judea (3 BCE)

The escape party met up with Priest Joseph less than a mile down the road from Herodium. Philip greeted the priest who then climbed aboard the wagon.

Philip, "There have been a change of plans."

Priest Joseph, "How so?"

"Instead of going south to Idumea we are turning north for Jerusalem."

"Jerusalem, is that wise?"

Mariamne again asserted herself insisting the baby was to be registered at the Temple. Priest Joseph didn't reply. He quietly acquiesced in his new wife's decision. An awkward silence persisted between Princess Mariamne and Priest Joseph. She knew he had been forced into the marriage by Heli and resented being dumped on Joseph like table scraps from the evening meal but there was not much that could be done about the situation. She needed the protection of a husband to travel. Finally she turned to Joseph saying, "Thank you for coming cousin. It is comforting to be among family in my hour of need."

Her soft words melted the resentment he too harbored about the arrangement. Priest Joseph replied, "It must be God's will cousin. Nothing else explains the extraordinary forces at work that brought us both to this point. God must have an important plan for the royal child you carry, whether boy or girl."

"Cousin, the baby I carry is a boy. I know this in my soul."

"Call me 'husband' Mariamne."

"Yes husband."

Thus began the married life of Joseph the Nazarite and Mariamne the daughter of King Antigonus. Despite their daring escape from Herodium, the night's excitement was far, far from over. The wagon wheels ground slowly onward as the desolate rocky terrain of Herodium gave way to the verdant hills surrounding Bethlehem. They saw crops and fields where sheep grazed. Philip of Rome asked Priest Joseph, "Say, where is this mysterious magi Gaspar I heard about?"

Priest Joseph replied, "He is leading a diversion of Parthian cavalry to the east of Herodium. I understand he wishes to show his face in a few villages to the east of here, then double back to find us."

Philip, "At our slow pace he'll have no trouble catching us." There was nothing Philip could do to speed up the donkeys. The obstinate beasts moved at their own leisurely pace. As the party neared Bethlehem the unthinkable occurred. Mariamne whispered to Joseph, "Husband, my water's broke." Amniotic fluid gushed down her leg. My mother huddled close to Mariamne but there was nothing she could do to help the situation.

Joseph had no experience with the birth of babies. No, this couldn't be happening. He prayed the first time mother was mistaken. He asked, "Are you sure?"

She placed his hand upon her leg to give him sensory proof of the truth of the matter. Their escape just went from bad to horrible. Philip stopped the wagon momentarily while they checked on Mariamne. In the stillness of night, they heard alarm bells clanging at Herodium miles away. The soldiers were rushing to their duty stations awaiting orders from their officers.

Priest Joseph, "We're done for. They will be on the road before we clear another quarter mile."

Philip was calm. He replied, "I think not that quickly."

Joseph wished to believe Philip's soothing words as he was going out of his mind with worry on two fronts. "Why?"

Philip, "Imagine you are the captain of the guard at the palace. One of your officers stumbles upon a dead guard at the servant's entrance. What's your first thought?"

Joseph shook his head. He didn't get the point. Philip continued, "The palace guard's main job is to secure the palace against intruders. They'll assume an assassin snuck into the palace killing the guard in the process. The first order of business will be to search the palace for assassins."

Joseph, "And when they find Princess Mariamne and the Lady Yohanna gone?"

"This is where Prince Joseph comes in. He will tell them intruders knocked him unconscious and kidnapped the princess. So they'll search the palace and all the out buildings surrounding the palace first. Then the last order of business will be to send out riders on the main roads in all directions from Herodium."

Joseph, "We'll never make Jerusalem."

Philip, "Bethlehem is upon us. Let's duck in there and see if we can find a place to hide for the night."

Joseph's mind still worried about the soldiers he was sure were on their trail. "Will they'll search the town?"

Philip replied, "Yes but I doubt they search the town at night, too easy for someone to slip away in the dark. My bet is first light. Our choices are to die on the road tonight or live to see tomorrow's sunrise somewhere off the road. Which do you choose priest?"

Mariamne grimaced with pain with another contraction. Joseph knew they had to get off the road. He looked to the heavens saying, "God, please lead us to shelter."

They arrived at Bethlehem finding it shut down for the night, doors locked, shudders closed. Joseph suggested, "Let's knock on the door of that inn over there."

Philip replied, "No Joseph, it will announce our presence to the entire town. Many of these people are surely employed in the palace. If the soldiers arrive, the townspeople will turn us in."

Joseph, "What about the stables? Nobody will be there at night."

They moved through the town to the stables located on the far edge of the village but Philip didn't stop. He just kept the party moving past Bethlehem out into the wilderness. Joseph protested, "Philip, we have to stop! Mariamne is giving birth. We need to go into town."

Philip was adamant that they stay the course. "We can't do it Joseph. Look there, the stable master's home is but twenty paces from the stables. Mariamne moans in pain already. They'll hear the screams in the night. The Herodian troops will be upon us at sunrise."

Priest Joseph spied stone cliffs in the distance by moonlight. Throughout Judea, sandstone cliffs were peppered with caves. Joseph thought the caves were a better alternative than allowing the baby to be born in a moving wagon. He made the case to Philip. "Friend, be reasonable, let's make for the cliffs in the distance. There are sure to be caves cut into those stone walls."

Philip mentally weighed the odds and decided Joseph was right but could he find a cave at night? They would need more light to traverse the open ground off road to navigate the wagon to the cliffs. The terrain was strewn with rocks and uneven ground. He got down from the wagon and lit a torch.

Joseph said, "What in the name of thunder are you doing? That torch will be visible for a mile in all directions. You're the one who said it was too dangerous to go into the town because we would be discovered yet now you light a torch."

Philip replied, "This is the only way for us to guide the wagon off road through the rocks. It's a dice game Joseph. We just have to let them fly and see what fortune has in store for us."

Philip didn't wait for a response. He walked out in front of the wagon guiding the donkeys through a rock-strewn field toward cliffs off in the distance. In thirty minutes time, they traveled enough ground that the torch was no longer visible from the road. Then the party's concerns shifted from soldiers to Mariamne's pregnancy as her contractions intensified. There was nothing Joseph could do to remedy the situation but pray his wife didn't give birth to her royal child in an open wagon under a starry sky in the Judean countryside. It took two more hours to reach the stone cliff and another hour searching along the ridgeline until Philip finally spotted a cave. They moved Mariamne inside. My mother threw down straw covering it with blankets in an attempt to make Mariamne as comfortable as possible. Joseph helped his very pregnant wife onto the makeshift bed. I was plopped down into a feed box for the animals while my mother attended to her mistress.

Priest Joseph tried to come up with an excuse to leave the cave. He'd never witnessed a woman give birth before and he sure as hell was too old to start now. He had no stomach for the blood and after-birth. One of the motivating factors in Joseph's decision to leave the Temple priesthood was the required ritual sacrifice of animals. The sight of blood made him ill. Philip came over speaking softly in Joseph's ear. "This isn't going well. Mariamne is struggling. The first child is always the most difficult. We need a midwife. You stay with the women, I'll go for help."

Joseph saw this as his way out and protested, "No, you stay and I'll go for help."

Philip, "But I can move faster than you. I should go."

Joseph had to get out of that cave. He pled his own weakness as an excuse. "You were raised in Rome. Judea is my homeland so I know the land. Besides, what help will I be if soldiers show up? You need to stay and protect the women."

Philip relented, "Alright, go then. Be quick about it." He waived Joseph away.

Once outside, Priest Joseph gazed up at the brilliant night sky and thought of his former life as a secluded Nazarite monk. He longed for that quiet life of secluded study and prayer. Such were Joseph's thoughts while stumbling over the rocky terrain in the direction of the main road. The sight of figures moving toward him in the darkness interrupted his thoughts. Joseph lay down upon the ground hoping to avoid detection. Where these soldiers from Herodium searching for their party? As the ghostly figures drew closer, Joseph realized they were not soldiers. These were Bedouins neglecting their sheep to stare into the night sky. What were they staring at? If spotted would they rob him? The Bedouin were opportunists taking advantage of situations as they arose. Well, he really didn't have much of a choice. Mariamne needed help and here were people who knew the area and were independent of the Jewish authorities. Perhaps a higher power had answered Joseph's prayers. He rose up from the ground showing his profile to the Bedouin. Two men came near and asked, "Do you follow the star also?"

Joseph replied, "What star?"

They pointed behind him in the sky above the cave. Jupiter, the star of kings, had drawn very close to Venus. They appeared as one massive star in the sky. The astronomical display was impressive but Joseph returned his attention to the urgent issue at hand, "Look, we need help. My wife is giving birth and it's going poorly. Do you have a midwife with your people?"

They nod affirmatively.

Joseph, "I beg of you to go and collect her. My wife is in a cave beneath the star you just pointed out. I'll light a small fire to better mark the cave entrance."

Two hours later in the dead of night, the Bedouin returned. Joseph ushered them into the cave. He waited outside the entire time ostensibly tending to the fire. Philip stood vigil next to Lady Yohanna as she tried to encourage an utterly exhausted Mariamne. The Bedouin midwife strode into the cave like a captain stepping onto the quarterdeck of a ship. Her presence conveyed such command that Yohanna cleared a way for the midwife without being told. The midwife put her ear to Mariamne's belly detecting a faint heartbeat.

She asked of Yohanna, "What is her name?"

"Mariamne."

The midwife turned her attention back to her patient. "Mariamne, I am Maia. You must listen to me sister."

Mariamne, drained of all energy, hovered in a state of semi-consciousness. The midwife shook Mariamne firmly by the shoulders. "Mariamne, you have to push."

Again, little to no response came from the princess. Maia was done with the gentle bedside manner. She reached back with an open hand unleashing a blow across Mariamne face with all the might her aging frame could muster. Mariamne's eyes opened this time.

Maia said, "Mariamne, your baby is dying. Unless you push for all you're worth right this instant the baby dies. Do you understand me?"

Mariamne shook her head up and down indicating she understood. Maia grabbed both of Mariamne's legs spreading them while jamming her knees toward her body.

"Push, for the love of Yahweh push sister!"

Through force of will, Maia brought the baby from the brink of death back to life. His difficult birth foreshadowed latter events in the life of this child. Yeshua emerged from his mother's womb drawing his first breadth with a slap on the buttocks from Maia, the Bedouin midwife. So it was that Yeshua known as the Christ was born.

Morning broke with Yeshua and I feeding side by side at our mother's breasts as the Bedouin huddled by the fire outside the cave's entrance. They gossiped amongst themselves. How did merchants traveling to Jerusalem end up in a cave over a mile off the road? Why hadn't they stopped in Bethlehem? The Bedouin concluded these people were on the run from the authorities. Very unusual, thought the Bedouin. And what of the star they saw in the sky last night hovering over the cave? What did it portend? What happened next confirmed their suspicions.

Philip came to the fire and stamped it out with his leather boots. The Bedouin noticed the fine leather workmanship of his boots and the Roman gladius that hung from his waist. Philip refused to answer when the Bedouin asked why he put out the fire while the morning chill was still upon them. Then Priest Joseph gave Maia seven Tyrian silver shekels for saving the child's life. That sealed it. This was not a group of middle class merchants. They were a party of royals. Herod's sons were surely hunting them.

The Bedouin thanked Joseph for the silver, congratulated Mariamne on the birth of her son, and then set off to put as much distance between themselves and the cave as possible. However, the Bedouin did not make it far when Magi Gaspar intercepted them. Two additional magi rode with Gaspar in search of Mariamne and her party. What in the name of the gods were Zoroastrian priests doing this deep inside Judea, the Bedouin wondered? The Bedouin wanted nothing to do with the royal baby back in the cave figuring it had imparted a bad omen upon them. One Bedouin preemptively inquired of Gaspar. "You come for the royal baby?"

Gaspar replied, "Yes. Does he live?"

Maia spoke up, "I delivered a healthy prince by Princess Mariamne just before daylight this morning. I left him suckling at his mother's breast not two miles in that direction." She gestured in the direction of the cave and started walking off. Gaspar smiled. He stopped Maia and placed three more Tyrian silver shekels into her hand. Fearing Herodian soldiers would arrive on the scene at any moment, Maia and the other Bedouin beat a hasty retreat back to their flocks without bothering to thank the magi.

Gaspar finally arrived at the cave sticking his head through the entrance. The sight caused Priest Joseph's body to shudder with an involuntary start. How did the magi find their party after they turned north from Herodium instead of south as agreed? The priest was unsure what to make of the magi and his mystical ability to appear as a ghost in the night like angels and demons. Gaspar and the two other magi ignored Joseph moving in a direct line for the baby. The three magi took to their knees with bowed heads in supplication to the royal being in their presence. After the presentation of gifts and blessings bestowed upon Yeshua, the men caucused at the entrance of the cave formulating strategy.

Gaspar said, "Why did you turn north? The ship awaits your arrival in Aqaba."

Priest Joseph, "The princess is determined to have the child registered at the Temple in Jerusalem on the fortieth day in accordance with Jewish law."

Gaspar, "Jewish law. I should have consulted you on the subject. Of course, the precepts of Jewish law must be followed."

Philip, "Do we stand a chance of making it to Jerusalem?"

Gaspar, "Providence has smiled upon your mission. Rebellion has erupted again in Jerusalem. All available Roman auxiliary soldiers in Judea have been recalled to Jerusalem to put down the revolt. The roads are, at this moment, clear of soldiers."

Joseph didn't bother asking Gaspar how he acquired this information, surely by some mystical means; however, this information begat another concern in the mind of Joseph. He asked, "But if all the soldiers are now in Jerusalem, won't it be dangerous for us to go there?"

Princess Mariamne gave Joseph a stern look and he became quiet. The priest learned the family power structure that morning in the cave. Yeshua had been born to reclaim the Hasmonean throne usurped by Herod. Joseph was not head of the household, Yeshua was. And Princess Mariamne acted as the boy's defacto regent until he reached adulthood. If Princess Mariamne, despite the risks, demanded the group go to Jerusalem, then the demand was met as if commanded by the king.

Gaspar replied to the now silent Priest Joseph, "The will of God shall prevail despite the danger."

It was too conspicuous for Gaspar to escort the family to Jerusalem so he left Judea for the east. Prince Joseph, Princess Mariamne, Philip of Rome, my mother, Yeshua and I traveled to Jerusalem during the commotion surrounding the renewed civil war. Due to the prevalence of robbers on the roads during the uprising, the men of our party buried the bulk of the treasure given to Princess Mariamne by the magi under a rock off the main road between Bethlehem and Jerusalem. Their fears turned out to be well founded as bandits robbed us as night fell before reaching Jerusalem. Priest Joseph pled with the men to leave them enough money to pay for the required sacrifices at the Temple but these men were hard of heart. They took everything except for a small amount in coin sufficient to cover the lowliest of lodgings in Jerusalem. The robbers certainly would have seized even this small amount of money as well had not Princess Mariamne hidden it within an unmentionable area of her garments. Despite this setback, fortune smiled upon us and we reached the holy city safely.

Caesarea Maritima, Samaria (3 BCE)

Brothers Archelaus and Antipas together with the vast army of Herodian royalty that sailed to Rome for the probate of Herod's last will by Augustus Caesar expected to have the matter concluded in a month or so and, in the case of those princes receiving territories to rule, return to their kingdoms in short order. This was not how the drama played out. Princess Malthace, mother of Archelaus and Antipas, died in Rome while Caesar deliberated how to slice up the Jewish kingdom. Family feuding over Herod's estate ground to a halt while all Jewish dignitaries in Rome went into mourning for Malthace. Princess Salome, sister of Herod and family rival of Malthace, couldn't stomach the faux sorrow over the death of Malthace. Salome despised the Samaritan ox. Having heard through back channels inside the imperial bureaucracy that she and her son Antipater ben Costobarus would receive only minor allocations when the final ruling came down on Herod's will, Salome departed Rome early to return home. She viewed herself as chief defender of the Herodian legacy in the absence of her departed brother Herod. Prince Philip, then only a teenager, remained temporarily in charge of the Jewish kingdom while his higher ranking brothers were in Rome and Salome had no faith her inexperienced nephew possessed the balls necessary to carry out the dirty business required to preserve the Herodian dynasty. She meant that literally as Philip displayed an overt femininity and never fathered children later in life.

The Hasmonean ghost resurfaced just prior to Herod's death with the potential to destroy all he built during his long reign. The Herodians mistakenly thought the seed of King Antigonus had been destroyed years ago in 37 BCE when Herod captured Jerusalem. However, Antigonus stashed his infant daughter Mariamne and cousin Elizabeth with priestly families inside Jerusalem just before the city fell. The ruse worked by fooling all the Herodians except for Pheroras. Instead of informing Herod about the two hidden Hasmonean princesses, Pheroras got greedy cutting a deal with the priests. In exchange for the power to name the husband of Princess Mariamne he spared the lives of the two royal babies. Because of this sin against the Herodian clan, Salome engineered Pheroras' assassination with the blessing of King Herod. In Salome's mind her brother Pheroras signed his own death warrant the day he joined the conspiracy to hide Princess Mariamne bat Antigonus and Princess Elizabeth.

The dying order of King Herod was to kill Mariamne after Caesar finishing probating his will. Herod tried to issue additional instructions from his deathbed but expired before getting out the words. Salome later learned what her brother was trying to say, Mariamne was pregnant. She attained this information from spies at Herodium just days before departing Rome. Princess Salome returned to Palestine from the comforts of Rome for the express purpose of seeing to it that the grandchild of Antigonus borne by Mariamne died an infant. Philip ben Herod evacuated Jerusalem for the safety of Caesarea during the revolt so he was there on the dock when Salome's ship entered the artificial port of Sebaste. Princess Salome came down the gang plank from a Herodian royal ship onto the dock as Prince Philip and his entourage looked passed her back up at the ship expecting to see Archelaus and Antipas emerge.

Philip, "Aunt Salome, where is the king? Did he not return with you from Rome?" Philip referred to his brother as the king because he fully expected Caesar to affirm Herod's will. But Herod's execution of Antipater against the private order of Augustus caused the princeps to later downgrade Archelaus' title to ethnarch (i.e., ethnic ruler).

Salome replied, "No, your brothers remain in Rome. As I am sure you heard by now, Malthace died and everyone is in official mourning. This delayed a ruling from Caesar on your father's will. There was still no word when I sailed from Brundisium."

Philip stood waiting for Salome to explain why she returned with no verdict from Caesar. The young prince knew the history of his aunt Salome. She brought charges against her first two husbands, which resulted in Herod executing both. She also led the charge in demanding prosecution of Crown Prince Antipater and these charges also resulted in his execution. Philip feared the witch of Judea.

Princess Salome continued, "I suppose you are curious as to the reason for my early return."

Philip tried to flatter the old girl, "It's always a pleasure to see you Auntie. Whatever the reason for Yahweh bringing you here to keep me company in Caesarea, I'm thankful for it."

In a twisted way Salome missed Crown Prince Antipater. The only Idumean among Herod's sons spoke directly, cut a fine figure on horseback and possessed the backbone necessary to lead soldiers in battle. This pretty Greek boy[54] had none of that and was the reason Salome allowed him to live. He could be intimidated. Antipater ben Herod stood as a strong political force inside Herod's palace and this was the reason the witch eliminated him on her path to power. Now she intended to finish the job by assassinating Antipater's posthumous child by Mariamne.

Salome grabbed her nephew by the arm pretending she needed support to walk. "Please do me the favor nephew of escorting me to the palace. I have a few matters to discuss with you as we walk. This concerns Antigonus' daughter."

Philip stopped walking and faced his aunt. "I'm sorry to inform you auntie that Princess Mariamne escaped from Herodium

---

[54] Philip the Tetrarch's mother was Cleopatra of Jerusalem. Her ethnicity is unknown. Obviously, her name is not Jewish but a dynastic name of the Ptolemies of Egypt who were ethnic Greeks; thus, the author identifies Philip as Greek. This identification falls into the category of reasoned guess.

yesterday. Our soldiers tracked her to Bethlehem but the trail grows cold there."

Salome exploded, "How could you be so stupid as to allow this to happen! Seal the Judean border in all directions this instant. Double the guard at all border crossings and ports."

Philip tried to calm the witch, "There is no need to get hysterical auntie. This has already been done. I feel confident she is still in Judea and we shall find her."

Salome, "Did you know she was pregnant?"

Philip grimaced. This next bit of information was sure to set off the witch like a volcano. "I heard the rumor previously but had been unable to confirm the information until this morning. Our soldiers questioned a Bedouin woman who informed them she delivered a son to a royal woman named Mariamne in a cave outside of Bethlehem. Our soldiers searched the cave but she was gone."

Salome exploded, "God curse that whore! A grandchild of Antigonus lives. What about Bethlehem? Have you tortured the citizens?"

Philip tried to rein in his aunt's emotions. Only the Lord knew what atrocity she would demand. Philip replied, "They are simple-minded peasants. The mere sight of the soldiers frightens them. Certainly they gave us any information about Mariamne they possessed."

Philip gently took Salome's hand into his own trying to walk her back toward the palace. "You must calm yourself auntie. The Jews have revolted again and we must be careful not to inflame their passions even further. All we can do for now is seal the border to make sure Mariamne does not escape and wait for this insurrection to die down. Governor Varus is on his way from Antioch with more legions. We should not act until Varus arrives."

Salome replied, "To hell with what the Jewish people think and we shall not wait for Varus to arrive. He might prevent us from executing the child. You send a century of fast cavalry to Bethlehem and execute every child in the town. If you don't have the balls, I'll sign the order myself. I am senior member of the Herodian family in the kingdom at this moment."

Philip was outraged. His aunt clearly intended to usurp his authority but the young prince didn't see a whole lot he could do about it. Proconsul Sabinus dismissed the entire Herodian army (some 15,000 strong) months earlier in Jerusalem. Philip retained but 1,000 men as a personal guard by promising to pay them out of his own funds, money he didn't currently possesses but expected to be granted whenever Caesar finished the job of probating Herod's will. Salome had money and estates apart from Herod. She had a long relationship with the Jewish military. Philip knew the 1,000 soldiers currently quartered in Caesarea who hadn't been paid in months would take orders from any Herodian royal who handed out coin. The only issue for Philip was whether to go along with the machinations of his aunt or oppose them. It took Philip no more than a fraction of a second to reflect upon the death and destruction Princess Salome authored inside the Herodian clan. This led him to conclude it was in the best interest of his future ability to walk among the living that he sign whatever order his aunt proposed.

Philip, "As you say auntie, you are the senior member of the family now in Palestine. I value your counsel. Tell me what you think needs to be done and we shall do it."

Salome smiled. The boy's spine broke after she had barely begun to push. Now that he was giving her free reign, she addressed another threat in addition to Mariamne and her child. Salome resumed walking up to the palace from the harbor as she continued explaining her plans, "I am honored that you value my counsel prince. First, eliminate the children in Bethlehem and search the surrounding region thoroughly for Mariamne and her baby. Next, send word to Jerusalem to interrogate priest Zechariah and his wife Elizabeth."

Philip, "Who is Zechariah of Jerusalem?"

"I've learned there is another Hasmonean princess loose in Judea, Princess Elizabeth bat Matthias. She too escaped execution when Herod first captured Jerusalem by hiding with a priestly family in the city. She is the great-granddaughter of Hasmonean

Yochanan Hyrcanus I. Zechariah is her husband and a Kohen priest. My informants tell me that Zechariah has fathered a child by Elizabeth. She and the baby must be eliminated."

As Philip suspected, auntie possessed an extensive list of assassination victims. He turned to a scribe who trailed behind them as they walked and motioned that he should take notes. Philip continued, "Alright auntie, so we have Mariamne and her child then this Princess Elizabeth and her child."

Salome, "Correct and don't forget the children in Bethlehem."

"Right, the children in Bethlehem. Let's discuss that for a moment. Is it necessary to kill all the children in Bethlehem? The Bedouin were adamant that Mariamne delivered a male child so shouldn't we limit the execution order to newborn male children?"

Salome, "The villagers should be punished for allowing this to happen on their soil."

"Yes auntie but my conscience is troubling me with the breadth of the execution. Can we limit the execution to males?"

"If that makes you sleep better at night prince then I shall go against my better judgment and agree to limit the executions in Bethlehem to male children."

"Excellent, now let us define the term 'children'; how about children under the age of one year?"

Salome was appalled by her nephew's lack of balls. How could a son of Herod be so weak when it came to the business of governing the Jewish kingdom? The people must know that retribution will be swift and painful whenever the interests of the crown are opposed. Salome replied, "Two years of age. Don't try and push me any further prince."

Philip was reluctant to continue the discussion further but decided it best to get on with Salome's complete list of those she demanded to be executed. "Anyone else auntie?"

She didn't need time to think about her reply, "Yes, whoever is responsible for Mariamne's escape from Herodium. The captain of the guard at Herodium who was on duty at the time of the escape, obviously, he must die. Did she have any help from inside the palace?"

This question brought the discussion to a delicate family matter. Philip broached the subject, "I'm not sure how to answer this question auntie. As you know, my father betrothed Princess Mariamne to Prince Joseph before the king died. Joseph was at Herodium when the escape occurred. He has stab wounds but a report I received from the military commander at Herodium questions Joseph's complicity in the escape. The tribune points out that the wounds to Joseph are quite superficial yet a palace guard who attempted to thwart the escape was run through with a well placed, lethal strike. Whoever killed the guard was well trained in the use of a sword and would not have inflicted the clumsy, superficial wounds that Joseph has."

"Meaning the tribune thinks the wounds were placed on Joseph to cover his participation in the escape?"

"Yes auntie, that is the allegation against Cousin Joseph."

The fool, thought Salome. How could he have been so stupid to risk his own neck to save Mariamne? The dazzling brilliance of Hasmonean royal blood seduced yet another member of the Herodian clan. Prince Joseph was the eldest son of Salome's brother Joseph who King Antigonus beheaded at Jericho during the civil war. This woman was the daughter of the man who murdered Joseph's father yet he risked his life to save her? Joseph, like Antipater, just signed his own death warrant. Salome said, "We shall deal with him. Who has custody of King Herod's seal?"

"Ptolemy does auntie. He is the last senior minister left in Palestine. All others traveled to Rome with Archelaus and Antipas."

Salome, "Prepare the orders we discussed then summon Ptolemy and tell him to bring the king's seal. Also summon Prince Joseph and whoever is in command of the Herodian troops currently here at Caesarea."

* * * * * * * * * *

Philip complied with the ~~command~~ request from Princess Salome. She presided over the subsequent meeting of the senior Herodians at Caesarea, which included Prince Joseph. Salome greeted him warmly pretending nothing was amiss. A scribe laid out the execution orders on the table before the dignitaries. Salome called the meeting to order. She addressed the men, "The dying wish of King Herod was to execute Hasmonean princess Mariamne and prevent her from having offspring. The worst has come to pass. Word reached us from Bethlehem that she bore a son. Prince Philip and I have agreed on orders that carry out the wishes of the departed king so that his soul may find rest in the afterlife. You have all been given an opportunity to review the orders. Does anyone object?"

Salome looked around the room and no one objected. "Very well. Since we are carrying out the wishes of the dead king and Augustus Caesar has not, as yet, confirmed Archelaus as the new king we shall issue these orders under Herod's seal. Philip and myself shall attest to the fact that these orders implement commands given by the king before his death. All of you shall sign as witnesses. Ptolemy, give me the seal."

Salome dripped wax onto each order then impressed Herod's seal into the wax. She, Philip, Ptolemy, Prince Joseph, and a military commander each signed. A well-dressed young man stood in the back of the room directly behind Prince Joseph. Salome noted his familiar face but couldn't place his name. Execution of the documents complete, she called forward the young man. Before Salome could utter a question to the man who looked to be in his mid-twenties, Prince Joseph spoke up. "Auntie Salome, this is my eldest son Joseph."

She looked the young man over thinking he might thank her one day. Before the day was out his father would be dead and he would become pater familias over the third richest private fortune in Palestine. Prior to convening this meeting, Salome and Philip secretly signed an order for the execution of Prince Joseph ben Joseph.

Salome, "Young prince Joseph, how come I don't recall seeing you around the palace?"

Young prince Joseph replied, "Because my father has tasked me with overseeing our estates in the countryside. I have a villa in Arimathea but mostly spend my days traveling from one property to the next including our mining interests outside of Palestine. I have traveled as far as the Roman copper and tin mines in Britain. I would be out doing my father's work this moment but he ordered me to Caesarea due to the revolt."

Prince Joseph was the Herodian family building contractor. He used the rich income obtained from Herod's vast building projects to purchase agricultural estates in Galilee, timber interests in Lebanon, and mining interests in far off lands of the Roman Empire. Salome thought it wise that Prince Joseph secluded his son from the palace in Jerusalem. His name had not cropped up in any of the elaborate plots that gripped the palace in the last years of Herod's reign.

Salome, "I am glad to see you again young prince of the House of Joseph. You bear a striking resemblance to my long deceased brother whose name you share. Perhaps you will spend time with your aunt while we are both in Caesarea and we can renew our acquaintance."

Salome then addressed the entire assembled group, "Prince Philip and I have business to discuss with Prince Joseph. We ask that everyone else excuse us."

As Ptolemy left the room, Princess Salome stopped the minister and whispered in his ear, "Send in the Modiin chief. He should be waiting in the hallway."

Prince Joseph grabbed his son and hugged him, which surprised the younger Prince Joseph. His father was not the affectionate type. His father's last words to him were, "You know I love you son." The elder Prince Joseph's fears were confirmed when Zechariah ben Eleazar, chief of Modiin, entered the room trailed by two very large men.

Prince Joseph addressed Salome, "Auntie is there not a way for us to negotiate this matter? Perhaps exile with a stiff fine? I can pay it directly to you for use as you see best for the benefit of the kingdom."

Salome stared at her nephew with eyes cold as the night sky in the desert. She replied, "I'm afraid not nephew. You will die before the sun sets this day. The only issue is whether we confiscate your estates to the royal treasury or not. Your son seems like a very nice young man. I'd hate to see his future put into jeopardy."

Prince Joseph ben Joseph (the elder) truthfully wrote out his confession then was strangled by Modiin operatives while Salome and Philip watched. Salome insisted that Philip witness the execution so that he fully understood the consequences of disloyalty to the Herodian clan. Seconds after Prince Joseph exhaled his last breath Princess Salome rose from her seat saying, "You will excuse me but I've been at sea these last two weeks and am dying for a visit to the baths." She then exited the room leaving Philip and Zechariah ben Eleazar staring after her.

Salome had misjudged her nephew Philip. She took his interest in art, literature, and fashion as a sign of weakness. Philip was not weak and proved to be the most effective ruler of the Herodian generation that followed Herod the Great. Philip harbored no illusions about his aunt Salome. She killed family members without giving it a second thought. Soon Caesar would bestow a kingdom upon Philip making him a potential target for a power grab by Salome. Philip had witnessed enough to realize that Salome posed a clear and present danger to his person. The young prince addressed Zechariah the Modiin chief, "Chief Zechariah, what say you about Salome's execution of the children in Bethlehem and the Temple priest who shares your name?"

The question rather surprised the Modiin chief. Herodians never inquired what he thought about the merits of an execution, they only gave orders leaving him to carry out their dirty work. Zechariah certainly didn't expect the young prince to tread upon such a sensitive subject with the kingdom's spy chief. He sensed the young prince had had enough of his overbearing aunt, a sentiment Zechariah shared. She engineered an endless string of assassinations and executions. If the Herodian Empire was to hold together in the generation after Herod, they needed to foster greater support among the Jewish people. So far, the second Herodian generation was off to a horrible start. Zechariah expressed a non-committal response attempting to gage which direction Philip intended to go with the conversation. He said, "These executions will only inflame the insurrectionists."

Philip continued, "My thoughts exactly chief. And of course you know this is only the first round of executions Salome has in mind. We finish with this batch of killings then the princess adds more names to the list."

Zechariah cut to the chase, "What do you propose prince?"

Philip swallowed hard and replied, "It's time for aunt Salome to go."

What he just said could be construed by Caesar as conspiracy against the state. He risked his own life by suggesting to the spy chief that his aunt Salome, sister of the king, be assassinated. Philip's heart pounded as he waited for a response from the stoic Zechariah.

The Modiin chief replied simply, "I agree."

Philip let out an audible sigh of relief. "Will you require a written order from me or is this conversation sufficient?"

"No order is necessary prince; however, I will need to trouble you for funds to finance this operation. For obvious reasons, I cannot use local contract agents. This job must be given to a foreign agent known to be effective and discreet in such matters. I have an operative in mind. He resides in Tyre and does not work cheap."

Philip, "Whatever sum you need just name it but this must be done quickly before Governor Varus arrives from Antioch with his legions. I want Salome dead and sealed in a tomb before Varus arrives."

The Modiin chief was efficient at his job. Princess Salome died seven days later, drowning in the baths she so enjoyed at Caesarea. Her attendants stepped away for a moment to get perfume for the princess and returned to find her floating face down in the pool. All agreed the old princess died of a sudden heart attack. The authorities recorded her death as natural and sealed her body in a tomb in Herodium the day after she died.

Jerusalem, Judea (3 BCE)

Our party with baby Yeshua was now in Jerusalem having traveled as two low level merchant families on a pilgrimage to the holy city for the coming religious feast of Pentecost. Philip of

Rome suggested no one make contact with family and friends while in Jerusalem as word of the princess's presence would spread like wildfire. The rebels controlled the majority of the city while the Herodians and Romans held Fortress Antonia and Herod's palace. The Jewish people understood the Romans would eventually send reinforcements but none knew when they would arrive or in what strength. So our party holed up in a rundown inn within a poor quarter of the city. Princess Mariamne remained sequestered for forty days after giving birth, as she was ritually unclean.[55] After the purification period ended, Mariamne and Joseph went to the Temple to present baby Yeshua as their first-borne son. Mariamne begged to be allowed to go to her father Heli's home to obtain the necessary money to pay for the required sacrifices at the Temple but Philip of Rome talked her out of it. His argument was that the safety of Yeshua was paramount and could not be risked by making an appearance at the home of Heli where a large number of servants would immediately become aware of her presence. Once the servants knew important information the entire city also knew.

Scripture required Jewish parents to offer the Temple priests a yearling lamb as a burnt offering to God at the birth of their first son for the life of the child and a young turtledove for forgiveness of sin; however, in the case of poverty, two doves could be offered instead. Unable to obtain money from their family, Mariamne and Joseph appeared as paupers at the Temple offering only the two doves.[56] Mariamne was well known at the Temple and, therefore, kept her head covered at all times. Priest Joseph lived in the desert as a monk for the prior five years and, for this reason, was less likely to be recognized.

Despite the warnings from Philip of Rome, Princess Mariamne desperately wished to see one person while at the Temple, her mother Anna. The now elderly Anna was the Temple mother and officiated in the court of women. She spent each day there from sun up to sun down. Mariamne and Joseph approached

---

[55] *Leviticus* 12:4-6.

[56] *Luke* 2:24.

her inauspiciously as possible but Mother Anna saw them coming in the distance and ran as fast as her ancient limbs could carry her. She placed her arms around her adoptive children and cried uncontrollably. Religious music and dancing occurred throughout the court of women yet people began to stare at Mother Anna attracted by the commotion. Still, Mariamne presented Yeshua to his adoptive grandmother. Mariamne pulled back her cloak revealing the infant Yeshua. Anna immediately fell to her knees prostrating herself before the newborn king. She looked skyward singing praises to Yahweh. Joseph took hold of his mother's arm begging her to stand upright and be quiet. Mariamne handed the child to Anna so she may have the pleasure of holding her royal grandson.

Anna said, "Thank you Lord! Oh, how I have prayed for this day. I may die now Lord for I have seen the new king." Antipater ben Herod was a blood descendant of Jewish kings Solomon and David, while his mother Mariamne was a royal daughter of Aaron. Thus, Yeshua embodied both branches of the messianic tradition from Judah and Aaron. There was no doubt in Anna's mind that she held the prophesied Messiah in her arms.

Mariamne had a favor to ask of her mother, "Mother, we need help. The boy must be recorded in the Temple as the son of Prince Antipater, his true father, otherwise he will be deemed a bastard. Talk to Heli mother. He can make it happen."

Anna very rarely spoke to her husband Heli. They lived in separate wings of his vast home and took their meals separately. She spent her days in the court of women while he was in the inner court reserved for priests. Heli would not lift a finger to help his wife but he would take action to help Princess Mariamne given the value of her bloodline to the family.

Anna said, "I will send a message to Heli and everything will be arranged. Wait here."

She returned an hour later to inform Mariamne that all had been arranged. Heli under his authority as a former high priest would personally register the baby in the Temple birth records.

Anna, "What name have you given the child?"

Mariamne responded, "Joseph and I thought 'Yeshua' an inconspicuous name. We do not wish to draw attention to him."

The old woman's face grew stern. She said, "That name is a disgrace. This is the grandson of the last Hasmonean king. He must have the name of a king. My grandson's name will be Mattatayah Antigonus ben Antipater!" Her voice boomed with more volume than was prudent. Heads turned but no one seemed to catch the dangerous name Anna uttered. They all assumed the Temple Mother was lecturing the younger woman on a matter of Temple protocol.

Mariamne, "That's too dangerous mother. The authorities will kill him."

"God has brought this child into the world my daughter. God protects his own. Call the child what you wish when at home but his official name in the Temple records must be that of his royal Hasmonean ancestor."

Princess Mariamne acceded to the demands of Mother Anna. Although we in the family called him Yeshua, the official Temple records listed the name as "Mattatayah ben Antipater". Priest Joseph sent a note to his father Heli suggesting the regnal name Antigonus was too dangerous to record at the Temple. Heli agreed.

After completion of the Temple ceremony, Anna stopped Mariamne and Joseph one last time with sad news and a warning. Zechariah, husband of Elizabeth and father of Yochanan the Baptizer, had been murdered on the Temple grounds shortly after Yeshua was born. Herodian soldiers grabbed him in the courtyard of the Gentiles and questioned him regarding the whereabouts of his wife and son. He had sent them into hiding at Bethany with relatives but lied to the soldiers claiming he had no knowledge of their whereabouts. A soldier stuck a sword to Zechariah's throat and asked the question again but Zechariah refused to yield information. They slit his throat leaving the noble priest to bleed to death on the Temple grounds. Anna begged her daughter to leave the country immediately as the Romans were sure to retake Jerusalem.

Chapter 11

Alexandria, Egypt (67 CE)

The smell of roasted goat wafted in from the kitchen momentarily distracting the old man from his story. Rhodopis stood over an open flame closely supervising the process of roasting their goat. Menelaus asked his grandson, "Shall I have Rhodopis bring us meat. You must be hungry?"

"A small taste of goat would be wonderful. I have a dinner engagement at the home of my friend Philo."

"Any relation to the writer and philosopher Philo?"

"Yes, his grandson. Did you know him?"

"Not personally. I was just one of the multitude who came to hear him speak on the steps of the library here at Alexandria. This was in the early days after I left the company of Yeshua."

Not wishing to interrupt Rhodopis from her cooking duties, Menelaus went to the kitchen to slice a few pieces of goat for Theudas and draw more wine for himself. The goat still needed more time on the flame to be cooked all the way through so he cut small portions for his grandson from the exterior of the carcass.

Theudas enjoyed the goat his grandfather brought him. "Please give my compliments to Rhodopis. The goat is excellent."

"You can tell her yourself if we ever get her out of the kitchen."

"Mother says you sleep with Rhodopis but, hey, that's your business."

The old man smiled. So the family knew his little secret. "And does this concern you?"

"Of course not grandfather but I thought I'd let you know it is not necessary to continue the charade of your relationship."

"As you have deduced, Rhodopis really isn't my servant. We coexist as equals here. This is in keeping with what Yeshua taught me."

Theudas couldn't resist teasing his grandfather further, "Yeshua taught you to have sexual relations with your servants?"

The old man laughed and threw back a healthy swig of wine. "No, Yeshua taught the aspirant to be celibate. I never knew a more resolute and upright man. What I meant was that Yeshua also taught us to respect one another as equals. He said we are equal because we are one. The concepts of master and servant are an earthly illusion."

This philosophical comment sorely tempted Theudas to follow up with questions as he heard similar teaching attributed to the ancient Greek philosopher Heraclitus regarding his concept of the Logos. Theudas was astonished to hear Yeshua taught a similar concept. The hour fast approached for Theudas to be off to his friend's house and he wished to hear the rest of the story. A discussion of the teachings of Yeshua must wait for another time. Theudas asked, "So your family and that of Yeshua made it out of Palestine?"

"Yes or so I am told. My first vague memories in life were as a child here in Alexandria with Yeshua. We stayed in this country for seven years. Only the Jewish revolt saved Yeshua's life allowing us to escape Palestine. What started out as demonstrations at the Temple for justice against those responsible for the rabbis being burnt alive in the golden eagle incident turned ugly when Archelaus released his military on the demonstrators killing thousands. Three times Governor Varus came to Palestine with legions to put down the revolt. Each time Varus quieted the revolt, Sabinus the incompetent succeeding in enraging the Jews, thereby, reigniting the blaze. Finally Varus set upon Judea with three legions and thousands of auxiliary forces. He also allowed the Nabateans to maul Galilee, an act they were happy to perform."

Theudas, "Quinctilius Varus, why do I know that name?"

Menelaus replied, "Commanding legate of the three legions completely obliterated by the Germans under Arminius in the battle of Teutoburg Forest. Augustus was said to have been near mental collapse when news of the defeat reached him in Rome."

Menelaus presented his grandson with another opportunity to veer off the discussion of Yeshua with his reference to the battle of Teutoburg Forest, a fascinating topic to be sure but not germane to subject at hand. Theudas turned the conversation back to the Jewish revolt of 3 BCE. He said, "What happened to Simon of Perea? You mentioned his forces burned down Herod's palace at Jericho."

"No matter the magnitude of the defeat, the Romans always regroup and return in greater strength. The legions under Varus eventually caught up with Simon and beheaded him, just as Marc Antony had done to King Antigonus."

"The Romans sure had a thing for executing Hasmoneans."

"The Hasmoneans personified Jewish nationalism which the Romans were determined to stamp out and replace with the Herodian royal family but the people never accepted the Herodians. The Jews always saw the Herodians for what they were, Roman puppets."

Theudas said, "So we are now at the point in the story where you and Yeshua are children in Egypt. Who taught Yeshua?"

Menelaus, "He studied with two groups in Egypt, the Essenes and the Therapeutae, who are still based near Lake Mareotis. Are you familiar with them?"

"I have very limited knowledge of this group. They are healers, right?"

"Yes, quite skilled in the healing arts but I think of them more as ascetic monks dedicated to the contemplative life. The Therapeutae eschew the comforts of this world requiring the barest essentials in food, clothing, and shelter. If you read Philo the elder then you may glimpse into the philosophy of the Therapeutae. They study sacred writings seeking the allegorical message that lay buried beneath the superficial meaning of the words. For them, there is an outer story for the masses but, for the initiated, an allegorical interpretation that holds the true knowledge of the text. Their teachings are similar in many but not all respects to the Jewish Essenes, of whom Priest Joseph was an adherent."

Theudas asked, "All manner of religious teachers are found at the agora here in Alexandria yet I never recall hearing a master Therapeutae addressing the people in the city. Why is that so grandfather?"

"Nor will you ever see a Therapeutae master holding forth in the agora. When one commits to the Therapeutae path, he must abandon his mother, father, sisters, brothers, even friends and seclude himself in the desert where the Therapeutae live in small communities. Cities are anathema to the Therapeutae. Why? Because the Therapeutae find it spiritual harmfully to associate with those engaged in the material world seeking fulfillment of their earthly desires. They call such persons spiritually dead and the Therapeutae permit only very limited interaction with anyone outside their own community."

"What is the origin of Therapeutae teaching?"

"To my knowledge the Therapeutae trace their roots back to followers of the Buddha who came to Egypt from India as missionaries in the days of the pharaohs."

Theudas, "Did you study with the Therapeutae?"

"Upon leaving Galilee, Yeshua first lived in Parthia with the royal relations of his maternal grandmother. At age 21, he went to Egypt to begin his training in earnest. The family sent James to study with Yeshua in the Egyptian desert for one year. I was the traveling companion of James to Egypt and stayed there one month so I did receive limited instruction from the Therapeutae as a young man."

"Yeshua lived in Parthia?"

"Yes, for almost ten years but he never spoke of it to me except for one event. Those years of his life are a mystery."

"One event?"

"It comes later in the story. First we must return Yeshua to Israel."

Theudas interrupted his grandfather, "One more question from your boyhood. How did the other children relate to Yeshua when he was boy?"

"They feared him. Magi Gaspar came for long visits to our home and taught Yeshua much of his art. By the time he was twelve, Yeshua's skills as a magician were known throughout the city of Sepphoris. Once in front of a hoard of kids in the neighborhood, he made a pigeon out of clay. He gave to it the children to inspect and confirm it was not alive. He then told them he would breathe life into the clay pigeon. He cupped the object in his hands, blew into it, and then pulled the clay apart. A white pigeon took flight from the remnants of the clay object."[57]

"Did you fear him?"

"Never, he was the gentlest human being I have ever known."

Rhodopis reappeared interrupting Menelaus. She addressed him as "master" and wanted to know whether Theudas would stay for the evening meal. Menelaus replied, "My dear, it appears the family has been in on our little secret for quite some time. We can be ourselves in front of them from now on."

Rhodopis, "Whether mistress or servant I still need to know how many there will be for dinner?"

"Just you and I my dear."

Rhodopis left as Menelaus returned his attention to his grandson, "Are you in a hurry to be with your friends? We could continue the story another day."

"No grandfather, I have more time. Please continue."

"We can dispense with further stories of the childhood of me and Yeshua. Let's skip forward to the adult life of Prince Yeshua. Our families returned from Egypt in the 32nd year of the reign of Augustus[58] but not to Judea as Archelaus ruled there.

---

[57] See *The Infancy Gospel of Thomas*, a work known to us from the Nag Hammadi library.

[58] 5 BCE.

Priest Joseph decided we should live in Galilee in the tetrarchy of Antipas thinking it a safer location."

"Safer?"

"When given the choice of entering a pit containing either a wolf or a wild dog, one chooses the wild dog. I meant relative safety given the alternative. We settled in the city of Sepphoris in Galilee. Herod Antipas knew of our residence in his territory yet left the family in peace during the early years. Sepphoris was substantially destroyed by the Nabateans during the revolt against Archelaus after Herod's death but Antipas rebuilt it as a Hellenized Jewish city. Although Galilee was something of a backwater in the Syrian province of the Roman Empire, Sepphoris had more of a cosmopolitan feel to it by comparison. I enjoyed my childhood days there but everyone must finally cast away the child and bear the mantle of adulthood. Yeshua spent his formative years studying in stoic seclusion in the deserts of Egypt. My education and experiences, on the other hand, tended more toward the epicurean."

Theudas, "So you enjoyed the years of your youth grandfather?"

"Yes grandson, I surely did!"

Chapter 12

Sepphoris, Galilee (32 CE)

Yeshua disapproved of my lifestyle when he returned to us from his religious training in Egypt yet he never stopped loving me. The rabbi did not judge others. He said, "Pull the plank out of your own eye before reaching to remove the speck from that of your brother."[59] Yeshua's stepfather Priest Joseph was serious and devout. He fathered three more children by Mariamne—James, Joses and Mariamne bat Joseph—then took a life-long Nazarite vow, which consists of three major elements. First, Nazarites consume nothing from the vine, including wine, grapes, and olives. This is why they do not put olive oil on their bodies. Second, the razor never touches the hairs of their head. And last, they never come in contract with a dead body. The final element of the Nazarite oath has a double meaning. Not only is a Nazarite under a vow to avoid physically dead bodies but it also means to avoid the company of those who are spiritually dead, meaning everyone who has not undergone a Nazarite initiation. This is why those under a Nazarite vow separate themselves from all other beings except members of their own community. They live simple, ascetic lives while under the vow. They devote themselves to spiritual purity. Priest Joseph retired to the countryside outside of Sepphoris, near the small village of Japhia, and gathered around himself others also following the Nazarite way. Several of the rabbi's older sons from his first marriage joined him there and,

---

59 *Matthew* 7:4.

later, his youngest sons James and Joses. This place came to be known as the village of the Nazarenes or Nazareth.

Having studied under the Essenes, Therapeutae, and the magi in Babylon, Yeshua joined the community at Nazareth also taking a Nazarite vow upon his return from exile although the elderly Priest Joseph had already passed on to the kingdom of heaven. After one year at Nazareth, Yeshua ritually presented himself in Jerusalem where his hair was shorn and sacrificed. He returned to us in Sepphoris a fully initiated rabbi. This marked the first stage in preparation for his public life when he would lay claim to the Jewish throne that was his birthright.

Tiberias, Galilee (32 CE)

Before Yeshua launched his political campaign, Herod Antipas called Yeshua to his vast palace at Tiberias on the western shore of the lake. He took the young rabbi of royal birth out onto the balcony with a spectacular view for many miles into his kingdom. Antipas offered to name Yeshua his heir and lobby the Romans to appoint Yeshua to the Sanhedrin in Jerusalem. In return, Yeshua was to publicly support Antipas' bid for kingship. Essentially, Antipas was asking Yeshua to supplicate himself to Antipas in return for the pocket kingdoms of Galilee and Perea upon the death of Antipas.

Antipas said, "All this will one day be yours Prince Yeshua. Just throw your lot in with me and I will make it happen."

Yeshua replied, "How can you give that which already belongs to me?" Yeshua saw the Jewish kingdom as his Hasmonean birthright, not something over which Antipas or the Romans possessed any authority. Further, as a purist Nazarene, it was utterly impossible for Yeshua to align himself with Antipas. It would have been a pact with the devil. The Herodian tetrarch was abhorrent to my master. Few ever understood the inner complexity of Prince Yeshua. He preached a relaxed application of Jewish law, washing the inside of the cup instead of the exterior, yet his discipline of body and spirit were unparalleled. He never compromised his principles in exchange for the easy path. Not for riches, not on pain of death. He remained upright never bending.

Antipas addressed Yeshua, "Do you reject me boy?"

Yeshua replied bluntly, "I do."

"Then we are enemies Yeshua. You shall be crushed should you ever challenge me."

Sepphoris, Galilee (32 CE)

The elder Princess Mariamne pulled her son aside after he returned from his audience with Herod Antipas. She said, "My son, it is time you took a wife. If you aspire to be king, you must have a queen." She had been prodding her son for years to end his Nazarite ways and take a wife but to no avail. Not only were Jewish kings expected to marry but also to procreate.[60] Fathering a child demonstrated to the people the strength of the royal line. She hoped now her son would see the importance of undertaking his duties as a future king.

The Nazarene way was marked by celibacy for all those who were full initiates. Many were called but very few became full initiates of the Nazarene faith. They never sought bodily pleasures, not even within the confines of marriage. However, Yeshua knew the political realities implicit in his mother's demand. A wife he must have although he felt a bit of resentment at his mother's bold course of action in tackling the subject head-on. He replied, "I assume you have a candidate in mind. Out with it mother."

She replied, "Princess Mariam bat Archelaus, daughter of Princess Mariam bat Aristobulus."

Yeshua paused to consider his mother's chosen bride, whom he had never met. She was the twenty five year old daughter of his uncle Archelaus, the former ethnarch who was Herod's prime heir. The Romans purged Archelaus from office in the thirty-second year of the reign of Augustus[61] after he divorced Mariam bat Aristobulus for Glaphyra, the famed widow of Archelaus' dead Hasmonean brother Alexander. All Herodian princesses lusted after Glaphyra and she finally belonged to Archelaus but at a terrible cost. Divorcing his popular Hasmonean

---

60 See the Torah's injunction to "Be fruitful and multiply." *Genesis* 1:28.

61 6 CE.

wife for a thrice-married Greek princess didn't play well with the Jewish people. Their simmering dislike of Herod Archelaus boiled over into open riots in Jerusalem, which forced the Roman hand to remove the young ethnarch. Not only did Archelaus lose his throne but Glaphyra died shortly after marrying the brother of her first husband. Rumors circulated that Prince Alexander (her dead husband) haunted Glaphyra nightly after her marriage to Archelaus leading to her untimely demise. A more plausible rumor was that the Herodian women united against the hated Glaphyra and saw to her quiet exit from this world.

Archelaus died in exile in Gaul at a young age. This chain of events worked to the advantage of Princess Mariam bat Aristobulus (Mariam Magdalene). She loathed her former husband Archelaus, who returned to her a massive dowry at the time of the divorce. This rich dowry had been provided by Caesar Augustus himself perhaps out of remorse over authorizing the execution of her father by Herod. Princess Mariam, the rich royal widow, was a curious case to Yeshua. She received numerous offers of marriage from politically ambitious Herodians yet remained unmarried after her divorce from Archelaus over twenty years in the past. Yeshua made her acquaintance on numerous occasions and found her to hold Jewish nationalist views. This was so despite Miriam's bloodline containing three-quarters Herodian and only one-quarter Hasmonean ancestry. She drew close with Yeshua's mother, the elder Princess Mariamne. Mariam retired from public life to Galilee where she owned an extensive villa in Cana, a short distance from Sepphoris. Clearly Yeshua's mother and Mariam already reached agreement on the betrothal of Miriam's daughter to Yeshua. The young princess Mariam held the highest ranking Herodian-Hasmonean bloodline of her generation. All Herodian princes of note sought her hand so it was quite a coup for Princess Mariamne to secure the prize for Yeshua.

The elder Princess Mariamne expected her son to at least be impressed with the high royal status of her candidate to be his queen. Would it hurt for him to show some appreciation for her hard work? He stared off into the distance momentarily ignoring his mother then inquired, "I suppose you have a meeting arranged with her family?"

His mother replied, "I invited Mariam and her family for the evening meal."

"When?"

"Tonight." Mariamne intended to strike while the iron was hot thereby denying her son the chance to wander off into the wilderness and change his mind about marriage.

Yeshua did not protest the invitation. He asked, "Who will be the senior male in her party?"

"Her brother Lazarus."

Yeshua, "I shall discuss the matter with Lazarus this evening." The rabbi then left his mother's house for a long solitary walk, as was his custom in those days. He could disappear into his thoughts for hours at a time.

Later that evening, Princess Mariam bat Aristobulus arrived in the company of her brother Prince Lazarus[62] and her daughter the young Princess Mariam. As an unmarried woman, Princess Mariam was under the legal protection of Lazarus. It was he who introduced his niece (the young princess) to Yeshua. She was demur and a ravishingly beautiful young woman. At that moment, I would have given anything I owned to trade places with Yeshua. My mother Yohanna came over scolding me for staring too intently at the young princess. Yeshua greeted her pleasantly but still distant. I couldn't understand his body language at the time. Did he disapprove of the girl?

Introductions concluded the men and women retired to separate rooms to recline and be served. Yeshua, his brothers, Lazarus, and I dined in one room while the four Mariamnes (Mariamne the mother of Yeshua, Mariam Magdalene, Mariam daughter of Mariam, and Mariamne sister of Yeshua) together with my mother Yohanna dined in an adjoining room. Although Yeshua had been released from his Nazarite vow, he only drank

---

[62] Eleazar is the Hebrew equivalent for the name Lazarus. However, this work operates under the theory that the Biblical Lazarus was Aristobulus ben Aristobulus, eldest son of Aristobulus ben Herod. The elder Aristobulus was one of the two Hasmonean sons Herod executed in 7 BCE.

wine at religious festivals and refrained from the eating of animal flesh. Those in his company drank in moderation out of respect for his upright ways.

Yeshua started the conversion, "Lazarus, tell us the news from Rome."

Lazarus, "The talk of the town is of Tiberius voluntarily leaving Rome for exile."

"Voluntarily? Who was left in charge at the palace?"

"It's all very strange. Caesar does not appear to desire to govern. He put Sejanus, prefect of his Praetorian Guard, in charge of the city and sailed for the Island of Capri. No one knows if the emperor is on an extended vacation or if this is something more permanent."

"And what of family? I understand your brother Agrippa is in Rome."

Lazarus was amused by the fact that Yeshua asked about Agrippa for the rabbi could pass as his twin.[63] Lazarus replied, "Yes rabbi. I stayed with my brother Agrippa while in Rome. In years past, he was forced to quit the city by his creditors but still lives an extravagant lifestyle he can't afford. Herod Boethus and Antipas previously subsidized him but even they could not sustain such a drain on their funds. I fear Agrippa will be forced into prison for his debts."

Such a lifestyle was antithetical to all Yeshua stood for yet he said nothing. Lazarus continued, "His one chance at salvation comes through his childhood friendship with Caligula. They whore together and are cut from the same cloth. Caligula may have the inside track to succeed his great uncle as emperor but no one can say with Roman politics. It is a blood sport."

Yeshua, "Are things any different in Jerusalem?"

---

[63] The Talmud at Tosefta Sanhedrin IX.9 appears to indicate that Yeshua had a twin who was a king and "ruled over the whole world", which I take to mean the entire Jewish world. *See* The Seductiveness of Jewish Myth: Challenge or Response? by S. Daniel Breslauer (SUNY Press 1997) at page 97. Herod Agrippa ruled over the entire Jewish kingdom and was a contemporary of Yeshua.

"No rabbi. It is the same. Family members poison one another while scratching their way toward power."

"And if Caligula does become emperor shall your brother rise with him?"

"There is no doubt. I saw the closeness of those two with my own eyes. Caligula will make Agrippa a king."

"And what sort of king do you suppose your brother would make?"

This was a dangerous question for Lazarus to answer. For Agrippa was not the sort to forgive slights. Should he denounce his brother, the words could come back to haunt Lazarus if and when Agrippa rose to the throne. Still, Lazarus spoke his mind. "Should my brother ascend to the Jewish throne, woe to his subjects. He'll tax them dry. Agrippa cares for no one but Agrippa. The Jews will not suffer him lightly I'm afraid. It will all go downhill in a hurry."

Yeshua said nothing although a faint smile crossed his lips. After conclusion of the elaborate meal the elder Princess Mariamne served to her guest, Yeshua asked Lazarus to join him for an evening walk. Lazarus expected he and Yeshua were to engage in the standard practice of haggling over young Princess Miriam's dowry but Yeshua surprised his future brother-in-law.

Yeshua said, "Cousin, thank you for informing me of the news from Rome. I enjoyed the conversation."

Lazarus assumed the soft-spoken rabbi found it difficult to initiate talk of marriage so he took the initiative. "I too enjoyed the conversation rabbi but I believe we have another topic for the two of us to discuss this evening."

Yeshua, "This is true cousin. I shall not be asking for the hand of young Princess Mariam."

Lazarus stopped walking to look Yeshua in the eye. The decision struck him as an insult and he expected an explanation. Yeshua touched Lazarus' shoulder in a gesture of friendship and motioned that they should continue their walk. Yeshua said, "I wish to ask for the hand of the elder Princess Mariam instead."

"You wish to marry the mother, not the daughter? Rabbi, I love my sister dearly and she certainly would serve you as a devoted wife but you do realize she is over forty years of age? It is unlikely she bears children again." Lazarus left unsaid the unseemly fact that Mariam had been betrothed to Yeshua's father as a child. The proposal struck Lazarus as unusual on several levels.

Yeshua replied, "I realize this cousin. I don't intend to father children by any woman. My destiny from birth has been to reclaim the Hasmonean throne. For this I require a wife and it is especially important she be of Hasmonean blood; however, I refuse to compromise my faith in the pursuit of temporal power. You know that I am Nazarene?"

"I confess ignorance in this regard Prince Yeshua. I was told you studied abroad in Egypt but I assumed you were a Pharisee."

"No cousin, my path is not that of the Pharisees. There is much to discuss of the spiritual message I bring but tonight is not the night for that topic. First there is the matter of Mariam. I do not wish to conclude a contract without speaking to her first. Do I have your permission to present my proposal to her personally? The two of us must be of one mind on the covenant."

"Of course rabbi, speak to Mariam."

Lazarus had no idea how she would react to the proposal for it truly came out of the blue. The two Hasmonean princes returned to the home of the elder Princess Mariamne where the women now joined the men for evening conversation. Yeshua and Lazarus reclined together on one side of the room directly across from Princess Mariam and her daughter. Out of deference, the women waited to be addressed before speaking.

Yeshua said to the elder Princess Mariam, "Your daughter has grown into a beautiful young lady."

Never one to mince words, Mariam replied, "Rabbi is that a pleasant compliment to your dinner guest or a marriage proposal for my daughter?"

Yeshua and Lazarus laughed, which upset Mariam. She did not think the betrothal of her royal daughter was a laughing matter.

Yeshua swatted the question away like a fly, "Lazarus and I spoke of your brother Agrippa earlier this evening. What thoughts have you on your brother?"

Now he wants to talk family gossip? Mariam decided to humor the rabbi figuring he would eventually get around to the subject of betrothal. She said, "Agrippa is a thorn in the side of all of us. He constantly writes demanding money. I no longer even respond to his correspondence. Herod Boethus cut the leach off so he begs my sister to lobby his case. No amount of treasure could satisfy the man. When we send him money, it falls through his fingers like water into the purses of the finest prostitutes in Rome."

Yeshua continued on to another member of the family, "Do you know Herod Antipas approached me offering an alliance?"

"Yes, I know that rabbi."

"Then you know my response."

"Yes."

Yeshua continued this line of questioning, "How does this sit with you? I understand your brothers Herod and Agrippa are on friendly terms with Antipas."

"Must I respond?"

"You don't have to do anything. I have no power over you. This is merely dinner conversation."

Mariam took offense at the remark. "Don't insult me rabbi. That question is loaded with serious political implications."

Yeshua got up and walked across the room to Mariam. "Come Mariam. Let us enjoy the breeze in the courtyard."

More than a few eyebrows were raised among the dinner guests as Yeshua and Mariam separated themselves from the rest. Once alone Yeshua said, "I was born for one thing, to be king. It was the sole reason my father and mother procreated. I am bound by that fate."

Mariam, "You forget that I was there when your father was laid in his grave. I know why you were born. And I expect no less from you than to seek the Hasmonean thrown that is rightfully yours."

"My goal will be mastery over all the Jewish lands held by our Hasmonean forbearers. It not only means war with the Romans but also deposing Antipas."

"The political realities of your mission are known to me rabbi."

"Then you are aware that my mission requires going to war with your brothers Herod and Agrippa should they side with the Romans. You do see the seriousness of what I am asking?"

Mariam understood that Yeshua intended to initiate a civil war to reclaim the Hasmonean throne. Until just now, she hadn't really thought through the implications for her own family. The civil war Yeshua intended would likely divide Mariam from her own brothers and sister Herodias. But what Mariam didn't understand was why Yeshua chose to address these questions to her instead of Lazarus as was customary. Concerns of the mother were addressed indirectly between the women of the family, not directly by the prospective groom. She asked, "Rabbi, you and I were born into a family at war with itself. The dangers you outline are something that has been part of my life these many years. My daughter and I are ready to stand at your side come what may."

Yeshua said, "I do not require your daughter at my side, only you."

Mariam stared into the eyes of her younger cousin not quite sure she heard him correctly. "What did you just say? I think I'm confused."

Yeshua, "I don't wish to marry the young princess. I asked Lazarus to sign a contract of betrothal between the two of us; however, I want your agreement to the proposal first."

"I don't understand rabbi. My daughter is ready to bear children. My time is past."

Yeshua responded, "You call me rabbi because I have undergone extensive training in Jewish law but I am a Nazarene and those of our order do not procreate. I cannot put aside my faith to claim the Hasmonean throne."

Mariam still didn't understand. If his faith forbade procreation and he refused to renounce his faith to seek the throne, why did he ask for her hand in marriage?

Yeshua continued, "I seek a partner in my life's mission. That means not only the quest for the throne but, also, my spiritual quest to grow in knowledge of the lord. My wife must be Nazarene. We shall both be bound by the rules of the order which forbid not only procreation but sexual relations of any sort. We shall be one in spirit but not in body. To achieve this, I require that my wife cleanse herself by living a Nazarite vow for one year prior to our marriage."

These terms were completely unexpected by Mariam. What was a chaste marriage? Now Mariam understood why the rabbi chose her instead of the young princess. Mariam already had a child. Further, she had lived a celibate life without a husband for the past twenty-five years. Continuing in this fashion would not be a burden to her. But Mariam was only willing to give up the freedom she enjoyed as an unmarried woman with her own estate if Yeshua proposed a true partnership. When she divorced Herod Archelaus, a very large dowry provided by Augustus Caesar himself was returned to her. Could this seemingly benevolent rabbi be after the money?

Mariam said, "Rabbi, you are proposing a partnership then, one where we share all things but intimacy. Is that correct?"

"Precisely!" Yeshua was relieved Mariam grasped the nature of the relationship he proposed.

"What about the dowry? Who shall control it?"

"I have no need to control your property Mariam. If you feel tradition dictates that a dowry price be named in the marriage contract then have Lazarus write the terms such that you retain control over the property. I find material possessions to be a burden."

He spoke words she had never heard from a rabbi. These men lorded over their women upon the authority they claimed from the Torah. She asked, "Who will instruct me in the ways of the Nazarene order?"

Yeshua said, "I shall instruct you personally. I wish for you to be an initiate of the inner wisdom."

None of the Jewish sects known to Mariam allowed women to be full members. "Women may be initiated rabbi?"

Yeshua, "Laws should never keep one from the path to God. The path is open to both men and women who enter through the straight gate. Those living a celibate life loose attachment to gender."

Despite the harshness of the ascetic Nazarene way, the prospect of studying with Yeshua inexplicably thrilled her. Miriam's father had been executed when she was a child. Her first husband, whom she barely knew, was also executed. Her second husband was a pompous ass. This man Yeshua walked a completely different path from any royal person she had encountered in life. He was upright, peaceful of spirit and noble. He treated her with respect. She had one last question, "And what of your political life rabbi? Will you consult me in your decisions? If I join you in this mission, then both of our lives shall be at risk when you claim the throne."

Yeshua responded, "This is true Mariam. As my wife you shall share the risk I am duty bound to take. For this reason, I shall consult you in all things." He proposed they share their lives completely, spiritually as well as politically. Yeshua sought the agápe of true spiritual love in his relationship with Mariam.

She said, "I accept your offer rabbi and look forward to studying under your guidance; however, you have put conditions on the marriage proposal and I wish to do the same."

"Oh?"

"You must agree not to take another wife and to adopt my daughter Mariam. As you know, her father Archelaus is deceased."

Mariam was no pushover. What Jewish princess was? Yeshua respected her strength and viewed it as a compliment rather than a threat to his own power. Yeshua replied, "Done." An embrace sealed the betrothal of Prince Yeshua to Princess Mariam Magdalene. Little did we know then where this union would lead us all. For in truth, the union of Yeshua and Mariam was the foundation upon which the Yeshua movement was built.

Chapter 13

Petra, Nabatea (34 CE)

Yeshua set out on a diplomatic mission to foreign leaders prior to launching his campaign for the throne. First stop was the nearby kingdom of Nabatea. We journey south from Galilee to the Dead Sea then southeast to the capital of the Nabatean Empire, Petra, home to King Aretas IV. Herod's mother was a Nabatean of noble birth from Petra, which meant Yeshua also carried a drop Nabatean blood. Despite the blood relationship, Herod continually battled this neighboring regional power striving, but never succeeding, to dominate Nabatea as the kingdom remained independent. Nabatea derived the bulk of its wealth from the sale of spices such as myrrh obtained from the far south of Arabia. The Silk Road also passed through the northern portion of the empire adding to the country's strategic importance. The plethora of temples devoted to the pantheon of gods habituating the Roman world devoured incense for use in religious and burial ceremonies thus fueling Nabatean trade. The Greek historian Strabo relates the story of Syllaeus,[64] chief minister to Obodas (immediate predecessor of Nabatean King Aretas IV), guiding a Roman general and 10,000 Roman legionnaires on a wild goose chase through the Arabian Desert seeking the source of the valuable incense Roman temples consumed. The incense source monopolized by the Nabateans was never located on this expedition while thousands of Roman soldiers perished in the desert. Such was the resourcefulness of the Nabatean people.

---

[64] This is the same Syllaeus who Salome, sister of Herod, wished to marry and the Romans later executed at the urging of Prince Antipater ben Herod.

In a bid for a lasting alliance with his Jewish neighbors Nabatean king Aretas IV married his daughter Phasaelis to Herod Antipas, tetrarch of Galilee and Perea. Despite over twenty years of marriage, correspondence from the king's daughter now suggested the union with Antipas was on the rocks. Antipas vacationed in Rome without his wife and all men of power philandered while on travel; however, sources told Princess Phasaelis that her husband's activities went beyond the usual dalliance with courtesans. The real power behind the Herodian dynasty was and always had been Rome. Thus, any Herodian seeking political advancement made frequent and lengthy trips to the power center of the western world. Herod Antipas had been in Rome for over six months and, rumor had it, was in the midst of a torrid affair with his brother's wife, Herodias (sister of Yeshua's wife Mariam). So our visit to Petra started off on an awkward foot—rumors swirling in the palace of Yeshua's sister-in-law fornicating with Aretas' son-in-law. Undaunted, Yeshua hoped to find King Aretas amenable to an alliance.

One entered the city of Petra from the Wadi Moses through the siq, a winding narrow path cut out of rock. The siq was no more than five meters wide in stretches, barely enough room for two camels to pass traveling in opposite directions. Petra was like no other city in the world, a marvel hewed from rock. Surrounded by sandstone cliffs of varying hues, it was a natural fortress cut directly into soft rock cliffs. The Nabateans crafted an ingenious hydraulic system of channels and cisterns to control and store water during the infrequent rainfalls. The natural fortifications and self-sustaining water supply made the city virtually impervious to attack.

Mariam Magdalene, her daughter Princess Mariam, I and six additional members from our community based in Galilee escorted Yeshua on his royal diplomatic mission. The purpose of this trip was to seek foreign alliances prior to Yeshua launching his public campaign for the Jewish throne. Upon arrival, servants directed our party to the throne room for an audience with King Aretas. We were seated waiting a short amount of time before a herald announced the entrance of the king, "Aretas King of Nabatea, Friend of his People."

A relatively succinct and unassuming title for an eastern king but of import. By "Friend of his people", Aretas intended a counterpoint to one of the many titles Obodas, his predecessor, used—"friend of Rome". Aretas never went to Augustus seeking Roman confirmation of his office and styled himself as a populist king. Aretas was his own man, something no Jewish king had been since the Hasmonean dynasty. Further, Aretas never claimed to be a god, another point of departure from the reign of Obodas. The king took his seat then stared intently at Yeshua. At the time, I mistakenly believed this act to be some sort of diplomatic ploy designed to give Aretas the upper hand in his future dealings with Yeshua. I was mistaken. Aretas possessed a keen interest in Yeshua, the man.

He finally spoke, "I knew your father well having first met him in Rome. He supported my petition to Caesar for the execution of my adversary, Syllaeus. Years later, then Crown Prince Antipater sought an alliance including intermarriage between our two families. He spoke of his impending marriage to the daughter of King Antigonus who was to be his queen and pledged the first son of that union as a husband to one of my daughters. Now, these many years later, that son of Antipater arrives in my court."

The opening statement of the king blew Yeshua away. He hadn't known just how close his father's prior association with Aretas had been or that the rabbi had been pledged to marry a Nabatean princess. What exactly did Aretas have in mind? On personal and religious grounds, taking another wife was out of the question. Yeshua fretted that diplomatic negations with the Nabatean king were dead in the water before even getting under way. Yeshua replied, "His highness knows my father died prior to my birth. It's rare that I speak with individuals who personally knew him so I thank you for the remembrance. But I must ask, does the king wish to hold me to the promise of my father?"

Aretas responded, "No prince. The promise died with your father. Forgive an old man for taking time to reflect on what might have been. Your father was a skilled politician, practical in his approach. He did our country a great service in helping to rid us of that villain Syllaeus. I never would have prevailed on Rome to execute the man without the support of your father. He dreamed of a broad alliance between the Jewish kingdom and Nabatea giving each of us greater strength in our dealings with Rome. Had he lived, I believe his dream would have been realized and this prince seated before me today would be my son-in-law. Our world lost a great king through the madness of Herod."

Yeshua, "Not a day goes by that I do not reflect on my father and what might have been. Thank you your highness for granting me a truer glimpse of that loss."

After the emotional exchange that opened Yeshua's audience with King Aretas, the meeting devolved into standard fare of court conversation: introduction of dignitaries, exchange of gifts, and speeches of greeting. King Aretas invited us to dine at his table that evening. The king was gracious but formal in his tone after the opening exchange. Prince Shimon, a grandson of King Aretas, showed our party to our quarters within the palace after the first audience with the king concluded. Aretas maintained only one wife so his grandchildren held greater status than in other eastern kingdoms where the rulers married multiple wives. As servants delivered our baggage, Yeshua discretely pulled me aside requesting I find out the exact position Prince Shimon held at court. In advance of our trip, I prepared a report for Yeshua listing all the prominent members of King Aretas' court. To my dismay, Prince Shimon was not on the list leaving my master in the dark. King Aretas selected Shimon to act as something of an advance scout / ambassador to Yeshua. Aretas knew Yeshua had not arrived on a social call so he sent his grandson to try and smoke out his visitor's intentions. During the commotion of settling everyone with their baggage, I slipped away to question a guard about Shimon. All he would divulge was that Shimon was highly regarded by the king and commanded an elite cavalry unit of the Nabatean army. Thus, I was not then able to inform my master of the relationship of Prince Shimon to King Aretas.

Prince Shimon invited Yeshua on a tour leaving the servants to sort out the baggage and room assignments.

The exposed stone walls of the buildings of Petra exhibited a rose color; however, little of the underlying stone could be seen as one walked through the city. Petra was a city of vibrantly painted colors. Every major public institution contained elaborate, Hellenistic murals on its interior walls. The god Dionysus was a favorite theme of local artists. Scenes of nature populated by flowers, birds and insects were found everywhere in the city. Shimon gave Yeshua a tour of the Nabatean royal treasury.

Yeshua said, "Your coins have likenesses of both the king and queen."

Shimon, "Yes, I know Jewish law forbids display of graven images but in Nabatea as elsewhere the king's image appears on coins."

"I understand prince but that was not my reason for asking. Other kingdoms may display the likeness of the king but I rarely see both the king and queen shown side by side. Does your father rule as an equal with his queen?"

"She does not rule but women have many rights under the law in Nabatea they do not enjoy in other kingdoms. Her likeness is depicted on our coins because in ancient times succession in tribes of Arabia was matrilineal. The queen's blood legitimized the king's rule."

"Is this so today?"

"The concept is followed less rigidly today yet the people still remember the old ways. My father's queen is of royal Nabatean blood so she appears on the coins as a reminder to the people."

Yeshua, "Our two peoples are not so different then."

Shimon, "The Jewish king must have a wife of Jewish royal blood?"

"It is the ancient ideal of King David who himself was not of royal blood yet legitimized his rule by marrying the daughter of the former king of the tribe of Benjamin, who was Saul. Herod also followed this model as he was a man lacking Jewish royal blood who legitimized his rule by taking a Hasmonean queen."

Shimon smiled and said, "I know all about King Herod."

Yeshua, "Yes, he was a famous ruler . . . ."

Shimon, "Cousin, it is one's duty to learn the history of his own grandfather. Don't you agree?"

Yeshua stopped and turned to look more closely at the face of Prince Shimon of Petra. He scolded himself for not making the connection sooner then said, "You are the son of Herod Antipas."

Shimon laughed, "We have never met so forgive my uncle for not altering you to this fact during the official introductions. We thought it might be amusing to see how long it took you to recognize me."

Yeshua hugged his cousin-german. "It is so very good to make your acquaintance. Why are you not in your father's tetrarchy overseeing his affairs while he is in Rome?"

Shimon replied, "My father refuses to give me official position with any real power. I'm allowed to command a century of horse with the rank of tribune but have received no authority in the palace. His manumitted slaves possess more authority in the palace than I."

"And does your presence here in Petra signify anything in regard to your father?"

"I have never been close with my father. I shall turn my back on him if he divorces my mother, which apparently is all but done."

Yeshua inquired further, "And King Aretas has appointed you to a command in his military in anticipation of you severing ties with your father?"

"That is correct cousin."

Shimon and Yeshua discussed the size and composition of the Nabatean military as they walked down a broad central street of the city to the Temple of Dushara, the principal god of the city. Yeshua changed subjects, "I see Temples to other gods besides Dushara worshipped in the city. How do the other gods relate to Dushara?"

"Dushara is the god without equal. All others gods are merely emanations or aspects of Dushara, the one true god for the Nabatean people."

"Is Dushara knowable?"

"A wise question Prince Yeshua. The common people who worship at the temples believe so but the initiate learns that a human only interacts with emanations from Dushara. One can no more know Dushara than know the sun. We feel the sun's rays as they reach us here on earth but the sun does not physically come down to earth and commune with humans."

Yeshua was pleasantly surprised by the deep religious conversation he was able to engage in with Shimon, who he understood to be a soldier. Yeshua said, "Possession of this knowledge marks you as an initiate in the mysteries of Dushara. I had thought you might be a practicing Jew."

"I am trained in both faiths. It is an easy trip from my father's fortress at Macherus to Petra. In truth, much of my adult life has been spent in Nabatea. My grandfather favors me more than my own father."

"Do you aspire to sit on a throne one day Shimon?"

"Does not every prince so aspire?"

Yeshua smiled for he knew the statement applied to them both. "So it is Shimon. So it is."

Shimon said, "But my road to the throne is blocked here in Nabatea. My grandfather the king has three sons."

"The road of life has many twists and turns. One never knows where a prince's path may ultimately lead."

"And what of your path Prince Yeshua?"

"I was born for one reason, to reclaim the throne of my grandfather Antigonus who was the last Hasmonean king and high priest."

"That is a lofty goal."

"As a man thinketh in the heart, so is he. One must first believe in his own heart Shimon."

The pair walked along quietly for a time. As they made their way past the temples and into the residential portions of the city, Shimon inquired, "I hear you are also an accomplished healer Prince Yeshua. Perhaps you will assist us with a troubling case."

Shimon stopped before the door of a modest house. He said, "This is the home of a soldier under my command. His child has been unable to eat for days. She's warm to the touch. The child is now very weak and our doctors fear for her life. Would you mind taking a look at her to see if anything can be done?"

Yeshua never refused to assist one in need. He said, "Show the way Prince Shimon." Yeshua followed the young prince of Petra into the soldier's home. They were greeted by the grim continence of James, father of the young girl clinging to life. Yeshua recognized the soldier as a Jew. The armies of the Near East contained many a Jewish mercenary as they were known to be fierce warriors and skilled in the art of death.

Shimon introduced Yeshua as a prince and rabbi of the Hasmonean dynasty. James formerly came to attention upon hearing the identity of his august visitor. Yeshua said, "At ease soldier. I come as a friend. What is your tribe?"

James replied, "Judah."

"Son of Judah, do you believe your daughter can be healed of this illness?"

"The doctors say she will die before the next sunrise."

"That's not what I asked. Do you believe?"

James fixed his gaze deeply into the eyes of Yeshua. What he saw therein, no one knows, however, his demeanor sharply changed. Calm replaced fear. Tension drained from his body. James said, "Yes rabbi, I believe."

Yeshua then turned to the Nabatean prince, "And you Shimon, do you believe? Our thoughts carry power. We must all be in agreement."

Shimon shuffled his feet apprehensive at being put on the spot. He didn't believe. The Nabatean doctors said the child would die, thus, Shimon fully expected the dark hand of death to visit this home shortly. Yeshua read Shimon's thoughts. No response was necessary. Yeshua said, "Please do us the favor Shimon of waiting outside while James and I attend to his daughter."

Prince Shimon did as requested but felt embarrassed in front of one of his men. His temper began to rise while he waited in the street for Yeshua's return. Who does this Jewish prince think he is? He possessed no kingdom, no estates, no army. How exactly did he think he was going to overthrow the Roman legions? Yeshua's plan seemed ludicrous to Shimon and that was what he intended to recommend to his father the king. Why should they waste fine Nabatean troops following some dreamer into battle? "Do you believe?" he asked. Shimon thought, "I believe in my horse, my sword, and the men I have trained."

James watched his commander walk out the door. He turned to Yeshua. "She is in the next room. Let me know if you require anything to treat her. I would move heaven and earth to save this child."

Yeshua replied, "Nothing is required beyond that which you have already given James."

Yeshua went into the next room where he found a pale, frail ten-year old girl nearly comatose in the bed. Yeshua took her by the hand commanding that she rise. He helped her to sit up. The fever suddenly left her body. She got out of the bed for the first time in four days.

"Father, I'm hungry," said the girl.

Under her own power, she walked into the next room to prepare herself a simple meal. James was known in his legion as Boanerges, or son of thunder, due to his rough and often violent demeanor. This son of thunder stood in the kitchen crying like a baby watching his daughter cook.

James said, "Rabbi, I owe you more than you can know. My wife died giving birth to this daughter. She is the sunshine of my life."

"You owe me nothing James."

Yeshua rejoined Shimon in the street. As he had only been in the home a few moments, Shimon assumed Yeshua had quickly seen the truth of the matter, that it was a hopeless case, and so informed the father. The two turned around walking back toward the palace as Shimon tried to check his anger. He said, "It was a lost cause Prince Yeshua. Sorry to have brought you into that home. I just thought you might be able to help."

Yeshua replied, "The cause was not lost. The girl is perfectly fine."

Shimon stared at Yeshua in disbelief. He ran back to the soldier's home and burst inside. James' daughter sat at the kitchen table greedily eating her meal. James, entranced by the vision of his daughter eating her food, barely noticed the reappearance of his commander.

Shimon asked, "James, what the hell happened?"

James came to attention, "I cannot say prince. The rabbi is a healer like none I have ever witnessed. Eternal thanks my lord for having brought him."

Word of Prince Yeshua healing the soldier's daughter spread around the neighborhood but did not cause much excitement at first. The residents of Petra thought it most likely mere coincidence that the child recovered while in the presence of Yeshua. The desert people were, by nature, skeptical. But a few were at least curious about the reported miracle. Aenaeas, chief minister to Aretas, informed me just prior to the scheduled evening meal with the king that a few dozen common citizens of Petra were at the main gate of the palace requesting an audience with Yeshua. He asked, "Does Prince Yeshua wish to grant an audience? I suggest tomorrow morning prior to the midday meal."

I replied, "Minister Aenaeas, I have been long in the employ of Prince Yeshua. Literally from birth. I can tell you he shall wish to see the citizens now."

"Now? But we are to join the king shortly."

"The audience shall be brief. Prince Yeshua would never presume to keep the king waiting."

A blind man could see the propaganda value accruing from Yeshua curing the sick of Petra. I witnessed the power his healing gifts many times in Galilee. As Yeshua authored the unexplainable, people became very emotional. Sometimes he was cursed as a magician of a false god. But most often people revered Yeshua to a degree that made those of us in his company uncomfortable. All who met him were touched in some way. Yeshua came to King Aretas with little to offer in exchange for the king's military support in the coming conflict with the Romans. In my mind, winning over the people of Petra was part of the campaign to win the support of King Aretas (and his soldiers). The smith strikes while the iron is hot. It was time for Yeshua to fan the burning embers of curiosity in the Nabatean people.

I went to him. "Prince Yeshua, the king's minister informs me a group of townspeople wait at the palace gates for an audience with you. Shall I send them in?"

"What do they wish?"

"I can only assume they have heard you cured the soldier's daughter and are here for a cure."

"Menelaus, did you put them up to it? More magic tricks for the locals?"

"I am wounded master. The people come of their own accord. If our political aims are met through helping those in need, how is that wrong?"

"The intention of the act always matters. If a man loudly drops silver coins into the offering chest at the synagogue for the sole purpose of impressing the dignitaries in the front row with the magnificence of his gift, the offering is useless in the eyes of God. Right intention is paramount."

I don't know why Yeshua bothered to preach to me. In those days, it was like preaching to a stone. I was absolutely uninterested in matters of the soul. I said again, "The people are at the gate. Do you want me to turn them away?" I knew he would never turn the people away.

He relented, "Send them in but make it clear the audience shall be limited as we are to dine with the king."

A man lame for many years regained the ability to walk that evening. The legend of Rabbi Yeshua the healer spread like a wild fire through the town of Petra over the following days. Each morning, a throng of people crowded the palace clamoring for Yeshua. The daily function of the palace nearly ground to a halt due to the size of the crowds besieging every gate. King Aretas had a problem on his hands. One of the king's many epithets was "he who loves his people." He could not help but notice the enthusiasm of his people for one Rabbi Yeshua, Hasmonean prince and claimant to the Jewish throne.

Not long thereafter, I received an invitation to share the midday meal with Minister Aenaeas in his private quarters. The

Nabateans knew through Shimon that Yeshua sought a military alliance in his coming insurrection against the Herodians and their Roman masters. Up to this point, we had received no hint of the king's intentions in this regard. He treated us cordially but never broached the subject. As I had hoped, the crowds clamoring for Yeshua forced the king's hand in the matter. The meeting with Aenaeas was the opening move in the diplomatic dance.

After a fine meal of tender goat, dates, and nuts, we reclined on the balcony outside his quarters sipping tea. As a guest, I was bound to wait for my host to bring up the subject we both knew was the reason for this meeting. Aenaeas said, "Tell me Menelaus, who commands Prince Yeshua's troops?"

"He has no troops to command minister. I thought this information was conveyed to Shimon?"

"Then explain to me the plan. How shall Prince Yeshua reclaim the throne of his forbearers? Certainly he does not intend to rely upon his magic tricks?"

"We will build a coalition of supporters just as King Antigonus did in expelling the Romans from Israel. The Parthians, the royal family of Tyre and the large Jewish Diaspora living outside Israel constitute our main allies outside the country. Inside the country we count the Galileans and Idumeans as our staunchest supporters. We are building support in Judea and, of course, hope to add the Nabateans to this alliance."

"And what of Antipas, the ruler of Galilee? Is he not Yeshua's uncle?"

Aretas had thought his grandchild would sit on the thrown in Galilee but Antipas spoiled the plan when he divorced the king's daughter in favor of Princess Herodias. Clearly the king still harbored designs on Galilee. I replied, "There is no love lost between Yeshua and Antipas. When Yeshua is king in Jerusalem, Antipas is out. King Antigonus, the grandfather of Yeshua, ruled Galilee as well as Judea. I am certain Yeshua intends to reclaim all lands ruled by King Antigonus."

"In the east, we have kings who serve under kings. Might not Yeshua appoint a subordinate king to rule over Galilee and Perea?"

Now I saw where the minister was heading with this line of questioning. I asked, "Why would he do this?"

Aenaeas replied, "To reward a valued ally." There it was. The cards were now on the table. King Aretas desired that a Nabatean of his choosing, surely his grandson Shimon, be named king over Galilee and Perea in exchange for his alliance in the coming Jewish rebellion against Rome. If one enjoyed diplomacy as I did, this was where it got interesting. The only mechanism to make the king's suggestion work politically was a marriage between the families of Prince Yeshua and King Aretas.

I said, "I shall communicate our discussion to my master. My thanks for a delightful meal Minister Aenaeas." We had been in Petra for a month waiting to engage the Nabateans in discussions of an alliance. Now that negotiations were upon us, I flew as fast as my clumsy feet could carry me to Yeshua and blurted out the proposal from King Aretas via Aenaeas.

Yeshua scratched his beard while pondering the offer. He said, "So they wish for me to crown Shimon as king of Galilee and Perea?"

I replied, "What is in a title my lord? King, tetrarch, does it matter?"

Yeshua gave me that stare of his. The one that said, "Pay attention for I am about to enlighten you with knowledge." He said, "The messiah is king first and, also, savior of his people from oppression. The messiah must abide in righteousness and possess the proper ancestry as designated in the scrolls. Do you believe Prince Shimon meets the requirement of a Jewish king?"

Yeshua knew I had never studied the scrolls sacred to the desert Hasidim so I was not familiar with the requirements of a messiah under the law of the scrolls. But why must Shimon qualify as a rightful Jewish king if he really was but a mere governor over Galilee and Perea? I replied, "Galilee and Perea were not part of the original Jewish homeland given to them by Yahweh. Why must Shimon be a king to govern these lands? It's only a title. He will be subordinate to you."

He let me know with his eyes that I still didn't understand his point. Yeshua said, "These lands were part of the kingdom ruled by my grandfather, King Antigonus. As messiah I cannot delegate authority over my grandfather's kingdom to someone who lacks the qualifications of a Jewish king. Herod usurped the Jewish throne knowing he lacked the proper legal qualifications. I will not engage in the same action. Shimon is neither Hasmonean nor a descendant of King David. I can't do it. He may hold the title 'governor' but no more."

King Antigonus had only a few small kingdoms in Syria and the Parthians as allies for his revolution. He ended up nailed to a Roman cross. To succeed against the Romans, we needed to build an even stronger coalition. The only other regional power we could hope to bring to the party was Nabatea. Yeshua knew it but he never compromised on his core principles. Many Jewish laws, such as restrictive rules relating to the Sabbath and dietary regulations, he found not to be properly rooted in commandments from God and, thus, ignored them. On the qualifications for kingship, however, Yeshua was steadfast. It was up to me to probe for a compromise position acceptable to both sides, for it was not Yeshua's nature to seek accommodation. He knew but one path to walk in life. I said, "What about a marriage between your royal house and that of King Aretas?"

"How will that solve the problem Menelaus? Even if Shimon marries into my family I cannot appoint him king of Galilee and Perea."

"Not king but regent for his child, a royal child Shimon shall father by his Hasmonean bride."

The smallest of smiles slowly crept across Yeshua's face as he contemplated my plan. It offered us a way out of the entanglements of Jewish law but required a Hasmonean bride for Shimon. Yeshua said, "And who do you propose for bride? The young princess Mariam?"

The young Hasmonean princess whose hand was offered in marriage to Yeshua had later been adopted by him. Yeshua now held the legal right to offer her hand in marriage to any man he so chose. Yeshua began pacing the floor while thinking hard on the matter. Finally he stopped pacing. His body remained motionless as his mind carefully weighed the pros and cons of the decision that lay before him. Finally he said, "Alright Menelaus, you've persuaded me. This might work. The situation with Shimon can be managed. He shall be named regent after fathering a Hasmonean child and have a seat on the Sanhedrin but the power to tax his territory shall be subject to veto by the king. A workable arrangement."

I said, "Well done."

"But final say on the proposal rests with my wife and Princess Mariam. I'll not force a marriage upon them."

"Certainly. I am sure you wish to discuss the matter with the princess privately. By your leave lord."

As I wheeled for the door, Yeshua stopped me. Another thought came to him. "Find out whether Shimon is circumcised. His mother is not Jewish and Nabatean blood predominates in his veins. A Hasmonean princess cannot marry a man whose body is impure under the law."

Donkey turds. I hadn't conceived of the potential elephant in the room. The Roman world viewed circumcision as a form of genital mutilation. They abhorred the practice and the Nabateans were no different. It stood as an enormous obstacle should the prince be uncircumcised. Would a prince have his penis cut on in order to gain a royal wife? I shuttered at the thought.

My worst fears were realized when I found out Prince Shimon was indeed uncircumcised. Two days later, King Aretas summoned Prince Yeshua to the palace throne room. The Nabatean king formally offered military backing in exchange for the marriage of his son Shimon to Princess Mariam together with the promise that Shimon be named regent of Galilee and Perea upon Yeshua's ascension to the Jewish throne but neither party would budge on the issue of circumcision. Shimon refused to have his phallus sheared.

King Aretas said, "Prince Yeshua, you do realize the seriousness of the situation, do you not?"

Yeshua replied, "I realize that our chances of success in retaking the Jewish throne are greater with a Nabatean alliance than without."

"And you know the consequences of failure?" King Aretas made a none-too-subtle reference to the fact that King Antigonus had been crucified and then beheaded when his insurrection against Rome failed.

"Sire, I am acquainted with the history of my own grandfather."

The king let out a gasp of air in frustration. He said, "Jewish law is such a labyrinth. Surely an avenue around this circumcision impasse must exist. I have consulted with our leading rabbis here in Petra and they tell me that there is a class of Jewish convert, the ger tzedek, for whom circumcision is not required."

"Your learned rabbis speak the truth your majesty but my royal daughter shall not marry a ger tzedek. This is a step below full conversion marking the individual as less than a full member of the Jewish community. Some rabbis hold that a ger tzedek may marry into the Jewish community while others forbid it. That's not the point though. Marriage to a ger tzedek is a stain on one's honor in Jewish eyes. A Hasmonean princess may only join with a husband pure under the law and above reproach."

The king said, "Then we are at a true impasse."

"I deeply regret it your majesty but this is where we find ourselves."

King Aretas ended the failed negotiations on a kind note saying, "You are always welcome in my kingdom Prince Yeshua. Go with my blessing."

Yeshua left the deal on the table departing for Babylon the following morning. At the time, I didn't understand his actions. Yeshua was never a rigid proponent of Jewish law. Instead of strict observance of Jewish law, Yeshua preached such things as the importance of love, right action in the eyes of God, washing the inside of the cup versus the outside. I later learned this wasn't about Jewish law. It had been drilled into Yeshua from birth that he came into this world with one purpose—to be king. That he owed an absolute duty to his ancestors to restore the Hasmonean dynasty. Regardless of his personal willingness for flexibility in interpretation of Jewish law, he would not dishonor the Hasmonean blood line. Yeshua was a complex man. Despite being in his company daily for many years there remained much I did not understand about him.

Babylon, Parthian Empire (34 CE)

We reached one of the oldest cities on earth after a long journey east on an ancient east-west trade route. Babylon sits on the fertile Mesopotamian plain between the Tigris and Euphrates rivers and is an important hub on the famed Silk Road. Our reception in Babylon was completely different from Petra. Not that the Nabateans were less than cordial but the Parthians and Jews of Babylon greeted Yeshua as a long lost king returned from the dead. The Jewish exiles viewed Yeshua as their rightful king. As Yeshua and his maternal half-siblings were the only human being on earth of both Jewish and Parthian royal blood, the Parthians treated him with the upmost respect. They fought numerous wars against the Romans over the last century with the promise of more to come. Establishing a friendly dynasty in Palestine as a bulwark against the Romans was a long-held political goal of Parthia. How better to bind Israel to Parthia than by placing a mixed Hasmonean-Parthian royal on the throne? With Israel in the Parthian sphere of influence, any invasion of Parthia must start well to their west in the Jewish homeland. It would be the Jews who first battled the Romans when war next came. If the Jews absorbed the heaviest Roman blows at the start of the next war, it diminished the strength of any Roman legions who later marched east to meet the Parthians in the field.

Five years before Julius Caesar crossed the Rubicon with his single legion to march on Rome,[65] Roman proconsul and triumvir Marcus Licinius Crassus invaded Parthia with 36,000 men. The Parthians slaughtered 20,000 of these (included Crassus and his son Publius) in the battle of Carrhae.[66] Triumvir Marcus Antonius invaded Parthia one year after Jerusalem fell to Herod seeking revenge for the mauling of Crassus and his legions. 70,000 Roman legionnaires and auxiliaries (30,000 more than Crassus had

---

[65] 54 BCE.

[66] Carrhae was also known as Harran. It is in modern day Southeastern Turkey and the ancient hometown of the Jewish patriarch Abraham.

under his command) marched with Antonius yet his legions were likewise swallowed by the vastness of Parthia. Marcus Antonius made it out alive but accompanied by only half the troops with which he started.

The suicide of Antonius in the palace of Queen Cleopatra paved the way for peace between Rome and Parthia. Future Roman emperor Tiberius concluded a peace treaty with Parthian King Phraates in 20 BCE. From that point forward, Parthia became chiefly interested in expanding its empire east and south into the Indian subcontinent. But they still watched their back to the west. What they saw disturbed them. In 6 CE, the Romans deposed King Herod Archelaus annexing Judea, Samaria, and Idumea into the Roman province of Syria, although administering it as a separate prefecture. This expanded the territory they directly controlled further east putting greater pressure on the Nabateans, a buffer kingdom between Rome and Parthia. However, all was not well within the Parthian kingdom during Yeshua's visit to Babylon. Artabanus II, a cruel king raised by barbarians, held a tenuous grip on the Parthian throne at this time with continuous revolts across the empire. So Yeshua walked into a dicey political situation when he arrived in Parthia. Tensions were high inside the Parthian royal house as they expected attack by the Romans while a weak king sat on the Parthian throne. Jewish princes descended from King David (remnants of the Assyrian exile) ruled a defacto pocket kingdom in Babylon at the acquiesce of the Parthian king. These Jewish nobles were the prime targets of Yeshua's diplomatic mission.

Babylon was a thoroughly cosmopolitan city of the east. I availed myself of the bountiful variety of exotic courtesans floating around the elites while Yeshua and Princess Mariam met with Jewish princes and priests of the eastern religions. Here I saw the blossoming of the relationship between Yeshua and Mariam beyond political partners. She applied herself in spiritual study as he desired. Yeshua preferred the Socratic Method whereby the student works for the knowledge attained. Often they went on long walks in the gardens of Babylon discussing spiritual topics. I caught snippets of these conversations while trailing behind the couple. I hated to interrupt Yeshua when in private conversation with Mariam for he truly delighted in her company.

Yeshua said, "Mariam, have you heard the phrase, 'passing from death to life'[67]?"

"No husband."

"Let us inquire upon it's then. How may one be physically alive in the flesh yet dead?"

She replied, "Without the spirit, the body is a hollow vessel."

Yeshua stopped and smiled at his wife so pleased was he by the response. She had grown much in wisdom. The master continued, "Might we further say that this physical vessel lacking the spirit is dead?"

"Truly husband. To be mindful only of the flesh is death."[68]

"And where do the scriptures tell us one finds life?"

"In the way of righteousness. In its path, there is no death."[69]

"And how does one walk in the path of righteousness?"

"Follow God's commandments."

"And is there a way to observe those who have entered through the narrow gate[70] walking on the path of righteousness?"

"I'm not sure husband."

He said, "We judge a tree by its fruit. So it is with man. We recognize those who have awakened from death to life by their acts."[71]

She asked, "The Pharisees follow the law yet you oppose them. Why are they different?"

"I do not condemn a man by party affiliation but by the fruit of their actions. What is the greatest of God's commandments?"

"To love one another."

---

[67] *John* 5:24; 1 *John* 3:14.

[68] *Romans* 8:6.

[69] *Proverbs* 12:28.

[70] *Matthew* 7:13-14.

[71] *Matthew* 7:15-20.

"Yes wife. The Pharisees and officials in the Temple are zealous for laws contrived by man yet, for the most part, neglect the royal law of God. He that loveth not his brother abideth in death."[72]

"But do not the Pharisees teach love?"

"The school of Hillel so teaches while the school of Maimonides does not. In any event, their lawyers have taken away the key to knowledge and buried it within their contrived law of man. They do not enter onto the path of righteousness themselves and, further, hinder the progress of others for they know not the power of love."[73]

* * * * * * * * * *

I entertained many an inquiry from potential suitors for the hand of young Princess Mariam during our stay in Babylon. The Babylonian princes of the House of David were keen to meet this Hasmonean beauty. I referred all such inquiries to Yeshua who ignored them at first. He finally relented allowing young Mariam to accept a handful of dinner engagements. A stream of marriage proposals followed prompting Yeshua to seek the counsel of Magi Gaspar.

Yeshua said, "I am faced with many a marriage proposal for the hand of Princess Mariam. Do you have a recommendation as to which proposal I should accept? I'm inclined to allow Mariam to choose."

The now elderly Gaspar replied, "And how was Mariam disposed to Prince Shimon of Petra?"

"Her mother tells me quite favorably. What young girl does not look fetchingly upon a strapping military officer? But, as I told you, this arrangement could not be consummated to my satisfaction. Shimon must be circumcised, which he refused to do."

---

[72] 1 *John* 3:14.

[73] *Luke* 11:52.

Gaspar said, "I am certain he has changed his mind. Stop in Petra on your return trip. I believe you shall find Shimon minus his foreskin."

Yeshua smiled then asked, "Gaspar, tell me how you work these wonders."

"Recall our conversations from long ago of the three elements of man—body, mind, and spirit?"

Yeshua, "God has three aspects. As it is above, so it is below. Man is made in God's image so he also has three aspects."

"Just so. Have you consciously left your physical body traveling in the etheric body?"

"We call this the garment of light.[74] I have put on the garment of light. This ability came to me during a long period of prayer and fasting in the desert."

"The Magi have exercises allowing the adept to move consciousness into the garment of light at will. Once your consciousness resides in the body of light, the limitations of the physical body no longer apply. You move about the earth merely by willing it to be so. In this form, I appeared in Petra in the dead of night to deliver a message to Prince Shimon in Petra then instantly returned to my bed in Babylon."

Yeshua laughed at the thought of Gaspar scaring Shimon in the dead of night. Yeshua said, "Thank you for the information Gaspar but I don't think I'll have need for this magic."

"As you wish Prince Yeshua but you may find use for the ability to escape from the physical body. It is bound to suffer in life. By moving your consciousness to the spiritual body, you may temporarily suspend the suffering of the flesh. I pray you have no need for this power but one cannot say what the future holds."

Yeshua reflected upon the execution of both his father Antipater and grandfather Antigonus. He knew not what life held in store for him but the fate of his ancestors hung over Yeshua. He replied, "I think you are right Gaspar. It never hurts to keep another arrow in the quiver. Please show me the exercises of the Magi of which you spoke." Upon our return from Babylon,

---

[74] See *Psalm* 104:2, *Matthew* 17:1-2 and the *Gospel of Philip.*

Yeshua possessed the power to consciously leave his physical body at will.

The main purpose of the trip was to consolidate support in Babylon among the Jewish Diaspora and Parthians. This task accomplished, Yeshua sent Princess Mariam (the elder), her daughter, and the bulk of our party back to Galilee to await his return. Yeshua stayed on a few extra months to study with the priests of the diverse eastern religions that resided in Babylon. He possessed a natural curiosity in the religions of the world and could not pass up the chance to trade information with fellow adepts.

Petra, Nabatea (34 CE)

Just as Gaspar predicted, we arrived in Petra finding a changed Prince Shimon. He and young Princess Mariam renewed their acquaintance during her second stay in Petra. She left a letter in Petra for her adoptive father expressing the desire to marry Shimon. Yeshua gave his blessing sealing the alliance with the Nabatean royal house. While in Petra, we also learned that Herod Antipas divorced King Aretas' daughter to marry Herodias. In response, Aretas began raising an army to make war on Antipas. The king's blood was up for revenge. The Romans never sanctioned wars between client states. Their leaders were expected to instead come to the Romans for an adjudication of any dispute. Aretas had no intention of going to Rome. Nabatean honor had been offended and no judgment from Tiberias Caesar could restore it. This coming war with Antipas moved King Aretas a step closer to insurrection against Rome. Yeshua and Aretas now had a common enemy. But the Nabatean king threw one last wrinkle into the agreement sealing their alliance. Yeshua went to the throne room for an audience with the king upon his arrival in Petra from Babylon.

Yeshua said to the king, "My minister Menelaus tells me all has been settled your highness in regard to the marriage of Prince Shimon to Princess Mariam and the alliance of our royal houses."

Aretas replied, "Presently, you're a king without a throne Yeshua. It's a grave hazard for Nabatea to openly support those in rebellion against the Roman Empire."

"I thought the issue of your support was settled."

"It is. Capture Jerusalem and you gain the support of my Nabatean army. We both know this rebellion goes nowhere without the backing of the Jewish people. If you can't take Jerusalem with your own men, it's a lost cause in any event."

Yeshua tried to rally the king to be more forceful in his commitment to the cause, "But you are preparing for war on Herod Antipas, a client ruler of the Romans. Does this not already put you at enmity with Rome?"

"True, I'm skirting the edge of a cliff. We war on Antipas in the Transjordan east of Palestine. Towns he claims in Perea belonged for centuries to the Nabatean kingdom but were taken from us in battle. That score has never been settled. I allowed Antipas to keep the Nabatean towns seized in the past so long as he was my son-in-law. Now that the marriage has ended we shall reclaim our rightful territory."

Yeshua, "Under Roman law the matter should go to the Syrian governor then on to the emperor for final adjudication."

Aretas, "And the emperor does not reside in Rome but on the Isle of Capri. Who can say when he would get around to addressing our grievances? Dushara helps those who help themselves."[75]

"Surely the Romans will eventually retaliate. Why not get off the ledge now and openly support us?"

"Prince Yeshua, I have complete faith that you, with the aid of my grandson, shall capture the city of Jerusalem just as your grandfather King Antigonus did before you."

Yeshua held no further ammunition for argument against the king's position. From the Nabatean standpoint, the risk versus reward equation didn't tilt in their favor until Yeshua captured Jerusalem. The entire success of Yeshua's mission now rested on successful accomplishment of that goal without Nabatean military support. In any event, Prince Shimon was now a member of Yeshua's inner circle. He traveled with us back to Galilee in the guise of a mid-level Jewish noble. The plan called for us to travel

---

[75] Poetic license borrowing from a Benjamin Franklin quote.

as a small band of Jewish private citizens returning from an extended trip to Babylon; however, Shimon met us on the day of departure from Petra accompanied by a platoon of forty-armed horseman.

Yeshua said, "Shimon, what is all this?"

Shimon seemed oblivious to the problem and replied, "All what?"

Yeshua, "The forty mounted soldiers."

"I never travel without armed escort."

"Your father's instructions are for us to hide Nabatean support for our cause until after we capture Jerusalem. What happens when we go through Roman checkpoints with your troops? The Romans are not fools."

"Do you expect me to travel without any sort of protection? Even wealthy private citizens travel with bodyguards."

Yeshua was firm, "Two men. Pick two of your men and strip them of armor. Just swords and keep those hidden. I prefer you bring Jewish soldiers."

Shimon turned to address his men, "Sons of thunder, fall out." James and Yochanan came forward from amongst the ranks.

"Prince Yeshua, you know James. The other is his brother, Yochanan."

Yeshua replied, "These men are acceptable to me. James and Yochanan, we wish to keep a low profile on our return to Israel. Control your passions. Don't do anything rash. Dump the armor, put on civilian cloaks and fall in behind Prince Shimon."

The men saluted Yeshua, took off their amour as instructed, then formed up behind their Nabatean prince. Our group rode out of Petra bound for Galilee. Once out of the city, Yeshua turned to the prince who was to become his son-in-law. He said, "Shimon is a Hasmonean name. There are several Shimones in my extended family. Menelaus over there already refers to you as Petra. I think it's an apt nickname as you are the military rock upon which I shall build my kingdom.[76] What say you to the name Petra?"

---

[76] See *Matthew* 16:18.

Shimon replied, "It is a name close to my heart. Call me what you wish Prince Yeshua."

Yeshua, "Those of our group call me rabbi. All except the obstinate one, Menelaus. He's stubborn in his use of 'master' or 'lord' as if he were some sort of servant. You are now a close advisor and member of the family. Please call me rabbi."

On our outbound journey from Galilee many months ago we first traveled east across the Jordan River then south through Decapolis on our way to the Nabatean capital of Petra thereby avoiding Judea entirely. On our return, Yeshua wished to stop in Bethany to meet with Lazarus, who promised to introduce Yeshua to several leadings Judeans.

We rode northwest from Petra for two days staying inside Nabatean territory until we reached Perea, on the northwestern shore of the Dead Sea. Israel and Nabatea had been at peace for almost forty years leading to a largely demilitarized border between the two nations. Hugging the coastline of the Dead Sea, we turned west toward Jerusalem. Our route took us just south of the Herodian palace at Jericho, then past the old Hasmonean fortress up on the cliffs near the Wadi Qumran. The Herodians had greatly expanded the small frontier fort turning it into an agricultural estate connected to the nearby plantation at Ein Feshkha. A few soldiers manned the watch tower at Qumran but they took little note of our passing. We turned west off the coast road onto a road which runs directly to Jerusalem; however, three miles to the west of Qumran sat the old Hasmonean fortress of Hyrcania, which the Herodians now occupied. With the sun low on the western horizon, our party reached Hyrcania. Roman auxiliary soldiers stopped our party outside the gate as we attempted to pass. The Romans understood Yeshua to be a middle son in the long list of offspring of Priest Joseph making him Hasmonean but not a Herodian royal, although there was some confusion in the Roman records. The Roman records in Egypt initially recorded Priest Joseph having a son named Mattatayah. Later in Galilee, Mattatayah disappeared from the tax records for the family and Yeshua appeared. Then Mattatayah / Yeshua disappeared completely from the Roman Empire for twenty years. He had gone into foreign exile. Later, a Rabbi Yeshua ben Joseph appeared in Egypt claiming to be a Hasmonean prince and descendant of King Antigonus. Thus, the Romans were a bit confused as to the true identity of the rabbi but he was on their list of Jews to be watched for potential subversive activity. Roman intelligence reports referred to him as "the Egyptian".

The Jewish authorities, on the other hand, knew all about Rabbi Yeshua. They were fully aware that the son of Princess Mariamne identified in the tax records of Galilee as Yeshua ben Joseph was the same individual listed in the Jerusalem Temple records as "Mattatayah ben Antipater". Herodian family members who met Yeshua in Galilee, which including Princess Herodias, recognized him as a member of their family due to his striking resemblance to Prince Agrippa (brother of Herodias). My master used the name "Yeshua" when he launched his public campaign for the Jewish throne to both throw off the Romans as to his true identity and mask his Herodian roots from the Jewish people. Very few people in Judea outside of the Herodian royal family knew Yeshua's true identity. The Jewish authorities desired to keep the Romans in the dark concerning the parentage of Rabbi Yeshua should he become a political opponent and the need arose to execute him. Yeshua's status as a grandson of Herod would constitute a stumbling block to execution. Hasmoneans who were not members of Herod's family (such as John the Baptist) could be disposed of by the Herodians / Sanhedrin as they wished without involving Rome.

Yeshua, for his part, wished to keep as low a profile as possible while he built alliances for his coming revolution in Jerusalem. Our party approached the Roman checkpoint cautiously. A decurion together with a squad of Roman legionnaires approached Yeshua. The decurion commanded, "Identify yourself."

"Yeshua ben Joseph, a citizen of Galilee. I am returning home to Sepphoris with my traveling companions. We are stopping in Bethany to visit family before returning home to Galilee." Yeshua gave what he judged to be the minimum amount of information necessary to get through the military checkpoint.

With any luck, the decurion would waive us along so he and his men could get out of the burning sun.

"Where are you coming from?"

Yeshua replied, "A pilgrimage to Babylon to meet with the leading rabbis of that city." This was technically true but left out the political nature of the visit and our side trip to Petra.

The decurion became suspicious. "If you come from Babylon returning to Galilee, then why are you on this road? You should have passed from Damascus to the north."

Yeshua, "I made an intermediate stop in Petra. It is a city famous the world over and I'd never seen their wondrous monuments so I made a side trip to Nabatea for sight-seeing."

That response only partially mollified the decurion. He began inspecting the rest of our party and something about Petra's appearance drew the officer's attention. Petra, although dressed as the others, didn't look like a rabbi's traveling companion. His saddle was richly decorated in the style of the Nabateans and he rode a valuable Arabian stallion. A careful soldier's eye detected a sword under Petra's robe. The decurion walked over to Petra for a closer examination and said, "Identify yourself. Are you a Jewish citizen?"

Petra was supposed to say he was a bodyguard but pride got in the way. He puffed out his chest and responded, "I am a Roman citizen! Prince Shimon, son of Herod Antipas, tetrarch of Galilee and Perea."

Yeshua shook his head. The damage was already done. Reacting would only make matters worse. The Roman officer asked, "And your destination?"

Shimon replied, "I ride with Prince Yeshua to Sepphoris."

The Roman decurion understood the significance of a high-ranking Herodian prince traveling with a Hasmonean prince to Galilee, a zealot hotbed. The Roman officer continued the questioning. "What business have you in Sepphoris?"

Petra replied, "I am to marry Princess Mariam, daughter of Ethnarch Archelaus and Princess Mariam bat Aristobulus. Princess Mariam is now the wife of Prince Yeshua." Petra nodded toward Yeshua to complete his identification. I wondered why Petra didn't just go ahead and condemn all of us as insurrectionists.

The eyes of the grizzled old officer widened with the news. This was the first information received by the Romans linking Yeshua with Herodian royalty, which vastly increased Roman interest in Yeshua the Galilean rabbi. This was also the first time, but not the last, that Petra's hard-headedness and lack of judgment cost Yeshua. The decurion moved on to question James and Yochanan. Thankfully, the two just muttered that they were bodyguards, end of story. The decurion ordered us to wait while he conferred with his superiors inside the fortress.

I internally fumed at Petra from atop my idled horse. Characteristically, Yeshua remained relaxed seemingly unconcerned with the turn of events. He got off his horse and walked away from our group toward the wall of cliffs situated behind the fortress. In one location, a large pile of rubble had been stacked up against the wall of the cliff. He turned to me and said, "Menelaus, come join me."

I got off my horse and walked over to him. I thought he wished to privately discuss the actions of Petra in conveying damaging information to the Romans. Instead he said, "Do you know who is buried at this site?"

I had no idea and just shook my head in reply.

He said, "My father, your father, and my grandmother. When our fathers were executed, our mothers escorted their bodies from the Herodian palace at Jericho here to Fortress Hyrcania for burial. My mother told me their bodies were placed in a tomb cut into the rock behind the fortress. This is the first time I have been to Hyrcania."

Now I understood why he chose this route to Jerusalem. There were less auspicious roads to travel. I pointed to the large pile of rubble stacked up against the wall of the cliff behind the fortress with the realization that my father's body likely resided behind those stones.

Yeshua said, "Yes, our fathers."

We both knelt praying to the men who gave us life in this world but were taken from us before we left the womb. This shared experience formed a special bond between Yeshua and I all our lives.

The Roman soldiers finally sent our party on its way. The kind heart of Yeshua prevented him from chastising Petra for his lack of discretion. I, however, had no such tenderness. After we moved out of earshot of the soldiers, I let my emotions get the better of me. Perhaps it was the experience of visiting my father's burial location. I said to Petra, "What in the name of Moses were you thinking?"

Petra seemed genuinely surprised at my outburst. He narrowed his eyes at me as if I'd lost my mind.

I continued my assault, "Don't you understand how damaging it was for you to tell the Romans you are the son of Herod Antipas and ride with Yeshua? Why didn't you just tell the Romans that all of us are planning a Jewish revolution?" I practically spit the words out of my mouth in the direction of Petra. I am certain no subordinate had ever before spoken to him in this manner. His face reddened.

He replied, "A Nabatean prince carries himself with honor and pride wherever he goes in life. It would dishonor my grandfather the king to deny my royal heritage before the Roman soldiers."

I kept hammering him, "Petra. It's a fitting name for you Shimon as there are rocks in your head."

Petra threw his cloak back and drew his sword. Yeshua rode between us and said, "That's enough Menelaus."

Petra wanted a piece of me. He said, "Get out of the way rabbi. That insult went too far. Give him a sword. We fight."

Just then, a Roman messenger overtook us riding hard in the direction of Jerusalem. He undoubtedly carried a report for the commanding tribune of the Roman garrison at Fortress Antonia in Jerusalem. Antonia sat adjacent to the Temple complex. We all watched the rider race past knowing the contents of the message he carried to our enemies. Rather than address Petra, Yeshua instead turned on me, "I say to you that anyone who is angry with his brother is guilty before God; and whoever says to his brother, 'You fool,' shall not gain entry into the kingdom of God."[77]

This rebuke from Yeshua probably saved my life that day on the road to Jerusalem. Petra meant business whenever he drew his sword and I lacked any experience with the business end of the weapon. Petra would have carved me up into little pieces had not Yeshua intervened. From that day forward, Roman interest in Rabbi Yeshua ben Joseph of Sepphoris jumped up several notches. In hindsight, it was inevitable.

Later that day during a moment when Yeshua and I found ourselves alone he said to me, "Emotions are like the currents of the sea. They throw us to and fro unrestrained by intention and reason."

"I'm sorry master but it is only human nature to get angry now and again."

"Blessed is the man who rises above human nature and walks upon the emotional sea." Yeshua rode on leaving me to contemplate the wisdom of his words. He walked on water but I lacked his level of self-discipline and was often drowned by emotion.

---

[77] *Matthew* 5:22.

Chapter 14

Alexandria, Egypt (67 CE)

Theudas exclaimed, "Grandfather, such a display of passion! I just can't see you yelling at a highborn prince. My reclusive, soft-spoken grandfather did this?"

"I was a near total idiot back then. Thank the gods for allowing me to live long enough to grow into a mildly offensive old man."

Theudas smiled at the self-deprecating humor. He said, "Where may I find a writing tablet? I wish to send a message over to Philo letting him know I shall miss our dinner but shall join him for wine later in the evening."

"The story draws you in I see."

"It's heating up. I don't wish to leave until we get to the crucifixion of Yeshua."

"You know the outcome yet you're on the edge of your seat. I must not have lost my touch as a storyteller."

Rhodopis brought a writing tablet and stylus while Menelaus trotted off to the pantry to retrieve more food leaving his grandson marking out a message in the wax. Theudas finished his message then hailed a boy in the street outside his grandfather's home, who agreed to deliver the message to Philo in exchange for a small payment. Theudas returned to the company of his grandfather finding him munching on bread drizzled with olive oil.

Theudas, "So, Yeshua had just returned to Israel on a trip east seeking foreign alliances."

"We stopped in Bethany to introduce Petra to Lazarus, meet a few Judean dignitaries, and then our party returned to

Galilee. Now Yeshua faced the hardest part of his mission—winning over the Jewish people. In the years after the death of Herod the Great, the Hasmoneans drifted into two camps, those working within the Roman power structure and their Pharisee allies in Jerusalem and those who were Jewish nationalists styling themselves as righteous leaders. Rabbi Yochanan ben Zechariah, the cousin of Yeshua known as the baptizer, was the most influential Hasmonean nationalist at the time Yeshua commenced his public ministry. Rabbi Yochanan was of royal blood free from the taint of Herod, although of lower Hasmonean rank than both Yeshua and his brother James the Just. Any serious Jewish opposition leader needed the blessing of Yeshua's influential cousin."

Theudas, "What was the standing of James the Just in Yeshua's community?"

Menelaus replied, "Yeshua once said when asked who shall be the leader should he die, 'You are to go to James the Just, for whose sake heaven and earth came into being.'"[78]

"If the bloodline of James was so august, why didn't he seek the throne instead of his brother Yeshua?"

Menelaus thought about the question for a moment, then said, "Jewish law is a labyrinth and I confess to lacking a rabbi's knowledge on the subject; however, it boils down to the qualifications of a messiah, as this is the position Yeshua sought. Crown Prince Antipater, the father of Yeshua, descended from King David through his son Solomon whereas James the Just, although of august priestly lineage, was not a descendant of King David. So even though Yeshua was born with the taint of Herod, his ancestry was still powerful."

"Grandfather, I have heard you use this term messiah a few times today but I don't understand its significance. Did not Yeshua wish to be the Jewish king? How is the office of messiah different from king?"

"The messiah must be a king but not every king is a messiah. Before getting into what Jewish law has to say about the

---

[78] *Gospel of Thomas*, Logion 12.

messiah and king, let me first speak of the method by which Jewish law comes into being. Yahweh authors all Jewish law; however, Yahweh only speaks through prophets. Thus, it is the prophets who propound the law. In turn, the rabbis interpret the law as given to the Jews by the prophets."

Theudas, "How is it determined whether an individual is a true prophet or a fraud?"

Menelaus, "Good question. A prophet must display gifts given to him or her by God, most notably the gift of prophesy. A consensus then emerges among the leading priests and rabbis that this individual is in fact a prophet, in which case all pronouncements from the prophet are treated as if they came from God. The prophet Samuel decreed that the throne of Israel shall evermore belong to the fruit of the body of King David so long as his children keep the covenant with God.[79] Well, King David's descendants did not keep the covenant with God and, therefore, Yahweh allowed King Nebuchadnezzar of Babylon to defeat the Jews in battle, sack the city of Jerusalem, and even destroy Solomon's temple. The Babylonians carried away into captivity Jewish king Jeconiah[80] and the entire Davidic royal family. Thereafter, the prophet Jeremiah decreed that none of the descendants of King Jeconiah could sit on the throne of Israel and rule."

"How long ago was this grandfather?"

"Over six-hundred years."

"And the Jewish people still concern themselves with such long ago events in the present day?"

Menelaus let out a long laugh at his grandson's incredulousness regarding the importance Jews placed upon the ancient history of their people. Menelaus replied, "The history of the Jewish people and its kings and prophets weighs down upon every pious Jew with every breath taken in life. The exploits of King Jeconiah are not ancient history to an observant Jew. Far, far older figures such as Abraham and Moses loom large in present

---

[79] *Psalm* 132:11-12, emphasis added.

[80] See Matthew 1:12.

day Jewish practice. Whatever is written in the scriptures becomes timeless."

"How did we get to Moses? Now I've forgotten how this part of the inquiry relates to Yeshua!"

Menelaus tried to calm his grandson who he perceived was getting impatient as the discussion wore on. Menelaus, "You wanted to know about the office of messiah."

"Yes, what is a Jewish messiah?"

"The Greek word 'christos' means the anointed one, which is roughly equivalent to the Jewish word 'mashiach' or messiah. It means a special Jewish king anointed by God who will deliver the Jewish people from oppression and injustice and defeat the forces of evil to restore righteousness in the land of Israel. For the common people, this means delivering them from Roman oppression. The messiah is also a prophet who sets the people back upon the righteous path."

"Do not all the Jewish people wish deliverance from the Romans?"

"The situation is not so simple grandson. The chief priests and the rabbis who sit on the Sanhedrin collaborate with the Romans. They have no interest in the emergence of a messiah for he would be an absolute ruler with the authority to strip the chief priests and rabbis of their power should he so choose."

Theudas asked, "Did the priests and rabbis play a part in the execution of Yeshua?"

Menelaus, "Now you are jumping ahead in the story. Patience. We arrive at the point where Yeshua is about to embark on his public campaign for the throne and present himself to the Jewish people as the messiah. His first public speech was in Galilee after the wedding feast of Mariam Magdalene's daughter in Cana."

Theudas, "Hold on, you still haven't told me why Yeshua was the messiah and not his brother James even though James had purer Jewish blood."

Menelaus replied, "I don't think 'purer' would be the correct word. James held higher standing as a Hasmonean and son of Aaron, which Jesus was not. Jesus' bloodline brought together the two traditions of King David and the Hasmonean dynasty. In hindsight, James may very well have been more acceptable to the Jewish people. But Yeshua was the eldest son of Princess Mariamne and, in the final analysis, it was she that determined which would claim the throne."

Theudas, "Weren't David's descendants invalidated by the decree of the prophet Jeremiah? I thought you said that a moment ago."

"Not all descendants of David, only those through King Jeconiah. Jeconiah and his extended royal family went into captivity in Babylonian; therefore, it was the royal descendants of Jeconiah in Babylon who were disqualified from the throne."

"What about Antipater, the father of Yeshua? Was he a descendant of King Jeconiah?"

"No, he was not."

Theudas, "So Yeshua had royal Davidic blood that James lacked, although they both were Hasmonean princes. Then Yeshua had the stronger claim to the Jewish throne, right?"

The intricacies of Yeshua's claim to the Jewish throne still perplexed Menelaus to this day. He tried his best to explain the situation to his grandson. He said, "The problem was Herod. Yeshua disavowed Herod as an ancestor because of his Roman collaboration."

"How does one disavow his own grandfather? If Yeshua did not claim Herod then he could not claim his father's Davidic royal blood."

"True, Yeshua refused to publicly speak of his father. The people assumed he was the son of Priest Joseph the Nazarite. For this reason Yeshua never claimed to be a descendant of King David. When the Pharisees questioned him about the office of messiah, he maintained the messiah was a descendant of the patriarch Levi and superior to David.[81]"

---

[81] See *Matthew* 22:41-45, *Mark* 12:35-37, and *Luke* 20:41-44; the Dead Sea Scrolls speak of two messiahs, one of Israel (thought to refer to the descendants of King David) and the other of Aaron (the priestly messiah of Levi).

"Grandfather, isn't that all a bit convoluted for an aspiring king to explain to the people in the streets? How did Yeshua convey his claim to the throne to the Jewish people?"

"He always spoke in simple terms to the Jewish people. He presented himself as the grandson of King Antigonus, who fought the Romans. His Hasmonean family members stood at his side supporting his claim to the throne. It was enough for them, at least initially."

"What about when he was arrested by the Romans? Didn't he tell them he was a grandson of Herod? I would think his case should have gone to the emperor in Rome or at least the Roman governor in Antioch."

Menelaus took a long drink of his wine then said, "Yeshua let the Romans nail him to the cross rather than confess he was the grandson of Herod. He never compromised his principles, not even to save his own life."

Chapter 15

Cana, Galilee (34 CE)

Petra and Princess Mariam bat Archelaus (step-daughter of Yeshua) completed their period of kiddushin (betrothal) and celebrated their wedding with a public feast at Princess Mariam Magdalene's villa at Cana, Galilee. Yeshua wished a simple feast but his mother Princess Mariamne overruled her son. She orchestrated a grand wedding feast at Cana.

This wedding brought together all the dignitaries of the Hasmonean and Herodian clans who were thought to be sympathetic to Yeshua's claim to the throne. Yeshua's younger sister (yet another Princess Mariamne) married a son of Herodian Prince Joseph ben Joseph (Joseph of Arimathea) five years prior to the wedding at Cana. This marriage of Yeshua's sister to Prince Joseph's middle son Clopas fulfilled a long ago promise made by the elder Princess Mariamne to the family of Prince Joseph. His extended family of Herodian royalty attended the feast as honored guests. Herod Antipas was not invited even though his son was the groom. Neither were Princess Mariam Magdalene's brothers Agrippa and Herod (the future kings), who sided with Rome. However, Prince Lazarus attended as the senior male member of Mariam's family.

Known as a shrewd business and political operator, Joseph of Arimathea was one of the five wealthiest Jews in Israel and a voting member on the Sanhedrin. Yeshua's political ambitions garnered a substantial boost with the marriage of his sister to Clopas ben Joseph. The allure of Hasmonean blood was sweet nectar to any ambitious Herodian prince. Joseph of Arimathea embraced the alliance with Yeshua despite the risks. He judged the young rabbi to be a sensible man not prone to lob political bombs as his cousin Yochanan the Baptizer was known for. Prince Joseph was then completely unaware that Yeshua formed alliances with the royal houses of Nabatea and Parthia pursuant and planned to initiate a revolt against the Romans. The family of Joseph of Arimathea prospered under Roman administration and he had no wish to see the relationship end.

Cana is located five miles north of Sepphoris down the rolling plain of Carmelion built into the side of a small mountain. Several dozen-country villas owned by wealthy individuals from Sepphoris sat scattered among this village of no more than one thousand. Cana boasts a synagogue and necropolis plus all the standard amenities of a Galilean town of its size. In addition to Joseph of Arimathea's large entourage of extended family and Yeshua's own large extended family, Prince Petra insisted on bringing his seventy soldiers to the wedding feast. Although Yeshua tried to divert Petra's attention to spiritual studies during our time together in Sepphoris, Petra saw his primary duty as forming a band of shock troops populated mostly by Jewish mercenaries who were veterans of foreign wars. Soldiers, wine, and young female wedding guests do not mix. Yeshua pulled me aside in the hours before the commencement of the wedding feast. As a Nazarene rabbi, Yeshua wished to make a pre-emptive strike against all out drunkenness.

He said, "There you are Menelaus. Do me a favor and round up the chief steward of this household. I need to have a word with him."

I replied, "The steward serves your wife. Perhaps we should involve Princess Mariam?"

The slightest hint of distemper showed on Yeshua's face as he responded. He trusted his wife implicitly and involved her in all major family decisions. It was his strong-willed mother he wished to avoid on this mission. Calling Mariam for consultation may attract the attention of his ever-hovering mother.

He replied, "If I wished for my wife's presence, I would have asked for her. Now, the steward please."

I didn't ask any more questions and did as the master requested returning within minutes, chief steward in tow. The man asked, "You wish to see me rabbi?"

Yeshua, "Yes, how much wine do we have on the premises?"

"Total including what we have in storage?"

"Yes."

"Twelve amphora. But I can quickly arrange for more if you are worried we shall run out rabbi. The chief steward at a neighboring villa will make a loan to us. "

Each amphora held twenty-gallons meaning the villa had 240 gallons of wine on hand, more than enough for the soldiers and others to drink themselves silly.

Yeshua commanded, "Too little is not my concern. Empty the stone water jars in the pantry and dump six amphora into the water jars."

The steward asked incredulously, "Dump wine into the water jars?"

Yeshua, "Yes, go do it now before the guests start arriving. I'll inform your mistress of this order. And tell the staff there is only water in the jars. They are to see only water."

"Yes rabbi."

The evening started off smoothly. Young Princess Mariam was a vision of modest beauty displaying the proper amount of deference to the elders in attendance. Petra stood at her side, very much in love with his new bride. The servants roasted the goats to perfection but the wine flowed freely, much to Yeshua's dismay. Drunks find each other at such events. I gravitated to the soldiers lounging in the overflow areas where guests of lesser station ate. As the groom, Prince Petra stayed up front with the wedding dignitaries leaving me with the Sons of Thunder and crew. We received only fleeting views of the royal ladies in attendance located far forward of our position. But it didn't matter after a few cups of wine as our attention honed in on the serving girls. As the sun went down, the wine ran out. The elder Princess Mariamne was mortified when Josephus of Arimathea requested the servant refill his wine cup only to be told there was none as only water remained. The elder Princess Mariamne was furious. That morning she confirmed there was ample wine at the villa by personally checking the stores. She knew who made the wine disappear and confronter her Nazarene son about the issue. She said to him, "They have no wine."

Yeshua replied nonchalantly, "And how does this concern me? I am a rabbi, not an innkeeper."

His mother's face turned red with anger as she struggled not to shout with guests close by, "You are the wedding host and the honor of our family is at stake. We'll not run out of wine at your daughter's wedding. Hear me son, our family shall not be embarrassed this way!"

I'd never seen the elder Princess Mariamne raise her voice and I'd known the woman from birth. Mother and son had an unusual relationship. Yeshua lived in exile outside of Israel for twenty years before returning to us. He studied with the Essenes and the Therapeutae in Egypt and the Zoroastrians in Parthia. He returned to us a philosophical and deeply religious man. The spiritual Yeshua stood in contrast to the earthly king his mother envisioned as his role in life. Left to chart his own course without the pull of family obligations I am certain Yeshua would have stayed in the desert living in poverty while dispensing wisdom to a select few seekers who came to him. This conflict over how much wine to serve to the banquet guests was a microcosm of the contrast between mother and son. Princess Mariamne the elder never studied the Nazarene way as had his wife, Princess Mariam.

His mother turned to the servants saying, "Do as he tells you." Then she stormed off.

Yeshua gave in to his mother's request, as he always did. The rabbi instructed the servants to go to the pantry and draw pitchers from the stone water jars located there. Upon return, the servants filled the cups of the guests desiring more wine. I hoped a little levity would lighten Yeshua's mood. I said, "Rabbi, this is your best magic yet. You've changed water into wine!"

Apparently I spoke loudly enough for many other wedding guests to hear the comment intended as a private joke. The guests picked up on the levity repeating it to one another. Months later we were still repeating the joke holding up our water cups during the evening meal beseeching Yeshua to change it into wine. Many other persons of note attended the Cana wedding feast including my brother Philip, son of Philip of Rome, and Yeshua's brother James. In both cases, Yeshua and myself viewed our half-brothers as having more desirable ancestry. In the case of Philip, he was full-blooded Jewish. My Greek half made me a Jewish outsider. In any event, Philip became one of Yeshua's core disciples.

James stood as a righteous Kohen priest respected by all who knew him but he lacked the magnetic leadership of Yeshua. James was a rare thing on this earth, a humble priest seeking only to enter through the straight gate and walk upright upon the Lord's path. He also adhered much more closely to traditional Jewish law than Yeshua, who was a reformer. Nonetheless, the two brothers were in agreement on their core teaching, something they called the royal law—love thy neighbor as thyself and the renunciation of material wealth. In their view, love was the key to an upright life. James believed suffering a helpful ingredient in one's pursuit of perfection. He said, "Count it as pure joy my brothers all the trials and tribulations you encounter for they build character."[82] I found James to be somber and conscientious in his spiritual pursuit, not the type of fellow you asked to join a bachelors' trip to Antioch. Oh, how I adored the delectable prostitutes in Antioch!

One more wedding guest deserves mention--Prince Phasaelus, a grandson of Phasael and Salampsio bat Herod. He was one of Herod's numerous great-grandsons.[83] Princess Salampsio was Herod's eldest Hasmonean daughter; therefore, Phasaelus possessed royal Hasmonean blood setting him apart from the hoard of Herod's progeny. He was also born into extreme wealth as the second son of Timius, a leading merchant of Cyprus. Phasaelus went by Saulus in these days but was later known as Paul of Tarsus after his conversion to the Nazarene movement. Phasaelus used his family connections to obtain

---

[82] *Letter of James* 1:2-3

[83] I present the reasoned argument in Herodian Messiah that Paul of Tarsus (Phasaelus in this work) was the grandson of Phasael and Salampsio, Herod's nephew and daughter, respectively. *See also* jjraymond.com/paul.

position with the Sanhedrin. At the time of the wedding, he held a nonvoting position within the Grand Sanhedrin although he rose to full voting status not long thereafter.

During the feast, Prince Phasaelus approached Yeshua and asked, "Good rabbi, what must I do to inherit eternal life?"

Yeshua previously received reports that the Pharisees in Jerusalem accused him of blasphemy. Knowing Phasaelus was Pharisee and sensitive to this charge, Yeshua replied, "Why do you call me good? No one is good except God alone. You know the commandments, do not commit adultery, murder, steal, bear false witness, honor your father and mother."

"All these I have kept from my youth."

Yeshua continued, "As you have been obedient to the Torah from your youth the final step to salvation should be easy for you. Sell all your material possessions and give the proceeds to the poor, then come follow me."

When Phasaelus heard these things, he became dejected for he was extremely rich. He walked away not willing to comply with the austerity imposed by Yeshua on his followers. As Phasaelus departed Yeshua commented to his followers then sitting around him, "Observe how difficult it is for those who possess wealth to enter the kingdom of God."[84]

Princess Mariam came to Yeshua after watching the exchange and said, "Husband, do you think it was wise to publicly rebuke Prince Phasaelus? His star rises in the Grand Sanhedrin and he has friends in Rome. Perhaps I should call him back and you could smooth over the misunderstanding."

Rebuking Phasaelus made no sense to Mariam politically as his position of power certainly could have been useful when the time came to claim the Jewish throne. But Yeshua never bent his principles in return for the easy path in life. He merely looked at his wife quizzically without replying further. Princess Mariam made one final attempt to change her husband's mind, "Husband, he is family."

---

[84] *Luke* 18:18-24.

Yeshua replied, "Herod Antipas is family yet you do not see him at this wedding feast. I did not come to make peace wife. No, I bring division. From now on a family of five shall be divided three against two and two against three."[85] This was not the last time Yeshua crossed paths with Phasaelus. He persecuted Yeshua and his followers during the revolt until inexplicably converting to the Nazarene faith later. We shall save the story of Phasaelus' conversion for another time.

In Cana, a throng of townspeople and workers from the surrounding countryside petitioned to hear Yeshua speak the morning after the wedding feast.[86] He instructed his disciples to sit the people on a small plain below the town. Yeshua stood on the mountainside addressing the people below. For me personally, this was the most moving speech I heard him deliver.

Yeshua said, "Blessed are those that hunger in this life for they shall be filled in the next. Blessed are those that weep in this life for they shall laugh later. Blessed are you whom men shall hate and cast you out for my sake, as your reward is great in heaven. But woe unto you that are rich, for your pleasures have been received in this life and shall not comfort you in the next. Woe to you that are now full, for you shall hunger. Woe to you that now laugh, you shall mourn and weep.[87]

"Blessed are the poor in spirit, for theirs is the Kingdom of Heaven. Blessed are those who mourn, for they shall be comforted. Blessed are the gentle, for they shall inherit the earth. Blessed are those who hunger and thirst after righteousness, for they shall be filled. Blessed are the merciful, for they shall obtain mercy. Blessed are the pure in heart, for they shall see God. Blessed are the peacemakers, for they shall be called sons of God.

---

[85] See *Luke* 12:52-53.

[86] The Bible does not explicitly give a location for the Sermon on the Mount; however, *Luke* 7:1 states that Yeshua went to Capernaum directly after giving the Sermon on the Mount. *John* 2:12 tells us Yeshua went from Cana to Capernaum. Putting the two passages together, it appears the Sermon on the Mount was delivered at Cana. However, the wedding at Cana is only found in John's gospel so the identity of Cana as the location of the sermon is suspect.

[87] *Luke* 6:20-25.

Blessed are those who have been persecuted for righteousness' sake, for theirs is the kingdom of heaven."[88]

Capernaum, Galilee (35 CE)

Prince Petra selected Capernaum, a small town on the shores of the Sea of Galilee, as the training and recruitment base for his band of warriors. Seventy mercenaries made up the core shock troop of what Petra hoped to expand into a complete cohort.[89] Yeshua paid little attention to the training of his new corps of soldiers but Petra implored Yeshua to travel to Capernaum to address the new recruits as the men desired a first-hand look at the royal prince they were expected to fight and die for. Thus, Yeshua decamped from Cana for Capernaum.

I was apprehensive when we arrived. Petra was in his element surrounded by soldiers, horses, and the weapons of war. Having known Yeshua from birth, I'd never seen the man raise his fist in anger. I could not fathom how he would manage to give a motivational address to, in my eyes, a hardened group of killers. My fears proved wildly unfounded. Yeshua addressed the recruits with a zest Julius Caesar would have been hard pressed to match.

Yeshua said, "I am the eldest grandson of the last true Jewish king, Mattathias Antigonus. He was a righteous son of Aaron who expelled the Romans from Jerusalem and the last Hasmonean monarch. Seated before you is my mother, the daughter of King Antigonus. The only male descendants of King Antigonus now living are I and my brothers James and Joses, who are also seated before you. James shall serve as high priest when we are victorious in Jerusalem. Also with us is my wife, Princess Mariam, who descends from two Hasmonean kings. She is the grandniece of Aristobulus, a Hasmonean high priest murdered by Herod. Our Hasmonean forefathers drove the Greeks out of our homeland, a land promised to us by God. The Hasmonean priests then cleansed the Temple desecrated by the impure Greeks and

---

[88] *Matthew* 5:3-10.

[89] A Roman legion consisted of roughly 5,500 men but was often augmented by local auxiliaries. Each legion was comprised of 10 cohorts generally containing 500 men except for the first cohort of the legion, which numbered 800 men.

their Jewish allies, the seekers of smooth things. You may think that I, a Nazarene rabbi, am here to impose peace upon the world. Then you do not recognize that it is division that I have come to impose—fire, sword, battle. Indeed, brother against brother, parent against child, and child against parent.[90] A man's foes shall be of his own household. He that loveth his father or mother more than me is not worthy. And he that does not take up the yoke and follow after me is not worthy. You shall find your life in losing it for my sake.[91]

"The Romans have taken the promised land from us. The Temple again stands desecrated with Passover almost upon us. Sharpen your swords for the time for battle draws near. During Passover, I shall take control of the Temple and again cleanse the Lord's house consecrating it to the most-high God. Who is with me?"

I never saw such a transformation in a human being. The champion of love and kindness became an insurgent rebel leader. The men bolted to their feet clamoring to swear allegiance to Prince Yeshua. Yeshua could have been a leading stage actor of his day. The man commanded an audience like no other.

A funny conversation occurred later during our stay in Capernaum. In nearly every city we visited, Yeshua enjoyed walking in the market or other public places the townspeople frequented striking up conversation with ordinary persons on the street. The only two royals I had ever observed possessing the common touch were Yeshua and Yochanan the Baptizer. As our party strolled on the wharf, Yeshua stopped to speak with a local boat captain as his crew worked on their nets in preparation for setting sail.

One of the crewmen asked the disciples, "So what line of work were you in before taking up with the rabbi?" All of Yeshua's disciples except the soldiers with Petra were of royal Hasmonean and Herodian blood. This uneducated man of the sea stood completely unaware of the awkwardness of the question

---

[90] *Gospel of Thomas*, Logion 16.

[91] *Matthew* 10:36-39.

leaving the disciples unsure how to respond. Yeshua heard the question from a distance and came to their rescue responding, "They were fishermen, every last one of them."

We let out a roar at the levity of the rabbi's pun. No Jew dared openly criticize the Romans. It was done indirectly through coded analogy that we understood but they did not. A "fisherman" in Jewish code of the day referred to one who reaps but does not sow. Fishermen do not plant nor otherwise tend to the raising of the fish. They merely put out to sea casting their nets to harvest fish. The Romans and their Herodian allies were tax farmers who did not grow anything. They showed up at harvest time casting their tax nets far and wide snaring bounty from the Jewish countryside. Most of Yeshua's disciples, save his brothers James and Joses, previously held positions within the Herodian royal administration of Palestine and, as such, fit the definition of "fishermen". They directly or indirectly benefited from the heavy Herodian / Roman tax of the Jewish people.

We stayed in Capernaum for several weeks before moving on. Yeshua spent his days preaching in the synagogue, healing the sick, and giving spiritual instruction to his disciples. The later task he found frustrating. James the Just left us at this point having returned to his ascetic life with the desert Hasidim. The remaining inner core of Yeshua's followers were trained in the Torah, knew the basics of Jewish law, but were completely ignorant of the Nazarene mysteries. Even the simplest of parables told by Yeshua to the townspeople escaped the understanding of his disciples.

One day while still in Capernaum, a great multitude gathered by the sea to hear Yeshua speak. He put out in a boat addressing the multitude back on the beach. He said, "A farmer went forth to sow his field but some seeds fell by the way side, and the birds came and devoured them. Other seed fell upon rocky ground with shallow soil. It sprouted quickly but withered under the scorching sun. And other seeds fell among thorns, which choked the crop as it grew. And the last of the farmer's seed fell upon good ground, and yielded grain in abundance. He that has ears let him hear."

Afterward the disciples came asking Yeshua, "Why do you speak to them in parables?"

Yeshua replied, "It is given to you to know the mysteries but they are not ready for this privilege. He that has abundance shall be given more but whosoever lacks knowledge, from him shall be taken away. Therefore I speak to them in parables; because seeing they see not, and hearing they hear not, neither do they understand." [92]

But the common people were not the only ones lacking ears to hear. The disciples begged Yeshua to explain the parable to them. He said, "All these months of teaching and you don't understand this simple parable? Not you Petra? Nor you Thomas? Please tell me someone understands."

They cast their heads down ashamed at their lack of understanding. Yeshua then said to me, "Menelaus, quit lurking in the back of the room. Come forward."

I complied with my master's wish and stood next to him in front of the disciples. Yeshua said, "This man stands before you an avowed agnostic. He also lacks the training each of you has received in the Torah yet I am confident his ears heard the message of the parable. Menelaus, explain it to them. I shall not cast more pearls before swine."[93] With that, the master stormed out of the room. This dramatic exit was stagecraft on the part of the master done hoping to a light a fire of desire within each disciple for greater knowledge.

I suspected for years that the master knew I intently listened to his words although feigning disinterest as he instructed others. I inwardly smiled at the revelation that Yeshua knew me so well. I said to them, "He that sows the good seed is our master. The fields are his kingdom. The good seeds, these are the sons of light. The bad seeds are the sons of darkness. They are the evil ones, enemies of he that sows righteousness."[94]

---

[92] Matthew 13:1-13.

[93] *Matthew* 7:6.

[94] See *Matthew* 13:38-39. The terms "sons of light" and "sons of darkness" come from the War Scroll found among the Dead Sea Scrolls.

Princess Mariam, wife of Yeshua, walked to the front from where she had been sitting with the other women. She continued explaining the rest of the parable, "And the harvest is the end of days when the angles of the Lord shall reap. The weeds, the evil ones, will be gathered up and burned in the fire. There shall be weeping and gnashing of teeth. The kingdom of heaven is like a treasure hidden in the field, ignored by the blind, but found by men with eyes to see."[95]

Petra chaffed at receiving instruction from a woman. He challenged her thusly; "Since you have explained it all to us, answer one more thing. What is the greatest sin in the world?"

Mariam replied, "That which you call sin is actually ignorance. One with true knowledge of God commits not an act we call sin."[96] She left the room in search of her husband eventually finding him seated on a rock by the seashore silently watching the waves wash in.

Mariam took a seat next to him and also watched the waves. She remained silent waiting for him to speak. Finally, she could wait no more and broke the silence. "Why are you so frustrated with them husband? These men are here to assist you in reclaiming the throne of your royal grandfather. They lack the years of spiritual training you have received."

"True wife. But I had hoped and prayed for more."

"More?"

"Claiming the throne is a task given to me from birth by my mother and father. Since embarking on my public campaign, I feel my father Antipater's presence with me every step. I shall obey their wishes but also desire to bring light to the Jewish people. The Pharisees hold the keys to knowledge yet they have not crossed through the door and, further, prevent others from crossing through the door. They neglect justice and the love of God.[97] I wish to open the door to knowledge for the people."

"Then name Menelaus one of your disciples. He has the knowledge."

---

[95] See *Matthew* 13:40, 44.

[96] *The Gospel According To Mary Magdalene.*

[97] *Luke* 11:42, 54.

"I cannot force the horse to drink, wife. I love Menelaus as my own brother, maybe even more so, but he is a stubborn horse. You are the only one in that room who has the knowledge and is willing to walk through the door. But men will not follow you because they are blinded by your gender."

Mariam said, "Why must there be another? You are here to teach us? The dam shall burst one day with light flooding through the darkness."

"I pray it is so wife. But your bridegroom shall not be here forever I'm afraid. Another is necessary to carry on the work."

"And what of James the Just husband?"

"I have complete faith in the righteousness of James but his path is one of secluded prayer with the sons of light in the desert. My fate is different. I must travel from village to village spreading the word to the common people."

Mariam knew that her husband, in his heart, much preferred the spiritual, contemplative life James now enjoyed to the public one he currently was engaged in. Family obligation thrust the quest of resurrecting the Hasmonean dynasty upon Yeshua. This path was not of his own choosing. She continued, "If it is truly necessary, then God will provide you a partner husband. When has he ever denied you?"

Yeshua smiled and hugged his wife. Without her, the burden of his mission may have been too great to bear.

Tyre, Roman Province of Syria (35 CE)

King Marion of Tyre sided with Yeshua's grandfather Antigonus in the war against Herod and, for this, Marc Antony deposed him shortly before the latter's own death. Descendants of the deposed king of Tyre still lived in the city and yearned for their family to regain its former glory. Yeshua traveled from Galilee to Tyre in order to seek the support of Marion's descendants. Tyre existed as an independent city for over one thousand years until Augustus Caesar removed that privilege due to attacks against Roman officials and leading citizens that occurred during the civil war between Augustus and Antony.

> Yeshua got up and went away from there to the region of Tyre. And when he had entered a house, he wanted no one to know of it; yet he could not escape notice. *Mark* 7:24.

Over three hundred years in the past, Alexander the Great conquered the city after a siege lasting seven months. To effect victory, Alexander's military engineers built a causeway from the mainland to the island. Yeshua's party walked upon Alexander's causeway to enter the old city. The swelling military force Petra assembled at Capernaum required funding. Anti-Romans of all stripe including both Jews and gentiles from throughout Phoenicia attended Yeshua's meeting at the house of Marion. The Hasmonean prince hoped to receive funding and pledges to join the rebellion from those in attendance. Herodian spies watched our every move while in Tyre.

In everyday life, Yeshua dressed as the simple rabbi he was. But this mission to Tyre required him to assume the mantle of Hasmonean royalty. As such, Yeshua and all members of our party were adorned in our best finery. Agents of the wealthy Jewish business community of Phoenicia met us in the public square in the old city. As they led the way to the meeting place, a Canaanite woman prostrated herself before Yeshua on the street begging and crying out for assistance. The encounter placed Rabbi Yeshua in an awkward situation. We were escorted by conservative Jewish nationalists to whom Yeshua intended to present himself as a patriot of royal birth, a descendant of the righteous Mattathias Maccabeus. A conservative Jewish rabbi does not speak with a woman unaccompanied by her male guardian and especially not a gentile woman. Even with this in mind, his words to the woman shocked me. He said, "It is not good to take the children's bread and throw it to the dogs."[98]

Yeshua walked on to the meeting but looked back at me giving a nod. I knew his intention; I was to slip away from the group and offer assistance to the Canaanite woman. I approached

[98] *Matthew* 15:26; *Mark* 7:27.

the woman who was now in tears. I said, "Woman, may I offer you a few coins?" I reached for my purse.

She replied, "I don't want your money."

I was at a loss for divining the correct course of action. She continued, "Why did he speak those words to me? My daughter is sick and we have no money for a physician. I heard he was a healer."

Comforting emotional women was not my specialty. I tried the best I could, "The rabbi meant no offense to you. He is a healer but he is also a patriot striving to free his country. Devotion to the Jewish people comes first. Please take these sestertii and I shall speak to the rabbi of your daughter's case."

Rabbi Yeshua possessed an abundance of kindness and love for his fellow man, all men and women including gentiles. He was never angry, nor cruel. Yet fate placed this kind individual into the role of nationalist leader in a coming war to recapture his country from Roman domination. In the role of Prince Yeshua campaigning to become King Yeshua, he said and did things that the humble rabbi who wore rags would never dream of doing.

Chapter 16

Bethany, Judea (35 CE)

Our entire membership traveled from Galilee to Judea for the first time during Yeshua's public campaign for the Jewish throne and stayed in Bethany at the home of Yeshua's brother-in-law Lazarus. This village sits just beyond the eastern slope of the Mount of Olives, a short distance from Jerusalem making it a nice staging area for our activities in the holy city during the coming Passover. Yeshua's party came to Jerusalem to take control of the Temple in a show of force to present Yeshua to the people of Judea. He intended this act as a reminder to the people of his Hasmonean ancestors cleansing of the Temple after reclaiming it from the Greeks. Lazarus greeted us having just returned from travel to Antioch where he consulted with the Roman governor, Pomponius Flaccus. Anxious to hear the news from Antioch, Yeshua pulled Lazarus aside for a private conversation. Yeshua said, "Tell me brother, what news have you from Antioch?"

Lazarus, "Flaccus is a nice enough sort but an old man long in the tooth. He doesn't strike me as the typical ambitious Roman politician."

"I assume your suggestion regarding the removal of Caiaphas from the high priesthood did not bear fruit?"

"I'm afraid not rabbi. Flaccus is a chair warmer, an old chum of Tiberius content to enjoy the sunshine and collect bribes. We don't have the funds at our disposal necessary to bribe Flaccus into sacking Caiaphas."

"A Roman governor who lacks ambition and drifts with the flow suits our purposes. We're unlikely to receive scrutiny from Antioch with Flaccus in charge."

"True but I understand Flaccus is to be replaced very soon by proconsul Vitellius."

Yeshua asked, "What do you know of Vitellius?"

"He is an experienced military commander and man of ambition, completely unlike Flaccus."

Yeshua reflected on the words from his brother-in-law for a moment then said, "I wonder if Rome sending an experienced general to Syria as governor signals its intention to conduct military operations against Parthia?"

"Rabbi, do you sense war coming?"

"King Artabanus of Parthia installed his own son on the throne of Armenia without consulting Rome. Artabanus views the aging emperor Tiberias Caesar as weak and disengaged in foreign affairs. I suspect Artabanus is in for a surprise from the Romans. The positioning of Vitellius in Syria tips their hand. What say you Lazarus?"

"I think it plays to our advantage that Rome and Parthia squabble over Armenia. With any luck, Vitellius will take the Roman legions of the Syria province east to confront Parthia leaving us in a stronger military position in Israel."

Yeshua smiled. "These are my thoughts as well."

Lazarus changed the subject, "I also have family news from Antiochl."

"Oh, Agrippa no doubt."[99]

"It comes as no surprise that he's already worn out his welcome with Antipas. Not even Herodias could stop our uncle from kicking Agrippa out into the street. The wretch then turned up penniless at the governor's palace in Antioch while I was there!"

"How did you both manage to coexist under the same roof?"

"Flaccus received us both with friendship and desired that we brothers repair our relationship, which I refused. The governor kept pressing the matter so finally I was moved to air Agrippa's dirty laundry to the governor, matters such as Agrippa accepting

[99] Herod Agrippa I, future king of the Jews and eldest son of Aristobulus IV.

bribes and defrauding numerous creditors from Judea to Rome."[100]

"And did Flaccus finally become wise to your brother's true nature?"

"Denouncing my own brother spurred the governor's advisors to also speak freely and corroborate Agrippa's low reputation throughout the empire. This convinced Flaccus to send Agrippa on his way. I heard he is in Alexandria begging for new sources of funds there."

"One reaps what he sows Lazarus. Your brother's harvest time will eventually come."

"I know rabbi. It's disturbing to see our family torn apart though. My brother Herod and sister Herodias stand by Agrippa while Mariam and I oppose him."

"It's the curse of royal blood Lazarus. Look at how our Hasmonean forbearers killed one another."

The next day Yeshua found his disciples seated in pious prayer along with others sympathetic to our cause. The scene caused Yeshua to break out in laughter, which, quite naturally, upset the disciples. Yeshua said in response to their protests, "Please forgive me. I do not laugh at you as men but at the motivation behind your prayer."[101]

One of them responded, "Rabbi, we are wounded at your words. Tells us where we strayed."

He said, "Let me respond with a story. Two men went up into the Temple to pray, the one a Pharisee, and the other a tax collector. The Pharisee stood and prayed in full view and hearing of the others there to worship, 'I thank thee Lord that I am not as the rest of men, extortionists, adulterers, and tax collectors. I fast; I give tithes; I obey your laws.' But the tax collector, standing off by himself, did not so much as lift his eyes to heaven. He beat his breast while uttering in a near silent voice, 'Lord, be merciful to me a sinner.' I say unto you, the tax collector left the Temple justified while the other's prayer was worthless in the eyes of God. For every one that exalts himself shall be humbled. No one shall enter

---

[100] Antiquities, XVIII 6:3.

[101] *Gospel of Judas.*

the kingdom of God who does not first become as a little child.[102] Do you understand what I mean by becoming as a little child?"

The disciples were silent for they did not understand. They cast their heads down expecting another rebuke from Yeshua as they recently received in Capernaum. Then a stranger stood up and said, "I understand rabbi."

Yeshua studied the young man with strong features standing in the back of the room. The rabbi approached him peering deeply into his eyes. They contained no fear and were pure. Yeshua said, "Tell me stranger, what is this life?"

The stranger replied, "Whence born of a woman then growing into an adult, man dwells in the vale of tears having been cast out of paradise for his sins.[103] He is asleep, dead to his true self until the time of his spiritual rebirth when his eyes are opened to truly see."

Yeshua's eyes widened for the stranger understood the distinction between the first and second birth. Yeshua asked, "And how does one pass from death to life?"

The stranger answered, "There is only one path to life rabbi, to be born again of the spirit. That which is born of the flesh is flesh. That born of the spirit is spirit."[104]

"Please, tell me your name."

"They call me Judas the Zealot. I am the son of Simon of Gamla."

"Are you related to Judas of Gamla who led the revolt against Rome during the reign of Archelaus?"

"Yes, he was my uncle."

"Come, we have much to discuss."

Yeshua and Judas went away for many hours talking in private. God had finally sent Yeshua a collaborator in his mission. In the back of the room sat an unnoticed man, ostensibly a potential recruit to Yeshua's cause, who mentally noted every utterance in the room. He silently slipped out of the room and

---

102 *Luke* 18:10-17.

103 *Psalm* 83.

104 *John* 3:5-6.

wrote a detailed report to his master back in Jerusalem, the chief of Modiin.

Eleazar ben Zechariah, son of the prior chief, took command of Modiin fifteen years ago. Eleazar extensively studied his father's files on the case of Yeshua ben Joseph a/k/a Mattatayah ben Antipater. In Eleazar's professional opinion, his father erred in failing to liquidate the baby Yeshua after his escape to Egypt. Eleazar worked under the philosophy that Modiin must error on the side of caution, when in doubt kill. Dead men never come back to bite you in the ass. The job of killing Prince Yeshua had become many orders of magnitude more difficult since the time of his father. Not only did Yeshua lead a messianic movement with many hundreds of followers but the Roman political landscape had changed as well. Rome now governed Judea directly. In the time of his father, the Roman governor based himself three hundred miles to the north of Judea in Antioch largely leaving the administration of Palestine to Herod the Great. Pontius Pilate now ruled from the port city of Caesarea, a mere sixty miles from Jerusalem. The Roman hand lay much heavier on the backs of all Jews in Judea no matter their station.

Eleazar ben Zechariah spied on the Yeshua movement as a precaution. His primary domestic surveillance target was Yochanan the Baptizer, whose followers numbered in the tens of thousands. The Yeshua movement was but an infant by comparison yet Eleazar recognized the threat of his bloodline. The Modiin chief was one of the few in Judea who knew that Yeshua was the grandson of not only King Antigonus but, also, Herod. That meant he was born of royal blood in Roman eyes whereas Yochanan the Baptizer was not. The Jewish authorities were free to deal with Yochanan as they saw fit but, should the Romans learn the secret of Yeshua's ancestry, his case was much more difficult to address should he become a threat.

That evening I got a message to meet privately with Yeshua. Once alone he said to me, "Menelaus, I have a favor to ask. I want you to go with our new member Judas to the Jordan River to observe the ministry of our kinsman Yochanan the Baptizer."

I replied, "You want me to go spy on Rabbi Yochanan?"

"All I want is for you to go there and report back what you see. Don't tell me you find this mission abhorrent to your tender sensibilities? Surely, if I asked for a complete and thorough report on the whore houses of Antioch you'd be off on the fastest Arabian horse your purse could procure."

I smiled knowing the truth of his words. I said, "It's just that I have fond memories of Yochanan during our youth when his mother would bring him to visit us in Sepphoris."

Yeshua, "It's a shame Princess Elizabeth left us at such a young age. We never saw Yochanan after her death. We may have remained close if she had lived."

"Are you political competitors now?"

"Definitely not competitors as we have the same enemy. The question is to what degree can we collaborate? That is the crux of your mission. Politics is a blood sport Menelaus. It's not a profession for the faint of heart. I need to know to what extent, if any, Rabbi Yochanan opposes my claim upon the throne. Please go with Judas."

"Yes master. And if you ever need the whorehouses of Antioch or Damascus investigated, be sure to call upon me. I promise a thorough job."

Judas and I traveled by foot carrying the barest essentials on our way to the ministry of Rabbi Yochanan. There was nothing but time to kill when traveling by foot. Luckily for me, Judas engaged me in conversation on a broad range of subjects during our journey. He was a staunch Jewish nationalist and zealot but, unlike others zealots I had come in contact with, he tolerated my own moderate religious views. As we neared our destination, I finally worked up the nerve to ask Judas a personal question that somewhat puzzled me, "My friend Judas, we've enjoyed pleasant discourse thus far on our journey so I hesitate to tread on ground that may be uncomfortable."

Judas said, "Allay your fears Menelaus. We are two travelers shooting the breeze as we walk. Let us speak in confidence."

"I don't understand your motivation for signing on with Yeshua. His chief disciples are all relatives. Also, Yeshua is a religious reformer yet you strike me as a hard-line zealot."

Judas replied, "Yeshua is out of daughters so what's in it for me is your question?" We both laughed although no joke had been told. He spoke the truth of my curiosity in his position. When someone parries your question, it means they would rather not answer. My habit in such circumstances was not to press the question but layback and leave it up to the other party whether they wished to respond. He who converses with ears open gathers the most information.

After walking for some time, Judas voluntarily responded further. "My initial attraction to Prince Yeshua was the foreign alliances. We Jews continually complain about Roman occupation. Every so many years, the grumbles turn into action. Where did the last revolt led by my uncle and father get us? It created many Jewish widows and orphans. My own father died with his brothers. I have no fear of death Menelaus but, if one is to sacrifice his life, should not there be some chance of the mission's success? Yeshua offers us that chance. His grandfather, King Antigonus, was the last true Jewish king. He expelled Herod and the Romans to restore Jewish control of our country. Yeshua was born to follow in his grandfather's footsteps. He is renewing the alliances made by King Antigonus."

I wondered whether Judas knew the secret, the huge dark cloud hanging over Yeshua's political campaign—that he was a grandson of Herod. Very few knew the truth. Judas spoke of Yeshua's grandfather the Hasmonean king but did he truly know the identity of Yeshua's other grandfather? Or did he believe Yeshua was the son of Priest Joseph as so many assumed? I avoided this subject and said, "Sorry to be contrarian but King Antigonus was later overthrown and crucified by the Romans. Is this the path you foresee for Yeshua?"

Judas, "King Antigonus died an honorable death. He overcame the Romans and held out as long as he could. Yeshua possesses an even stronger foreign alliance than Antigonus. The key is Prince Petra, grandson of King Aretas. With the Nabateans on board, we have a real shot to make this work. That's all I ask for. We all die eventually. I fear it not. All I ask of God is that my death have purpose."

I switched subjects, "What do you make of Rabbi Yochanan? He is very popular with the people."

Judas replied, "An interesting study Menelaus. Essentially, Rabbi Yochanan intends baptism as a symbol of repentance for sins. But the rabbi does not preach one attains admittance into the kingdom of God merely through baptism. Righteous action is also required. I'm not sure the people understand the subtlety of this distinction. They appear to believe Yochanan's baptism in the Jordan is an alternative to ritual sacrifice at the Temple, that it removes their sins. The poor cannot afford to make offerings at the Temple. Yochanan's baptism costs nothing and the people believe God forgives their sins. From an organizational standpoint, very shrewd."

"On religious grounds, what do you think of Yochanan's baptism?"

"There are legal requirements for water used in a mikveh. It cannot contain water drawn from a standing lake. Spring water, such as flows in the upper Jordan is acceptable but below the Sea of Galilee, the spring water of the upper Jordan mixes with the ritually impure waters of the Sea of Galilee.[105] I am sure the Pharisees will adjudge Yochanan's baptism to be against Jewish law."

"Will the people care what the Pharisees adjudge?"

"The common people have simple minds and simple beliefs. I doubt the doctors of the law will make much headway trying to convince the crowd that the lower River Jordan is ritually impure."

I asked, "Then you've heard him preach?"

Judas, "Yes, I have visited his Jordan ministry many times."

"But you did not join?"

---

[105] See Washing In Water: Trajectories of Ritual Bathing in the Hebrew Bible by Jonathan David Lawrence (Society of Biblical Literature 2007) at page 144, footnote 159. Lawrence cites Mishnah, Parah 8:8-10 on this point.

"No, his movement lacks a military wing. They're just a bunch of peasants with knives and wooden staves for weapons. They stand no chance against the Romans."

"What of the rumored Hasidim army out in the desert east of the Jordon?"

"You mean the fabled Hasidim heavy infantry that saved King Jannai at Shechem?"

Menelaus, "Precisely, do they still exist?"

Judas replied, "I have often speculated that an Hasidim army fought beside King Antigonus to expel the Romans from Israel but, for some reason, did not come to his rescue three years later when Herod besieged Jerusalem. Does this army still exist? Legend has it that a fortress built generations ago by Hyrcanus the Tobiad lies somewhere out in the desert south of Damascus. The Hasidim army we speak of was probably in truth a Tobiad army. Hyrcanus the Tobiad was a Hasmonean ally but I have not seen evidence that a Tobiad or Hasidim army still exists."

"Judas, you seem to be well informed on Rabbi Yochanan. Why again are we making this trip?"

"How strong a position would Rabbi Yeshua be in if we could meld Rabbi Yochanan's populist movement with that of Yeshua? Right now, Yeshua holds popular support in Galilee, Idumea and pockets of the Jewish upper crust in Judea through family connections. He needs the numbers Yochanan draws in Judea."

We arrived at Yochanan's camp by the Jordan in the early hours of the morning. Rabbi Yochanan presented quite a sight wearing a garment made from camel hair drawn by a leather belt. The hair on his head was unshorn in the manner of the Nazarites. He ate not meat nor drank alcohol subsisting on locust and wild honey.[106] We joined the crowds gathered to hear the rabbi speak prior to performing baptisms. This was my first and only opportunity to hear Rabbi Yochanan preach.

---

[106] See *Matthew* 3:4.

He said, "I am the voice of one crying in the wilderness. Make ye ready the way for the coming of the Lord.[107] Repent, for the kingdom of heaven is at hand.[108] To repent is the first step toward God. But you must then exercise virtue, both to one another and piety towards God. The soul shall be thoroughly purified by righteousness.[109] Having repented and put aside wickedness, you must prove yourself as doers of righteousness and not merely hearers of the word who delude themselves. For if anyone is a hearer of the word and not a doer, he is like a man who looks at his natural face in the a mirror; for once he has looked at himself and gone away, he has immediately forgotten what kind of person he was."[110]

Switching from doctrine to politics, the rabbi blasted Antipas' marriage to Herodias as unlawful in the eyes of God. Herodias was the former wife of Antipas' brother (Herod Boethus) who yet lived. The crowd bobbed their collective heads up and down in total agreement. What Jew of the underclass wasn't all for bashing Antipas or any Herodian for that matter? I wondered how many of these people knew that Princess Herodias, whom Rabbi Yochanan referred to only as "that whore", was the sister-in-law of Rabbi Yeshua?

Yochanan continued, "The crooked shall become straight and the rough shall become smooth. All eyes shall see the salvation of God. Repent, walk on the straight path, and God shall forgive. Those who repent are to come and be baptized in the cleansing waters of the Jordan."

Then the people asked Rabbi Yochanan, "What shall we do?"

The rabbi replied, "He that has two coats let him share with he that has none. And he with food, likewise, share with he who has none."

Then a tax collector came forward and asked, "What about me rabbi?"

---

107 *John* 1:23.
108 *Matthew* 3:1-2.
109 Antiquities, XVIII 5:2.
110 See *James* 1:22-24.

Yochanan said, "Take no more from the people than the legally required tax. Do not extort sums from the people to line your own pockets or those of your master."[111]

A party of chief priests from the Temple in Jerusalem rode up behind us as Yochanan spoke. They came to hear the words of the rabbi for themselves. Yochanan noted their arrival and unleashed a flurry of invectives upon them.

Yochanan jabbed with his staff at the chief priests as he said, "You brood of vipers. Who warned you to flee the coming wrath of God? Do not suppose you shall escape the wrath merely by claiming Abraham as your father. God can raise up children of Abraham from stones. The axe is already laid bare. All trees that fail to bear fruit shall be cut down and cast into the fire. He'll not preserve your lot."[112]

One of the chief priests responded for the group, "We have received reports on you Yochanan. Now with our own eyes and ears we confirm the reports are true. Son of Aaron, you are leading the people astray from Yahweh with your illegal baptism. Your ritual means nothing. And who appointed you to speak for God? Only the prophets speak for God. Your actions smack of blasphemy."

With that, they wheeled their horses around and rode off back toward Jerusalem. It was clear to me the religious police from the Temple would appear on the banks of the Jordan sooner rather than later to shut down the ministry of Rabbi Yochanan. But the rabbi showed no outward concern for the confrontation with chief priests of the Temple. If anything, the exchange heightened Yochanan's standing with the people. Did not the chief priests ride off after being rebuked by the rabbi? Many a tactical retreat has been mistaken for victory only to be crushed under marching boots when the enemy later returned in greater strength. The Temple power structure would not stand for this populist rejection of Temple sacrifice promoted by Rabbi Yochanan. Trouble loomed on the horizon for his movement.

---

[111] See *Luke* 3:3-14.

[112] See *Matthew* 3:7-10.

Later in the day, a senior disciple of Yochanan spotted Judas among the crowd and greeted him warmly. The bonhomie disappeared when Yochanan's disciple learned that we were both disciples of Rabbi Yeshua. The man agreed to arrange a private meeting with Yochanan that evening then left our company as if we were lepers. A messenger came for us just before sundown. He directed us to what I would describe as no more than a shelter, leather stretched across a few sticks suitable to keep the rain off but otherwise open to the elements. We found Yochanan seated by a fire drinking a brew that looked for all the world to be seasoned with dirt.

He said, "Brothers, please sit."

We placed out butts upon the naked ground as there was nowhere else to sit. The rabbi continued, "Judas, it is good to see you again. Who is this visitor you bring? He looks familiar."

I answered for myself, "It's been many, many years rabbi. We are age mates and knew each other as children when you visited Sepphoris with your mother."

Yochanan closed his eyes mentally traveling back to a different time and place. The warm glow of recalling fond memories appeared on his face. "Yes, yes, I remember you, the kinsman of Yeshua. Please help me with the name."

"Menelaus ben Bathyllus. My mother is Lady Yohanna." As Philip of Rome had adopted me, I could have given my name as "Menelaus ben Philip" but I was stubborn that way. The Jews didn't fully accept me so I invoked the name of my Greek father whenever possible in protest.

Yochanan reached across the fire grabbing my hand with genuine enthusiasm. Yochanan said, "It's been many years Menelaus. Welcome. And I assume you are both here as representatives of Yeshua."

Rabbi Yochanan didn't beat around the bush, no small talk. He dove right into the heart of the matter leaving Judas and I staring at one another wondering how to proceed with this delicate subject. Judas was the senior member of our embassy so I deferred to him. Judas replied, "Yes rabbi. I have pledged myself to be of whatever assistance I may to Rabbi Yeshua and his wife, Princess Mariam." Yochanan was direct, Judas replied in kind.

Everyone knew what the rabbi thought of Princess Miriam's sister, Herodias. Would he lambaste Yeshua and Mariam by association? This was Judas' concern. Mine went deeper. Did Yochanan know the family secret? That Yeshua was the son of Prince Antipater ben Herod and not Joseph the Nazarite? My heart stopped beating as I listened for the response. Yochanan asked, "Judas, have you met Princess Mariam bat Aristobulus?" [113]

"Yes rabbi."

"I expected a better choice of wife from a leading rabbi." Yochanan obviously referred to her prior marriage to Herod Archelaus.

Judas replied, "Do you not teach the doctrine of repentance rabbi?"

"You know I do Judas but one's actions reflect on their character. We know you by your fruit."

"Of course Rabbi Yochanan but Mariam was a child when King Herod betrothed her to Herod Archelaus."

Yochanan sat silently weighing the words of Judas. He appeared to have an open mind on the question of Princess Mariam.

Judas pressed on, "Archelaus is now dead and, prior to her marriage to Rabbi Yeshua, she lived under a Nazarite vow for one year during which time he personally instructed her. You shall find her possessed of deep spiritual knowledge."

This news surprised Yochanan. He said, "Yeshua instructs women?"

"Yes rabbi."

The conversation jumped from Princess Mariam and prior husbands to potential doctrinal differences. This reinforced my impression Yochanan didn't know the identity of Yeshua's true father. I began to relax as the conversation continued. As Yochanan himself baptized women, I couldn't fathom why he would make an issue on this point. But anything could happen in

---

[113] She was also known as Mary Magdalene.

Jewish political negotiations. Yochanan sat contemplating something. What, we hadn't a clue.

Judas finally broke the silence. "Rabbi, you know Yeshua has gathered disciples and is actively recruiting followers. Menelaus and I are but two of many."

Yochanan, "To what end?"

"Reclaiming the throne of his grandfather, King Antigonus." How would Yochanan respond? Both he and Yeshua were princes of the Hasmonean dynasty whose kings sat on the Jewish throne for over one century. Certainly Yochanan, as a Hasmonean prince, favored the resurrection of the Hasmonean dynasty or so we both assumed. We thought the only issue for discussion was whether the proper candidate for the throne was Yeshua or Yochanan. Yeshua was the grandson of a Hasmonean king while Yochanan the great-grandson of one. Would Yochanan support Yeshua on the basis of his higher Hasmonean royal blood? What came next confirmed my worst fears.

Yochanan replied, "I would be more than happy to see Yeshua lead a revolt to expel the Romans as did his grandfather but he cannot be our king. Yeshua is not Kohen. He is not a son of Aaron and, therefore, cannot be the Messiah of Aaron."

Judas was dumbfounded. Obviously he did not know the truth of Yeshua's ancestry. He looked at me seeking an answer but there was none for me to give. I made an ill-advised effort to reason with Rabbi Yochanan, "Rabbi, Yeshua descends from King David on this father's side and from the righteous Aaron on his mother's side. Do not the scriptures speak of two messiahs and does not the ancestry of Yeshua fit the prophesied messiah?" It was like a young student trying to lecture the teacher.

Yochanan merely shook his head saying, "Yeshua should know this as well as I. We both descend from Mattathias, the righteous teacher who set forth the law we follow. The people are to be led by the Kohanim. There are no exceptions to this rule. Yeshua is eligible to serve as Nasi of the Sanhedrin but not as king."

The entire Yeshua movement and his recruitment of foreign allies centered on his claim to the Jewish throne once held by his grandfather, King Antigonus. It was on this basis that Prince Petra signed on to the program and married Yeshua's stepdaughter. Parthian and Nabatean support hinged on Yeshua becoming king. The re-establishment of the Hasmonean dynasty was at the heart of the Yeshua movement. To accept Rabbi Yochanan's offer would require Yeshua and Yochanan to go back and consult with all their foreign allies, without whom the revolt against Rome could not succeed. Years of work went into building these alliances but Rabbi Yochanan was completely unknown to the allies. He lived his entire life as an ascetic in the Transjordan region with little to no contact with persons outside of his Hasidic community, much less foreign dignitaries. Judas graciously thanked Yochanan for his time and promised to report their conversation to Yeshua but Judas thought the chance of compromise with Yochanan was slim. Yeshua had the foreign contacts. Yeshua was building an army while Yochanan walked around the desert in animal skins carrying a wooden stick. Yet the Judean people revered Rabbi Yochanan. The history of Jewish political discord stretched back to Cain and Abel and never much improved. For this reason the Jews are one of the most conquered people on the face of the earth. A house divided falls.

Jerusalem, Judea (35 CE)

Nasi Gamaliel summoned Eleazar ben Zechariah, chief of Modiin. Nasi Gamaliel was president of the Grand Sanhedrin and grandson of Hillel, the famous Pharisee rabbi.[114] Upon being ushered into Gamaliel's private chambers, Eleazar gave a nod of recognition to Gamaliel's acolyte, Prince Phasaelus ben Timius (Paul of Tarsus), seated in the corner of the room. Eleazar then addressed the Sanhedrin president, "Nasi Gamaliel, how may I be of assistance?"

Nasi Gamaliel replied, "As I am sure you are aware, Yochanan the so-call baptizer has become more than a thorn in our side. The ranks of his followers continue to increase."

---

[114] According to Rabbinic tradition, Hillel and his descendants (including Gamaliel) were said to have held the post of president of the Sanhedrin from 30 BCE to 70 CE.

Eleazar, "I have informants imbedded in his movement and am closely monitoring the situation on the Jordan."

"The chief priests demand we shut down Yochanan's ministry. What course of action do you recommend?"

Eleazar said, "I agree it is time to end this movement. My recommendation is for the Grand Sanhedrin to charge the Baptizer with blasphemy. He pretends to speak for God. Nasi, get me that indictment and I'll personally handle the arrest."

Gamaliel sat contemplating the recommendation from the Modiin chief. The president of the Sanhedrin was too compassionate for Eleazar's tastes. In his view, performance of God's work was often a nasty business. Gamaliel replied, "I think not chief. Find a lesser charge to arrest the baptizer on, not a capital offense. He is a rabbi of priestly descent. We must guard against the possibility that we are fighting against God himself."[115]

The chief of Modiin replied, "But he enflames the passions of the people Nasi. It will be dangerous to hold him at Fortress Antonia."

"Better to enrage the emotions of the people than the anger of God."

Eleazar knew better than to attempt to debate a preeminent rabbi once he invoked the will of God. He nodded his assent to the position of Gamaliel and left his office having other fish to fry. On his way back to the Modiin section of the Temple compound, Eleazar felt the presence of someone walking beside him. He turned to find Prince Phasaelus at his elbow. His political future appeared bright in Jerusalem given his Herodian connections and Hasmonean bloodline.

Phasaelus, "I hope I'm not disturbing you chief."

Eleazar replied, "Not at all prince. What's on your mind?" Eleazar didn't bother to stop walking to address the prince. If the prince wished a private audience away from his master, a little chat while walking on the Temple grounds drew the least attention.

Phasaelus said, "I agree with you chief. The baptizer is dangerous."

---

115 See *Acts of the Apostles*, 5:34-40.

"Well you heard the nasi, no capital offense."

"And the baptizer's fame shall spread like fire in the countryside after we place him in our jail here in Judea. It's a bad move."

"I've been ordered not to kill him so assassination of the baptizer isn't a smart career move. Now, if you want to take on that job, I might be willing to lend a small hand."

Phasaelus stopped and faced the chief. They were alone in the Temple courtyard without a pair of ears within 20 yards.

Phasaelus offered, "Perhaps there is another way."

"Another way?"

"I understand the baptizer rails against tetrarch Herod Antipas at every opportunity. Perhaps Uncle Antipas would be interested in prosecuting Yochanan? That way the blood stays off our hands."

"But how does Antipas gain jurisdiction over Yochanan? Antipas' kingdom is in Galilee and Perea while Yochanan operates in Judea."

"An easy enough legal hurdle to overcome chief. You arrest Yochanan in Judea on lesser charges as ordered by the Sanhedrin. But instead of bringing him back to the Hall of Hewn Stones for trial, transport him across the Jordan to Antipas in Perea. Once in that territory, Yochanan comes under the jurisdiction of Antipas."

The Modiin chief was impressed with the strategic thinking of this young Herodian prince. Eleazar said, "How do we know Antipas will accept the Baptizer as a prisoner and execute him? Antipas might view holding him as dangerous as we do."

Phasaelus replied, "I am close to my cousin Herodias, wife of Antipas. I will make the arrangements with her and she will ensure that Antipas does that which is required."

Eleazar bar Zechariah knew he was in the presence of a rising star in the Herodian clan and made a mental note to keep an eye on the career of Gamaliel's apprentice. He said, "You have a deal Prince Phasaelus. Notify me when arrangements have been finalized with Princess Herodias."

Bethany, Judea (35 CE)

Judas and I reported back to Yeshua on our embassy to the Jordan River. We may have been surprised at the words of Rabbi Yochanan but the master was not. Yeshua said, "Yochanan lives by the rules the Sons of Light. The Kohanim dominate their society."

I still held out hope for finding a negotiated settlement and said, "He did offer the office of Nasi of the Grand Sanhedrin. Judas told me on our return journey that the Teacher of Righteous decreed that the king should not also be high priest. If Yochanan cannot be both king and high priest, perhaps he would accept James the Just as his high priest?"

Judas added, "Under this arrangement, you and James would hold two of the three most important offices in the nation."

Yeshua thought about our proposal in silence. I was relieved to see that he at least thought about the suggestion rather than dismissing it out of hand. He said, "In theory what you suggest is workable; however, in practice, the king holds authority to replace the president to the Sanhedrin and the high priest at any time. And the king appoints all the members of the Sanhedrin."

Judas countered, "But we would also control the military. I suggest Petra would be national military commander."

Yeshua, "Judas, you have studied the scrolls of the Dead Sea Hasidim as have I. Under their rules, the sons of Aaron ride into battle with the military commanders. Who selects the priests for positions of authority throughout the government? It is the prerogative of the king."

Judas did not back down from this line of inquiry. He threw out another idea. Judas said, "What if a member of our community acted as a senior minister to the king and was to be consulted on such decisions?"

Yeshua paused to consider the suggestion. The more we talked the more it appeared there was at least a small window through which compromise with Rabbi Yochanan was possible. Yeshua asked, "And who do you propose for this important position of minister to the king? This individual would need to be held in the deepest trust by myself and James."

Judas, "You know who I propose for the office. Do you trust me rabbi?" Judas the Zealot was born a son of Aaron so he possessed the right blood line for leadership in a kingdom headed by Yochanan the Baptizer. Further, Judas was known to Yochanan. Still, we had no idea whether Yochanan was willing to compromise.

Yeshua cut off further discussion on the issue saying, "Allow me time to contemplate and pray on this issue. The proper course of action will discern itself in due time."

As events played out, our political strategizing about a compromise with Rabbi Yochanan became a useless exercise. News arrived days later that the Temple authorities from Jerusalem arrested Rabbi Yochanan and turned him over to the custody of Herod Antipas in Perea. We were all devastated upon hearing the news.

I indulged myself that evening by transformed a few cups of water into wine after the evening meal. The soothing embrace of Bacchus carried me away to dreamland. As I slept in the dead of night a hand gently shook my shoulder. Was I dreaming? Had one of the servant girls accepted my unspoken offer communicated with a friendly smile during the evening meal? God forbid, Magi Gaspar, was that you? I took in a great gasp of air ready to exhale a mighty scream when Yeshua's hand forcefully wrapped itself across my mouth smothering any sound. He motioned with his finger across his lips not to make a sound. I followed him in the inky blackness to a lamp lit room at the back of Lazarus' home. There in the faint light I found Princess Mariam, her brother Lazarus, and Judas seated on cushions. These were the true disciples of Yeshua, the chosen few privileged to receive Yeshua's inner teaching. Yeshua and I joined them on the floor.

Yeshua said, "Are you awake Menelaus?"

"Yes master."

He continued, "Do you know why we meet in this small group in the darkness of night?"

"No master."

"My disciples disappoint me. They aren't ready to receive the higher message. But those of us here are spiritually awake. We have passed from death to life. I can speak freely here knowing that all have eyes to see and ears to hear."

"But why me? I commit many sins master and am agnostic."

"Yes, you are a sinner Menelaus. Lying happens to be one of your favorite sins for you are not agnostic. I have looked at your inner being and know the truth. You carry on this pretense to be excused from the burden of walking the straight path. It is time for you to awake and join us in the light."

"Yes master."

"As each new member joins our circle, I ask a question to help prepare this person for higher thought. So I ask you Menelaus, where does one find the kingdom of God?"

I'd never pondered this question before, quite fundamental yet infinitely deep. The Pharisees preached that Yahweh resided in the Temple in Jerusalem. But I knew this was not the answer Yeshua looked for. I said, "In the heavens master."

He replied, "If the kingdom is in the heavens then the birds of the sky shall get there before you Menelaus. And if you say it is in the sea, then the fish shall precede you. The kingdom is inside of you and all around you.[116] If you bring forth what is inside of you, it shall save you. Failure to gain knowledge of yourself means you remain asleep, spiritually dead."[117]

I felt like a drunken man lying on the ground having a large bucket of cold water splashed over his face.

Yeshua said, "It is I who am the light of the world. Split a piece of wood, I am there. Lift a stone, and you will find me there as well.[118] Do you find these words blasphemous Menelaus?"

He identified himself with a higher force, something beyond the God of the Torah. This was not the alternatively paternalistic, wrathful God of the Pharisees. I replied, "No master. You have found that which is inside of you. But I don't know

---

[116] *Gospel of Thomas*, Logion 3.
[117] See *Gospel of Thomas*, Logion 70.
[118] *Gospel of Thomas*, Logion 77.

what to call this thing inside of you. Is this what the Greek philosopher Heraclitus spoke of, the logos?"

He replied, "The logos is but an emanation from the source of all. The source is not one thing. It is everything and it is nothing. Words fail in describing the source as it is ineffable. The first emanation from the source is the unbegotten monad, that from which all in the material and spiritual worlds came into being."[119]

Yeshua enlightened me to that which I thought I knew but did not know. I asked, "Where did we come from?"

"It is from the light that we have come. We are its offspring.[120] And it is back to the light we shall go. Become acquainted with your inner light and even greater works than I shall you do."[121]

I asked, "How did this light get inside of our bodies?"

He said, "A question for which I have no answer. It amazes me how this great spiritual wealth has come to dwell in the poverty we call the human body.[122] Fear not the flesh nor love it. If you fear it, it will gain mastery over you. If you love it, it will swallow and paralyze you."[123]

Those words were spoken to me thirty years ago yet I reflect upon them each day and they haunt me every night.

The next day, preparations for our assault on the Temple complex progressed. Petra's shock troops joined us in Bethany. As the time for battle drew near a question nagged at Judas. Judas asked Yeshua, "Rabbi, can I beg a moment of your time in private?"

"Yes Judas."

The two left Lazarus' house walking alone on the streets of Bethany. Once away from the others Judas continued, "The

---

[119] The word "monad" is not found in the Gospels. It was used by Clement of Alexandria. The term "unbegotten monad" was used by Hippolytus in the 3rd century CE while denouncing hereicies. He traced the concept to Pythagoras. *See* Hippolytus, "The Refutation of All Heresies", 06. Concerning Valentinus.

[120] Ibid, see Logion 50.

[121] See *John* 14:12

[122] See *Gospel of Thomas*, Logion 29.

[123] *Gospel of Philip.*

people here in Judea are asking who you are. What should we tell them?"

Yeshua, "Of course, tell them I am the rightful Hasmonean king, grandson of Mattathias Antigonus."

"Yes rabbi but the common people are not very well versed in our history. Antigonus has been dead over 60 years. They know King David and King Solomon from teaching received at the Synagogue but the less educated do not remember King Antigonus. His reign was brief."

Yeshua replied, "The more educated among the people will enlighten the less educated."

Yeshua stopped and faced Yeshua. He said, "Why didn't you tell me you were the grandson of King Herod before I went to meet with Yochanan?"

"I am sorry Judas that the information came to you in this fashion. My assurance the speed of events caused my failure to speak with you on this subject until now. Priest Joseph is not my biological father. I am the son of Antipater ben Herod, the former crown prince and coregent executed by his father Herod."

Judas, "And he was a descendant of Kings David and Solomon! You descend from both King David and from Aaron. The scriptures of the Hasidim speak of two messiahs, one descended from King David and the other from Aaron. You are the grandson of Jewish kings on both sides, the true messiah. I wish to proclaim this to the people."

"No Judas, I have no intention of announcing this to the people. The only way for me to invoke David is to also claim Herod. And another thing, the Idumean royal house of my father also intermarried with the Egyptian Pharaoh. The Pharisees would have a field day with that information. Can you hear the taunts Judas? Yeshua is an Egyptian king. He descends from worshipers of false gods."

"Yes, a two-edged sword rabbi."

Yeshua concluded, "Never have truer words been spoken. When the time is right, I shall be anointed and ride into Jerusalem on a donkey in the prophesied manner for the king's return to Jerusalem but you'll never hear me invoke David or Solomon."

Judas knew how important it was politically to control the message to the people. He said, "And what if the people proclaim you to be the son of David as you walk through the streets?"

"And where would they get this information?"

Judas smiled and said, "A few men in the know might just happen to mingle among the crowd and whisper such words into many ears."

Yeshua replied, "This is a dangerous issue Judas."

"Sedition against Rome is a dangerous game rabbi. Those who play it inherently take risks. I must sell your credentials as the messiah to the people."

Yeshua, "Then do what you must."

Jerusalem, Judea (35 CE)

The seven-day celebration of Passover began. On the Sabbath, Yeshua ventured into Jerusalem with a small group of his disciples. In the city by the Sheep Gate was a spring-fed pool having five porticoes called Bethesda. The sick, blind, lame and afflicted came there for a cure thinking the angels stirred up the waters whenever gasses bubbled up into the pool from the spring below. Yeshua walked by the pool of Bethesda coming upon a man in pain lying on a mat who appeared to have been in this state for a long time. Yeshua said, "Do you not wish a cure? Why don't you get into the water?"

The man replied, "Every time the angles stir the water, it takes me a moment to call a man for help getting into the water. By then, the pool is full of others who rushed in ahead of me leaving no room for me to make it to the spot where the angels touched the water."

Yeshua said, "Do you believe in a cure?"

"Yes, with all my heart."

"Then pick up your mat and go. Your faith has cured you."

Immediately the man was well. He picked up the mat and proceeded on his way only to be stopped by the religious police.[124]

---

[124] See *John* 5:9.

They said, "You there, why are walking around carrying that mat? What's the matter with you, don't you know it's the Sabbath?"

"The man who cured me told me to pick up the mat and go. Before I was lame but now I am cured as you see. I am only following his orders."

The religious police asked, "Who is the man who cured you on the Sabbath?"

"I don't know his name. He walked up to me out of the blue."

"Show us this man."

So the man who had received his cure led the two religious police officials back to the pool at Bethesda looking for Yeshua. After a brief search, he found Yeshua speaking to a small crowd. "There he is. This is the man who cured me."

The religious police went to Yeshua and rebuked him saying, "You there, are you ignorant of the law? You told this man to carry his mat on the Sabbath and he says you cured him as well. These are unlawful acts on the Sabbath."

Yeshua replied, "The Sabbath was made for man, not man for the Sabbath.[125] Is it lawful to do good works on the Sabbath? Or do you counsel evil deeds on the Sabbath?"[126] The hardness of their hearts grieved Yeshua bringing him to anger. Petra backed by James and Yochanan, the sons of thunder, came beside Yeshua ready to confront the religious police. Sensing a fight, the people drew near to see what would come. But Yeshua put his arm out holding back Petra and the others.

Yeshua told them, "Now is not the time." Yeshua and his followers withdrew from Jerusalem returning to Bethany in order to regroup and plan for further operations during the Passover festival.

---

125 *Mark* 2:27.

126 *Mark* 3:4.

Chapter 17

Bethany, Judea (35 CE)

Word of Yeshua's confrontation with the religious police in Jerusalem accelerated the pace of our plans. Rabbi Yeshua put out the word to his men--the planned assault on the Temple complex was on for the next day. Judas' family reputation as a zealot leader greatly aided the recruitment drive as there were large numbers of zealots in Jerusalem for Passover. But the zealots joined only on an ad hoc basis for this single mission against the Temple. They didn't know quite what to make of Yeshua, the Hasmonean prince who appeared to be taking on the establishment. In zealot eyes, the Temple priests were hopelessly corrupt due to their alliance with the Herodians and their Roman overlords. The zealots were not yet sure how far Yeshua was willing to go in overturning the established order. Further, his wife Mariam was a Herodian princess, which made them suspicious of the rabbi.

Despite these doubts, the day of action finally arrived. Petra, together with his Nabatean lieutenants James and Yochanan, prepared the seventy and many new recruits for battle. We had one thousand men and expected members of the crowd to join us once we took action in the Temple. Our people armed themselves lightly with short swords in the style of the Roman gladius and daggers but no armor. Our core fighters under Petra were in high spirits having trained many months with no live action. Judas took command of the zealot wing. Most of these men were green but what they lacked in military experience they made up for with religious fervor. These were sons of men who died in Jewish uprisings against Rome in past generations. The zealots feared not death.

Just before pulling out of Bethany, Petra took me aside. "Menelaus, here, take this dagger."

I replied, "I wouldn't know how to use it."

He said, "Look, you have no military training but everyone should be armed. Take the dagger but only unsheathe it as a last resort."

I took the weapon and placed it under my cloak.

Petra summoned my half-brother, "Philip, come here."

Petra said to Philip, "Do me a favor and stay close to your brother when we get into the Temple. Things could get rough in there." Philip's father had been a soldier and imparted the craft to his son as part of his early training.

I said to Petra, "I'm touched by your concern but don't worry about me. If it is God's will that I leave this world today, so be it."

Petra replied, "It's not you I'm worried about. Rabbi Yeshua is overly attached to you and would be in morning for weeks if you died on this raid."

"So your concern is not to upset the rabbi. As for me, you could give a donkey turd?"

"Exactly."

I smiled as Petra walked away. The big rock head couldn't admit he was concerned for my safety. It was nice to know some small dose of compassion lurked within him. We set off for Jerusalem in waves rather than in one body to reduce the attention we drew while on the road and planned to reform just outside the Temple gates. Success or failure of the rabbi's entire mission hinged on our ability to overwhelm the Temple guards that day. The zealots required proof of Yeshua's bona fides as a rebel leader. Capturing the Temple's outer courtyard would burnish his anti-Roman credentials and strengthen his credibility with the average citizen of Judea. But given the reservations the zealots already harbored about Yeshua, if this mission failed, zealot support would disappear like grains of sand in the wind. And if Yeshua lost the zealots, the average citizens would desert as well. Yeshua engaged in an elaborate dice game that day at the Temple.

Petra commanded 400 fighters; Judas roughly 600. Intelligence pegged the standard number of lightly armed religious police patrolling the Temple grounds at 100. Immediately to the north of the Temple stood Fortress Antonia housing 500 heavily armed Roman legionnaires. One quarter of a mile away stood Herod's majestic palace with another 1000 soldiers. The plan was to quickly overwhelm the lightly armed religious police stationed on the grounds of the Temple's outer courtyard (also known as the Court of the Gentiles) affording Yeshua the opportunity to make a speech to assembled worshippers. He hoped to gain sympathy with the anti-Roman Jews among the crowd. As news spread throughout the city of the activities transpiring in the Temple, we expected thousands of additional festival goers to stream into the Temple joining the rally staged by Yeshua thereby giving us sufficient numbers to hold off the Roman legionnaires stationed at Fortress Antonia. The Roman military acted according to a tightly controlled command structure. Our plan allowed for several hours between taking control of the Temple outer courtyard and orders arriving for the Roman legionnaires to deploy against us as our lightly armed fighters would be no match for them.

Yeshua remained in Lazarus' compound at Bethany until the last man departed. Princess Mariam saw him off. Mariam made a last plea to Yeshua, "Husband, please take no unnecessary risks. Leave the soldiering to Petra and Judas."

He replied, "If I am to be king, I must be there in the thick of things. The people know a coward when they see one." Mariam didn't respond. She hung her head so Yeshua wouldn't see the tears. They shared a tender kiss and Yeshua was off with his men.

Jerusalem, Judea (35 CE)

Our force arrived in two waves that simultaneously stormed through the gates of the outer walls of the Temple complex. The first hint of something amiss came from the number of Temple police on duty that day—double the expected tally. Nonetheless, Petra's veteran mercenaries pushed aside the police with little difficulty. The Temple complex contained three sets of walls. Inside the outermost lay the Court of the Gentiles, by far the largest open area in the Temple complex. The level of commerce within the Temple walls gave one the impression of having entered a bazaar, not a place of worship. Ritual sacrifice of animals to Yahweh for forgiveness of sin was the activity around which all commerce in the Temple revolved. The Temple priests approved of only Jewish or Tyrian money for purchase of sacrificial animals. The Greek and Roman coins carried by the average Jew were marked with graven images making them impure for Temple commerce, according to the priests. This spawned a cottage industry changing Greek or Roman money into Tyrian silver shekels that were acceptable to the priests. And only animals declared ritually pure by the priests could be sacrificed requiring a heavy trade in approved animals on the grounds of the Court of the Gentiles.

What followed after we subdued the Temple police in the outer courtyard had a few of us scratching our heads. Yeshua made a whip from the cords of his belt and began pummeling the moneychangers. He overturned their tables causing coins to fly everywhere. The crowd pounced on the loose money like vultures descending on a kill. Yeshua bellowed with a force I had not heard before. He said, "It is written, 'And my house shall be a house of prayer', but you have made it a den of thieves."[127] He gave the same measure to the sellers of animals for sacrifice saying, "Take these things away and stop making God's house one of commerce."[128]

Yeshua cleansed the Temple complex of the corrupting influence of the merchants in much the same fashion as his Hasmonean forefathers had cleansed the Temple of Hellenistic influences after the defeat of the Seleucid Empire. The theatrics of Yeshua's attacks upon moneychangers and sellers of sacrificial

---

[127] *Luke* 19:46.

[128] *John* 2:16. In the *Gospel of John*, Yeshua expels the money-changers during the first of two or three visits to Jerusalem during Passover. The Synoptic Gospels present Yeshua attending but one Passover during his public career.

animals occurred with no serious injuries. The performance demonstrated to the Jewish people that Yeshua stood ready to oppose the authorities but the rabbi didn't stop there. He went on to lambaste the very foundation of Temple worship—animal sacrifice. He proclaimed, "The prophet Hosea said, 'God desires mercy not sacrifice.'[129] I came to abolish sacrifices, and unless you cease to offer sacrifice of God's creatures, the wrath of God shall not cease upon you."[130]

Those words marked Yeshua as a walking dead man in the eyes of the high priest and the chief priests of the Temple hierarchy. Ritual sacrifice at the Temple was the only approved way to buy forgiveness of sin from God under Jewish law. And revenue derived from animal sacrifice at the Temple largely funded the Temple priesthood, their scribes, the religious police, and even the Sanhedrin. The entire Jewish religious establishment depended upon the mother's milk of korban.[131] The Temple priesthood would defend this institution with the last drop of blood in their veins. In essence, Yeshua declared war on the entire Temple establishment that day. Moments after we seized control of the Court of the Gentiles, Roman troops in full armor began forming up outside the Temple complex's northern gate. It appeared to be an entire cohort, five hundred soldiers. Even worse, I saw an officer strutting around in front of the Roman formation with a plum of feathers coming out of his helmet. Judas predicted a comfortable amount of time would elapse between first sight of Roman troops and a high-ranking officer arriving on the scene but he was mistaken.

While Yeshua continued whipping up the crowd with his rhetoric, Petra and Judas caucused off to the side. They'd obviously seen the Romans. Although not part of the military command, I joined their discussion anyway. Certainly, they had not missed the officer's presence but I was nervous and wished reassurance from these two that we would be safe.

---

129 *Matthew* 9:13.

130 *Gospel of the Hebrews* preserved in quote from Epiphanius.

131 Sacrificial offerings at Temple, which included items other than animals.

Judas said, "No Petra, I'm for immediate withdrawal from the Temple complex. Look, there's an entire cohort of legionnaires right there."

Petra pressed his case, "We can take them brother! Mark how Yeshua has the crowd eating out of his hand. Look at the size of the crowd, thousands and thousands of people. All Yeshua has to do is point at the Romans and yell 'attack'. Our people will lead them."

James and Yochanan, the Jewish mercenaries turned disciples, both threw back their cloaks exposing their weapons. They appeared eager for battle. Judas argued reason, "You're thinking too narrowly Petra. Suppose we defeat the Roman cohort and seize the entire Temple complex. There are two thousand Roman auxiliary troops stationed in the Jerusalem district. How long before they show up at the Temple? Do you wish to fight them with the mob as well? And if we stay here, the Romans will have an entire legion marching from Caesarea by sun up tomorrow. We don't have enough manpower to seize control of the entire city of Jerusalem and defend the walls until relieved by our allies. That could be weeks."

But Petra was adamant, "No, I can have five hundred Nabatean cavalry here in two days. In two weeks, five thousand infantry. In a month, I can recruit an army of Jews. We can make it work."

Judas dug in his heals, "No Petra. I'm going to Yeshua. We pull out now." In retrospect, Petra may very well have been correct. That was the time to seize the moment throwing caution to the wind and let the dice fly. We were unprepared but our enemy was less so. They knew of our arrival in Jerusalem through informants but underestimated Yeshua's appeal with the crowd. The Romans, the Temple establishment, and their Herodian allies never again underestimated the threat Yeshua posed to them. Yeshua sided with the counsel of Judas that day and ordered his followers off the Temple mount. We retreated to Bethany. The Romans held fast at their defensive positions allowing us to exit the Temple complex without bloodshed.

Not long after we pulled out of the Temple complex, Prince Phasaelus paid a visit to chief Eleazar ben Zechariah of Modiin. With him came another Herodian-Hasmonean prince, Costobarus ben Antipater. Phasaelus said, "Chief, I know you have a new problem on your plate with the Yeshua movement but I wish to discuss Rabbi Yochanan. First, let me introduce my cousin, Costobarus ben Antipater."

Chief Eleazar couldn't keep track of the multitude of Herodian princes without a chart. He reasoned the strapping young prince seated next to Phasaelus was the grandson of Costobarus and Salome, the great Herodian witch. If this young man possessed an ounce of his grandmother Salome's malevolence, then he would be very useful in carrying out Yahweh's work. The chief dispensed with preliminary pleasantries cutting right to the heart of the matter. The chief said, "The explosion of the Yeshua movement today at the Temple adds urgency to the baptizer situation. We can't have these two insurrectionist movements running amok in Judea at the same time. They may coalesce into one powerful juggernaut."

Phasaelus, "I am in agreement with your thinking chief. Antipas and his wife Herodias are here in Jerusalem for Passover. Costobarus and I were able to secure a private audience with Herodias and she is completely on board with eliminating the baptizer. His words condemning Antipas' marriage to Herodias are whispered among courtiers in his palace and Herodias has had enough."

Chief Eleazar replied, "But how much sway does she have with her husband?"

Phasaelus, "Your question is whether Antipas would execute a rabbi clad in animal skins to keep his Hasmonean wife happy? You can take it to the treasury chief. Antipas wishes above all things to be a Jewish king. For that, he requires a Hasmonean wife."

Chief Eleazar, "Tell Herodias to do whatever is necessary to persuade Antipas to execute the baptizer."

Phasaelus, "It shall be done chief."

The fathers of both of these young princes did not descend from Jewish kings; therefore, their prospects for one day ruling even minor kingdoms were bleak. Although they both possessed priestly Hasmonean blood through their mothers, their fathers were not of the tribe of Levi meaning neither Phasaelus nor Costobarus were eligible for positions as Temple priests much less the office of high priest. The word around Jerusalem had young Phasaelus' grandmother, Princess Salampsio, angling to marry off her grandson to a daughter of the high priest Caiaphas.[132] In Chief Eleazar's opinion, the prospects for Phasaelus and Costobarus marrying into the families of high priests were minimal. Jewish law dictated that status as Kohen passed from father to son. No high priest would marry off his daughter to a man lacking the proper priestly lineage absent massive political leverage. Princess Salampsio was a daughter of King Herod but he had been dead for thirty years. His bloodline meant little to the Temple priests. Late in life, Salampsio lacked the political juice to arrange a high level marriage into the upper reaches of the priesthood. Chief Eleazar wondered if the zeal young Phasaelus held for the destruction of rival Jewish political parties would wane once it became clear he couldn't marry his way any higher in Jewish society than voting member of the Sanhedrin. That was the highest rung open to Prince Phasaelus. Would it be enough to satisfy his ambition or would Phasaelus switch allegiances when this realization sank in? Chief Eleazar made a mental note to keep an eye on Phasaelus.

Bethany, Judea (35 CE)

A jubilant mood prevailed back at our base in Bethany. We briefly held the Temple complex while rubbing the noses of the religious police into the ox dung without suffering a single casualty. All were merry except for Petra. He sulked like a child due to being overruled on whether to attack the Romans troops at the Temple. This was not what Yeshua had in mind when he instructed his disciples to become like little children in order to

---

[132] According to Epiphanius, an Ebonite tradition holds that Paul of Tarsus came to Jerusalem to marry the daughter of a high priest who rejected him.

enter the kingdom of God. The situation gnawed at Petra's ego producing venom he directed at Judas. Under Petra's compact with Yeshua, he was to be undisputed military commander yet Judas held greater confidence in these matters with Yeshua. Petra asked for a private audience with Yeshua. He said, "Rabbi, as you know, my grandfather the king declared war on my father Herod Antipas. I ask your leave to return to my command in the Nabatean army to fight in the coming battle."

Yeshua held a serious stake in the outcome of this war. If Antipas defeated Yeshua's allies the Nabateans, his entire plan for capturing the Jewish throne became untenable. Yeshua could not prevail without the support of Nabatea. It was in the best interests of all concerned for Petra to return to Nabatea and offer what assistance he could in prosecuting the war. But how many of the few troops they had assembled did Petra plan to take with him? Yeshua ascended to a much higher profile the day of the great Temple raid and, correspondingly, his need for personal protection rose. Yeshua asked, "What of your mercenaries? They provide protection for our group."

"I request only twelve men as a personal guard for my trip back to Nabatea. Command of the seventy passes to the sons of thunder who shall stay."

"And your wife, Princess Mariam? She cannot return home to Galilee while you war on Herod Antipas. Are you taking her to Nabatea?"

"No rabbi. She is with child. I have spoken to Prince Lazarus who has offered her protection here in Bethany during the war."

"I will miss your company friend."

Petra embraced Yeshua then immediately made preparations to leave for Nabatea. Fate diffused the tension between he and Judas. We did not see Petra for several months during which time he commanded an elite unit of the Nabatean cavalry in their war against Antipas. Before quitting Bethany, Yeshua issued instructions to his disciples. The community shall dress and conduct themselves more closely to the Nazarene ideal, whose members were referred to as "the poor ones".

Yeshua said, "Do not acquire gold, or silver, or copper for your money belt. You'll not require a bag for your possessions, as no one shall carry an extra tunic or sandals.[133] Do not worry from dawn to dusk about what you wear.[134] For it is easier for a camel to pass through the eye of a needle than a rich man to reach the kingdom of God.[135] To bring about truth, justice and uprightness on earth, one enters God's community by placing his money in a common purse."[136]

With my customary impertinence, I replied from the back of the room, "I'm not shaving the hair from my head like the Nazarites when their vow ends."

Yeshua and the rest took the comment in good humor having a laugh at my joke. Yeshua replied, "Never in life Sampson would I ask for you to give up your precious locks."

Prior to our departure, Yeshua authorized the initiation of Lazarus into the mysteries. Judas, also an initiate, agreed to stay behind in Bethany for a few days to officiate during the ritual, which was to last three days. I'm under vow not to reveal the particulars of this sacrament but I can say it involved symbolic death to body and rebirth in spirit.

Jerusalem, Judea (35 CE)

I slipped back into Jerusalem the next day to mingle among the crowd at the Temple trying to judge their reaction to the appearance of Yeshua and his followers the prior day but my mind wandered from the intended mission. There was music and dancing in the Temple outer courtyard during the festival. I watched the girls with interest. It had been over a year since I had been with a woman. The last opportunity presented itself at the Cana wedding but I got too drunk to try my luck with the serving girls that night. There I stood in the most sacred place in the Jewish universe during the second most important religious festival with carnal desire glowing inside me. Religious festival or not,

---

133 *Matthew* 10:10.

134 *Gospel of Thomas*, Logion 36.

135 *Mark* 10:25.

136 *The Rule of the Community* (Dead Sea Scrolls).

wherever on earth men gather in numbers women of a certain type follow. I walked with purpose to the main open-air market outside the Temple. My eye knew what to look for--women not really shopping who were holding empty baskets and dressed more fashionably than Jewish matrons of the middle to lower classes. I spotted a group of three women huddled together engaged in idle conversation with empty baskets. They wore imported silk scarves. Their jewelry was fine silver, perhaps from Tyre.

Jewish religious law contained extensive rules regarding marriage. Further, the law recognized the relationship of pilegesh, a concubine who was something of a quasi-wife with protected contract rights. Rabbis in Babylon also allowed for, but never officially sanctioned, yet another class of male-female relationship, that of the temporary wife.[137] We Jews in Palestine adopted this eastern practice on the sly as a way of giving legal cover to our prostitutes. The fig leaf of entering into a temporary marriage contract allowed a female prostitute to serve clients with some protection against being hauled before the Sanhedrin on the capital charge of adultery.

I approached the most attractive of the three women. She had dark hair, olive skin, and almond-shaped eyes. She had the look of the women of the desert. I really didn't care. She could have been born on the moon and I still would have pursued her. As I drew near my nostrils were filled with the fine sensuous scent of her perfume.

She said, "Hello friend. Can I help you?"

She had me at shalom. Of course she could help me. I desperately needed the weight of male desire lifted from between my legs. The only question was how much? Yeshua's Nazarene austerity program meant that I was dressed in near rags that day and had no money. I'm sure my prospective temporary wife wondered whether I had even one shekel in my pouch. I mumbled a greeting of some sort. She took my arm and said, "Not here. Talk to me while we walk about the market."

---

137 Jewish Marriage In Antiquity by Michael L. Satlow (Princeton University Press, 2001) at page 193-95.

I asked, "What is your name?"

"Batsheba."

This was certainly a nom de guerre but I didn't care to know her real name. Batsheba was confident and worldly. Her voice put me at ease. No tension or shame lingered between us as our casual discussion of the services to be rendered reached the issue of compensation. She named her price and asked me if this was acceptable. I am sure she expected me to decline due to inability to pay.

What I said next surprised even me, "The price is acceptable however I don't have coins with me. I shall need to acquire funds from my mother. Please do me the favor of waiting here until I return."

"Your mother?"

I smiled, "She knows her son and shall not be shocked by the request."

My step-father, Philip of Rome, died years ago leaving my mother a relatively young widow of Hasmonean blood. However, her prior marriage to a Greek freedman somewhat tainted her stock on the Jewish marriage market. Herod Antipas' chief minister Chuza, also of Greek ancestry, pursued my mother and married her. She thereafter lived a lavish lifestyle in the home of Herod Antipas.

I went to Antipas' mansion in Jerusalem and found my mother in residence. She knew the reason for my appearance without my saying. Mothers intuitively know these things. Neither the price of the services nor the pendency of a holy festival upset her. She assumed I was buying a high-level prostitute so the price was within reason. The act itself did not concern her, only the public perception should my activities attract notice.

She said, "Someone will see you coming from this whore's tent. There are so many people in Jerusalem now. Can't you wait until after the festival?"

I tried to explain to her that Yeshua planned to stay in Jerusalem only for the festival then we would be off for the Judean desert or Galilee, where we lived as celibate monks. I needed this.

Lady Yohanna, "Need? Are your swollen testicles more important than family honor? If you get caught word will spread and I'll never be able to find you a suitable wife. You'll have to marry one of those village tramps who follow Yeshua around the countryside."

I protested her assault upon the virtue of the young women who traveled with our company. These were sisters of male members of our community meaning they traveled with a male escort from their family as required by Jewish custom. That didn't stop people from gossiping about the immorality of Yeshua's circle of traveling companions. Not only did young, unmarried women accompany us but we also ate communally as opposed to segregated by sex in accordance with custom. This reinforced the perception of immorality within our community.

My mother swatted aside my protest and moved on to another of her favorite irritants, "Why do you never have money? Doesn't Yeshua pay for your services as his chief steward?" Apparently my mother was more concerned I had no money than the fact that I was buying a prostitute over Passover. She had changed since marrying Chuza. The humbleness, the soft warmth of her person were now gone. This conversation with my mother brought home to me the exemplary virtue of Mariam Magdalene and the other women instructed by Yeshua.

Behind me I heard an excited small voice, "Father!"

It was my five-year-old daughter Theudosia. She ran to me and hugged me tightly despite the fact that I had not seen her for many months. I was a miserable father who did not deserve love from his daughter. Theudosia and I sat in the palace garden talking for more than an hour, then I left not to see her again for another year.

Batsheba was mildly upset when I returned to the market having been gone for almost two hours but the money resolved the situation. I spent three glorious days and three wicked nights with my temporary wife Batsheba. When it was over, I returned to my life as a celibate Nazarene monk catching up with our party in the Judean countryside. Yeshua never asked me where I had been. He could read any man's soul to the core. We took a walk during which he said nothing until we were alone. His only words were a parable, "A farmer sowed his field. As he sowed, some seed fell on hard ground and the birds of the air devoured it. And some fell on stony ground with little soil. It sprang up but was withered by the sun. Other seed fell among the thorns and their yield was choked. The rest feel on fertile ground and brought forth an abundant harvest. He who has ears to hear, let him hear."[138] Yeshua walked away leaving me to ponder his message. I was the rocky ground. Yeshua gave me the seed but my stubbornness refused to let the seed take root.

Jericho, Judea (35 CE)

Yeshua led our party to the Jordan River valley after Yochanan the Baptizer had been arrested. His people had moved north along the Jordan River out of Judea and into Decapolis, near Aenon. We set up camp outside of Jericho just north of the Dead Sea not far from the old Hasmonean fortress at Qumran. Yeshua delegated his disciples with the task of baptizing in the river, while he told parables to the people and healed the sick. Yeshua attracted large crowds soon after setting up camp near the Jordan. The groundwork laid by Yochanan in this same area accrued to Yeshua's benefit. The people already understood ritual baptism as an alternative to expensive ritual sacrifices at the Temple. The concepts of forgiveness, love, renouncing material possessions were all preached by Yochanan and dovetailed into the program presented by Yeshua. The poor and uneducated mostly came to us in the wilderness seeking redemption. These people were an important constituency in Yeshua's bid for the throne.

Shortly after our ministry of baptism started up near Jericho, Herodian princes Phasaelus and Costobarus arrived with prominent Pharisee rabbis. In search of distinction among his peers, Phasaelus engaged Yeshua in debate before the crowd. He said, "Rabbi, we know you are a man of truth and teach the way of God so tell us, is it lawful to pay taxes to Caesar?"

---

[138] *Mark* 4:3-9.

It was a loaded question designed to trap Yeshua. If he denounced the payment of taxes to Caesar, the Romans might arrest him for insurrection. But speaking in favor of paying taxes to the Romans was political suicide with the common people who virulently hated taxes of any kind. Yeshua responded, "Show me the coin used to pay the tax."

Someone from the crowd handed him a denarii, which he inspected. Yeshua continued, "Here is Caesar's likeness on the coin. Pay to Caesar what is Caesar's, to God what is God's, but give to me that which is mine.[139] Woe unto the Pharisees for what they resemble is a dog sleeping in the manger of cattle, for it neither eats nor allows the cattle to feed."[140] Yeshua deftly parried the question while countering with a jab back at the Pharisees. Only Phasaelus among the Pharisees caught the meaning of Yeshua's phrase, "give to me that which is mine." Yeshua referred to the Hasmonean throne of his grandfather King Antigonus.

Members of the Sadducee party had likewise ridden out from Jerusalem and now wished to join the debate. One asked, "Tell us rabbi, if a man dies leaving a wife, the law says his brother should marry the wife. Let's suppose the brother also dies and yet another relative marries the woman and dies. Later the woman dies as well. In the resurrection, whose wife shall she be under God's law?" The question was intended to mock Yeshua. For his wife Princess Mariam had been thrice married and her fist two husbands were brothers (i.e., Antipater and Archelaus, who were both now dead). Few in the crowd understood reference in the question to Princess Mariam Magdalene but those who did chuckled to themselves.

Yeshua replied, "You do not understand the scriptures or the power of God. The god of Moses is god of the living, not the dead. For the dead, when they rise up, they do not marry. They are like the angels in heaven."[141] The Sadducees had no response for they did not understand Yeshua's reference to those who rise

---

[139] *Matthew* 22:15-21; *Gospel of Thomas*, Logion 100 adds the phrase "give to me that which is mine" to the quote.

[140] *Gospel of Thomas*, Logion 102.

[141] See *Mark* 12:18-27.

from the dead. He meant that individuals who spiritually rise from the dead live celibate lives and do not marry.

Phasaelus again addressed Yeshua, "Rabbi, sorry to be the bearer of bad news but your cousin Yochanan was executed by Herod Antipas yesterday." The news of Rabbi Yochanan's execution rippled through the crowd horrifying the people. A great murmur rose up among them. The sons of thunder, James and Yochanan, had heard enough. Together with a detachment from the seventy, they physically removed the mixed Pharisee / Sadducee contingent from the crowd sending them forcefully on their way back to Jerusalem.

The next day, Princesses Mariam Magdalene and young Mariam (wife and stepdaughter of Yeshua, respectively) arrived at our camp near Jericho. They appeared in an excited state exclaiming that Lazarus was dead. The women begged Yeshua to return to Bethany immediately to aid Lazarus. Princess Mariam, like I, was not an initiate of the mysteries yet she knew Lazarus was in the midst of a special Nazarene sacrament the specifics of which were beyond her grade in the order. His wife's appearance at the Jordan River with her pregnant daughter left Yeshua unamused. No emergency existed in his mind. He said, "Wife, I told you Lazarus was undergoing initiation. I also told you to leave he and Judas in complete peace."

Princess Mariam did not appreciate the public scolding. She replied, "I realize that husband but an important letter arrived from our mother in Rome and I thought Lazarus would wish to see it immediately."

Yeshua took his wife by the arm to speak with her privately, "So you invaded the ceremony?"

"Yes."

"And what did you see?"

"They were in a stone tomb cut into a hill. It was a burial tomb. And Lazarus was laid out for burial wrapped in white linen. Judas sat praying."

"And this startled you?"

"Of course husband. I ran to my brother Lazarus and grabbed his hand. It was cold to the touch. His skin was bluish. I pulled back the shroud to see his face. His eyes were rolled back in his head. He's dead." Mariam then fell to the ground sobbing violently.

Yeshua said to her, "Get up wife. Here take my hand. Get up." He helped Mariam to her feet and embraced her. Once she calmed down, he spoke to her further. "What did Judas do when you screamed?"

She replied still sobbing, "Nothing, he just kept praying."

Yeshua said, "Listen, the brother you knew is dead. Just as Jonah rose from the belly of the fish after three days and nights so too will your brother Lazarus rise again."

"In heaven?"

"No, here in this world. Do you believe in me?"

"You know I do husband."

"Then return to Bethany and keep everyone away from the tomb. Lazarus is in good hands with Judas."

It took two days for us to cover the relatively short distance from just east of Jericho back to Bethany. Yeshua stopped to preach and cure the sick at every miniscule village we encountered along the way. The disciples were truly perplexed by his reaction to the news that Lazarus, his brother in law and close companion, was dead. Yeshua acted as if he had all the time in the world to return to his family in Bethany.

Bethany, Judea (35 CE)

After Lazarus had been in the tomb three days and nights, we arrived back at Bethany. Throngs of wailing women lined every corner of Lazarus' home. Relatives, and relatives of relatives, made their way from all over Judea to mourn the loss of the young Hasmonean prince. Mariam was extremely upset with her husband for taking so long to return to Bethany. She thought any chance of saving Lazarus died days ago. A throng of people followed Yeshua to the tomb upon his return to Bethany. He ordered the large stone blocking the tomb be rolled back. Mariam tried to stop him. "Husband, it has been three days and three nights. The stench in the tomb will be terrible. Please stop."

Yeshua replied, "I thought you believed in me wife. You men, go ahead and roll back the stone." When they had finished moving the stone, Yeshua commanded in a booming voice, "Lazarus, arise and come forth."[142] In response, Lazarus exited the tomb still wrapped in his burial shroud. Mariam and her daughter fainted in shock. The people proclaimed they had seen Yeshua raise Lazarus from the dead. They shouted news of the miracle throughout the country.

[142] *John*, Chapter 11.

Chapter 18

Alexandria, Egypt (67 CE)

Menelaus paused telling his story as, truth be known, several hours of discussion had worn the old man down. His days were now filled with silence and peaceful reflection. He'd not spoken so many words in more years than he cared to remember. Perhaps his grandson should be on his way to meet up with his friends? Menelaus recalled the long gone days when he felt his oats, a virile stag primed to join the rut. What he wouldn't give to trade places with his grandson for just one evening! Instead, the old man satisfied himself with vicarious pleasure through imagining the conquests of his grandson.

Theudas said, "Grandfather, stop grinning! I know you are thinking about your prostitute in Jerusalem. What was her name?"

Menelaus replied, "Batsheba was her working name. You knew her as Tanith."

"Wait a minute! My grandmother was a prostitute?"

There was much for Menelaus to explain about his grandson's Jewish ancestry but it would have to wait if Menelaus was to complete the story up to the crucifixion of Yeshua before Theudas left for the evening. Menelaus said, "Tanith was not your grandmother. Your grandmother was a minor Hasmonean noble from the village of Mod'in, just as was my mother Yohanna. She died in childbirth when your mother was born. When I left Israel for Egypt, I brought with me your mother Theudosia and Tanith."

"Now I know why sadness comes over my mother whenever I ask her about her life in Israel."

"Your mother is a strong woman, whom I love deeply. She never complained about her lot in life. I pray she has passed that strength on to you."

Theudas was deep in thought. He said, "I have so many questions about my mother's family."

Menelaus, "Please hold them. I cannot finish the story of Yeshua up to the crucifixion before you leave this evening unless I press on. And there are things about your mother's family back in Israel that cannot be fully explained until I first relate the story of Yeshua. Is that acceptable to you grandson?"

Theudas, "Yes grandfather, this is acceptable but I'm off with father for a trading trip to Cyrus on the morning tide. We may go from there to Antioch as well, thus, we could be gone a month or more."

The old man collected himself realizing circumstances dictated the best course of action was to tell of the climatic events surrounding the crucifixion of Yeshua in Jerusalem before his son set sail in the morning. "I'm pleased to hear that you will be joining your father on a business trip. Perhaps this will be a first step into your father's world of commerce?"

"Perhaps grandfather but perhaps not. I don't understand why my grandfather the philosopher urges me to join my father in business? Won't that take me away from intellectual pursuits?"

"Yes grandson, for a time it will. But I have found man does not emerge from the womb fully prepared for philosophy. First he must gather experience in the world of men before retreating to the inner world of spiritual thought. Jonah must first be swallowed by the whale before his spiritual rebirth."

"Jonah?"

Menelaus knew his grandson lacked even a basic understanding of Hebrew scripture, something he hoped to remedy one day but tonight was not the time. He said, "Jonah is a figure from Hebrew scripture. Let us return to the story of Yeshua. The execution of Yochanan the Baptizer highly incensed the emotions of the Jewish people. One hates to benefit from another's misfortune but Yeshua's movement picked up converts after the execution. The core disciples of Yochanan, however, refused to recognize Yeshua as their new leader. They carried on as before but without their leader."

"Grandfather, what about Petra and the Nabatean war against Antipas?"

"Thanks for reminding me. In a short campaign, the Nabateans soundly defeated Antipas on the field of battle east of Perea. The forces of Antipas retreated back to Galilee in disarray. Had King Aretas been so inclined, he could have overrun all of Perea and Galilee."

"Why didn't he?"

"The Romans. They always return in greater numbers for payback. The bigger the offense, the greater the Roman payback. King Aretas played it right. He bloodied the forces of Antipas restoring family honor, seized a few border towns, and then returned home to a hero's welcome declaring victory."

"And did the defeat of Antipas by the Nabateans help Yeshua?"

"Definitely. The Jewish people saw Antipas' defeat at the hands of the Nabateans as God's punishment on the Tetrarch for beheading the righteous Rabbi Yochanan. The people knew Yochanan and Yeshua were cousins; therefore, the people's sympathy for Yochanan helped Yeshua. With Yochanan dead, the Temple priests now focused on Yeshua by nipping at his heals wherever he preached in Judea. Arrest appeared imminent so we retreated to Galilee. Herod Antipas wasn't in a position to move against Yeshua with his depleted army having recently been crushed by the Nabateans and our numbers swelled by the influx of zealots recruited by Judas. We traveled about Galilee freely growing ever stronger after the Nabatean defeat of Antipas. We also received funds from our Parthian allies. These were happy times for Yeshua and his political movement."

Theudas, "Did Yeshua stay in Galilee where he was safe?"

"No grandson. Jerusalem was always the prize. He was just biding his time in Galilee waiting for the right moment to make his move. The right moment came the next year. The sympathy of the Jewish people for Yeshua was at its high point. Antipas had been weakened. Further, the Romans sent two legions east out of their Syria Province to attempt to put their puppet on the Parthian throne. The time for Yeshua's grand dice throw against the Romans had arrived."

"When was this?"

"Passover in the year before Tiberius Caesar died."[143]

---

[143] 36 CE.

Chapter 19

Capernaum, Galilee (36 CE)

In first days of the New Year, Petra returned to us after ably assisting his grandfather in the Nabatean defeat of Herod Antipas. King Aretas played his game pieces prudently by springing his attack on Antipas just as two of the four Roman legions in the Syria province received orders to move out for Parthia. Roman governor Lucius Vitellius[144] marched two legions east picking up allied forces en route for the campaign. Artabanus ruled as an unpopular Parthian king. He made an aggressive political move grabbing the throne of Armenia to appear stronger to the Parthian people. Tiberius Caesar did not take the posturing of Artabanus lightly. He countered the Parthian aggression by ordering proconsul Vitellius to invade Parthia and install Phraates, a Roman tool, on the Parthian throne. This order came down from Caesar during the winter of the previous year.

Prince Petra returned to us from the Nabatean victory accompanied by an additional five hundred mercenaries plus a chest loaded with denarii from King Aretas. Months spent in the field commanding troops changed Petra. A more seasoned, less emotional man now stood before us. Whatever animosity existed between he and Judas was gone. They clasped each other's shoulders like brothers. A small feast was had to celebrate the return of our Nabatean prince. To the surprise of many, Petra and Judas reclined next to each other during the meal deep in conversation. Yeshua came to them and said, "Gentlemen, please

---

[144] His son Aulus Vitellius briefly became Roman emperor in 69 CE during the year of the four emperors.

excuse my intrusion into your conversation but I wish to hear any news Petra brings of our Parthian allies."

Petra, "The Roman and Parthian armies have not yet engaged rabbi. My last report has the Romans camped west of the Euphrates with three legions. They are joined by rebel factions from within the Parthian Empire. Artabanus sits uneasily on the Parthian throne and may not survive."

Yeshua inquired further, "How do you think the situation will play out?"

Many more followers of Yeshua now gathered around as we were all anxious to hear the news of the Roman foray into Babylon. All ears turned to Petra as he continued, "I discussed this issue at length with my grandfather's generals before leaving Nabatea and all agreed that the Parthians will use the same strategy they employed years ago against the Roman invasion under Crassus."

Marcus Licinius Crassus was the wealthiest Roman of his day, a successful general, and the third member of the First Triumvirate (Pompeii Magnus and Julius Caesar being the other two). Crassus invaded Parthia seeking a capstone military achievement; however, the Romans were slaughtered by the Parthians at Carrhae losing 20,000 killed and 10,000 captured.[145]

No one spoke waiting for Petra to elaborate further. He continued, "Crassus also led Roman legions from Syria overland into Babylon just as governor Vitellius has done. In the case of Crassus, instead of directly engaging the heavy Roman infantry the Parthians retreated into the wilderness stretching the Roman supply lines out further and further. Then they used their superior cavalry and mounted archers to continually harass the Romans thereby weakening the integrity of the Roman formation as the engagement dragged on. Crassus sent his son Publius out on a cavalry charge against the Parthians to clear his flanks from harassment but the Parthian cavalry annihilated the Romans under Publius. They decapitated Publius and paraded his head on a pike in front of the Roman lines. Discipline broke down even further

---

[145] The invasion occurred in 53 BCE.

after that debacle and the Romans were routed. The Parthians killed Crassus at Carrhae, the birthplace of our patriarch Abraham."

All eyes turned to Yeshua who listened intently to the words of Petra. Finally Yeshua spoke, "So you expect the Parthians to suck Vitellius deeper into Parthia where they can use their mobility to advantage against the heavy Roman infantry?"

Petra replied, "It is not just my opinion Yeshua but that of all the leading Nabatean generals. Why wouldn't they follow a strategy twice proven successful against the Romans?"[146]

Yeshua said something next that I didn't credit at the time but perhaps he had a premonition, "Because men left to their own devices often do that which is imprudent. They focus on short term gain sacrificing that which is clearly the most beneficial long term course of action. Remember that Petra."

Petra didn't know what to make of Yeshua's comment but he clearly viewed that year as the proper time for our movement to seize the Jewish throne. He asked Yeshua, "So do we march on Jerusalem?"

Yeshua replied, "We no longer can expect Parthian troops coming to Jerusalem to aid us in fending off the Romans yet you recommend we move on Jerusalem?"

Petra replied, "Yes rabbi. Now is the time. We cannot count on Parthian soldiers but they are engaged with two standard Roman legions plus an auxiliary legion from the Syria province far to the east of Palestine. These are legions no longer available for deployment in Judea. The Romans have only two legions currently in the entire province. It creates an opening for us."

Yeshua, "Let me sleep on it Petra. The sands shift beneath our feet." With the next sunrise, Petra and Judas sought out Yeshua finding him seated alone on a rock outside of town silently staring out at the Sea of Galilee. The burden of his mission weighed on him. Wherever we went in Galilee, hundreds, even thousands of well-wishers crowded around Yeshua seeking cures

---

146 The Parthians used a similar strategy to defeat Roman legions under Marc Antony in 36 BCE.

for this or that illness. The size of the crowds made it ever more difficult for him to preach. His ministry had become more magic act and less spiritual instruction. Even at this early hour of the morning, dozens of villagers from the rural areas of Galilee waited outside Yeshua's home for an audience hoping for cures. Petra and Judas stood silently beside the rabbi waiting to be addressed. They hated to interrupt his moments of solitude but first light was their only chance for a private audience until well after nightfall.

Finally Yeshua addressed them, "Yes my brothers, what brings you to the seashore at this hour? A day of fishing perhaps?"

"No rabbi. We come to petition you to move against the Temple in Jerusalem this Passover."

Yeshua asked, "Petra just returned to us from the war against Antipas. Shouldn't we build up our forces before attacking?"

Petra replied, "When Antipas went down in defeat, half the Roman auxiliaries from Israel were lost with him. At last report, three Roman legions from the Syria province are at the Euphrates River. The Roman emperor Tiberius still resides on the Isle of Capri. A purge of Roman bureaucrats appointed by Sejanus rages in the provinces weakening the position of Pilate who was appointed by Sejanus. Now is the time to strike while Herodian and Roman forces are at their most vulnerable and our Nabatean allies at their most powerful. Consider further that we now employ eight hundred mercenaries. Denarii drain from our purse each day just feeding them, much less meeting the monthly payroll."

Yeshua, "Do you both agree that now is the time?" Just then my brother Philip walked up with a message from Joseph of Arimathea. Yeshua opened the scroll and read it privately. He sat staring at the scroll as if he didn't quite understand the words.

I had followed Philip to Yeshua and asked, "What is it master?"

"The Sanhedrin has condemned me to death for the practice of sorcery and seducing Israel to idolatry."[147]

---

[147] *Talmud*, b Sanh 43a; *see* translation by Dr. Peter Schafer at pages 64-65 of his book Yeshua in the Talmud (Princeton University Press, 2009).

Judas exclaimed, “How can they have a trial without your presence? This can’t be!”

Yeshua replied, “Apparently the chief priests so fear the great Egyptian sorcerer that they tried me in absentia without even giving me notice of the charges.” Yeshua looked each of us in the eyes to measure our reaction to the news. His gaze found no fear among his closest followers. Instead, he found determination. He said, “Well then, it is done brothers. The Sanhedrin has made our decision for us. We march on Jerusalem. May God’s will be done!”

Judas and Petra smiled while nodding their agreement. The sons of thunder strapped on belts containing their armament as if the battle were upon us that instant. The die was cast for Passover in the twenty-second year of the reign of Tiberius. None of us were quite prepared for the events that later unfolded in Jerusalem.

Shechem, Samaria (36 CE)

We moved south from Galilee into Samaria on the ancient road to Jerusalem, more an army than a rabbi and his followers. Petra led two thousand Jewish mercenaries some of whom carried kits of armor while Judas walked at the head of three thousand Galilean Jewish zealots, five thousand men total. We had hoped to take double that number south with us from Galilee but, when the time comes for action, men become weak. Many more in Galilee came to hear Yeshua speak and cheered his healing of the sick and other miracles but were nowhere to be found as we marched toward destiny. Tepid Galilean support forced Yeshua’s hand. We entered Samaria en route to Judea in search of converts to the movement. Just the prior year when sending his disciples out as ambassadors to the Jewish people Yeshua issued explicit instructions regarding the Samaritans. He said, “"Do not go in the way of the Gentiles, and do not enter any city of the Samaritans; but rather go to the lost sheep of the house of Israel."[148] Yeshua knew his decision to recruit Samaritans wouldn’t sit well with Judas

---

148 *Matthew* 10:5-6.

and his zealot followers (or the Hasidim for that matter) so Yeshua kept the decision private until the matter was a fait accompli.

Jews held the Samaritans in contempt due to their mixed race and hybrid religion. The Assyrians defeated the Northern Kingdom of Israel (the land now known as Samaria) over seven hundred years ago in antiquity. After the defeat, the Assyrians took a large portion of the Jewish population of the northern kingdom into exile. Those left behind intermarried with Assyrian settlers. The Samaritans ceased worshipping at the Temple in Jerusalem and, instead, erected their own temple at Mount Gerizim. The Samaritan brand of Judaism blended elements from the local Assyrian religion, something anathema to the Jews. Hasmonean King Yochanan Hyrcanus, a Hasmonean ancestor of Yeshua and Yochanan the Baptizer, conquered Samaria and destroyed the temple at Gerizim. Jewish kings ruled Samaria as colonizer thereafter. The Jews thought of Samaritans as second-class mix-breeds, while the Samaritans thought of the Jews as foreign occupiers. Further, the Samaritans refused to join the great Jewish revolt that raged in the years after the death of Herod the Great. For this act of loyalty, Herod Archelaus reduced the tax burden on Samaria, a point further stirring Jewish animosity.

Customarily, Jews traveled from Galilee to Jerusalem by avoiding Samaria all together taking a more circuitous route east through Decapolis then south through Perea finally crossing the Jordan River west into Judea. On this fateful journey, Yeshua chose to travel directly through Samaria hoping to gain acceptance by its people in the process. We arrived at Shechem, near Mount Gerizim, the first major town in Samaria south of the Galilean border. Judas requested we stop so he could go to the market at Shechem to buy food as we traveled light and there were many mouths to feed. Yeshua agreed. While the bulk of our party rested on a hillside and Judas went to buy food, Yeshua wandered off to the nearby well of Jacob. There he encountered a Samaritan woman who came to the well alone without the company of a male member of her family as required by Jewish law. The well was deep requiring a bucket and rope to draw water which Yeshua lacked. He said to her, "Give me drink."

Usually Jews did not speak with Samaritans. She replied, "You are a Jew. Why do you ask me for a drink?"

He said, "If you knew who it is that asks for water, you would have asked him to give the living water. Whoever drinks the living water shall not thirst again."

She didn't quite know if the Jewish stranger was joking with her or was a traveling mystic of some sort but she decided it could not hurt to ask for this mysterious living water. She replied, "Sir, give me this water so that I may not thirst again and won't have to come to draw water at this well."

Yeshua, "Call your husband to come here."

This request caught the woman off guard for she was a prostitute. She said, "I have no husband."

Yeshua peered through her eyes down into the depths of her soul. The Samaritan woman felt naked before Yeshua. He said, "It is correct that you have no husband for you have five temporary husbands."[149]

The truth of these words shocked the woman. She ran back into the town of Shechem as fast as her legs could carry her proclaiming to anyone who would listen that a Jewish prophet was at Jacob's well. The town elders and a multitude of townspeople came out to meet Yeshua at the well. Many believed in him because of the word of the woman. Yeshua identified himself as the Messiah of Levi, a descendant of the last Hasmonean king. In private discussions with the Samaritan elders, he promised the Samaritans political and religious autonomy from the Jewish kingdom if they supported his cause. Autonomy was the long sought-after goal of the Samaritan people who were receptive to the offer. Also, the position of leadership in our cause held by Prince Petra (aka Shimon ben Antipas) helped win the Samaritans over to the Yeshua movement. The mother of Herod Antipas, thus the grandmother of Prince Petra, was a member of the Samaritan royal family.

We stayed in Shechem for two days recruiting many followers into our ranks for the coming assault on the Temple at

---

149 See *John* 4:4-42.

Jerusalem. We continued our travels south through Samaria recruiting thousands from that country. And an amazing thing occurred as our ranks swelled with Samaritans—Galileans heard the news and came south to join our party. Success breeds success.

Shiloh, Samaria (36 CE)

The last town of consequence we came to before leaving Samaria was Shiloh, often discussed in Hebrew scripture as an important religious center that even hosted the Arc of the Covenant for a period in the ancient past. The once great Shiloh was no more than an oversized village when we arrived. It is written in the Torah that, "The scepter shall not depart from Judah, nor a lawgiver from between his feet, until Shiloh come."[150] Yeshua hoped to accrue the propaganda value of showing up in Jerusalem with the mayor of Shiloh to show the people that, "Shiloh has come."

Yeshua sent ahead Petra and the sons of thunder to announce to the citizens of Shiloh that the grandson of King Mattathias Antigonus approached. I suppose Yeshua selected Prince Petra for the mission so as not to hurt his feelings given his old rivalry with Judas. But I knew immediately that sending Petra on a diplomatic errand was a bad idea. He was a head basher, not a diplomat. Petra and the sons of thunder were born for combat. The three rode back to us a short time later to report their dealings in Shiloh.

Petra said, "The elders of Shiloh refuse to receive you rabbi. They closed the village gate as we approached and would only speak with us from the tops of their walls. We must make an example of this village. Give the command and we shall rain fire down upon them."[151] Petra sought permission to burn down the village.

Rather than dress down three senior military commanders in front of their troops, Yeshua motioned that Petra, James and

---

150 *Genesis* 49:10.

151 *Luke* 9:54.

Yochanan should follow him to a place away from the others. He said, "I appreciate your efforts but you three have not, as yet, been reborn of the spirit. I did not come to destroy men's lives but to save them. We shall never win the hearts and the minds of the people through fear tactics. Our war is against the Romans. We win over the common people through kindness."

Judas joined the group and unexpectedly came to the defense of Petra and his men. "Rabbi, we are now at war. Desperate times call for desperate measures."

Yeshua performed the impossible on a regular basis during our travels in Galilee yet Judas challenged the wisdom of his master's decision. The rabbi stepped back to gaze each of his followers in the eye. "And the four of you think killing Samaritans will help our cause? How many Roman soldiers do you expect in Jerusalem for the festival?"

Judas was sure Yeshua knew one Roman cohort was stationed in Jerusalem at all times, thus, the question puzzled him. Why ask the question if the rabbi already knew the answer? Judas replied, "Five to seven hundred."

Yeshua said, "And what about Roman auxiliaries soldiers under the command of either Antipas or other Herodians?"

They reviewed Roman troop strength endlessly before departing Galilee. The rabbi knew full well the totals. Judas replied, "An equal number rabbi, five to seven hundred stationed at Herod's palace although as many as an additional two thousand could be in summoned to Jerusalem on short notice from fortresses at Jericho, Hyrcania, Massada, Herodium and elsewhere in Judea."

Yeshua continued, "And Judas, what numerical advantage do you think we must possess as lightly armed fighters to overcome the heavily armored and professionally trained Romans?"

Judas, "Five to one at least, maybe more."

Yeshua paused for a moment to let those words sink in. "By your own account we can expect to face up to 3400 Roman soldiers in Jerusalem counting auxiliaries that could arrive within two days march. Further, a lightly armed opposition force requires a five to one advantage to defeat Roman heavy infantry. Add in the military assistance the Romans will receive from their Jewish allies in the Sanhedrin and we need at least twenty thousand fighters in our ranks to capture Jerusalem. Turn around and look behind you Judas. How many men do you estimate followed us out of Galilee? Do not count the Samaritans."

Petra responded, "About five thousand rabbi."

Yeshua, "You are all just as capable as I of doing the math." We only had about one-quarter of the necessary fighters from our base in Galilee. We needed fighters from other Jewish lands to join us.

Petra, "What about James the Just and the Hasidim? Is the legend true of the Hasidim legion in the desert?"

Yeshua, "Yes, the legend is true. The Hasidim legion joined forces with my grandfather King Antigonus to drive the Romans out of Israel but we can't count on them."

Judas, "Why? They hate Rome and the Herodians."

Yeshua, "You have given the answer yourself. They hate Herodians. I am Herodian by birth. James is pure Hasmonean, a son of Aaron, so they accept him while rejecting me. Our only hope is that the Hasidim agree to march on Jerusalem with James even though they do not accept my leadership."

Judas still felt Yeshua overplayed the weakness of our force for its assigned goal of seizing Jerusalem during Passover. "Rabbi, we only need enough men to foment rebellion among the people. Thousands shall join us after we demonstrate at the Temple. Our five thousand shall quickly multiple into tens of thousands."

Yeshua said, "Just like the loaves of bread on the shores of the Sea of Galilee? Men are not loaves of bread my brothers. They act more like the sands of the desert blowing to and fro with the wind. Do you suggest we stake our lives on the grains of sand blowing about with the wind inside the Temple courtyard during Passover? If we project strength in the Temple then the grains of sand shall be swept up in our current. Look at all the Galileans who have had a change of heart after hearing about the large numbers of Samaritans we recruit and joined us on the road. The same thing will happen in Judea yet you wish to offend our Samaritan brothers?"

Judas protested because the Samaritans were despised by the Jews of Judea and, therefore, the existence of Samaritans in our party makes Judas' job of recruiting zealot allies all the more difficult. Like Judas, Petra didn't think the Samaritans were necessary. Yeshua was part Idumean through his father's ancestry and we expected to be met by a considerable contingent of allied Idumeans in Jerusalem. Petra said, "Rabbi, your analysis left out the Idumeans under bar Babas that shall rendezvous with us in Jerusalem."

Yeshua replied, "My last correspondence from bar Babas indicated about 3000 Idumeans were to meet us in Jerusalem. Let us assume Judas can raise 3000 more among the zealots in Judea. Adding the fighters from all sources except the Samaritans leaves us 10,000 short of our target strength yet here we walk through the land of people oppressed by Rome same as the people of Galilee and you come to me asking whether we should burn down a Samaritan town? Five thousand Samaritans have already joined our ranks. Go count them for yourself."

Yeshua stared down Petra and Judas, who remained silent. We passed by Shiloh without burning the town and marched into Judea with seven thousand Samaritans in our party. These new recruits boosted the confidence of our men as we continued south into Judea.

Jericho, Judea (36 CE)

Parable of the Minas

Yeshua did not lead us on a direct route to Jerusalem once we crossed into Judea. Instead, our party turned east to the Jordan River and territory previously frequented by Yochanan the Baptizer. The poor people of this area were Yeshua's strongest supporters in Judea and he hoped a good number of the local men of peasant stock would follow him to Jerusalem for Passover. The closer we came to Jerusalem, the thicker in our midst stood the army of spies marking down Yeshua's every move and utterance. The local people easily spotted the Herodian interlopers and alerted us to their presence. Rather than be alarmed, Yeshua used the spies to send a thinly veiled message back to Jerusalem. It was aimed at the wealthy Pharisees and priests who principally opposed him, especially Herodians such as Antipas and Phasaelus ben Timius.[152] To confuse the Romans, Yeshua wrapped his political message within a parable we heard several times before, that of the master going on a journey and entrusting silver pieces to his servants while he was gone.[153]

Stripping away the spiritual portion of the revised parable Yeshua told in Jericho that day left the following words, "A certain nobleman went to a distant country to receive a kingdom that was his birthright. The citizens of this country hated the nobleman and sent a delegation rejecting him as king. The nobleman replied to the delegation saying, 'These enemies of mine who did not want me to reign over them, bring them here and slay them before me.'"[154] The fighting men in our group knew exactly what Yeshua meant by these words and cheered wildly upon hearing them. Yeshua said, in so many words, that they intended to kill his Herodian and Pharisee enemies in Jerusalem once he secured the kingdom. The Galileans, Samaritans, and Jewish mercenaries from abroad that comprised our ragtag band of fighting men were more than willing to kill powerful and wealthy Judeans who stood in our way. The men oozed piss and vinegar that day as we approached Jerusalem. Thousands of Judean peasants from the Jordan River valley pledged to follow Yeshua to Jerusalem for Passover. Little did they know how the worm would turn in the coming days.

---

152 Paul of Tarsus.

153 *Matthew* 25:14-29.

154 *Luke* 19:11-27.

Chapter 20

> Then the Pharisees went out and began to plot with the Herodians how they might kill Yeshua. Mark 3:6.

Bethany, Judea (36 CE)

Yeshua pushed on to Bethany accompanied by Petra and one thousand of his most experienced warriors. These men served as Yeshua's personal guard. He didn't wish to parade our full numbers until the moment we marched to the gates of Jerusalem. The bulk of our followers stayed in Jericho to follow in the coming days.

My master planned the last details of his insurrection in Bethany at the home of Lazarus, his Hasmonean brother-in-law; however, Yeshua was still a rabbi first and claimant to the Jewish throne second. His wife Mariam Magdalene pulled Yeshua aside the moment we arrived in Bethany. She said, "Husband, I have need of your services in a family matter."

He replied, "Why must you take me from my father's work?" For those unfamiliar to his idioms, my master was sometimes difficult to follow. He often used the phrase "my father" to refer to his spiritual father dwelling in another realm beyond the physical world of men. In this instance, however, he meant his deceased father Antipater ben Herod whose dying wish was that his son one day sit on the Jewish throne. In a private moment during our journey in Samaria, Yeshua confided to me that he felt the presence of his deceased father Prince Antipater constantly at his side since our group departed Galilee for Jerusalem. The hopes and dreams of many ancestors who came before Yeshua rested on his shoulders these final days leading up to Passover.

Yeshua gazed off in the distance consumed by thoughts of his father when Mariam called him back to the land of the living. She said, "Must I say more than you are a rabbi and my husband? My niece Salome requires your gifts husband. When among the poor people in the villages in Galilee and Judea do you ever refuse to cure the sick or feed the spiritually deprived with a meal of knowledge?" They both knew the answer to this question. Yeshua gave of himself to the point of physical exhaustion whenever called upon by strangers.

She continued, "My niece Salome is in a bad way, completely uncontrollable. She defies all authority."

Yeshua asked, "Herodias' daughter?"

Princess Herodias was the moving force behind Antipas' execution of Yochanan the Baptizer. The news that the daughter of Herodias was a headstrong demon surprised no one. Salome's first husband, Philip the Tetrarch,[155] died two years previously leaving her a childless and young widow. Between marriages Salome lived with her mother in the palace of Herod Antipas. There Salome performed a seductive dance inspired by the goddess Ishtar ostensibly for Antipas at his birthday feast. The true target audience for Salome's dance was Herodian-Hasmonean prince Aristobulus ben Herod, her cousin and future king of Chalcis. The seductive dance of Princess Salome yielded two results. Herod Antipas so enjoyed the performance that he told the young widow to ask for any reward she desired. Herodias prompted Salome to request the head of Yochanan the Baptizer on a platter, a request Antipas granted.[156] Young Prince Aristobulus was so intoxicated with his cousin that he married Salome.

Mariam replied, "Yes Herodias' daughter. She is married to the son of my brother Herod. Will you help her?"

---

155 Two gospels incorrectly name Herodias' first husband as Philip--*Mark* 6:15-29; *Matt.* 14:1-12. Per Josephus, Herodias' first husband was Herod, grandson of the high priest Boethus. Her daughter Salome took Philip the Tetrarch as her first husband.

156 See *Mark* 6:15-29; *Matt.* 14:1-12.

Yeshua, "Where is her husband?"

Mariam led Yeshua to another opulent home in Bethany. It belonged to Mariam's brother King Herod of Chalcis. His son, Prince Aristobulus, greeted them at the door. He was young and handsome yet haggard looking. Deep circles ringed his eyes from sleepless nights and tormented days. He said, "Rabbi Yeshua thank you so much for taking time to speak with me."

Aristobulus kissed his aunt Mariam and clasped hands with Yeshua, a cousin he had never met. Aristobulus lived in Rome at the time of the wedding at Cana, the last time Mariam's clan gathered. Mariam excused herself to allow the men to speak privately and went to Salome. Aristobulus led Yeshua to his study where the rabbi took a seat waiting for the young prince to divulge what problem he was having with his marriage. Rabbis often mediate family disputes, a job the itinerant Yeshua rarely performed.

Aristobulus had trouble unburdening himself so Yeshua started the conversation, "Cousin, what is it I can do for you today?"

Aristobulus let out a large gasp of air as if a huge weight rested on his chest. "My wife, I can't take it any longer rabbi." He threw his head into his hands unable to continue further.

Yeshua, "No one ever said marriage was an easy matter." After that vague statement, Yeshua just sat silently waiting. The young man was in such obvious distress Yeshua knew a tale of woe would be forthcoming; however, it must not be rushed. The words would come when Aristobulus was ready to speak them.

Aristobulus finally said, "Salome is a beautiful woman, just enchanting to look at, but it hides pure evil. It took me a few months to smoke out her true nature. After the wedding, we went to Rome where I introduced her to my relatives there and our Roman friends at Caesar's palace."

Yeshua continued to remain silent merely listening and giving the occasional nod.

Aristobulus continued, "She just went crazy sleeping with every important Roman she could dig her nails into. I had no clue. She threatened and bribed the servants not to tell me. Finally, an old servant who was my nursemaid when I was a child broke down and informed me of my wife's habits. I've confined Salome to the house yet she attempts to seduce even the servants."

Yeshua knew his father, the king of Chalcis, to be a respectable man even though he aligned himself with Rome. "Have you spoken on this matter with your father?"

Aristobulus, "Yes, his only concern is family honor. He forbids me from going to the Temple and denouncing Salome as an adulterer. He also forbids me from divorcing Salome until I produce an heir by her. How can I copulate with someone I loathe? I'm trapped rabbi, trapped!" Aristobulus broke down in tears. Yeshua decided it was best to leave the young, distraught prince in the hands of his wife Mariam and confront Salome. He gave Aristobulus an embrace then left the study. He found Mariam and Salome in the main greeting hall reclined on couches eating dates. As Yeshua entered the room, the two women became silent. He perceived they had been engaged in family gossip, a practice Yeshua abhorred and previously instructed Mariam upon. This woman Salome corrupted my wife in a matter of minutes, thought Yeshua. He looked about the person of Salome using the spiritual sight of an adept and detected an evil apparition hovering next to her. Young Salome was possessed by an evil spirit.

Mariam said, "Husband, please meet my niece Salome."

Yeshua merely nodded in her direction. "Wife, I think it best if I speak with Salome in private. Please go to your nephew. He requires consoling."

Mariam left the room as instructed. Salome was a sensual and erotic creature craving attention. By giving in to her charms, men surrendered power to her darkness. Yeshua sat down on the couch next to her sampling the plates of food on the table. He refused the entreaties of her eyes looking only at the food as if she didn't exist. Salome nudged closer to Yeshua but still no response from the rabbi.

Without making eye contact, he finally spoke. "Two recline on a couch. One is alive, the other is dead to self."

What kind of statement was that, thought Salome? This man desires me. Every man with a functioning penis does. Yet here he sits afraid to even look at me. She would have him just like the other rabbis Aristobulus send to her.

Salome said, "Yes rabbi, I think you need to counsel me. Why don't you look at me rabbi?"

But he continued to eat from the table seemingly oblivious to Salome's existence. "These dates are exquisite. I bet they come from Damascus."

She replied, "Who are you? Like a stranger you sit on my couch and eat from my table!"[157]

"I am integrated with the father and hold knowledge of that which resides within each of us. As a consecrated Nazarene, you have no effect on me."

Salome lifted her head upward and screamed. This was the sign Yeshua waited for. The battle was on. Finally, Yeshua turned toward her. Aristobulus heard the scream from the other room and tried to go see what was happening with his wife. Mariam stopped him and ordered the servants to keep everyone away from the room where Yeshua confronted Salome.

Yeshua, "Give me your hands cousin."

Salome smiled for she finally received attention from this man and supposed the physical interaction would lead somewhere sexual. They clasped both hands together.

Yeshua continued, "We must pray. Bow your head and close your eyes."

Now Salome was certain she would have sex with Yeshua for this was how it started with the last rabbi. She did as instructed but instead of a sexual encounter, Salome bat Herod Boethus fell unconscious. Having calmed the girl, it was now time for Yeshua to do combat with the evil spirit resident in her body. He crossed over to the etheric plane donning his garment of light coming face to face with the evil spirit.

The evil spirit said, "You want the girl rabbi, I can taste it in the air. She is there before you. Take her!"

Yeshua, "Do you know who I am?"

---

[157] See *Gospel of Thomas*, Logion 61 for short exchange between Yeshua and a woman only identified as Salome.

"Yes, you silly little rabbi but do you know who I am? I am the one who caused Herod to kill your father Antipater and I have the power to kill you as well."

Yeshua then realized he confronted the spirit of Princess Salome, sister of Herod, the witch of Judea. Through the dark arts, she had gained influence over the physical and mental person of her great-granddaughter of the same name. He laughed at the witch, "Kill me? Don't be ridiculous. So you believe my father Antipater is dead, do you? Look."

Yeshua pointed across the room where another spirit appeared. This apparition wore a purple cloak with a royal diadem upon his head. It was his father Antipater. Yeshua continued, "Do you have eyes to see witch? What you destroyed is but the flesh that clothes the man. My father lives and has always been with me from birth."

Antipater drew near gleaming in royal splendor. The witch let out an eerie cackle then tried to strike Yeshua's garment of light.

He said, "You have no power over me." Then a heavenly angel outfitted in etheric battle armor appeared behind Yeshua. Light gleamed as if from highly polished metal. The angel was more powerful than any spirit the Judean witch had ever encountered. She trembled before the mighty angel summoned by Yeshua.

He continued, "This angel from my father's house confronts you here and now. I can summon a legion of the same with but a word. I command you to leave Jerusalem at once and to have no further interaction with the girl Salome. This angel shall watch over you relentlessly night and day. He will follow you to the gates of hell and ensure you stay there. Whatever evil you attempt to project on the world, it shall come back to you sevenfold. Be gone!"

The evil spirit of the long-deceased Princess Salome screeched and moaned in great distress as if gored with a spear then departed as commanded by Yeshua. The girl Salome fell into Yeshua's arms now awake and sobbing violently. Her entire body shook with the after effects of the witch's departure. Yeshua comforted her like a father comforts his young daughter.

Finally, she looked up into his eyes. "Thank you for saving me rabbi."

"No girl, it is I who must thank you for through you I was able to rebuke an evil spirit who haunted our family for generations."

Salome said, "Please accept me as a disciple. I am your servant."

Yeshua called for Mariam who came at once. "Your niece is now ready for spiritual instruction. I ask that you instruct her immediately for she is an empty vessel thirsting to be filled."

Yeshua then went to Aristobulus putting his arms around the broken man. "Your wife Salome has been healed. I cast an evil spirit from her. Mariam is with her now and shall give her spiritual guidance. The woman you knew before is dead. She has been reborn this day. A new woman awaits you. Please put from your mind the past. Blessed are the merciful for they shall receive mercy."[158]

Young prince Aristobulus looked up at Yeshua with tears in his eyes. "You have performed a miracle rabbi!"

* * * * * * * * *

That night Petra woke me with a firm jab to the ribs. He said, "Wake up. You better not have gotten into the wine again."

There was nothing gentle about this man. I said, "Is there some emergency?"

"The king needs you. Come, bring your cloak."

I threw on a tunic, grabbed my cloak, and followed Petra out a side entrance of Lazarus' Bethany estate. Assembled in the courtyard were Yeshua, Princess Mariam, Princess Mariamne the elder (mother of Yeshua), Princess Mariamne the younger (sister of Yeshua), Joses (younger brother of Yeshua), Lazarus, the Sons of Thunder, and seventy other armed men. The seventy were the elite soldiers of our army. I was confused by what greeted my eyes. Sneaking away in the dead of night under heavy guard indicated a diplomatic mission of some sort, perhaps to meet with leaders of a

---

158 *Matthew* 5:7.

dissident Jewish faction in Jerusalem. But why were the women going on a mission that could turn dangerous? We were days away from launching a revolution and stood within easy walking distance of a Roman garrison. Our every move outside of the protective gates of Lazarus' compound was dangerous as spies were everywhere.

Yeshua came to me and said, "The night air will do you good Menelaus. Please join us for a walk."

Our party moved out taking the road for Jerusalem. The elder Princess Mariamne walked next to me. She was in her seventies but still spry of spirit. I couldn't image what destination required the aging princess to leave her bed for a moonlight walk of this distance. She said, "Menelaus, give me your arm. I'm not a young woman anymore."

I did as instructed. Years ago while Yeshua was away in exile, my primary duty was to attend to the household needs of Princess Mariamne. Since Yeshua's return, I spent little time with her as Yeshua's requirements completely occupied my waking hours. She said as we walked, "Have I told you how much you resemble your father?"

"Not for many years princess."

"You and Yeshua have been prepared from birth for the day that is soon to come. The road has been long but we are finally here Menelaus." The princess radiated excitement. She saw her sole mission in life as putting Yeshua back on the Hasmonean throne. Here we were in Jerusalem with a massive army ready to complete the task. But why were we sneaking around in the dead of night in such close proximity to a Roman barracks? I had to ask, "Princess, where are we going?"

She whispered, "To the tomb of my father."

King Antigonus? The news shocked me. I did not know he was buried in Jerusalem. A loyal Kohen priest carried King Antigonus' body into exile in Babylon after his execution by Marc Antony. The king's bones were repatriated to Jerusalem during the civil war that broke out after the death of Herod the Great, which was exactly when Yeshua was born. We turned north walking past the western slope of the Mount of Olives and the Garden at

Gethsemane. However, we did not turn west at the entrance to the city of Jerusalem and instead continued north entering a city of the dead. We passed one tomb after another. Finally, we stopped at the entrance to an unassuming tomb with no special exterior adornment. Yeshua instructed the guards to station themselves outside. It was then I realized that only the family of Yeshua entered the tomb with me the singular exception. I was humbled by the honor paid to me by the master that night.

That dank smell of a chamber not entered by the living in decades hit my nostrils as I passed over the threshold. The tomb was modest with two rooms joined by a narrow passage way. The first, larger room contained an ossuary but Yeshua walked past it to the smaller room where a second ossuary sat in a locus, a small chamber hewn from the rock. Above the ossuary was an inscribed tablet that read, "I, Abba, son of the priest Eleazar, son of Aaron the great. I am Abba the tortured and persecuted; Born in Jerusalem, exiled to Babylon and raised Matatai son of Judah and buried him in a cave, which I purchased by deed."[159]

Everyone knelt in prayer. Yeshua touched his hand to the ossuary of his grandfather the king and said, “Sire, I have come as you wished me to do. We are here to honor your memory and all actions we take are in your name. Please grant us your blessing in this righteous mission we are about to embark upon.” He continued his prayer silently. When Yeshua finished, Princess Mariamne the elder came and touched the ossuary but broke down in tears immediately. Yeshua came to her assistance. This was the first time she had been in the presence of her father since his execution seventy-two years in the past. Lastly, each of us came and touched the ossuary saying a silent prayer to the former king.

Jerusalem, Judea (36 CE)

9 Nisan, Yom Ree-Shon / Dies Solis (Sunday)

Judas arrived midday at Bethany trailed by an army. Perhaps five thousand Judean peasants from the Jordan River

---

[159] See Corpus Inscriptionum Iudaeae/Palaestinae by Hannah M. Cotton, Leah Di Segni, Werner Eck (De Gruyter 2010) at page 99.

valley followed behind our Galilean and Samaritan recruits. Yeshua took up position at the head of the column eliciting cheers from the men, which then totaled 20,000. We marched toward Jerusalem in a light mood confident in our numbers. Yeshua stopped near the Mount of Olives sending two disciples on an errand. He said, "Go to the house up ahead and you shall find a donkey colt tied there. Untie it and bring it to me. If anyone says anything to you, tell him the king requires it and they shall be compensated."[160]

After acquiring the donkey colt, Yeshua led our party west crossing the Valley of Kidron toward the gates of the city. The spirits of those marching with Yeshua rose to even greater heights when Hasmonean prince bar Babas met us outside the city gate at the head of over five thousand Idumeans. Bar Babas saluted Yeshua and the two Hasmonean princes embraced. An army of 25,000 now marched at Yeshua's back. It truly appeared that the stars had aligned and the Hasmonean dynasty was about to be reborn this Passover. Yeshua mounted his donkey and entered the city. People are like sheep in many respects, they followed the herd. Hours before, Judas ordered a party of his zealot followers to go ahead and infiltrate themselves into the vast multitude of observant Jews then assembling in Jerusalem for the religious feast. They stood ready to incite the passions of the crowd when Yeshua appeared on his donkey. On cue, the zealots took branches from palm trees waiving them as they went in front of Yeshua crying out, "Hosanna! The King of Israel comes,[161] the anointed one comes!" The ~~sheep~~ people took the bait stampeding to Yeshua's route in order to glimpse him atop his donkey colt. A grand procession of Yeshua's followers trailed in his wake making for magnificent political theatre.

Petra asked me, "Why is he riding that little donkey?"

I said, "Us Jews go through life weighed down by our history like a milestone around our neck. King David's son Absalom authored a revolution against his father driving David out

---

[160] *Matthew* 21:1.

[161] *John* 12:13.

of Jerusalem. At the Mount of Olives, David was given a donkey to ride away into exile.[162] Later, some ancient prophet of our people foretold that the true king would one day return riding into Jerusalem on a donkey colt."[163]

On this day at least, everything went off according to our plan. Thousands of ordinary Jews already inside the city for the holiday joined our ranks as we processed through the city swelling our numbers to perhaps 30,000. The people proclaimed Yeshua king as he paraded through the city. The exercise acted as a formidable show of force to the Jerusalem authorities. All they could do was stand and watch Yeshua, the condemned criminal, parade through the streets of Jerusalem like a conquering hero. Mission accomplished, we withdrew from the city. This was merely a show of force. We marched with heads held high up to the summit of the Mount of Olives where the bulk of Yeshua's followers based themselves for Passover week. The inner circle of the movement returned to the comfort of Bethany in triumphal spirits.

The number of followers marching with Yeshua in the city that day shocked the Romans, Herodians and Sanhedrin members. Pontius Pilate, Roman prefect of Palestine, got sweaty palms looking down from the roof of the Praetorium seeing the joyous crowd following Yeshua through the city. Pilate's advisors previously assured him that their intelligence reports indicated this man they called "the Egyptian" had a smaller following than Yochanan the Baptizer and was a less charismatic speaker. The reasoning went that the Baptizer was easily disposed of so the prefect shouldn't be overly concerned about this new nationalistic rabbi of Hasmonean blood. The Romans called Yeshua "the Egyptian" because they weren't quite sure who he was. They had no record of his birth surmising the birth occurred either in Judea or Egypt during the Jewish revolt that followed Herod's death. He first showed up in Roman census records as a citizen of Egypt and the son of Joseph the Nazarite and Mariamne bat Antigonus.

---

[162] 2 *Samuel* 16.

[163] *Zechariah* 9:19.

However, the Roman records from Egypt listed his given name as Mattathias. Later, the family moved to Sepphoris in Galilee. The Roman census records for Galilee during this period did not list Joseph having a son named Mattathias but, rather, he then had a son named Yeshua of the same age. Were they the same person? Confusing matters further, reports indicated the boy known as Yeshua ben Joseph left his family in Sepphoris for Egypt before reaching adulthood. Apparently he studied with priests during this period. Roman spies in Parthia filed reports during the lost years of Yeshua stating that a young Jewish prince thought to be the grandson of King Antigonus appeared in Babylon under the tutelage of Jewish rabbis and Zoroastrian priests. Was this Mattathias / Yeshua, the son of Mariamne and Joseph? Was the man riding the donkey around Jerusalem even the same individual Roman reports referred to as the Egyptian? There were many royal pretenders in the empire. The Romans were not certain of the answer to either question.

Pontius Pilate needed answers and all his Roman staff could manage was to point fingers at one another assigning blame for the breakdown in intelligence on the Egyptian. They knew a rebel Nazarene rabbi was coming to Jerusalem from Galilee for Passover this year; however, they expected him to arrive with no more than five or six thousands followers in his entourage, not the thirty thousand that paraded with Yeshua in Jerusalem that day. This constituted a massive intelligence failure on the part of the Roman administration in Judea and Pilate feared the shit would splatter on his toga.

The prefect barked to a nearby aide, "Summon Prince Phasaelus ben Timius! I wish to speak to him this instant."

If the career Roman bureaucrats of the Palestine prefecture couldn't provide Pilate correct intelligence on the threat level posed by the Egyptian then he needed to seek counsel from his Jewish allies. Herod Antipas was still away in Babylon assisting proconsul Vitellius in his negotiations with the Parthians so Pilate turned to young Prince Phasaelus. In any event, the relationship between Pilate and Antipas soured over the business of the Nabatean war. The whole Nabatean affair was the idea of Antipas yet Pilate authorized the use of Roman auxiliary troops, which meant a portion of the blame for that defeat would land on the prefect when proconsul Vitellius returned from Parthia.

Prince Phasaelus was a rising Herodian star and now a full member of Sanhedrin. Pilate came from a military family of Roman Equestrian stock. The cognomen "Pilate" derived from the legionnaire's spear known as a pilum. He was tall and bald in the fashion of Julius Caesar with tufts of hair surviving on the sides and back of his head. Pilate obtained his Palestinian office ten years earlier meaning the now fifty-year old Pilate was in his tenth year as prefect. Sejanus, the former top minister to Tiberius and prefect of the Praetorian Guard in Rome, acted as Pilate's benefactor within the imperial court. Tiberius purged Sejanus five years ago so Pilate knew his remaining days in office were short. Still, he hoped to avoid marring his career with a Jewish revolt. He further wished to rake in as many bribes as possible during his last days to allow for a comfortable return to private life in Rome.

Pilate re-read the Egyptian's file while waiting for the arrival of Phasaelus. The confident young Herodian prince entered Pilate's office after being announced. He sat down without being invited to do so. Every Jew in Palestine waited for the prefect to address him before speaking; however, headstrong Phasaelus didn't play by the rules. His Latin was atrocious, barely comprehensible, and he spoke the Greek of the common people, not the high Greek of the stage used by elite Roman society. This was because the impatient Phasaelus refused to take instruction from his tutors nor perform his required studies. He instead spent his youth on the docks and in the warehouses owned by his father in Cyprus. There he learned Greek from the laborers. Upon his arrival in Judea to study the Torah, the brash Herodian prince asked the leaders of the two most prominent Pharisee schools of the day to recite the Torah to him while standing on one foot because he didn't have time for instruction with long-winded lectures on the subject.

Phasaelus said to Pilate, "Prefect, might I suggest wine. It's been a long day and I think we both could use a drink."

Pilate found the confidence displayed by the Jewish prince unexpectedly reassuring. He clearly kept his head in the face of the public display by Yeshua and his followers. Pilate motioned to an aide to bring wine.

Pilate, "Our intelligence reports on Rabbi Yeshua state that they expected him to arrive in Jerusalem with five or six thousand followers yet my eyes perceived upwards of thirty thousand people parading behind him as he rode his donkey through the streets today. Can you explain to me this sudden jump in popularity?"

Phasaelus, "Yeshua turned to Samaria for recruits after he left Galilee heading south. He apparently has formed alliances with the leaders of several Samarian towns. Only Shiloh turned him away. Thousands of Samarians came south with him. Also, a previously unknown Hasmonean prince from Idumea, bar Babas, rendezvoused with Yeshua just outside the city gates bringing another five thousand followers. The rest are Galilean and Judean peasants caught up in the unexpected display of force by this populist poser."

"Bar Babas, why does that name sound familiar?"

"The name is mentioned in the histories of Nicolas of Damascus on the reign of Herod the Great. Perhaps you read it there."

As recommended by his predecessor in office, the first thing Pontius Pilate did upon arriving in Palestine was to read the histories of Nicolas but that had been a decade ago. Pilate said, "Yes but refresh my memory."

Phasaelus continued, "Herod ordered the execution of all members of King Antigonus' family and the Hasmoneans who aligned themselves with his government after gaining control of Jerusalem. Babas was of royal Hasmonean blood and a close associate of Antigonus that Herod executed. Unbeknownst to Herod, two sons of Babas escaped to Idumea and remained there in hiding until Herod discovered them nine years into his reign. Herod's brother-in-law Costobarus gave sanctuary to the sons of Babas under his authority as governor of Idumea. Herod executed both the sons of Babas and Costobarus."

Pilate now saw the connection, "And this bar Babas just arrived in Jerusalem is a descendant of the sons of Babas executed by Herod long ago?"

"Yes prefect. Herod succeeded in executing the criminals but must have failed in locating their offspring. The Hasmonean ghosts connected to Antigonus have risen from the dead and are now in Jerusalem."

It was clear to Pilate that his ministers greatly underestimated the threat posed by the Egyptian. Pilate, "How do we know this man who rode into Jerusalem today on a donkey is truly a grandson of Antigonus? The Roman Empire is awash in false royal claimants."

"From a practical and political point of view I'm not sure it matters."

"Explain Phasaelus."

"He arrived in the city with two Hasmonean princesses who are his wife and mother respectively, Mariam bat Aristobulus and Mariamne bat Antigonus. The people will accept his claim to be the grandson of Antigonus based upon the presence of two high-ranking Hasmonean princesses at his side. But the proof of the Egyptian's identity runs even deeper."

"How so?"

"Have you met my Hasmonean cousin, Prince Agrippa ben Aristobulus?"

"Not in a number of years. I heard rumors that he was running from creditors."

"Yes, Agrippa has no sense of money. He spends it as camels drink water. Anyway, Agrippa normally is clean shaven in the Roman style but, when he does grow out his beard, Agrippa and the Egyptian could pass for twins."

"Twins!"

"You will see soon enough. I have word that Agrippa landed in Caesarea yesterday. His beard is grown out in honor of Passover. He will arrive in Jerusalem tomorrow."[164]

---

[164] *See* Tosefta Sanhedrin IX.9; The Seductiveness of Jewish Myth: Challenge or Response? by S. Daniel Breslauer (SUNY Press, 1997) at page 97.

Pilate began to pace the room acid churning in his stomach. He said, "This Egyptian has cobbled together a following of tens of thousands of Galileans, Samarians, and Idumeans. Is that correct?"

"I'm afraid so prefect."

"Then he poses a serious threat to our administration of the Jewish nation. Yochanan the Baptizer never marched upon Jerusalem and had few followers outside of the Jordan River valley. One item in the Egyptian's file puzzles me though. Perhaps you can shed light on the matter Prince Phasaelus. Princess Mariam bat Aristobulus, who you say is now the Egyptian's wife, is the former wife of both Antipater ben Herod and Archelaus ben Herod. She is the highest ranking Herodian princess of her generation, the older sister of Herodias. I can't fathom why Princess Mariam and a senior male member of her family would agree for her to marry the Egyptian? Is there something I'm missing in his background?"

"We believe the person you Romans call the Egyptian is Herod's grandson by Prince Antipater."

The news shocked Pilate. "On what grounds do you believe the Egyptian is a grandson of Herod?"

Phasaelus, "Herod Antipas has known the Egyptian since he was a boy and swears that he is the son of his dead brother Antipater. My grandmother Salampsio also says the same."

Pilate slammed his fist down on the table. "How could this information not be in the files of the Roman prefecture?"

The conversation now arrived at an uncomfortable area for Phasaelus. The Herodians tried mightily to kill Yeshua when he was born almost forty years ago but narrowly failed. They went to such lengths as to kill all the young male children in Bethlehem just in case his mother hid him there among the townspeople. Phasaelus said, "I had a long discussion on this very topic with my uncle Philip the Tetrarch when he was last here in Jerusalem before his death. According to Philip, King Herod knew Princess Mariamne was pregnant before he died and left orders to his sons to kill the child when born. Archelaus, Antipas, and Philip wished to carry out their father's orders but feared retribution from Caesar if he found out they executed a child who was potentially of Herodian royal blood without first getting authorization. To be frank, Antipater was very close to Augustus Caesar and there was concern among the Herodians that Caesar would raise the child in the royal palace at Rome and give him a kingdom when he reached adulthood."

Pilate interrupted, "You say 'potentially of Herodian royal blood'. Is there some question about the paternity of the Egyptian?"

"According to Uncle Philip, his mother and Antipater were both imprisoned at Jericho on separate floors of Herod's dungeon when she conceived Yeshua. Some say one of Herod's soldiers took pleasures with the princess resulting in the child. Who can say?"

Pilate inquired further, "So Archelaus, Antipas, and Philip kept the information from Rome because they were trying to kill a potential rival to Herod's throne without authorization from Rome?"

"That is correct prefect."

"And what is the thinking of the Sanhedrin on the matter of his paternity?"

"It's difficult to say prefect as we have never debated the matter. The majority of the Sanhedrin views him as a threat regardless of parentage. The size of his following here in Jerusalem this Passover bears that out."

"Does he have supporters on the Sanhedrin?"

"Yes prefect. A middle son of Joseph of Arimathea known as Clopas is married to Yeshua's sister. As you know, Prince Joseph is a senior member of the Sanhedrin. He allies himself with Yeshua. Also Princess Mariam's older brother Aristobulus ben Aristobulus, known within the family as Lazarus, is a devoted follower of Yeshua. He is not a member of the Sanhedrin but a private person of wealth and influence who can sway opinion of the members." Phasaelus neglected to mention that he himself had tried to join the Yeshua movement two years ago but was rejected. This public embarrassment by Yeshua fueled Phasaelus' rage against the Nazarenes in general and Yeshua in particular.

Pilate sat down at his chair deep in thought then lifted his head after having reached his decision, "I am leaving for Caesarea tonight. When Vitellius returns with his legions, we'll have the manpower to deal with this Egyptian problem."

The old man was getting jumpy at the end of his career, thought Phasaelus. The Roman praetorium sat inside Fortress Antonia, itself large enough to house an entire legion and with walls as tall and stout as those of the Temple it overlooked. All Pilate had to do to secure his safety was to order the gates of the fortress closed. The Jewish ruffians who followed Yeshua lacked heavy weapons and siege equipment. Phasaelus saw Pilate's decision to withdraw an extreme act of cowardice that would give aid and comfort to the enemy. He set himself upon reversing the decision.

Phasaelus said, "Prefect, I beg that you do not do this. The Judean peasants must return home tonight so that they may be in the fields or at the bench in their workshops when the sun rises on Dies Lunae (Monday). If you leave now, the Jewish people will take it as a sign of weakness and Yeshua's followers will swell."

"Those criminals could have taken the city today if they had so wished trapping me inside. This is risky Phasaelus."

"That rabble is no match for the trained and heavily armed soldiers we have at our command prefect."

Pilate's voice rose a notch. "No match? I think you underestimate their chances. The danger lies not just with the thugs carrying daggers that march with the Egyptian. We must also account for the tens of thousands of ordinary Jews milling around the city during Passover. The soldiers at my command as we speak cannot withstand all the Jewish peasants in the city if they join Yeshua. These are simple people whose passions are easily enflamed. You haven't been in Jerusalem all that many years young Prince Phasaelus so perhaps you are unaware of the indignities I faced at the hands of the Jews during my time here. It started my first few months in office. I ordered rotation of the Roman cohort stationed in Jerusalem. The new cohort came from a different legion and placed its standard with images of Caesar outside the entrance to the fortress as they would wherever billeted. The Jews went berserk. We have every legal right to display the image of our emperor outside of Roman buildings everywhere in the empire. Not so say the Jews. The entire city is holy to them. They wouldn't listen to reason. When I tried to disperse the protesters with Roman troops, hundreds knelt down with necks exposed daring us to execute them. These insane people would rather have their throats slashed than endure the sight of an image of our emperor in this city. They're raving lunatics I tell you!"

Phasaelus sat still trying to restrain his temper. Jews often quarrel amongst themselves using harsh language in the process. Phasaelus himself held contempt for the average Jew in the street. But they were all God's chosen people and no self-respecting Jew could stand by and listen to a mere gentile put down the Jewish people as a race. When attacked, Jews rallied around one another. He didn't care for Pilate but, while this Roman clung to office, Phasaelus had no choice but to deal with him. Phasaelus said with an even voice belying his resentment, "Give me one day prefect. I will challenge Yeshua before the people when he speaks tomorrow."

Pilate, "Challenge him? How?"

"Yeshua is playing a political game with the people. He has a Herodian wife, his sister is married to a Herodian prince, yet Yeshua has not acknowledged to the people his lineage from Herod. He uses his Herodian ancestry to recruit wealthy and important followers but he hides this information from the people."

"You are going to tell the people he is Herod's grandson?"

"Yes prefect, at the Temple tomorrow. What will the people think when Herodian prince Agrippa stands next to Yeshua, his twin?"

Pilate again began pacing around his office. This too was a risky tactic Phasaelus intended to engage in. If the Egyptian truly was a grandson of Herod, then Pilate should rightfully send to Rome for instructions on how to deal with a royal Herodian prince who appeared to have become an enemy of Rome, which would call into question how Pilate allowed a high ranking Herodian prince to gather such a large following in Palestine without previously reporting the situation to his superiors. Pilate intended to put as much distance between himself and the problem with the Egyptian as he possibly could. "I give you one day Phasaelus. If you are not able to suppress the number of people rallying behind this man tomorrow then I am withdrawing my administration to Caesarea. Now go." Pilate dismissed Phasaelus with a wave of his hand. Herodian treachery in withholding information on the Egyptian's ancestry put Pilate in a bind and his anger over the entire situation was now directed at Phasaelus.

As Phasaelus turned to leave Pilate added a thought, "Another thing, this conversation never officially happened. As far as I know and the Roman records indicate, the Egyptian's parentage is vague with the most likely father being Priest Joseph the Nazarene. Is that clear?" Pilate had no intention of incriminating his administration for its intelligence failure in the case of this possible renegade grandson of Herod.

"Yes prefect, this conversation never occurred." Phasaelus turned and left. Romans were always guarding their ass and ducking for political cover. A part of Phasaelus would be very happy to see Yeshua succeed at ousting the Romans from Israel but his contempt for Yeshua the man prevented him from following through on that thought.

Jerusalem, Judea (36 CE)

10 Nisan, Yom She-Nee / Dies Lunae (Monday)

The sun dawned that day like any other but it was different from the day before. Dies Lunae (Monday) marked the turning point leading to the downfall of the Yeshua movement. We were still basking in the warm glow of Yeshua's coronation parade through Jerusalem as we broke fast in the morning. Yeshua again departed Bethany with his inner core of followers making his way to the Mount of Olives where the bulk of his followers waited. Cheers greeted his arrival. As expected, most of the Judeans who participated in yesterday's festivities retreated home to work the fields but promised to return on Dies Veneris (Friday), the day

Yeshua intended to take control of Jerusalem and proclaim himself king to the people.

We marched proudly from the Mount of Olives into Jerusalem. Yeshua led us into the outer courtyard of the Temple. There was no need this time to take his belt and physically expel the money changers as he did the prior year. The merchants closed up shop the minute we arrived in the Temple. At the time we thought this marked a show of respect for Yeshua but were wrong. The Temple guards knew a confrontation was coming and they passed this information on to the merchants. The crowd was strangely sparse that day considering it was the start of a holy festival but we thought little of it. Yeshua began to preach at the Temple and the people gathered around to hear what he had to say.

A mass of Pharisees, Sadducees and Herodians appeared at the Temple with the intention of opposing Yeshua; however, Nasi Gamaliel was not among them. Yeshua took note of their arrival and launched a preemptive verbal assault upon them, "Woe to you, scribes and Pharisees, hypocrites! For you observe the minutiae of the law yet neglect the weightier provisions such as justice and mercy and faithfulness. These are the things you should place primary importance upon. You are blind guides who clean the outside of the cup but leave the inside full of self-indulgence. Outwardly you appear righteous men but inside you are full of hypocrisy and lawlessness. You claim to honor the prophets yet you are sons of those who murdered the prophets. Your fathers murdered the Teacher of Righteousness! Fill up, then, the measure of the guilt of your fathers. How will you escape the sentence of hell? It is you and your fathers who murdered the righteous Zechariah here at the Temple just as he left the altar of our Lord."[165]

Yeshua invoked both his righteous ancestor Mattathias Maccabeus and Priest Zechariah, the father of Yochanan the Baptizer who the Herodians murdered with the contrivance of the Pharisees on the holy Temple grounds. A leading Pharisee took up

---

[165] See *Matthew* 23:23-35.

the challenge from Yeshua in front of the crowd. He said, "By what authority are you doing these things? The Sanhedrin has not proclaimed you king."

Yeshua replied, "I will answer your question if you can answer one of my own. What was the source of authority for the baptism of Rabbi Yochanan, of God or man?"

The Pharisees conferred among themselves on how to respond. They knew Rabbi Yochanan was highly popular among the people. If they denounced Yochanan at that moment with the crowd already charged with emotion, they may spontaneously stone the Pharisees. Fearing for their lives, the chief priests determined evasion as the best course of action. They said, "We can't speak for Rabbi Yochanan. We don't know the source of his authority."

Yeshua replied, "Well then, neither will I answer your question."[166]

The Pharisees fell silent bickering among themselves on how to proceed. Into this confusion stepped Prince Phasaelus to challenge Yeshua. Lazarus moved next to Yeshua whispering into his ear to make sure the rabbi knew the identity of the man about to address him. Yeshua had only met Phasaelus one time at the wedding at Cana. Phasaelus was elegantly attired this day as he posed for the crowd. I tensed up with anticipation as the two prize gladiators stepped into the ring to do battle by oratory.

Phasaelus said, "Rabbi, are you a Samaritan?"[167] A murmur rose up in the Judean crowd at the mention of Samaritans. The existence of a large contingent of Samaritans among the followers of Yeshua had gone largely unnoticed until Phasaelus made them aware of this fact.

Yeshua replied, "Phasaelus, you know very well I am the grandson of King Mattathias Antigonus. I honor my grandfather and you dishonor me."

"Rabbi, you claim to be the anointed one yet the Hasmoneans are of the tribe of Levi. We are kinsman Yeshua. I

---

166 See *Matthew* 21:23-27.

167 See *John* 8:48.

myself descend from Hasmonean kings yet am not a descendant of David. How can you claim to be a descendant of David? And if you are not a descendant of David, on what authority do you claim to be the messiah?"

Every Jewish sect, and there were many, had varying traditions on the identity of the messiah. Phasaelus presumed to have Yeshua in a box but appeared only to have knowledge concerning the teaching of the Pharisees on this matter. The common people, on the other hand, were blissfully ignorant of such technical differences in scripture. They sought deliverance from the Romans and understood a righteous warrior messiah who was a king would appear to do the job. The Hasmoneans were the last warrior kings who expelled both the Greeks and Romans from Israel. The sword match by oratory was on.

Yeshua replied with a question of his own, "What do you think about the anointed one, whose son is he?'

Phasaelus replied, "David."

Yeshua brilliantly parried the thrust, "In the Psalms, why then is King David said to call the anointed one lord? If King David calls the anointed one lord, how can the messiah be David's son?"[168]

Phasaelus intended to bash Yeshua's skull with scripture yet found himself fumbling for a reply. Phasaelus' point was that, as a Hasmonean, Yeshua did not descend from David and therefore could not be the messiah. However, Yeshua fell back on an obscure prophesy from the Hasidim Jewish sect of the Dead Sea region that two messiahs would appear, one from the line of David and the other a priestly messiah descended from Levi. Under these prophesies the priestly messiah of Levi took precedence over the messiah descended from David. As the Hasmoneans were priests of Levi, Yeshua identified himself as the priestly messiah. Phasaelus lacked the necessary training in sectarian scripture to engage in this battle of words. He shifted tactics.

Phasaelus, "Do you claim to be a priest of Levi?"

---

[168] See *Matthew* 22:41-45, *Mark* 12:35-37, and *Luke* 20:41-44; see also *Psalm* 110.

Yeshua's father Antipater was not a Levitical priest; therefore, under Jewish law, he could not claim to be a Levite. Yeshua counterpunched, "Just as Melchizedek was a priest, so too am I."[169]

Phasaelus didn't have a clue upon the identity of the obscure Melchizedek. Again, he found himself out of his depth trying to argue scripture with Yeshua. Melchizedek had been both king and high priest before the time of David and, on this authority; the Hasmoneans claimed the right to both offices simultaneously. Phasaelus, though bruised, remained calm for he held an unseen dagger up his sleeve. It was time to spring his surprise on the self-proclaimed king of the Jews. Phasaelus said, "You spoke a moment ago about your grandfather King Antigonus but all men have two grandfathers. Let us now speak of your other grandfather. Tell me this Yeshua, was Herod the Great a priest of this order of Melchizedek?"

Yeshua momentarily froze. His reaction told Phasaelus his thrust finally found its mark! Yeshua did his best to recover and counter his enemy saying, "Listen to me. The scribes and Pharisees have seated themselves into the chair of Moses. They tell you to observe this and that law yet their own deeds are otherwise. And they place heavy loads on the shoulders of men they themselves are unwilling to carry. And they love the place of honor at banquets and the best seats at the synagogue and respectful greetings in the marketplace. There is only one teacher and one leader, the anointed one. But count me as eternally your humble servant for whoever exalts himself shall be humbled and whoever humbles himself shall be exalted. And woe to the scribes and Pharisees, these hypocrites, because they shut off the kingdom of heaven from men."[170]

Phasaelus didn't take the bait by trading insults with Yeshua. He stayed poised resuming his assault on Yeshua's Herodian ancestry. "Nice speech oh humble anointed one. But please tell me, the despised hypocrite that I am, how is it one can

---

[169] See *Hebrews* 5:6.

[170] See *Matthew* 23:2-13.

be the grandson of King Herod yet enter the Temple claiming to be the messiah? What reference have you in scripture for that oh anointed one of Levi?"

The crowd was strangely silent. They couldn't quite comprehend or believe that this populist rabbi normally adorned in rags was a grandson of Herod. Yeshua did not immediately respond and denounce Phasaelus, which seemed a confirmation of the allegation. Murmurs began to rise up among the crowd. Now Phasaelus went for the dagger. He called forward Herodian Prince Agrippa to stand before the people. Phasaelus said to the people, "Here is my cousin Agrippa just arrived from Rome. He is a grandson of King Herod yet Yeshua appears as his twin!"

The people were stunned realizing the truth of the accusation made by Phasaelus. Now Phasaelus pressed his advantage with the crowd. He said, "Excuse me, I hear gasps in the crowd. So you did not know that our exalted self-proclaimed messiah is the son of Antipater, the former crown prince and eldest son of Herod the Great? Prince Agrippa is his cousin-german. How could Yeshua have failed to mention the identity of his father? I tell you brothers, this man has deceived you!"

All hell broke out then and there. Several members of the zealot party followed by rabble among the crowd stormed the platform on which Yeshua stood seeking to kill him. Petra and his band of seventy quickly drew their swords forming up into a protective screen around our king. Petra secreted Yeshua out of the Temple complex and we retreated to the safety of the Mount of Olives.

Phasaelus marched directly from the Temple to the nearby Roman praetorium in an elated state. In his mind, he succeeded in putting the haughty Yeshua in his place. "Priest of the order of Melchizedek," what kind of gibberish was that thought Phasaelus? Pontius Pilate viewed the events in the Temple's outer courtyard from the top of the walls of Fortress Antonia and saw Yeshua turn to flee from the mob. Phasaelus' triumph in winning over the Jewish mob greatly calmed the prefect's nerves. He ordered the very best amphorae of wine be cracked open to toast Phasaelus.

While Pilate hosted Phasaelus, Yeshua met in counsel on the Mount of Olives with his closest advisors (including bar Babas) to access the damage wrought upon their movement that day. Petra and bar Babas argued it was a momentary setback, nothing more. Bar Babas previously knew the identity of Yeshua's father, an Idumean prince, and used this information as a recruiting tool among the Idumean people. They saw it as putting one of their own on the Jewish throne and expected special treatment under the administration of King Yeshua. Bar Babas promised several thousand more Idumeans would arrive in Jerusalem over the coming days. Petra made the same argument about their Galilean recruits. They wouldn't care who Yeshua's father was as they viewed him as a Galilean and more of them were to arrive later in the week. The Samaritans made a political alliance with a Jewish prince. They really didn't care if he descended from Herod or not. Petra further expected Nabateans of Jewish blood, who likewise didn't care if Yeshua was Herod's son, to arrive in Jerusalem during the coming the days. Only the Judeans were in an uproar over the news of Yeshua's Herodian ancestry. Both Petra and bar Babas were confident our movement's numbers would swell leading up to Friday despite the defection of the Judean zealots. Among his inner core of advisors, only Judas saw it as a major blow to their chances of success. He pointed out that if their ultimate goal was the overthrow of the Romans, they needed the support of the Judean people. The mission would never work if the Jewish people viewed our movement as a foreign operation spearheaded by Galileans, Samaritans, and Idumeans. Judas spoke truth but few appeared to listen. Yeshua did not respond in front of the others but pulled Judas aside after the meeting broke up.

Yeshua said to Judas, "Brother, walk with me a moment."

Once they separated themselves from the others Yeshua continued, "Your point is well taken brother. A kingdom divided against itself is laid waste and a house divided against itself falls.[171] But what group comprises the vast majority of the Judean population?"

---

[171] *Luke* 11:17.

Judas wasn't sure what he meant. "You mean party affiliation, like the zealots or Pharisees?"

The vast majority of the people of Judea didn't affiliate themselves with any particular religious or political party. That was the point Yeshua tried to make. He said, "The average Jew is a poor peasant who is neither Pharisee, Sadducee, Essene, nor zealot and knows very little of the Torah. He believes in God and hates the Romans and waits for a righteous king to deliver him from Roman oppression. The last king to deliver the Jewish people from Roman oppression was Mattathias Antigonus. I am his eldest grandson. Are these words true?"

"Yes rabbi."

Yeshua continued, "The zealots are passionate people. How many would you say rushed the podium when I spoke at the Temple today?"

It was a hard question to respond to accurately. Everything became a blur of bodies once the melee commenced. Judas said, "I'm not sure rabbi, probably no more than two hundred. I was too busy avoiding getting bashed over the head with a stave to make a count."

"Judas, do you wish me to abort my mission here in Jerusalem because two hundred zealots became enraged?"

"It's not just these two hundred rabbis. The event has far deeper implications. These two hundred will sway thousands of other Jews. Their combined fury can sway the average Jew in the crowd. And what of the desert Hasidim? Will James be able to sway them?"

Yeshua replied, "James will arrive in Jerusalem from the desert just before the start of Passover. Last word I received is that he does not know how many Hasidim will follow, if any."

Judas, "We can't win this war with Galileans, Samaritans, and Idumeans alone."

Yeshua didn't respond at first. He too was concerned by the day's events but refused to make an emotional and hasty decision. Yeshua said, "Many, many years of planning and preparation have brought us here to Jerusalem for this Passover. My entire life has been a preparation for this day. It is the reason my parents brought me to this earth. I owe them a duty not to turn tail and run at the first sign of trouble. I understand that the zealots are not pleased; however, we have 30,000 followers at our backs. We shall hold fast keeping our eyes and ears open for developments. If a storm appears on the horizon, we shall take appropriate action then. Do you agree Judas?"

Judas knew the master's words rang true. Judas had a bad, bad felling in his stomach but it could just be the swirl of emotions surrounding the day's events. The rabbi rightly decided to hold fast and see what fortune brought on the morning breeze.

Jerusalem, Judea (36 CE)

11 Nisan, Yom Shelee-She / Dies Martis (Tuesday)

Yeshua returned to the Temple but with a much smaller band of followers. The Temple guards strangely treated us with ambivalence. Yesterday our presence put them on edge yet today they acted as if we were no threat. Did they know something we did not? Yeshua didn't dwell on it. He went about doing what he did best, granting audience to individuals and small groups of Jews that wished him to heal the sick or give instruction regarding their problems. In this setting, his humbleness and compassion won over all but his harshest enemies.

The scribes and Pharisees pushed their way to the front of the line of those seeking an audience with Yeshua. They brought a woman allegedly caught in adultery and asked, "Rabbi, this woman has been caught in the act of adultery. The law of Moses commands us to stone her. What say you?" The Pharisees knew forgiveness was a hallmark of Yeshua's teaching and thought they had cornered him with this case. He would be forced to condemn this young mother of two children or fail to apply God's law.

Yeshua ignored them stooping down to write on the ground with his finger. The Pharisees refused to be put off so easily and pressed Yeshua for an answer. He straightened up and said, "He who is without sin among you, let him throw the first stone at this woman." He returned to writing on the ground.

The Pharisees were perplexed and argued amongst themselves on how to proceed. The crowd clearly favored freeing the woman thinking the punishment of death by stoning too harsh. Deciding the crowd was against them and not wishing to stir up sympathy for Yeshua, the Pharisees withdrew leaving the woman with the rabbi. Yeshua then address the woman, "Where are your accusers?"

She said, "They have all gone."

"I do not accuse you either. Go in peace child and sin no more."[172]

My eyes followed the accused woman as she walked away from Yeshua. She joined a group of women all wearing scarves covering their faces who hung back from the rest of the crowd. They greeted her with great enthusiasm as she finally broke down in tears, overcome by how close she came to death. Then I noticed a set of attractive eyes staring at me from behind a veil. This woman approached me cautiously, careful not to draw attention to herself. The gentle sway of her hips beneath her robe told me who approached.

The woman stopped at my side. The scent of her perfume filed my nostrils. She said in a soft voice, “Shalom Menelaus.”

I melted with lust and reached out to touch her hand. She pulled away from me saying, “I just came to ask you to thank the rabbi for what he did. We all wish to thank him.”

“Of course, I shall tell him.” What did she expect me to tell Rabbi Yeshua, the prostitutes of Jerusalem salute you? I asked her, “When can we meet?”

Batsheba replied, “I am under contract for the remainder of Passover. Then, I go to Jericho. If you wish to see me, I can be found there.” She slipped back into the crowd and disappeared.

* * * * * * * * *

When Yeshua finished speaking to the crowd at the Temple, a leading Pharisee invited him to eat at his home so he went. There were two schools of Pharisees in Judea at this time—Beit Hillel and Beit Shammai. Rabbi Hillel was of noble Davidic

---

[172] *John* 8:2-11.

descent having been born in Babylon. His return to Judea marked one of the few instances of a descendant of David living in exile in Babylon returning to Jerusalem to take up position in the government of the country. He served as president of the Sanhedrin during a portion of Herod's reign and was known for a liberal reading of the Torah. Beit Shammai taught a conservative, hard line view of the Torah. Bet Shammai were conservative hard liners. The dinner invitation Yeshua accepted came from a member of Beit Hillel. Yeshua reclined at table without first performing ritual purification, which surprised his Pharisee host.

Yeshua turned to him and said, "Now you Pharisees clean the outside of the cup and the platter as well but inside you are full of wickedness."[173] The meeting got off on the wrong foot for Yeshua declined to brook any insults from his Pharisee hosts regardless of which school they were from. Just then Nasi Gamaliel entered the room. He was the grandson of Rabbi Hillel and the current president of the Sanhedrin. He greeted Yeshua warmly and without malice lightening the mood in the room.

One of the leading Pharisees in attendance asked Yeshua, "Rabbi, why do you have so many Samaritan and Idumean followers? I've heard whispers you have even brought Nabateans here for Passover. These people are not part of the congregation of the Lord." Jewish law imposes strict requirements regarding who was a Jew and how a non-Jew went about the process of conversion. Those groups outside of the chosen ones where collectively called "the nations". Descendants of Idumean converts were not considered full Jews until three generations after conversion. The Nabateans were of Arabian stock and, thus, were lumped among "the nations".

Yeshua responded with a thinly veiled parable, "A man threw a big party and invited many guests. His servants dutifully delivered the invitations to every invited guest yet, as the dinner hour arrived, the dining hall was not filled. Many of the guests sent excuses to the host for why they could not attend the banquet so the master turned to his servants and told them, 'Go out into the

[173] *Luke* 11:39.

highways and along the hedges, and invite whoever you meet to come to my house, sit at my table, and enjoy the bounty. For I tell you, none of those men who were invited and chose not to attend shall taste the food I give.'"[174]

Nasi Gamaliel smiled for he was impressed with the rabbi's eloquent reply. He said to Yeshua, "Rabbi, if you welcome Samaritans, Idumeans, and even Nabateans with open arms, why don't you become Jewish ambassador to the nations? The Torah requires we at least try to spread the word to those left without a path to heaven."

Yeshua did not immediately attack the suggestion from Gamaliel so it was an improvement on the tenor of prior discourse at the table. He asked, "What are you proposing Nasi?"

Gamaliel said, "I believe I could pass a resolution in the Sanhedrin appointing you teacher of the Torah to the nations. Further, I heard you told Prince Phasaelus yesterday that you were a priest of the order of Melchizedek although not a son of Aaron."

Gamaliel steered away from the contentious issue of Yeshua's parentage. He continued, "Establish your new priesthood Yeshua but it is not a Judean priesthood based on the traditions of Levi and Aaron. Take your priesthood to the gentiles and extend salvation to them. I will back you in that mission."[175]

Essentially, Nasi Gamaliel offered a compromise or, more accurately, a face-saving avenue for Yeshua to abandon his dangerous quest to expel the Romans from Israel and reclaim the Hasmonean throne of his grandfather. Yeshua rejected the offer saying, "I have come for the lost sheep of Israel.[176] Thank you for your hospitality." He got up and left.

Jerusalem, Judea (36 CE)

12 Nisan, Yom Re-Ve-ee / Dies Mercurii (Wednesday)

My mother invariably came to Jerusalem for Passover as the wife of Chuza. Herod Antipas and his entourage occupied King Herod's old palace when in Jerusalem. I intended to pay my

---

[174] *Luke* 14:16-24.

[175] See Yeshua The Pharisee by Harvey Falk (Paulist Press 1985) at chapter 5.

[176] *Matthew* 15:24.

respects to my mother and see my daughter Theudosia but had not yet found the time this particular Passover given the momentous events that took place. Yeshua tasked me with logistics; the minutiae that make an organization operate. And as Judas held the common purse, this meant I needed to go through a very busy individual to complete all the many purchases necessary to keep our organization running. Also, we stayed nights in Bethany, which was a manly walk from Herod's palace on the west side of the city. Traveling back and forth from Bethany, climbing up the Mount of Olives several times a day, complicated my job.

Thus, it didn't completely surprise me when I saw my mother approaching while I stood at Yeshua's side as he preached to the people in the Temple. I assumed she was taking the bull by the horns in coming to find her son. Seeing her reminded me of the last time we spoke and I asked her for money. Was she still made at me? She dressed resplendently in the finest imported garments and carried herself with great dignity. I expected a smile on her face as she approached a son she had not seen in one year but her countenance was stern. I kissed her and said, "Greetings mother. Thank you for taking the time to come visit me. I had every intention of calling upon you at the Herodian palace but I have many duties assigned to me by Yeshua."

Instead of asking whether I intended to squander money on a prostitute again this Passover, she said softly but forcefully, "Get your brother. I want to speak to both of you now. It is important."

Philip was a short distance away engaged in some sort of debate. He studied the Torah much more thoroughly than I ever had so I assumed that was the nature of the debate. I politely interrupted his conversation not wishing to appear the overbearing older brother and pointed to our mother. After greeting Philip, she pulled both of our faces close to hers and said, "Proconsul Vitellius has struck a peace agreement with the Parthians. There will be no war between Rome and Parthia this year. He marches for Jerusalem with his two legions as we speak."

I was too stunned to speak. This news changed everything. Philip asked, "How do you know this information mother? Is it a reliable source?"

She replied, "My husband was with Vitellius and Antipas in Babylon. He personally attended the negotiations with the Parthians. He and Antipas arrived back in Jerusalem late last evening. This information came directly to me from my husband."

Philip and I stood silent as we tried to process the staggering implications of this turn of events. Our mother had her own ideas about what we should do. She said, "Now listen my sons. You have both served Yeshua ably and loyally but this whole venture has now turned into a suicide mission. Your band of peasants does not stand a chance against one Roman legion much less two. Please, I beg of you. I could not bear to see my sons nailed to a Roman cross." She began to weep uncontrollably as the deep concern she held for her sons gushed forth.

Despite the crowds of people constantly approaching him for a cure or for advice, Yeshua took note from a distance of the interaction of my brother and I with our mother. As soon as she left the Temple complex, he called me over. I relayed my mother's exact words to the rabbi. He looked to the heavens and said, "Father, why have you done this to me?" A short time later he continued ministering to the people as if he had no care in the world. Such was his gift at controlling his emotions and focusing upon the task at hand.

While I was with Yeshua, Philip began telling our men about the Roman legions marching on Jerusalem. The news spread like a wild fire.

Bethany, Judea (36 CE)

12 Nisan, Yom Re-Ve-ee / Dies Mercurii (Wednesday)

That evening we ate a communal meal at the home of Lazarus in Bethany attended by all the rabbi's brothers and other disciples, except for James the Just who was still with the Hasidim. As Yeshua reclined at the table after the meal, Princess Mariam took a pound of very costly perfume of pure nard and anointed the head and feet of Yeshua then wiped them with her hair. The house filled with a wonderful fragrance. This ceremony marked Yeshua as a Jewish king in the same manner that Samuel anointed King David.[177] Lazarus called for all present to stand and hail the king, the grandson of Mattathias Antigonus has returned to claim his throne. Drinks were served out followed by toasts to the king. The alcohol lightened the men's' spirits. For the moment, they forgot about the Roman legions.

Ever faithful to the frugal Nazarene way, Judas raised a mild protest about the extravagance of costly oil used for the ritual anointment. He said, "We could have sold this perfume for three hundred denarii and given the proceeds to the poor.[178] Shall I take what's left and sell it?"

Yeshua responded, "Let her be. She may need it for my funeral. The poor you shall always have to assist while I might be leaving you shortly."[179]

Yeshua's comment turned the conversation morbid so I ventured gallows humor attempting to lighten the mood. I said, "Judas, better give Mariam more money. If Yeshua is to be buried soon, then they'll be having funerals for all of us. She'll need an amphora full of that oil." My humor fell flat with the crowd. All were silent contemplating their fates as the news of two Roman legions marching for Jerusalem weighed heavily on our minds. Yeshua sought private counsel with Judas.

Yeshua asked once they were alone, "What counsel do you give me brother?"

Judas replied, "You realize our position here in Jerusalem is untenable? The people will flee from our banner like rats jumping off a sinking ship the moment word circulates that two Roman legions are marching on Jerusalem."

Yeshua didn't respond immediately wishing for Judas to finish his thought, "Go on."

Judas, "Rabbi, I recommend a tactical retreat out of Judea. We need to reposition our movement to a sanctuary. Nowhere in Israel is safe. Perhaps we could go to Nabatea to regroup?"

---

177 1 *Samuel* 16:1-13.

178 See Mark 14:5.

179 John 12:1-7.

Yeshua replied, "And if we go to Petra will not the Roman legions merely follow us there? Then we bring destruction on the Nabatean kingdom."

"Then Parthia."

Yeshua tried to make Judas see the futility of the suggestion, "King Artabanus just sold us out to the Romans with this peace treaty. We should no longer expect held from the Parthians."

Judas thought for a moment but couldn't come up with a safe location. "I don't know the answer rabbi. I am prepared to die but only if my death has meaning."

Yeshua continued, "We could break up into small groups and go into hiding in that fashion but to what end?"

Judas seemed heartened by this suggestion, "Yeshua, you are the king. You must save yourself to continue the fight."

Yeshua replied, "Socrates didn't flee Athens when the city fathers ordered him to commit suicide. He drank the poison. I have played the role of royal prince my entire life, a role thrust upon me by my parents. If I hide to continue my quest for the throne, many of the people I love in this world will be destroyed. I always preach do unto others as you would have them do unto you. It is time to live the words Judas."

"Is this the only way rabbi?"

"Yes, it is. My flesh must be sacrificed to save those who follow me. I shall become the Passover lamb. For this, I require your help brother Judas. I want you to go to the chief priests and negotiate a deal—turn me over to them in return for the promise to spare my followers, all of them including Lazarus and Petra."

"But they'll stone you rabbi!"

"Only the man that clothes the true self dies. You know this Judas."

"Yes rabbi."

"And I doubt the priests kill me. You heard Phasaelus declare before the crowd that I am the grandson of Herod. The Sanhedrin does not have the authority to kill a grandson of Herod. The priests cannot deny what has been revealed by Phasaelus thus requiring them to turn me over to Pontius Pilate."

"And Pilate may yet kill you as well. The Romans killed your father and your grandfather. Rabbi, it means crucifixion!"

Yeshua and Judas often had long philosophical discussions about the nature of life and man's place in it. This was the last such conversation they shared together. Yeshua said, "My fate is what it is brother. On a visit to Babylon many years ago, I had the chance to read scriptures from the eastern religions. One of these tells the tale of a young prince speaking with his spiritual guide, Krishna, on the eve of battle in a civil war. The young noble laments in despair over his kinsmen arrayed for battle with the opposing force. He tells Krishna he cannot fight. Krishna replies, 'The wise grieve not for those who live and they grieve not for those who die, for life and death shall pass away.'[180] The spirit within us never dies so the prince should prepare for battle with peace in his heart. The prince was born a warrior so duty and honor dictated that he not flea the field of battle. One must walk the path of action to find enlightenment. Faith alone is dead and meaningless without right action.[181] We are required to carry out those duties life assigns to us. Perhaps my fate is to be executed under Roman law as my father and grandfather before me. We shall find out the day after tomorrow."

Judas stopped walking for a moment to soak in the wisdom. "Why Friday?"

"Because they won't act during the high holy day. Time is running out. Our enemies have until sundown Friday. We just might yet make it Judas. Many wheels are turning."

Judas turned to a troubling subject, "I had a dream. In it, Petra and the other disciples were stoning me."[182]

"If fate requires that you turn me over to the authorities, you may also die brother. Are you willing to accept that fate to assist me in saving our people?"

Judas replied without hesitation, "Gladly rabbi. Perhaps we both shed the man that clothes the true self very soon. I have no desire to survive on this earth if you do not."

---

[180] Bhagavad Gita 2:11, translated by Juan Macaro (Penguin 1962).
[181] See *Letter of James* 2:17.
[182] See *Gospel of Judas*.

Yeshua said, "Then we will be together in my father's house." The rabbi did not respond further for he knew that God had granted Judas a view of the future in his dream. He gave his friend a hug and they parted ways each with many tasks to perform on the morrow.

Jerusalem, Judea (36 CE)
13 Nisan, Yom Hah-Mee-Shee / Dies Jovis (Thursday)
The Last Supper

Early that morning Judas walked into the southeast quarter of the city to the home of Joseph Caiaphas, the high priest. He inquired at the front door but, being an unknown individual of no particular standing in the city, was made to wait while a servant made inquiries up the chain of command. Finally the chief steward of Caiaphas, a freedman named Malthus, came to the door. He said, "I am chief steward to the high priest. What business have you with his Excellency?"

Judas replied, "As I tried to explain to the half-dozen other servants who have interviewed me, I am a disciple of Yeshua the Nazarene. I wish an audience with Caiaphas to offer a deal."

"What sort of deal?"

"That information is reserved for his Excellency. Please, time is short. I promise your master shall be in a foul mood should he find out you have kept me at the door waiting this long."

Malthus was not gone long. Upon return, he whisked Judas with great speed through the elaborate home of Caiaphas toward the reception room where the high priest waited along with several other members of the anti-Yeshua caucus on the Sanhedrin.

Caiaphas was direct, "Why are you here?"

"I come on behalf of King Yeshua with a proposal."

"Proposal? Your self-proclaimed king is in no position to negotiate."

"I am glad to hear your Excellency say this as I have tried to dissuade King Yeshua from negotiating with the Temple authorities. Our mercenaries together with the Galileans, Samaritans and Idumeans look ready for a fight so I suppose we shall meet one another on the field of battle. Thanks again for your time."

Judas turned and began to leave but Caiaphas stopped him, "Hey, hold on there. What is your name again?"

Eleazar bar Zechariah, chief of Modiin, stepped forward from the back of the room to address the meeting. Having compiled a thick file on each of the key disciples of Yeshua, he enlightened the group on the identity of their visitor. The chief said, "Your Excellency, this is Judas ben Simon the Sacarii, a native of Galilee. He is the nephew of Judas of Gamla, another who claimed to be messiah in the reign of Herod Archelaus. His father and two uncles were executed by Governor Publius Varus for insurrection. This man has been a zealot from birth. My informants tell me the zealot party has deserted Yeshua but I humbly recommend that we listen to what Judas the Sacarii has to say."

Caiaphas, "Your insight is welcome chief. Come forward Judas. State the offer of your master."

"King Yeshua is willing to turn himself in peacefully for trial. In exchange, you must promise no charges shall be brought against any of his family and followers. That specifically includes Prince Lazarus and Prince Shimon of Petra."

Caiaphas looked over at the Modiin chief for help as he was unfamiliar with Petra. "Shimon of Petra?"

Eleazar, "Middle son of Herod Antipas and the brother-in-law of Yeshua. His grandfather is King Aretas of Nabatea and I should mention that intelligence reports have a Nabatean army massing on our eastern border. In fact, an advance cohort may have already pierced our border into Perea."

The high priest returned his attention to Judas saying, "Wait in the courtyard while we discuss the proposal of your master."

No sooner had Judas left than pandemonium erupted in the room. Some thought Judas came under false pretenses seeking to delay Yeshua's arrest and buy time for the Nabatean army to march on Jerusalem. Others claimed the whole thing was a trap. Still others adamantly argued that Lazarus should be executed along with Yeshua as the uneducated people stubbornly clung to the idea that Lazarus had been raised from the dead through the power of God. Phasaelus stood and asked permission from the high priest to speak. Permission was granted.

He said, "Your Excellency, esteemed members of the Sanhedrin. My personal opinion is that we risk little by accepting the offer so long as Yeshua turns himself in tonight. We must begin the trial immediately to convict and execute him prior to tomorrow's sundown. This offer actually plays into our hands. We stand little chance of succeeding with a night assault on Yeshua's followers on the Mount of Olives. We would have to wait for Vitellius and his legions to assault their position allowing the enemy to flee. And what crime can we charge Lazarus with in any event? Has he claimed to have risen from the dead? It is the people in the street who gossip about such things."

Another member of the Sanhedrin jumped up to voice his opinion but the high priest raised his arm cutting off discussion. Caiaphas said, "I agree with Prince Phasaelus, we have little to lose and the capture of a dangerous heretic to gain."

They called Judas back into the room to hammer out the specifics of the handover. Judas was to lead a group of Temple priests and police at midnight to a spot where they would find Yeshua under light guard for arrest.

Caiaphas, "It is agreed then Judas. You hand over Yeshua to us in the last hour before sunrise at the Garden of Gethsemane. We promise, in return, that no charges shall be brought against members of his family and his followers."

Judas, "I want to hear you swear this in an oath before God to which the members of the Sanhedrin here assembled shall bear witness."

Caiaphas repeated his pledge as an oath before all assembled then said to Judas, "If this comes off as promised and we capture Yeshua, your reward shall be 30 silver Tyrian shekels. Go now to your master and confirm his acceptance of this agreement."

Judas left feeling sick to his stomach at having made a bargain with a man he regarded as the devil's helper here on earth.

As the meeting broke up in the home of Caiaphas, the high priest motioned for Prince Phasaelus and the Modiin chief to wait behind until the others departed. Caiaphas said to them, "The three of us shall need to work together to finalize the execution of Yeshua. First, let's not be fools. This could be a trap. They might be luring us out from the walls of the city to be attacked, so we need backup from the Romans. Phasaelus, you go to Pilate and get the Roman soldiers to escort us to the arrest site. Let Pilate know we have a deal in place for a peaceful arrest. All they need to do is protect our back while we make the arrest. Eleazar, Yeshua has allies in this revolt. Arrest the leaders of his Samaritan and Idumean allies. Do you know their identities?"

Eleazar, "Yes, Your Excellency."

Phasaelus, "Your Excellency, does this violate the agreement with Judas? You agreed <u>not</u> to arrest the family and followers of Yeshua?"

Caiaphas replied, "His family and followers are Galileans so we agreed not to arrest Galileans. These other people are political allies not subject to the agreement."

Phasaelus smiled at the ingenuity of the double-cross. The meeting broke as there was much work to be accomplished before effecting the arrest.

* * * * * * * * *

Yeshua's followers didn't see Judas that day, which was odd. Our offensive against the city of Jerusalem was planned for the next day on the eve of Passover and one of our top commanders was inexplicably absent. People began asking questions. I suggested he was desperately trying to bring the zealots back into our alliance. Yeshua carried on as if it were any other day. He conducted his ministry in the open courtyard at the Temple as before. The Temple guards gave us no trouble, a false calm before the impending storm. Late that afternoon, we walked to the Jerusalem home of Joseph of Arimathea, who reserved an upper room in his vast estate for our use. Only the inner core of the movement attended this dinner while Yeshua's many thousands of followers returning to their camp on top of the Mount of Olives.

Joseph pulled Yeshua aside and said, "I just received word, Caiaphas plans on arresting you tonight. I recommend you flea your highness."

This, of course, was no surprise to Yeshua. He replied, "No Joseph, my disciples and I shall have our evening meal here in your home as planned. If the authorities come to arrest me, do not resist. I shall peacefully submit myself to them. All I ask is that you speak for me in the Sanhedrin if the arrest occurs."

Joseph replied, "As you wish your highness."

The rest of us were not informed regarding the state of affairs. At mealtime, we reclined on lush carpets and cushions in an expansive room. The host was unable to join us having been called away on urgent business we were told. In truth, Joseph of Arimathea left us to frantically lobby his allies on the Grand Sanhedrin to oppose the arrest planned by Caiaphas. We proceeded with our meal thinking all was well with the rebellion. Judas rejoined our group just as food was served. Yeshua ritually broke the bread and said, "Blessed are you, our God, king of the universe, who has brought forth bread from the earth."

You could sense something special in the air that evening. Yeshua dealt with us in an unusually formal manner. Wine was unexpectedly served with the bread. Yeshua abstained from alcohol at all times except for the day of the Passover feast, which was to occur the next day. We talked amongst ourselves during the meal but, before everyone had finished their food, Yeshua called over Judas saying, "Go now and do what you must do."

Judas said, "Are you sure rabbi?"

Yeshua nodded affirmatively then pulled Judas close whispering into his ear, "When and where?"

Judas whispered in reply, "The last hour before sunrise at the Garden of Gethsemane."

Yeshua nodded indicating he understood the time and location. Judas then left without saying another word. None of us were quite sure what the little exchange was all about at the time. As Judas held the common purse and preparations for the Pascal

Feast were under way, some thought Yeshua commanded Judas to leave us to complete preparations for tomorrow's Passover meal. After the departure of Judas, Yeshua spoke to us on into the evening about many different spiritual subjects. It was the longest speech I had ever heard him give. As I listened, my mind wondered why some of this could not be saved for after-meal speeches in coming days. Obviously, Yeshua knew this was very well his last chance to impart wisdom to us in this life.

Yeshua concluded with these words, "Shortly, the world will behold me no more but you will behold me because my inner self shall live. You shall not be alone for the spirit shall be upon you. He who does not love me does not keep my word. Stay true to my word and I shall live in you."[183]

We got the sense during Yeshua's speech that danger was afoot. I asked, "Master, will there be trouble tonight?"

He did not reply directly but said, "If you have a bag, bring it. Also bring whatever weapons you possess. If you don't have a sword, sell your cloak and buy one."[184]

After singing a hymn, we decamped from the home of Joseph of Arimathea.[185] It was night as we passed through the east gate of the city, traversed the Valley of Kidron, and rejoined our company on the Mount of Olives. No one stopped us along the way. All appeared calm to our eyes; however, many unseen wheels where in motion that night. Yeshua hoped against hope that the cup would somehow be lifted from his hands allowing him to escaped arrest.

Mount of Olives, Judea (36 CE)

14 Nisan, Yom Shee-Shee / Dies Veneris (Friday)

It was now past midnight and into the very early hours of Dies Veneris (Friday). Upon arrival at the Mount of Olives, Yeshua turned to Lazarus and said, "Brother, please return to Bethany. The women are in your charge and your presence with them is required this night." Lazarus agreed to the king's request

---

183 See *John* 14:19-26.

184 See *Luke* 22:36.

185 See *Mark* 14:26.

without question. Yeshua then turned to me and said, "Menelaus, old and dear friend, please accompany Lazarus to Bethany."

I replied, "No master, I stay with you."

He started to argue with me but decided against it. "Stay up here with your brother Philip and you shall be safe."

An uneasy feeling permeated the air. The Roman legions were still a week's march away to the east. None of us knew exactly why but all felt the disturbance of spirit. The words Yeshua spoke at our evening meal concerning his departure from us troubled everyone. Yeshua started to descend from the summit. Petra went to Yeshua and said, "Rabbi, where are you going that I cannot go with you? I shall follow you anywhere, even lay my life down for you."

Yeshua replied, "Will you lay down your life for me? Truly, before the cock crows with the sunrise you shall have denied me three times Petra."

Petra protested, "This is not true rabbi. The others may fall away but I will not."[186] The rest of us raised our voice to also protest that we would follow Yeshua to Sheol and back.

Yeshua smiled and replied, "Yes, I am sure you will all gladly follow me to hell. But it is not necessary for all of us to descend into the depths of the pit. It serves no purpose." Yeshua instructed us to recline on the Mount of Olives with our best infantry posted as guards on the perimeter of our encampment. Yeshua called over my brother Philip to impart instructions, "I am going into the garden to pray. Petra is coming with me. You shall be in charge of the mercenaries and all our armed men while we are gone. Should Roman soldiers appear, my orders are to hold your position. Do NOT attack under any circumstances. Our people may draw their swords only in self-defense. Is that understood?"

Philip replied, "Yes your highness."

"I know I can count on you Philip."

He took Petra and the two sons of thunder, who were the most aggressive and militaristic of his disciples, and went down

---

[186] *John* 13:37-38 and *Mark* 14:29-31.

into a ravine just west of the Mount of Olives to a spot called the Garden at Gethsemane. Yeshua said to the small group of disciples who accompanied him, "My soul is deeply troubled brothers. Please sit here with me while I pray."

In the dead of night at the north gate of the Temple complex, Judas met the high priest and Temple officers who came there with torches and weapons backed by an entire Roman cohort of heavy infantry.[187] The arrest party of close to one thousand moved east out of the Temple complex, then south along the Valley of Kidron. The tribune commanding the Roman cohort ordered them to take up positions at the base of the Mount of Olives thereby cutting off our mercenaries from interfering with the arrest of Yeshua at the Garden at Gethsemane. Had Petra remained behind with the mercenaries, he certainly would have given the command to attack the Romans despite whatever order Yeshua issued. Philip, on the other hand, carried out his orders from Yeshua to the letter. Our army held fast on the Mount of Olives. Yeshua stood alone in the garden while Petra, James and Yochanan lay fast asleep up against a nearby tree. Judas led the chief priests and Temple police through the ravine to the garden.

Yeshua prayed, "Father, let your will not mine be done."[188] He now saw the arresting party coming through the ravine with torches. He nudged his three disciples asleep on the ground and said to them, "Could you not stay awake with me but one hour? The spirit is willing but the flesh is weak. Behold, the hour has come. The king is being arrested."[189]

Petra jumped up shaking the sleep from his eyes not quite able to comprehend the large force arrayed against them. He said, "Come your highness, let us run. We can make it back up the mountain to the safety of our people."

Petra grabbed the king's arm but Yeshua would not move. He said, "No Petra. If the Jewish people wish to destroy me, then so be it." Yeshua didn't try explaining to Petra that he was

---

[187] *John* 18:3.
[188] *Mark* 14:36.
[189] *Mark* 14:37, 41.

sacrificing himself to save everyone else for he would not have understood.

Now Judas approached the garden leading the arrest party. As a signal to the high priest, he came to Yeshua and kissed him.[190] Yeshua addressed the arresting party saying, "Why have you come out at night with clubs and swords to arrest me like a common criminal? I was at the Temple teaching for many hours today yet you didn't approach me."[191]

Unable to control his anger, Petra drew his sword and struck the ear off Malchus, chief steward and freedman of the high priest. This rash and pointless action set up a tense situation. The sons of thunder drew their swords, as did the Temple police who greatly outnumbered the companions of Yeshua in the garden. The Roman soldiers would have killed Petra where he stood for such an action but they were fearful of our 30,000 followers stationed above them on the mountain. The king defused the standoff. He said, "Petra, James, Yochanan, put your swords into the sheath. This is the cup my father has given to me. Shall I not drink it?"[192]

The three proud men refused to sheath their swords. As soldiers, they viewed it as cowardice to allow their king to be captured without a fight. Yeshua addressed them one last time, "Petra, I hoped at least you would understand. I have already defeated death. These men here have no power over me."

Finally, Petra, James, Yochanan backed away allowing the chief priests to take Yeshua into custody, although they had no clue of the true meaning of the master's final words. Yeshua intended to impart a spiritual message saying that he had risen above bodily life and death in this world. Put another way, Yeshua defeated death by his acceptance of, and dedication to, the path. He spoke of the second birth all true initiates must undertake of which Petra and the others lacked knowledge. To defeat death, one must not only accept God but, also, perform all the works required to walk the path. That path requires detachment from the

---

[190] *Matthew* 26:47-50.

[191] *Mark* 14:48-49.

[192] *John* 18:11.

material world. Yeshua made these works abundantly clear for all with ears to hear: give away your material possessions to the poor, love your neighbor as yourself, blessed are the peacemakers, blessed are the gentle, blessed are the pure in heart, et cetera. Many heard the words, few listened. Yeshua feared not death of his body for his true self, as with all of us, was spirit. This spirit cannot be defeated by any man.

The arrest party cautiously moved away from the garden turning for the city with Yeshua in custody. Caiaphas kept his word by handing over 30 silver pieces to Judas in full view of Petra, who seethed with anger.

Trial and Crucifixion of Yeshua

In the hour before sunrise, the Temple guards bound Yeshua without further incident and led him back into the city. They took him to the home of high priest Caiaphas for interrogation. Those on the Sanhedrin in alliance with Joseph of Arimathea were denied entrance to the home of Caiaphas. Yeshua had already been convicted by the Sanhedrin in abstentia so there was really no need for a formal trial. Still bound, Yeshua stood before a Sanhedrin ad hoc committee. The actions of the high priest were unrestrained among his allies inside his own home. Caiaphas said, "Tell us rabbi, did you proclaim that you would tear down the Temple and build it back up in three days?"

The Sanhedrin members chortled at what they perceived as an outlandish statement from Yeshua. It had taken Herod forty-six years to rebuild the Temple.[193] But the chief priests lacked spiritual insight into the words of Yeshua. The true Temple of God is within each and every human being. He spoke of spiritual death and rebirth that ritualistically occurs over a three day interval as was the case with Jonah. After the second birth a spiritual seeker enters through the narrow gate gaining eyes to see and passing from death to life. Such a topic was far beyond the ability of any in the room to comprehend so Yeshua didn't bother to respond.

---

[193] *John* 2:20.

Caiaphas, "Rabbi, have you become mute?"

Yeshua said, "I have spoken openly to the world. I've taught in the synagogues and in the Temple where all the Jews were free to hear me. Nothing was said in secret. Why do you question me now?"

Phasaelus and Eleazar ben Zechariah sat to the left of Caiaphas. The Modiin chief nodded to one of his men standing next to Yeshua. The Temple guard wound up and struck a blow across Yeshua's face with his fist. The guard said, "Is this the way you speak to His Excellency, the high priest?"

Yeshua turned to the guard saying, "If I have spoken wrongly, bear witness of the wrong. But if not, why do you hit me?"[194]

Caiaphas continued his questioning. "Are you the Christ, the anointed one?"

Yeshua, "If I tell you, you will not believe. If I ask you a question, you will not answer. But the son of man shall be seated at the right hand of the power of God."

Caiaphas, "Are you then the Son of God?"

Yeshua responded in a loud and clear voice, "Yes, I am."[195]

Upon hearing these words Phasaelus stood up tearing his clothing with high emotion. "What further evidence do we need? You have heard the blasphemy for yourselves!"[196]

Costobarus then stood up and shouted, "He deserves death!" All Sanhedrin members present agreed. Some began to spit at Yeshua and to beat him with their fists. They said, "Tell us Christ, which one struck you?"

At the back of the room sat Yeshua ben Caiaphas, youngest son of the high priest. He shared the name of the accused. Both men were of Hasmonean blood. Both had a daughter named Mariamne.[197] Both grew up following paths set for them by their august fathers yet one stood condemned to death

---

[194] *John* 18:20-23.

[195] *Luke* 22:67-70.

[196] *Mark* 14:63-64.

[197] A Second Temple ossuary recovered from looters in 2009 bears the inscription, "Miriam daughter of Yeshua son of Caiaphas, priest".

and the other lived a comfortable life of luxury as a chief priest. Yeshua ben Caiaphas couldn't help but look across the room at his distant cousin Yeshua the Nazarene and wonder, "There but for the grace of God go I."[198]

Petra waited through the night outside the home of Caiaphas warming himself by a fire while the interrogation continued. A servant girl approached Petra saying, "You are one of them. I saw you with Yeshua the Nazarene."

Petra lied, "No, no, you are mistaken girl. I am not one of his followers."

Several others now jumped into the conversation saying that they too had seen Petra with Yeshua in the Temple. Petra twice more denied the accusers. Just then the sun broke the eastern horizon and the cock crowed. Petra ran off in tears realizing the words spoken by Yeshua hours earlier had come true.

* * * * * * * * *

Judas knocked on the door of the home of Joseph of Arimathea. The servant answering the door, recognized the visitor, and admitted him. Joseph came to meet Judas in the entrance hall asking, "I heard Yeshua was arrested by Caiaphas but was unable to see with my own eyes. Is it true?"

Judas replied, "Yes, he was arrested. Will he be executed?"

Joseph, "Caiaphas controls enough votes in the Sanhedrin to do as he pleases. My only hope is to invoke Roman law and demand Yeshua be sent to Pilate for trial as a Roman citizen and grandson of two Jewish kings."

"But Pilate could crucify him?"

"Roman citizens cannot be crucified. If Yeshua proclaims that he is a grandson of Herod to Pilate that should force his case to Rome. We are only left with hard choices."

Judas paced the entrance hall of Joseph's grand home thinking. He finally stopped and turned to the Herodian prince, "I have a contingency plan in case he is crucified."

---

198 Quote attributed to John Bradford of Britain (1510–1555).

Joseph didn't understand, "What plan?"

Judas, "The inner disciples of Yeshua are initiated through a mock death and rebirth ceremony. Lazarus and myself are initiates. Certain herbs are used in this ceremony that simulate death."

"I don't follow you."

"Lazarus will know what I have in mind. Please send a messenger to him in Bethany to come and bring all that is necessary for a secret Nazarene initiation."

"But they might arrest Lazarus. It is dangerous for him to come."

Joseph of Arimathea was correct. The authorities could very well renege on their agreement and arrested Lazarus. Judas needed to minimize the danger to Lazarus. He asked Joseph, "Do you have access to a burial tomb near the city?"

"Yes, my own tomb has been cut and waits for my body."

"If Yeshua is crucified today, send a message to Lazarus instructing him to wait for us at your tomb with all the necessary ingredients for a secret initiation. He can hide inside the tomb. Under Jewish law, the body must be down from the cross before sundown. Our job will be to drug Yeshua while he is on the cross to give the appearance of death."

Joseph, "This sounds very risky. I pray it does not come to pass."

Judas, "This plan is only to be implemented as a last resort. Please argue for Yeshua before the Sanhedrin. I shall make additional arrangements and wait for Lazarus at your tomb. The two of us together will try to heal Yeshua if the worst transpires."

After the arrest of Yeshua, his disciples with the exception of Petra and the sons of thunder, went into hiding for fear that they too would be apprehended by the authorities. As for myself, I needed wine to deal with the situation. I begged the god Bacchus to come and rescue me from this nightmare. I returned to Lazarus' home in Bethany and broke into his storeroom helping myself to the Passover wine. Consuming a proper share for three men, I passed out on the floor. At sunrise, someone shook me. He said, "Wake up you drunk."

I had no idea even who I was at that moment. My only reply was to vomit the contents of my stomach out onto the floor. Lazarus told a servant to draw a big bucket of water and pour it over me. This raised my consciousness to the state of the walking dead. My eyes opened but I was not there. They dragged me out to the fountain in the courtyard dunking my head many times under the water.

Lazarus finally said, "That's enough. Bring him water to drink." Slowly I became human again. Lazarus wished for me to accompany him to a tomb just outside of Jerusalem. My hazy brain couldn't quite comprehend what it was we were supposed to be doing there, something about saving the king. My stomach revolted with spasms as we took to the road making for Jerusalem. I saw a body hanging on a tree in the Valley of Kidron as we approached the city. Lazarus and myself went to investigate. The person hanging by the rope looked to have been stoned. His face swelled in places marking the landing spot of rocks. Judging from other marks on his body, the man had been kicked as well. We took the body down from the tree. Slashes in his skull oozed blood. I thought I saw his head move slightly so I lifting him up. It was then I recognized the person who had been stoned and hung. It was Judas. I asked, "Brother, who did this to you?"

He could manage but one word, "Petra". With that, his head collapsed into my hands and he died. As we laid the body of Judas on the ground, I heard the jangle of coins in his purse. Thirty pieces of silver tumbled to the ground. I paid a hugely exorbitant sum, three Tyrian shekels, to a nearby mortician to bury Judas immediately. By doing so, the mortician became ritually impure unable to partake in the Passover feast that evening. The rest of the silver I put into my purse. We would need this money if forced into exile, as appeared likely at that moment. Despite the shock of watching Judas die, Lazarus instructed me that we had to continue with our mission and worry about who killed Judas later. We continued on our hunt for Joseph's tomb eventually locating it with the help of his servant.

Lazarus said, "Go now into the city and discover the fate of Yeshua. I am too well known in the city to enter. If he is to be crucified, come back here to me in the tomb for further instructions."

Case of Yeshua before the Grand Sanhedrin

> Now when morning was come, all the chief priests and the elders of the people took counsel against Yeshua to put him to death. *Luke* 27:1.

The Temple complex teemed with thousands of lambs and hundreds of priests ready for the coming sacrifice as the sun broke over the eastern wall. All the lambs were to die before sundown that day. The members of the Grand Sanhedrin rose from their seats as His Excellency Joseph ben Caiaphas, the Kohen Gadol, strode into the Hall of Hewn Stones. He was the one person on earth allowed to enter the holy of holies during Yom Kippur to atone for the sins of all Jewish people by performing an elaborate ritual that included sprinkling the blood of a sacrificial bullock within the Temple. King Yeshua stood before the high priest with hands bound, the figurative bullock whose blood the high priest desired to spill. Caiaphas brimmed with confidence knowing he possessed sufficient votes to do as planned and quickly execute Yeshua on the charges of sorcery and blasphemy then proceed with the Passover feast. The high priest immediately called the hearing to order and, without so much as an introductory speech, turned the case over to Prince Phasaelus, who acted as chief prosecutor.

Phasaelus said, "Yeshua the Nazarene, self-proclaimed king of the Jews, you stand before the Sanhedrin previously convicted of the crimes of sorcery and blasphemy. Do you have anything to say before your sentence is carried out?"

Yeshua replied, "You have no authority over me. This is an illegal assembly. The high priest and each of you sitting here today owes his position to the Roman occupiers. You have no power under God to judge me."

A Temple guard reached out with an open hand and struck a heavy blow across the face of the prisoner. The guard said, "Do not speak to His Excellency in such a manner."

Phasaelus had orders from Caiaphas to conclude the hearing with lightning speed. He said, "I will take that response from the prisoner to mean that he contests the charges. Even though not required to do so by the procedures of the Grand Sanhedrin, we will present the most damning evidence to the accused to see if he can refute it. Is that acceptable Your Excellency?"

Caiaphas, "Yes Prince Phasaelus but be quick about it. This man's guilt is known to all and Passover is almost upon us."

Phasaelus turned to Yeshua and said, "Prisoner, are you the son of God?"

Yeshua replied, "Yes, I am."

The prosecutor threw his hands in the air gesturing to the members of the Sanhedrin allowing the words of the accused to register with his audience. He continued, "Then do you deny that you are a sorcerer?"

"Is it black magic to heal the suffering of one's fellow man?"

"Yes, if the power to heal comes from a dark source!" Phasaelus strutted around the front of the chamber shooting a confident grin to the chief priests seated in the chamber. He stopped and turned to face the prisoner yet again, "Cousin, I know all the family secrets. Your power comes from a foreign God because you bear a mark upon your flesh placed there by Zoroastrian priests, the magi. Do you deny it?"

The marking of flesh was forbidden by the Torah.[199] A murmur arose in the room. All eyes riveted upon the pretender to the Jewish throne, who chose to remain silent in the face of a devastating allegation. Phasaelus called over the high priest then pulled back Yeshua's tunic. The prosecutor pointed to a tattoo marked into the flesh of the accused's thigh.[200] Magi Gaspar put

---

199 *Leviticus* 19:28.

200 See *Talmud*, Shab 104b; *see* Dr. Peter Schafer <u>Yeshua in the Talmud</u>, ibid at pages 15-16.

the tattoo on the thigh of Yeshua as a new born baby so he could distinguish the king later in life and avoid the chance of an imposter. Gaspar had not known the prohibition against this act by Jewish law.

Upon seeing the scratch mark on Yeshua's skin, Caiaphas cried out, "It is the mark of a foreign god!" The murmur in the courtroom now erupted into a roar.

Phasaelus, "The prisoner has convicted himself! My work here is done. The prosecution has no more."

Caiaphas, wishing to publicly demonstrate his fairness before stoning Yeshua, asked, "Does the accused have anything else to say for himself?"

He waited for a reply but none came from Yeshua. Caiaphas belittled Yeshua's silence, "Apparently the Son of God has gone mute." The Sanhedrin broke out in laughter.

Joseph of Arimathea rose from his seat addressing himself to Nasi Gamaliel, the Sanhedrin president, who had been uncharacteristically quiet during the proceeding. Joseph said, "Point of order Mr. President."

Caiaphas protested that the case was already closed. All that remained was a vote to carry out the punishment. Nasi Gamaliel overruled the objection allowing Joseph to speak.

Joseph continued, "Thank you Mr. President. As I understand the evidence, the main cudgels in the arsenal of the prosecution are the miracles worked by the accused, that the accused was heard to say he is the Son of God and, also, the appearance of a scratch mark upon his thigh. I have seen this man's good works in Galilee and Judea. He heals the sick. Goodness comes from God. As to the other charges, have not all Jewish kings been called sons of God in scripture? In fact, are not all Jews children of God? How can this be blasphemy? And putting scratch marks on one's flesh is not a capital offense! You can't put a man to death for that!"

The face of the high priest turned dark red, almost purple with rage. He stood then loudly banged his hand on the table. "This isn't a point of order. Debate on the guilt of the prisoner is closed. No more debate!"

Phasaelus interjected, "Your Excellency, I would be happy to address the objection of our esteemed Joseph of Arimathea."

The high priest had screamed so loudly that his vocal cords were strained as he tried to recognize Phasaelus and give him the floor. All he could muster was a hand motioning for Phasaelus to proceed. Phasaelus said, "It is one thing to call oneself the 'Son of God', quite another to claim that you shall ride a heavenly cloud at the right hand of God on judgment day. That is to equate himself as a prophet of God and presume to speak for God. Many members of the Sanhedrin have asked Yeshua for a sign of his power to speak on behalf of God but he refuses to give us a sign. You have witnessed his magic out in the countryside but here in the holy city of Jerusalem though, this magician is unable to perform his magic for us. He is a sorcerer and his power comes from the dark arts! Did not he spend decades studying in the Egyptian desert? Does he not bear the mark of a foreign god on his flesh? His guilt is undeniable." Shouts of approval for the prosecutor's words came from around the room.

Joseph replied, "He's a gifted healer! Clearly his power comes from God."

Caiaphas finally regained enough of his voice to call a halt to further debate. "That's enough. The man is a sorcerer who has tried to lead Israel astray. Enough talk. We vote. Who votes to carry out the sentence of death by stoning on the charges of blasphemy and sorcery?" By custom, voting began with the most junior member of the Sanhedrin. Phasaelus cast the first vote for guilty as the most junior member of the assembly. Yeshua ben Caiaphas, to the surprise of all, voted for excommunication. The vote continued but the end result for execution was never in doubt, although a surprising number of the Sanhedrin members voted not to execute Yeshua, most notably, Nasi Gamaliel. The chief scribe of the court recorded the vote of each full member of the Sanhedrin and read the verdict, "42 votes for death, 28 votes for excommunication."

Caiaphas stood and said, "Yeshua the Nazarene, the verdict of the Grand Sanhedrin is that you are guilty of the charges of blasphemy and sorcery. Your punishment of death by stoning has been confirmed by vote here today. I hereby order the captain of the guard to carry out the prescribed punishment of stoning. The chief prosecutor shall escort the executioners to witness the sentence being carried out." The guards advanced to grab Yeshua intending to publicly stone him that very moment. Joseph of Arimathea bolted out of his seat closing the distance between himself and the high priest. The aggressive move startled the members of the Sanhedrin. Would two senior members of the Sanhedrin come to blows?

Joseph of Arimathea said, "Caiaphas, you have no authority under Roman law to execute this man and you know it. He is not only a Roman citizen but, also, the grandson of two Jewish kings. Here is his birth record from our Temple archives proving the identity of his true father, Crown Prince Antipater ben Herod. Maybe Pilate is in league with you but the family of Yeshua has connections in Rome. Yeshua's brother-in-law, Prince Lazarus, was educated in Rome and retains many friends in the Senate. I also have many friends in Rome."

A Pharisee of Beit Shammai shouted out in reply, "For all we know Yeshua's father was one of Herod's soldiers at Jericho. This man was conceived while his mother was imprisoned. How do you know Herod's soldiers didn't have their way with her? There is a reason the law forbids the high priest from being married to a woman who has been in prison."

The Sanhedrin erupted in private debate regarding this new line of argument. Joseph of Arimathea made his rebuttal, "Yeshua's certificate is signed by the high priest Matthias ben Theophilus and names the father of Yeshua as Antipater ben Herod! So by claiming Yeshua was born of a common soldier you also defame the high priest Theophilus."

That was a particularly skillful rebuttal which completely took the chief priests by surprise. The family of Annas dominated the high priesthood since the end of the reign of Herod Archelaus. Caiaphas himself was the son-in-law of Annas. And everyone in the room knew that the granddaughter of high priest Matthias ben Theophilus married high priest Annas ben Seth, the patriarch of the entire Annas clan of high priests. This granddaughter of

Theophilus was of Hasmonean descent, which served as a matter of great dignity for the family of Annas. The wife of Caiaphas was herself a descendent of Theophilus. All of Caiaphas' sons were descendents of Theophilus. To disparage the dignity of Theophilus was to disparage the lineage of both the house of Annas and Caiaphas.

Joseph of Arimathea then gave his final argument for the life of Yeshua, "Caiaphas, I swear as God is my witness that if you stone this man the Romans shall remove you from office just as prefect Gratus removed your father-in-law Annas."

All knew Joseph of Arimathea for years yet no member of the Sanhedrin had ever heard him swear an oath of any sort. He was a mild-mannered, smooth negotiator. They also knew of his fabulous wealth and Herodian connections. Caiaphas realized Joseph was deadly serious, which gave the high priest pause to reconsider his plan of action. He was torn for he very much wished to remain in office. Phasaelus quickly determined what had to be done. He leaned across the table to whisper to the high priest, "Your Excellency, go ahead and give Joseph what he asks for. You send Yeshua to Pilate and I will see to it the Romans crucify Yeshua."

Caiaphas, "On what charge Phasaelus? Blasphemy is not a crime under Roman law."

"Insurrection, Yeshua has declared himself Jewish king."

"How can you guaranty a conviction?"

"Pilate is greedy. Uncle Antipas will bribe Pilate. Whatever the price, he'll come up with the money."

Caiaphas had been high priest for eighteen years, nine more than his august father-in-law Annas ben Seth. Caiaphas enjoyed the power of the high priesthood and wished to retain it. This Galilean wasn't worth the risk of losing power. Phasaelus was right, every Roman had his price. This was the safest play. Caiaphas nodded to the chief prosecutor signifying he agreed with the proposal. The order was given and, instead of taking the prisoner out to the courtyard to be stoned, they marched Yeshua to the Praetorium inside Fortress Antonia. Before leaving the Hall of Hewn Stones with the prisoner, Phasaelus grabbed Eleazar ben Zechariah, the Modiin chief, for a quick strategy session.

Phasaelus said, "You escort the prisoner to the Praetorium, while I arrange for Herod Antipas to pay a bribe to Pilate. Oh, and another thing, you better come up with some reason why Yeshua is not legally a Roman citizen before I arrive at the Praetorium."

Second Hour, Trial Before Pilate

> They led Yeshua therefore from Caiaphas into the Praetorium: and it was early; and they themselves entered not into the Praetorium, that they might not be defiled, but might eat the Passover. *John* 18:28.

The Temple guards took the prisoner into the Praetorium where Pilate conducted the public business of the prefecture while in Jerusalem. However, the chief priests waited outside refusing to enter the building. The Praetorium contained graven images of Caesar making the build unclean under Jewish law. To enter the Praetorium was to become ritually unclean and, thus, ineligible to partake in the Passover feast with one's family that evening. The chief priests stood outside waiting for the prefect. Seneca, chief minister to Pilate, approached his master in his chambers. He said, "Prefect, the chief priests are here with a prisoner, Yeshua the Nazarene."

"The Egyptian? Why is he here? The Jews told me they would try this man in the Sanhedrin and execute him. Give me a moment to put on my toga."

After donning the proper attire for a Roman official, Pontius Pilate entered the Praetorium judgment hall expecting to find a throng of Jewish officials but instead found only Seneca, the prisoner, and guards. Pilate said, "What charge has been brought against this man?"

Seneca replied, "Insurrection prefect. He claims to be king of the Jews."

Pilate addressed Yeshua, "I am told you are the king of Jews prisoner. Is this so?"

Yeshua, "It is as you say."

Pilate maintained an extensive file on Yeshua the Nazarene, also known as the Egyptian. Pilate knew full well that the prisoner standing before him was born of the truest Hasmonean blood through his mother Princess Mariamne bat Antigonus. The identity of his father was somewhat hazy although Phasaelus informed Pilate of the rumor that Yeshua was the son Antipater ben Herod, the former coregent of the Jewish kingdom. Antipater had been named successor in the last will Herod left under seal in Rome with the Vestal Virgins. That potentially made Yeshua, under Roman law, the legitimate Jewish king. Either way, Yeshua was a hot political problem. Executing him risked retribution from Rome.

Pilate said to those assembled in the Praetorium, "I find no fault in this man. Where are this man's accusers?"

Seneca, "They wait outside in the forum prefect."

Pilate, "Why in the blazes are they out there? If the chief priests have a complaint against this man, then tell them to come in here before me."

"I have told them prefect. Apparently, it is against their law to enter the Praetorium on the eve of a high religious holiday. Caiaphas and the rest refuse to enter."

Pilate rose from the judgment seat. As he strode to the forum Pilate vowed to himself that Caiaphas was done as high priest. The prefect had not dismissed a high priest during his ten-year administration of Judea but the move was past due. Caiaphas treated the prefect, an official appointed by personal command of the emperor, like some sort of underling. He demanded a Roman prefect come to the forum in his toga to hear formal criminal charges. Unheard of!

Caiaphas stood stoically in the forum waiting for Pilate to appear outside but internally his stomach was in knots. Phasaelus promised a Roman conviction of Yeshua yet still no Phasaelus. The high priest turned to the Modiin chief and said, "Where is my chief prosecutor?"

Eleazar replied, "I can only guess he is still negotiating with Herod Antipas your Excellency."

'Well get him here immediately. There is Pilate coming out to greet us now!"

Eleazar ben Zechariah left the forum but didn't go in search of Phasaelus as ordered. Disobeying orders generally was a bad career choice but, on rare occasions, led to a commendation from one's superior. He knew Phasaelus would return from the palace of Antipas as soon as humanly possible. Instead of harping on Phasaelus to come to the forum, the Modiin chief entered the Praetorium in search of the Roman official in charge of the tax rolls. He had a hunch—Yeshua, although a grandson of Herod according to the Temple records, was not listed in the Roman records as a Roman citizen. Shortly after Yeshua's birth, Prince Joseph and the elder Princess Mariamne fled for Alexandria, Egypt where they sought refuge. They and their children were absent from the Jewish kingdom when the Romans took the census after the death of Herod. Did they return in time to register in the Roman census of Quirinius?[201] Did Yeshua appear on the Roman tax records at all? Eleazar needed answers to these questions and needed them quickly.

Pontius Pilate didn't bother to walk down to ground level to greet the chief priests. Instead, he spoke down to them from the portico of the Praetorium. He inquired, "Your Excellency, a pleasure to have you visit us on the eve of a Jewish holy day but why are you here?"

The high priest replied, "Prefect, we come to press charges against Yeshua the Nazarene."

"Isn't that a kick in the balls?" thought Pilate. These Jews asked my assistance to arrest the fellow telling me that was all the help they required. The trial and execution of Yeshua were supposedly arranged for in the Sanhedrin. Now these brainless donkeys stood here in the forum creating a public scene asking for Yeshua to be executed under Roman law. The public veneer of an amiable civil servant began to drain from Pilate's face. He said, "I can see you are here to press charges. The man stands shackled

---

[201] The census of Quirinius occurred in 6 CE after Herod Archelaus was removed from office.

under guard in the Praetorium. The point is why have you not tried him under your own laws?"

Caiaphas replied, "He is a Roman citizen prefect. We lack the authority to execute him." So there it was. The high priest just exacerbated a public mess that now lay at Pilate's feet. He retreated back into the Praetorium for consultation with Seneca. By the will of Jupiter, Pilate was determined to find a way out of this morass. If Pilate executed Yeshua as called for by the chief priests, he risked censure from Rome for execution of a Roman citizen and local of royal blood without prior authorization of the sentence by the emperor. If he left the man locked up in Jerusalem throughout Passover, local sentiment would likely flare up like a wildfire. The common people could rally behind a Hasmonean prince sitting in a Roman jail. Yeshua was just too hot of a political commodity to keep locked up.

Pilate bellowed, "Seneca!"

"Yes prefect."

"Get my head out of this vice. The gods damn me either way I rule—guilty or innocent. Find me a way out."

"I have given the matter thought and offer the following potential solution. The Modiin chief came to me just now and suggested we go through our tax records. I have done this and found that Yeshua, although born in Judea, appears to be a citizen of Galilee."

"Galilee? How does that help?"

"Prefect, Antipas rules Galilee. You rule Judea, Samaria and Idumea. Yeshua is a subject of Herod Antipas. Send him to Antipas for a ruling on the matter."

Pilate's face lit up with joy. He hugged his trusted advisor. "Pure genius! Guards, send the prisoner to Herod Antipas."

Yeshua Before Herod Antipas

> Now Herod was very glad when he saw Yeshua; for he had wanted to see him for a long time, because he had been hearing about him and was hoping to see some sign performed by Him. And he questioned him

> at some length; but he answered him nothing. *Luke* 23:8-9.

Phasaelus' interview with Herod Antipas had not gone according to plan. Chuza,[202] chief minister to the tetrarch and my mother's husband, lobbied against paying an extravagant bribe to Pilate for the execution of Yeshua. He said, "The Nabatean war left you very short of funds tetrarch. We just can't afford a bribe of thirty talents of silver,[203] not even close."

Herod Antipas turned to his Herodian kinsman, "You see Phasaelus, my minister says I lack the treasury to make the bribe you suggest. Why don't you go to the other Herodians and see what funding they are willing to contribute to this enterprise? How about the high priest? He is the one who refused to execute Yeshua in the Sanhedrin, which leaves this problem on our hands."

Every ruler pleads poverty when asked to pay a bribe to the Romans. Phasaelus knew Antipas had money stashed away as insurance against the day he was pushed into exile. Every ruler of a kingdom subject to Roman jurisdiction prays that day never comes but, realistically, knows the probabilities are high they will eventually be dethroned. Antipas knew this better than most as he was the last of Herod's sons with a crown still upon his head. As Phasaelus formulated his response, Roman soldiers entered the audience chamber of Herod Antipas bringing with them a bound prisoner, Yeshua the Nazarene. The sight sprouted a huge smile on the face of the tetrarch.

Antipas said, "My dear nephew Yeshua! Or should I say Mattathias? It has been many years since my eyes have been upon you." Antipas got up off his throne for a closer viewing of his nephew. He examined the wounds about his face delivered by the Sanhedrin guards.

Antipas, "You don't look well nephew. And these clothes are in tatters. You need a better tailor. Chuza, fetch one of my

---

202 Chuza is mentioned in Luke 8:3.

203 "And they gave 30 talents to Pilate that they should kill [Yeshua]." Josephus' Jewish War and Its Slavonic Version: A Synoptic Comparison by Flavius Josephus, edited by H. Leeming and K. Leeming (Brill 2003) at p. 261-262.

fine purple robes for my nephew, the king." Herodias and her women (including my mother) entered the audience chamber to view the spectacle.

Antipas said to them, "Wife, we have a visitor, your brother-in-law the Jewish king. My, how he resembles Agrippa. Where is Agrippa my dear?"

Herodias replied, "It's just past the second hour husband. Three of Hannibal's war elephants couldn't rouse Agrippa from his bed at this hour."

Antipas, "I pray he is sober for Passover." He then turned to Yeshua saying, "My wife and I have heard so much about the miracles your highness. We hope you will indulge us with a sign, just a small one like raising someone from the dead or curing of a leper."

All the women but Herodias and my mother laughed at Yeshua thinking it was all grand fun. My mother was in sympathy with Yeshua despite her position in the court of Antipas. She had helped raise Yeshua as a child. Herodias, for her part, agreed with Phasaelus that Yeshua posed a clear and present danger to their power. Word previously reached her that Yeshua converted her daughter Princess Salome to the Nazarene faith. The thought appalled Herodias. She said, "It's no laughing matter husband. Yeshua is Yochanan the Baptizer come back to life. He is a sorcerer and a danger to us all."

Seneca, chief minister to Pontius Pilate, pulled aside Chuza explaining that Pilate wished for Antipas to rule on the matter of Yeshua on the grounds that Yeshua was a citizen of Galilee. Chuza spoke to his master, "Tetrarch, the prefect desires for you to rule on the fate of the prisoner. The Roman records indicate this man is a citizen of Galilee and, as such, the prefect believes he is under your jurisdiction."

Phasaelus said to Antipas, "I recommend we caucus privately on this case before responding to the prefect." The tetrarch withdrew to a private chamber just off his main audience hall. Herod Antipas and Herodias followed him.

Once away from the others, Antipas said, "This solves my problem. I'll just execute Yeshua and I don't have to pay thirty talents to Pilate."

Herodias, "Husband, don't be foolish. If you execute a Herodian of Yeshua's bloodline without approval from the emperor you'll be exiled."

Phasaelus, "I must agree with my cousin."

Antipas' jolly mood turned grim. He sorely wished to execute his nephew and to do so without dipping into his reserve fund. The man stood bound in the other room subject to his orders. Antipas could order the prisoner moved to Perea for immediate execution. The tetrarch turned his back on Herodias and Phasaelus and gazed darkly out the window. His wife came to his side and stroked his brow.

She said, "Husband, money comes and money goes but while you sit on the throne there is always a source of fresh coin at your fingertips. Why don't you pay Pontius Pilate his bribe, my dear. Then when we return to Galilee you can seize the estates of my brother Lazarus and sister Mariam which are within your jurisdiction. I'm told Mariam owns a very fine villa at Cana. They are conspirators with this villain Yeshua. A Roman conviction gives you grounds to seize the property of his co-conspirators and thereby recover your lost silver." It excited Antipas when his wife spoke of evil deeds. She excelled in this department.

Phasaelus said, "Joseph of Arimathea is also an ally of Yeshua."

Herodias drew her body close to her husband gently kissing the old man's leathery, wrinkled neck. She said, "Think of it husband, all the possessions of Joseph of Arimathea in Galilee. They will all be yours. Think of the wealth."

A smile returned to the corpulent face of Antipas. The idea of seizing the vast wealth of Joseph of Arimathea gave Antipas a primal erection, which he intended to implant in every orifice of Herodias at the first available instant.

Yeshua Again Before Pilate

> While Pilate was sitting in the judgment hall, his wife sent him a message: "Have nothing to do with that innocent man, because in a dream last night, I suffered much on account of him." *Matthew* 27:19.

Seneca returned from Herod Antipas to the Praetorium with the prisoner Yeshua, who he left in an anteroom adjacent to Pilate's private chambers. Seneca appeared before Pontius Pilate to make his report. Pilate said, "Ah Seneca, what word do you bring from Antipas? Is Yeshua on the road to Perea as we speak?"

Seneca replied, "I'm afraid not prefect. Yeshua is here in the Praetorium awaiting trial before you."

The veins in Pilate's neck began to bulge as his emotions rose with anger directed toward Herod Antipas. The prefect slammed his fist down on the table and said, "If that is the way Antipas feels about it, then release the prisoner. I find him innocent."

Pilate waived his hand indicating Seneca was dismissed. The prefect returned his attention to his correspondence but his minister remained in the room. Seneca motioned to a slave standing in the back to come forward with a box he carried. The slave set the box before Pilate who opened it. Inside sat one silver talent that weighed nearly 60 pounds.

Seneca said, "Antipas promises to deliver a total of thirty silver talents if you execute Yeshua."

One talent was equivalent to 6000 silver denarii. Each denarius was considered fair pay for one full day of labor. Thus, 30 talents was equivalent to wages for 180,000 man days of labor. Money affects every man and Pilate more so. The prefect greedily rubbed the massive silver bar in his hands. Thirty talents were more money than Pilate had ever possessed at one time. This sum, when added to the hoard accumulated by Pilate via bribes over the last ten years, would provide him with a comfortable retirement back in Rome. He said to his aide, "That's a fortune Seneca! Did Antipas truly promise it?"

"Yes prefect."

"I could return to Rome in style with that silver." Whereas earlier in the day Pilate looked for someone, anyone to remove the Yeshua problem from his courtroom, now Pilate was ready to sentence the self-proclaimed Jewish king to death. Money talks.

Seneca was not enthused by the idea. He cautioned his superior, "What if this man really is Herod's grandson?"

The Roman discipline of rhetoric was in truth the art of obfuscation and every Roman above a certain political rank excelled at obfuscation. Pilate possessed the necessary rank to have mastered the art. He paced his chambers raking his brain for a way to distance himself from the potentially dangerous fallout from Yeshua's coming execution. The leading rabbis and priests were also masters at manipulating the law. Perhaps they saw a path around the predicament. Pilate said, "Come Seneca, we shall go see what the Jews have to say about this issue."

Pilate returned to the forum outside the Praetorium to meet with the Jewish leaders who still refused to enter the Roman building. He again stood on the portico and addressed the high priest, Caiaphas. "Your Excellency, I endeavor to accommodate your request that Yeshua the Nazarene be executed on the charge of insurrection against Rome; however, an odd rumor is whispered in the alleyways of Jerusalem that the Nazarene is a grandson of Herod. What say you in response?"

Caiaphas said, "Prefect, our response shall come from Prince Phasaelus who has looked into this matter." This was just the person Pilate wished to hear from.

Phasaelus stepped forward from the crowd and said, "Prefect, I believe two issues are at work here. What evidence have we of the prisoner's status as a Roman citizen?"

Pilate looked over his shoulder at his minister Seneca who shook his head indicating he had no idea. The prefect said, "Apparently, he bears a resemblance to a Herodian noble."

Phasaelus, "Let us examine the evidence prefect. Rumor is not evidence. Our chief of Modiin, in the company of your treasury officials, has searched the local Roman census records going back generations. There is no Antigonus ben Antipater,

Mattathias ben Antipater, Yeshua ben Antipater or Yeshua ben Joseph listed as a Roman citizen in Palestine. And if we reflect on this a moment it makes sense. We are not even 100 percent certain of the parentage of Yeshua but let us assume, for the sake of argument, that his father was Prince Antipater ben Herod. Yeshua was born after Antipater died a condemned criminal. Is it not the practice in such cases that children of condemned criminals in the provinces are stripped of their Roman citizenship? Further, the individual who we assumed these many years was his father, Priest Joseph the Nazarene, was never a Roman citizen but a citizen of Galilee. There is no evidence of Roman citizenship in this case. The prisoner is a citizen of Galilee according to Roman law, period." Pilate smiled and moved his head in agreement.

Phasaelus continued, "For all we know prefect, the prisoner was born of fornication. His alleged father was locked up in prison at the time of the Yeshua's conception. His mother was also a prisoner. No one really knows the identity of his father. How do we know the Herodian palace guards at Jericho did not have their way with his mother?"

That last comment brought laughter to the crowd. Grandson of two Jewish kings though he may have been, Phasaelus argued that the official Roman records for Judea and Galilee contained no record of Yeshua holding Roman citizenship. Without Roman citizenship, he could not be considered a "friend of Rome" even if he was of royal birth. Roman officials often executed local royalty who opposed them. These were treated as enemies of Rome and could be executed when apprehended.

Pilate instructed, "Seneca, go to the treasury and personally confirm the contention of Prince Phasaelus." He then returned his attention to the up and coming Herodian prince saying, "Cicero himself couldn't have said it better. No doubt there is quite an impressive career ahead of you Prince Phasaelus."

Little did Pilate know the prophetic quality of his words. The prefect returned to the Praetorium awaiting confirmation from Seneca that the treasury archives contained no record of Yeshua possessing Roman citizenship, the last obstacle between Pilate and thirty silver talents. No sooner had his buttocks landed on the judgment seat in the Praetorium than a servant brought him a note from his wife. It read, "Have nothing to do with that innocent man because, in a dream last night, I suffered much on account of him."[204] Great Jupiter! The message threw Pilate into mental panic. Julius Caesar himself died after ignoring a warning received by his wife in a dream. Pilate's wife, Claudia Proculla, came from an old Roman family of the equestrian class and was not given to emotional outbursts or flights of fancy. He took note of her counsel. Pilate heard the rumor that the Egyptian practiced black magic and this note from his wife just confirmed it. The Jews were right, Yeshua was dangerous! A large din coming from the forum outside the Praetorium interrupted the prefect's thoughts.

Seneca returned from the treasury to report his findings to Pilate. He said, "Prefect, your treasurer confirms the words of Prince Phasaelus. Yeshua is not enrolled as a Roman citizen."

Pilate, "Very good Seneca but what is all that damn noise coming from the forum? Are they Yeshua's people calling for his release?"

"No prefect, those are Idumean nationalists calling for the release of their Hasmonean prince, bar Babas, who they claim to be the rightful king of Idumea."

Pilate shook his head with disgust and said, "There is a Hasmonean king under every rock in Palestine." Pilate sat in his judgment seat reflecting for a moment. The germ of an idea was forming, one that could absolve him from blame for the execution of Yeshua while still allowing him to collect the fortune in silver Antipas offered.

Pilate said, "Tell me Seneca, you say the core supporters of this bar Babas are Idumean but how are the rest of the Jews disposed to him?"

Seneca, "I don't claim to be an expert on what the Jewish mob thinks prefect. Perhaps Prince Phasaelus could be of assistance?"

Pilate again went to the portico outside the Praetorium overlooking the forum where the Jewish public gathered awaiting

---

204 *Matt.* 27:19.

news on Yeshua and the other condemned men held in the Roman prison. Pilate said to the Herodian prince, "You must come to me here on the portico. If your precious religious rules do not permit you to step foot on the portico to converse with me then to hell with the case against Yeshua. I'll release him."

Reluctantly Phasaelus came to meet with Pilate just outside the Praetorium. Phasaelus could give a donkey's turd for Jewish religious laws such as the prohibition against graven images but he very much cared what impression he conveyed to the other members of the Sanhedrin. It wasn't meeting with Pilate at the Praetorium that was the problem. It was doing so in full view of his collogues.

The prefect asked, "How popular is bar Babas with the Judeans?"

Phasaelus said, "Bar Babas is one of the very few Hasmoneans alive not a blood relation of Herod. Although Yeshua possesses higher royal blood, bar Babas lacks what the common people view as the taint of Herod. Bar Babas' popularity went to the heavens after being convicted of killing a Roman soldier. He is hugely popular with the average Jew on the street at this moment."

Pilate, "Is he more popular than Yeshua?"

Phasaelus replied, "Today, yes. Tomorrow, who can say? The people's sentiments change with the wind."

Pontius Pilate motioned for Phasaelus and Seneca to draw close so they could speak privately. He said, "I want to wash my hands of the Egyptian while still performing a service to the Sanhedrin and to Herod Antipas. A subordinate reminded me that we have a tradition of freeing one Jewish prisoner on the eve of Passover. We generally let the Jewish people decide who is to be released."

Phasaelus smiled as he saw the evil genius behind the plan. Pilate would let the crowd condemn Yeshua to death! Pilate continued, "The two candidates for release will be bar Babas and Yeshua. The Jews shall decide--one goes free, the other is crucified. When my report goes to Rome, no one can be heard to say that I condemned Yeshua. It was the Jews themselves who made the final decision. Phasaelus, go stuff the crowd with your people ensuring it is bar Babas who goes free. You have little time to prepare, go now."

Pontius Pilate ordered bar Babas brought up from his cell in the dungeon. As Pilate gave a speech to the Jewish people assembled in the forum, the prisoners bar Babas and Yeshua briefly stood next to one another waiting presentation to the crowd.

Bar Babas asked, "King Yeshua, what is happening?"

Yeshua, "One of us is to be freed by the Romans. Pilate shall let the people decide."

"My ancestors served your ancestors in defense of Jerusalem against the Romans many years ago. It is you who must go free. You are the king."

"The Judeans have rejected me as their king. It is I who must die so others may live. As it was before, so it is now. My grandfather the king was executed by the Romans yet your grandfather escaped. Go in freedom brother."

Pilate gestured to the guards for the two prisoners to be brought out before the people. Pilate addressed the crowd, "Now I ask the Jewish people to decide who it is they wish for me to release to them on the eve of their momentous religious holiday of Passover. Shall it be Yeshua, king of the Jews?"

After his arrest, the majority of Yeshua's followers were either hiding behind barricades atop the Mount of Olives or back in Bethany fearing arrest. Still, many hundreds of common people who had seen Yeshua's miracles in Galilee and Judea were on hand in the forum. Each called for Yeshua with a loud voice but most of the crowd remained silent when asked to cheer for Yeshua.

Then Pilate asked, "Or shall it be bar Babas?" The followers of bar Babas from Idumea and the Judean zealots who now hated Yeshua for his Herodian heritage went crazy with their cries for the release of bar Babas. Added to these were the voices of the Pharisees and their allied supporters rounded up by Phasaelus and Costobarus in the short time afforded before Pilate's little show. Together, the acclaim for bar Babas unmistakably rose well above that for Yeshua.

Finally, Pilate asked the crowd, "What shall I do then with Yeshua the Nazarene?" Phasaelus and Costobarus pushed their supporters to the front of the crowd in the forum so their voices could be heard. They shouted with all their might, "Crucify him!"

Pilate turned to his aide, "Seneca, make certain the official record of this day reflects the Jewish crowd called for the release of bar Babas and for the crucifixion of Yeshua the Nazarene, their king. Bring me water and a towel." In a theatrical flourish, Pilate washed his hands in front of the still screaming mob. He turned to them while toweling off and said, "I wash my hands of this man's fate. His blood shall be on your heads."[205]

Pilate then gave the order for bar Babas to be released. Upon being unbound, bar Babas knelt before Yeshua and said, "I pray to meet you in God's kingdom."

Yeshua replied, "Rise my friend. The kingdom lies within. Become acquainted with it and you shall be saved."

Pilate commanded, "Centurion, prepare this man for crucifixion. Be quick about it now." Herod Antipas approached Pilate on the portico near the forum as the soldiers took Yeshua into the Praetorium to be scourged. The two had not spoken since Herod Antipas lost a Roman army in the border war with the Nabateans.

Antipas said, "Hail Pontius Pilate." The two embraced like long, lost brothers with huge elephant sized grins on their faces. Neither knew it then but both men were destined to leave office in the near future. Before the next Passover, Pontius Pilate was removed from office by the Roman governor of Syria and ordered to return to Rome. Before he arrived in Rome, Tiberius Caesar died. Gaius, better known as Caligula, succeeded his grandfather and promptly appointed his friend Agrippa to Philip's old tetrarchy. Two years later, Agrippa accused Antipas of planned insurrection against Rome for which Antipas was sent into exile. Herod Agrippa thereafter became king of the Jews.

This part of the story is difficult for me to describe for crucifixion is the most extreme and pitiful of deaths. The Romans

---

205 *Matt.* 27:24-26.

delivered a savage beating to the condemned before allowing him the privilege of dying on the cross. They stripped the prisoner then tied him to a post whereupon they whipped his body with a device called a flagellum, which consisted of several braided leather thongs knotted at the end with iron balls. The flagellum ripped the flesh completely off the body of the condemned leaving his body a bloody pulp. I was there in the forum outside the Praetorium, a useless spectator to my master's wrongful conviction. As they led Yeshua away to be scourged, I spied Joseph of Arimathea with the other members of the Sanhedrin. He was the only ally of Yeshua I saw in the forum that day. I ran to him and said, "Prince Joseph, I have come with Lazarus."

Joseph, "Where is he?"

I replied, "Waiting in your tomb outside the city walls. Lazarus could not enter the city as he is too well known."

"And Judas?"

"He is dead prince. What shall we do?"

"Come, the three of us shall deliberate together."

Joseph led me back outside the city to the tomb where we found Lazarus. He set out linens, oils and spices as if it were a medical operating theatre. Joseph said, "Menelaus told me that Judas is dead. He had some sort of plan for saving Yeshua but the details are a mystery to me."

Lazarus replied, "I believe I know his intention. During the initiation ceremony into the Nazarene mysteries, the aspirant experiences a ritual death. To assist in this process, various herbs are used to bring about a simulated death. I have the necessary herbs and potions here with me. I know the formula."

Joseph, "That's all well and good but how do we get the potion to Yeshua's mouth?"

Lazarus, "Bribing a Roman guard is the only idea that came to me but I'm too well known to get that close to Yeshua. You're a member of the Sanhedrin and will draw too much attention." Both men stopped talking and looked at me.

I said, "Just tell me what to do."

The Crucifixion of Yeshua

> And they brought him to Golgotha, which means Place of The Skull. And they gave him wine mingled with myrrh to drink but he would not receive it. Then the Romans crucified him and parted his garments casting lots upon them what every man should take. *Mark* 15:22-24.

I arrived at Golgotha outside the city walls finding three men hanging from crosses, each badly bloodied by their scourging such that I couldn't tell which one was Yeshua by sight. The arms and feet of the condemned were lashed to their crosses with ropes. Also, nails pierced through their hands.[206] The nails were relatively small. Their sole purpose appeared to be increased pain rather than to support the weight of the condemned on the cross. Above the head of Yeshua the Romans placed a sign reading, "Yeshua Nazarene King Jews."[207] Off in the distance sat Princess Mariam Magdalene, Yeshua's mother, his sister (Clopas' wife), and Salome (daughter of Herodias). All of the leading disciples of Yeshua were in hiding from the authorities leaving the women to grieve alone at the cross. I hoped to see my mother there comforting Princess Mariamne, her dearest friend in life, yet Lady Yohanna was absent at the cross. However, someone I did not expect see was in attendance. Our eyes met and I walked to a place away from the crowd hoping she would follow.

Batsheba said, "I am so sorry for the rabbi and his family. Is there any assistance I can offer to his relatives? To cook or clean, anything."

I replied, "I might need your help. We are going to try to save the rabbi."

She grabbed my arm and pulled me close to her saying, "How can I help? What is the plan?"

---

206 *See John* 20:25-27 referencing nail marks in the hands but not feet of Yeshua.

207 *John* 19:19.

That was the problem. There was no plan. The soldiers stood between me and Yeshua and I really didn't have any idea how I would get past them to deliver the potion. I said, "I need you to distract the soldiers. Can you do that?"

She smiled, "Of course. It will be like taking sweets from a child."

At least one of us had confidence. I told Batsheba to wait for my signal. A battered, nearly unrecognizable Yeshua hung upon a Roman cross clinging to life yet I had to wait. Each minute watching him in agony killed me but sufficient time needed to elapse for the Romans to plausibly believe Yeshua had died once I slipped him the potion. God forbid, he died on the cross before I gave him the herbs but the ruse had to be believable. At the appointed hour, I looked back toward the city gate waiving to a servant of Joseph of Arimathea who had been positioned there to receive the signal. The servant ran to his master who would then approach Pilate for the body of Yeshua.

I held the potion in a vial hidden under my tunic. Most of the morbid gawkers already lost interest in the trio of bodies on their crosses allowing me to elbow my way to the front. The Roman soldiers joked amongst themselves pointing out attractive women in the crowd. I'm convinced that had one of these grizzled legionnaires been up there nailed to the cross himself, his eyes would still have scanned the crowd for a pretty female with thoughts of fornication. A soldier's brain rides in his scrotum. I must have been a Roman legionnaire in a previous life.

I gave Batsheba a sign to make her move and waited for her to get into position. Up close, Yeshua looked even worse. He could barely lift his head to breath. Ever so subtly, I moved over to the spot where his eyes pointed to the ground. He gave me the barest hint of recognition whereupon I briefly removed the potion out of my tunic to show Yeshua what I was up to. I spied a bowl of common wine sitting next to the soldiers. I slipped the potion given to me by Lazarus into the wine bowl just as Batsheba made her entrance. The soldiers' eyes transfixed upon her allowing me easy access to the wine bowl. Yeshua observed my actions from the cross. He then called out from the cross for drink. I went for the bowl of wine but was pushed back by one of the legionnaires. He said, "You there, back off!"

I pulled a single silver denarius out of my pouch discretely passing it to the legionnaire saying, "He's my cousin. Just a quick drink of wine to ease his pain."

Batsheba skillfully kept the other legionnaires occupied in conversation allowing me to negotiate with just one soldier. He motioned with his hand demanding more money. I slipped him a second denarius.

The soldier said, "One more and I'll get your king there a drink."

This was the critical part of the operation. I didn't want to let the soldier know how desperate I was for Yeshua to drink the wine spiked with herbs so I played along with the haggling ritual. It was crucial to avoid the appearance of being too eager to make a deal without suspicion being raised. I said, "Give him the drink and I'll pay you when his thirst has been quenched."

The soldier ran a sponge through with his spear, poured wine over the sponge, and then stuck it in front of Yeshua's mouth. Yeshua suckled on the sponge as best he could. I had no idea whether Yeshua ingested enough of the potion to be effective but it was all I could do under the circumstances. I paid the soldier his final denarius for completing our deal but the commander of the unit caught sight of the transaction. He said to the soldier I had bribed, "Hey, what in blazes is going on here?"

"Nothing decurion."

"Don't be an asshole every minute of your life Marcus. I saw you take a bribe from this man. You know the rules, we all share."

The decurion turned to me, "Jew, how much did you pay him?"

Even thieves have rules. With no personal interest in protecting the soldier, I ratted him out to the decurion and made sure to knock over the bowl of spiked wine so the soldiers would not discover the drug it contained. The decurion extorted another denarius from me for spilling the wine then berated the soldier for trying to keep a bribe for himself, allowing me to slip away. Batsheba likewise disappeared into the crowd.

I intended to stop only briefly to comfort Princesses Mariamne and Mariam but Yeshua caught sight of me next to his mother. He gathered his little remaining strength to lift himself up on the cross and said to me, "Behold your mother!" Then he turned to his mother and said, "Behold your son." I suppose Yeshua feared that all of his brothers would be arrested by the Romans and, further, that my mother Yohanna's connection to the household of Herod Antipas gave me greater protection from the Romans. I bowed my head to Yeshua to signify that I accepted the assignment. With that Yeshua let out a cry and uttered these words, "Father, into your hands I commend my spirit."[208] Thereafter he went limp on the cross.

The decurion who was in charge of the execution party said, "What the hell, the king could not have died already. It's only been a few hours." The situation didn't look good as the Roman soldiers now grew suspicious. The decurion grabbed a lance and thrust it into the side of Yeshua, who received the blow without uttering a sound or twitching a muscle. Blood and water flowed from the open wound left by the lance.

The decurion said, "I'll be damned. The Jew king is frigging dead. Lucky buggar kissed off quickly."

I learned very little of the medical arts despite my close association with Yeshua those many years; however, I did remember one fragment of medical knowledge imparted to me by the master. He said the body stops bleeding when the heart stops. Thus, the wounds of a dead person will not bleed. I peered intently at the wound in the side of Yeshua. Blood continued to drip out ever so slightly. I knew he was still alive but for how long?

Unable to help Yeshua further, I begged the women to move with me further back into the crowd. Princesses Mariam and Mariamne refused. They would stand by Yeshua's side until his body came down from the cross. I spied two hulking, young

---

[208] *Luke* 24:46.

brothers from Galilee among the crowd that I knew and begged them to stand by the princesses until Yeshua was removed from the cross. I intended to honor my pledge to Yeshua to look after his mother but my first priority was to see if Yeshua's life could be saved despite the slimmest of possibilities. I raced to Joseph of Arimathea.

* * * * * * * * *

Pontius Pilate needed a printed roster in hand to keep track of all the descendants and relations of Herod parading into his office on a daily basis demanding an audience. Joseph of Arimathea did not reign over a territory but made up for it by being fabulously wealthy. He was the most successful businessman of the Herodian clan. Pilate got along with Prince Joseph. His requests were reasonable, promised bribes were always delivered, and he possessed an even temperament (something unusual among the Herodians). If the god Yahweh had fashioned all the Jews in the mold of Joseph, administration of this god-forsaken land would not be so burdensome in Pilate's opinion. He said to Joseph, "Dead already? Your king didn't perform well on the cross."

Joseph replied, "As a senior male member of his family I ask for release of his body for burial. Our law requires that he be off the cross before sundown this evening. We are cousins and our children are married to one another. I ask this as a personal favor in recognition of past generosities prefect."

"How presumptuous," thought Pilate. You come before me asking for favors and demand they be granted for free? The empire doesn't work that way and you should know better!"

But Joseph wasn't being cheap. His words were a calculated move. If he barged into Pilate's audience chamber immediately offering a huge bribe to get the body of Yeshua down off the cross, the prefect would smell something out of place. Having served in Palestine for a decade, Pilate knew Jews always haggled.

Pilate, "My dear Prince Joseph, I can't start giving away official favors or every Jew in the territory will show up at my door requesting the same. I'm sure you see the gray hairs on my head. It's time to plan for retirement. Let us help each other Joseph."

Prince Joseph, "Perhaps we can call this a donation to your retirement fund then prefect. Would thirty denarii help to fatten your retirement?"

They settled on fifty denarii, a hefty price for the simple right to bury a family member. A strange feeling gnawed at the pit of Pilate's stomach as he congratulated himself on extracting bribes from the Jews for putting Yeshua on the cross and then to take him off the cross. The priests would demand Yeshua's body come down from the cross immediately due to the Sabbath. Normally the soldiers then tossed the bodies on the side of the road leading to the main gate of the city where family members retrieved them. Joseph paid fifty denarii merely to retrieve the body more expeditiously? Joseph was a wealthy man but the prefect's gut was twittering with the feeling that the prince had just played him. As Joseph strode across the audience chamber making for the exit, Pilate called to his minister in a loud voice. Pilate said, "Seneca, go personally to Golgotha and order the centurion to run the body of Yeshua through the heart with his gladius before releasing it to Prince Joseph. We wish to be sure the sentence is complete."

Joseph stopped in his tracks. This told the prefect all he needed to know. Yeshua still lived. The prince returned to the prefect. Pilate said, "Seneca, hold on one moment. It appears Prince Joseph has further words for me."

Joseph of Arimathea returned to Pilate, who said, "Prince Joseph, fifty denarii was it for the body?"

"Prefect, the family wishes no further damage to the body. Please, no public desecration."

"Desecration? Come my good man. The prisoner surely received upwards of forty lashes with the flagellum. His body is a bloody pulp of torn flesh yet you concern yourself with a small entry wound from a gladius?"

At first, Joseph was at a loss on how to attack the problem. Pilate now knew Yeshua still lived. A simple bribe wouldn't work.

He needed leverage against the Roman. He said, "It's in your best interest prefect to allow me to retrieve the body of Yeshua and do it quickly."

Pilate was surprised by the aggressive tone coming from the normally deferential Joseph. He said, "Oh, so you have lied to me about Yeshua but for my own good? How thoughtful on your part."

Joseph, "As things now stand, the Hasmonean supporters of Yeshua shall all petition Rome for your removal. These include Prince Lazarus, Princess Mariam, Princess Salome and myself. Salome grew up in Rome and is personal friends with the niece of the emperor. We shall all sail for Rome at the conclusion of Passover unless we get the body of Yeshua now and unharmed."

"Then he still lives?"

"I don't know. He might live; he might not. If we get him off the cross now there is a chance."

"Our agreement was for a dead body, Joseph. What you now seek is only half-dead."

"Then I offer double the price plus my personal assurance that no family member of mine shall petition Rome for your removal."

"A half-dead king is worth substantially more than a fully dead one. Two-hundred denarii plus more conditions."

"More conditions?"

"You surely know I took a huge bribe from Antipas to execute Yeshua. If Antipas finds out the man lives, he'll demand a refund and denounce me in Rome. Yeshua must disappear from the Roman Empire."

Joseph said, "If he lives through this, I further guaranty Yeshua leaves the Roman Empire for the east as soon as he is fit for travel."

Pilate slapped his hand on the table and exclaimed, "Done!"

Just as the sun set in the western sky, two servants of Joseph of Arimathea pulled a handcart carrying the body of Yeshua past the city walls. Nicodemus walked behind the cart ready to offer assistance. He was a Pharisee member of the

Sanhedrin and a secret follower of Yeshua; therefore, it surprised me to see him helping with the burial of Yeshua. I wasn't sure how much he knew of the plan to save Yeshua though. He brought with him a mixture of myrrh and aloes, which weighed nearly one-hundred pounds. I overtook the party as they slowly made their way toward the tomb where Lazarus waited. Nicodemus said, "Menelaus, thank Yahweh you are here."

I replied, "What's all the stuff in this sack?"

"Medicines for Lazarus to use in closing Yeshua's wounds. That is, if he still lives." So Lazarus had included Nicodemus into the inner circle of those with knowledge of our attempt to save Yeshua. If Lazarus trusted Nicodemus then I decided to do so as well.

I said, "The one physician gifted enough to bring forth a cure is himself the patient lying on the cart. We are in a desperate situation brother." Our party came to a halt in front of Joseph's tomb. Nicodemus and I carried Yeshua inside laying him on a stone slab cut into the wall. Joseph of Arimathea arrived just as Lazarus put his hand to Yeshua's heart.

I asked, "Is he alive?"

Lazarus said, "I don't know. There is no discernible heartbeat. How much of the potion did you give him?"

I replied, "I am unable to give an accurate estimate. I dumped the entire vial into a bowl of wine. A soldier dunked a sponge into the wine bowl, which Yeshua sucked on. It was the best I could do under the circumstances."

Lazarus was alarmed. He said, "The entire vial? You were supposed to just give him a few drops! I pray you haven't killed him."

I protested but only briefly. All attention returned to nursing Yeshua with the hope he still lived. I got my first good look at the injuries after laying him out in the tomb. The sight horrified me. His back resembled the hide of a flayed animal at the butcher shop. One saw lumps of exposed flesh everywhere. The deep gash in his side from the spear thrust lay open. Lazarus and Nicodemus worked feverishly to close the wounds with ointments, herbs and bandages. I then caught sight of Yeshua's hands. The nails had been driven clean through the knuckles in between the phalange bones of his hands without piercing any bone.[209] As the others were busy attending to more serious wounds, I pulled the small nails out of Yeshua's hands. Rope burns marked his arms and feet. His face was battered beyond recognition. It was difficult to fathom how anyone could survive such injuries. After dressing the open wounds, we completely washed the body with a mixture of water and natron, an astringent. Next, aloe and honey were applied liberally into Yeshua's wounds. Lastly myrrh was applied then we wrapped the body in fresh linen. Just as we finished up, Roman soldiers appeared outside the tomb. They ordered us out, rolled a stone across the entranceway, and then took up guard positions at the entrance. The sun disappeared over the western horizon marking the official beginning of the Sabbath. Our first opportunity to check on Yeshua would be Sunday morning, meaning Yeshua would be alone in the tomb for two nights. These were the longest days of my life.

---

[209] Only one set of bones have been found in Jerusalem from the Roman period with nails through the hands, those at the so-called Abba Tomb. I contend these remains are that of King Mattathias Antigonus, the grandfather of Yeshua.

Chapter 21

Alexandria, Egypt (67 CE)

Theudas, "Why have you stopped grandfather? So Yeshua lay in the tomb. Was he alive or dead? You can't stop the story here!"

"It is getting late for an old man and, besides, you have friends to meet."

"But I leave the country tomorrow for a trip with my father. It will be over a month before I return. What about my great-grandfather Theudas? You said he was part of the story of Yeshua yet not a word about my ancestor."

"The story of your ancestor Theudas comes after the crucifixion. We'll save it for next time. There is still much to tell."

"Just a few quick words before I go grandfather, does Yeshua come out of the tomb alive?"

"I know my grandson shall visit me promptly when fate brings him home again if I save the ending of the story for later. May the gods grant you fare weather on your journey and a safe return. Please give my regards to your father and mother."

"Yes grandfather."

The two embraced and smiled for they shared one of the greatest stories ever told that evening. It warmed the old man's heart knowing his memories now lived on in his grandson. Menelaus escorted his grandson to the door then slipped into bed next to Rhodopis, who was already asleep. He knew his friend Yeshua would again visit him after he drifted off to the dream world. The day approached when he would leave the material world to join Yeshua in their true home, the realm of eternal life.

Chronology

This chronology contains dates for events accepted by scholars and those backed by my own theories.

47 BCE	Herod bar Antipater marries Doris, Idumean princess.
46 BCE	Antipater born to Herod and Doris.
41 BCE	Herod divorces and exiles Doris (along with her son Antipater); betroths Mariamne bat Alexander, Hasmonean princess.
40 BCE	Herod crowned king of the Jews by the Roman senate.
37 BCE	Herod marries Hasmonean princess Mariamne; Jerusalem captured by Herod and Romans; King Antigonus, the last Hasmonean king, executed by Marc Antony at urging of Herod.
36 BCE	Herod appoints his brother-in-law Aristobulus ben Alexander high priest; Herod assassinates Aristobulus (drowned in the palace swimming pool at Jericho).
35 BCE	Marc Antony acquits Herod of the murder of Aristobulus (trial held in Antioch). Herod executes his uncle Joseph, who he left in control of the Jewish kingdom, upon return to Judea.
35-31 BCE	Herod captures Fortress Hyrcania and executes the members of Antigonus' family besieged there.
31 BCE	Octavian defeats Marc Antony and Cleopatra at Actium.
30 BCE	Herod executes Hyrcanus II, the former high priest and grandfather of his wife Mariamne.
29 BCE	Herod executes Queen Mariamne bat Alexander; Herod recalls and remarries Doris; restores position

	of his son Antipater.
28 BCE	Herod executes Alexandra, mother of his wife Mariamne and daughter of Hyrcanus II; Herod also executes his brother-in-law, Costobarus, for harboring the Hasmonean sons of Babas.
9 BCE	Herod prosecutes border war with Nabatea; Caesar demotes Herod from "Caesar's Friend" to "Subject King" as punishment for unauthorized Nabatean war; Obadas dies and Aretas IV becomes king of Nabatea.
7 BCE	Herod executes Aristobulus and Alexander, his Hasmonean sons by Mariamne; Herod elevates Antipater to coregent and prime heir; Antipater marries Mariamne bat Aristobulus, the young daughter of his dead Hasmonean brother.
6 BCE	Antipater secretly marries Mariamne bat Antigonus, daughter of the last Hasmonean king.
5 BCE	Antipater sails for Rome as word of his secret marriage to Mariamne bat Antigonus leaks out to his Herodian enemies.
4 BCE (spring)	Pheroras poisoned; Antipater returns to Judea from Rome and is arrest the moment he lands in Caesarea; Antipater tried in Jerusalem before Quinctilius Varus for conspiracy to murder Herod; Varus finds Antipater guilt and sends his verdict to Augustus Caesar for confirmation.
4 BCE (winter)	Antipater conceives a son by Mariamne bat Antigonus while imprisoned; Augustus Caesar confirms Antipater's death sentence but suggests Herod exile Antipater rather than execute him; Herod defies Caesar by executing Antipater, then dies himself five days later; Herod's last will names Archelaus his successor as Jewish king; Herod buried in elaborate ceremony at Herodium.
3 BCE	Archelaus marries his niece Mariamne bat Aristobulus (Mary Magdalene); Archelaus turns his soldiers loose on the crowd in Jerusalem at first Passover after death of Herod, then departs for Rome along together with

	Antipas leaving Herod Philip in charge of kingdom; Varus believes he has suppressed the Jewish revolt touched off by Archelaus and returns to Antioch; Mattathias Antigonus ben Antipater (aka Yeshua Christ) born to Mariamne bat Antigonus at Bethlehem (near Herodium) in late summer; Actions of procurator Sabinus revive Jewish revolt against Rome.
3-1 BCE	Major Jewish revolt rages in the Jewish kingdom eventually suppressed by Roman governor of Syria, Publius Quinctilius Varus; Caesar probates Herod's will naming Archelaus Ethnarch (not king), Antipas and Philip are named tetrarchs.
6 CE	Archelaus divorces Mariamne bat Aristobulus to marry Glaphyra of Cappadocia; Archelaus deposed by Romans and sent into exile in Gaul; Judea, Samaria and Idumea become prefects of Roman province of Syria; Annas ben Seth named high priest by the Romans.
11 CE	Phasaelus ben Timius (aka Paul of Tarsus) born.
26 CE	Pontius Pilate appointed prefect of Judea.
29 CE	Rabbi Yochanan (John the Baptist) begins his public ministry.
31 CE	Sejanus, chief minister to Emperor Tiberius, executed.
32 CE	Emperor Tiberius issues decree throughout the Roman Empire not to mistreat the Jews.
34 CE	Herodias divorces Herod Philip and marries Herod Antipas. In order to marry Herodias, Herod Antipas divorces Phasaelus, daughter of Nabatean king Aretas IV. Rabbi Yochanan condemns marriage of Antipas to Herodias on religious grounds. Yeshua begins his public ministry—wedding at Cana. Rabbi Yochanan arrested by Herod Antipas. Rabbi Yochanan executed by Herod Antipas.
35 CE	King Aretas declares war on Antipas; Aretas attacks and defeats the forces of Herod Antipas in battle.
36 CE	Proconsul and president of Syria, Lucius Vitellius,

	takes several legions into Parthia deposing the Parthian king; Yeshua declared king in Jerusalem just prior to Passover; Yeshua crucified in Jerusalem by Pontius Pilate.
37 CE	Pontius Pilate removed as prefect of Rome by Proconsul Vitellius; Emperor Tiberius dies; Claudius becomes Roman emperor.
38 CE	Stephen stoned to death in Jerusalem by order of the Sanhedrin.
39 CE	Herod Antipas removed by Caligula. Herod Agrippa becomes king of the Jewish kingdom.
41 CE	Caligula assassinated. Herod Agrippa assists Claudius in securing Roman throne. Paul's first trip to Rome to meet Peter and James; begins first missionary journey.
43 CE	Herod Agrippa executes James ben Zebedee.[210]
44 CE	Paul's second trip to Jerusalem. Herod Agrippa dies.
46 CE	Famine starts in Judea.
49-50 CE	Paul goes to Corinth finding Aquila and Priscilla after their expulsion from Rome by Claudius.
51 CE (summer)	Paul hauled before Roman tribunal of proconsul Lucius Junius Gallio Annaeus (brother of Seneca) in Corinth. Paul leaves Greece for Judea.[211]
52 CE	Council of Jerusalem.
54 CE	Arrest of Paul in Jerusalem by Felix; Claudius dies and Nero becomes Roman emperor.
56 CE	Festus succeeds Felix as prefect of Judea and deports Paul to Rome.[212]

[210] *Acts* 12:1. I assume this event occurred in the last year of Herod Agrippa's reign as it is related in the text just prior to the death of Agrippa.

[211] *Acts* says Paul sailed for "Syria" but I believe they use the word to indicate the Roman province of Syria (which included Judea), not the modern-day country of Syria. *Acts* 18:18.

[212] We date this event from a change in Roman prefects in Judea. *Acts* tells us Paul was first tried before the Roman prefect Felix and, then, new charges were brought when Porcius Festus succeed Felix in office. See *Acts*, Ch. 25. We

57 CE	Paul arrives in Rome after ship wreck in Malta.
59 CE	Paul's two-year Roman house arrest ends.
63 CE	James the Just executed by Sanhedrin.
64 CE	Great fire of Rome blame for which Nero put on the Christians as scapegoats.
65 CE	Nero orders Seneca to commit suicide.
66 CE	Great Jewish revolt against Rome begins.
68 CE	Nero dies, succession unsettled.
69 CE	Four successive emperors reign in Rome until the tumult is ended by the ascension of Vespasian.
70 CE	Romans capture Jerusalem and level the Temple.

know from external sources that Festus succeeded Felix as prefect of Judea in 59 or 60 CE.

Afterword

A small, seemingly insignificant loose thread in the New Testament's biography of Yeshua gnawed at me for years. Why didn't the Sanhedrin execute Yeshua after finding him guilty of blasphemy? It was a capital offense under Jewish law whose required punishment was execution by stoning. One day after reading the sentence officials of the Sanhedrin should have dragged the prisoner outside of the Hall of Hewn Stones and stoned him to death.[213] The New Testament book of *Acts* records Stephen, a follower of Yeshua, being stoned to death after conviction by the Sanhedrin.[214] Likewise, Josephus records the Sanhedrin executing James the Just, the brother of Yeshua.[215] Why was the case of Yeshua treated differently? Instead of executing Yeshua the chief priests took him to Roman prefect Pontius Pilate declaring they lacked authority to execute the accused. Even Pilate found this action by the chief priests odd for upon receiving Yeshua into his custody at the Praetorium he told the chief priests, "Take him yourselves and judge him by your own law."[216]

A potential solution to the paradox comes from the case of Paul of Tarsus. He too stood trial before the Sanhedrin and, when it appeared the Jewish authorities may execute Paul, Roman soldiers intervened taking him into protective custody.[217] The

---

213 "According to the *Mishnah Sanhedrin* 4.1 capital cases are to be held during the day and the verdict must also be reached during the day. * * * If the verdict was guilty they must wait until the next day [to execute the prisoner]." CSI: Gethsemane to Golgotha by Steve Rush (PublishAmerica, 2005) at page 25.
214 *Acts* 7:54-60.
215 *Antiquities* XX 9:1 (201).
216 *John* 18:31.
217 *Acts* 22:30 – 22:10.

reason given in *Acts* for the Romans saving Paul from execution at the hands of the Sanhedrin is that Paul possessed Roman citizenship making him immune from prosecution by local tribunals. If Yeshua were a Roman citizen this fact explains why the chief priests declared they lacked authority to execute him. However, very few Jews born in Palestine during the reign of Herod the Great were Roman citizens. The son of a poor Galilean carpenter would not normally be among the small number of elite Jews holding Roman citizenship during the first century of the Common Era. The actions of the Roman prefect of Palestine recorded in the New Testament support the theory that Yeshua was of Jewish royal blood. Pontius Pilate nailed a board to the cross proclaiming Yeshua to be king of the Jews.[218] The chief priests protested that Yeshua only claimed to be king of Jews yet Pilate refused to change the wording of his proclamation.[219] How does a Galilean carpenter's son of ambiguous parentage come to be recognized as a legitimate Jewish king by the Roman prefect of Palestine?

Adding to the mystery, we have this passage from the Talmud:

> On (Sabbath eve and) the eve of Passover Yeshua the Nazarene was hanged (tela'uhu). And a herald went forth before him 40 days (heralding): Yeshua the Nazarene is going forth to be stoned because he practiced sorcery and instigated and seduced Israel (to Idolatry). * * * They hanged him on (Sabbath eve and) the eve of Passover. * * * *With Yeshua the Nazarene it was different, for he was close to the government.*

Yeshua In The Talmud by Prof. Peter Schäfer (Princeton University Press 2007) at pages 64-65 translating b Sanh 43a, *emphasis added.*

---

[218] *John* 19:19.

[219] *John* 19:21-22.

Something is wrong with the accepted biography of Yeshua handed down to us by the New Testament. Alternative evidence indicates Yeshua was not born into the humble circumstances we have been led to believe. I argue Yeshua was instead the scion of a noble, wealthy and royal Jewish family. Modern scholarship widely presumes Yeshua's claim to the Jewish throne rested upon descent from King David. That position ignores the fact that a descendant of King David had not sat on the Jewish throne for more than 600 years at the time Yeshua was crucified by the Romans. Even more troubling, the synoptic Gospels of *Mathew*, *Mark* and *Luke* each record Yeshua saying to the Pharisees that the Messiah was NOT a son of King David of the tribe of Judah.[220] Here is *Luke*'s formulation.

> Then Yeshua said to them, "How is it that they say the Christ is the Son of David? David himself declares in the Book of Psalms: 'The Lord said to my Lord, sit at my right hand until I make your enemies a footstool for your feet.' David calls him 'Lord.' How then can he be his son?"[221]

Obviously, Yeshua refers to himself in the third person as "the Christ". Thus, the first sentence quotes Yeshua saying, "How is it that they say I am the Son of David?" Yeshua then goes on to use *Psalm 110* to support the argument that the Christ (i.e., another name for the messiah and the office held by Yeshua himself) was a position higher than that held by King David and, therefore, the Christ was not a Son of David.

This line of reasoning brings us to a difficult hurdle to clear—how could Yeshua claim to be the Messiah and a Jewish king if he was not a Son of David? What other Jewish clan held legitimate claim to the Jewish throne? The answer to the second question is the Hasmonean dynasty. Josephus uses the phrase Jewish "royal blood" only in reference to the Hasmoneans and never in reference to the descendants of David.[222] The

---

220 See *Matthew* 22:41-45, *Mark* 12:35-37, and *Luke* 20:41-44.
221 New International Version.
222 See *Vita* 1(2) and *Antiquities* XIV 16:4, two of many examples.

Hasmoneans were high-ranking Kohanim priests of the tribe of Levi who spearheaded the overthrow of Greek Seleucid reign in Israel.[223] The Hasmonean triumph over the Greeks and their Hellenized Jewish allies lead to the cleansing of the Temple in Jerusalem. This act is celebrated in the present day feast of Hanukkah. Decades after capturing Jerusalem and the high priesthood, the Hasmonean rulers also claimed the Jewish throne thereby simultaneously holding the office of high priest and king, the only time this occurred in Jewish history. The Hasmoneans were extremely powerful rulers during their brief reign of roughly 100 years. "Maccabees" is another name applied to the Hasmoneans, whose exploits are recorded in books 1 and 2 *Maccabees* found in the Roman Catholic bible (but not protestant Christian bibles) and, also, in the works of Josephus.

The best evidence for the theory that Yeshua was a Hasmonean prince comes to us from the *Gospel of Luke*. The Gospels of *Matthew* and *Luke* contain inconsistent genealogies for Yeshua. The Roman Catholic Church explains the inconsistency by asserting that the genealogy given in *Luke* is actually that of Mary the mother of Yeshua while *Matthew* records the ancestors of Joseph the carpenter. I accept this premise regarding *Luke*. Three early names found in *Luke*'s list of Yeshua' ancestors point toward Hasmonean royalty. Below appears *Luke*'s list of ancestors opposite the ancestry of the last Hasmonean king, Mattatayah Antigonus.[224]

Luke Chapter 3	Hasmonean Rulers
Heli	
Matthat ←	← **Mattatayah Antigonus**
Levi	**Aristobulus II**
Melchi	**Alexander Jannai**
Jannai ←	
Joseph	**John Hyrcanus I**
Mattathias ←	← **Mattathias Maccabee**

[223] The Hasmonean triumph over the Seleucid Empire and subsequent cleansing of the Temple in Jerusalem is celebrated in the present day feast of Hanukkah.
[224] Mattatayah is a variant of Mattathias.

The name "Melchi" means king in Hebrew and appears in *Luke* in a generation corresponding to the Hasmonean dynasty (i.e., the only Jewish kings of this period were the Hasmoneans). Melchi's son was named "Levi", the priestly tribe to which the Hasmonean kings belonged. Further, Melchi's father was given as Jannai, the name of a specific Hasmonean king (Alexander Jannai). According to *Luke* an ancestor of Yeshua named Jannai had a son named Melchi (king) and a grandson Levi (priest). The only kings from the tribe of Levi were the Hasmoneans and Jannai was the best-known king of this dynasty.

But isn't the messiah supposed to be a descendant of David of the tribe of Judah? Judaism of the first century CE was more pluralistic than today's Rabbinic Judaism. Texts from the Dead Sea Scrolls such as *Jubilees* speak of two messiahs, one from Levi and the other from Judah. The *Aramaic Levi Document* (fragments of which were also found at Qumran) goes a step further naming the messiah of Levi as the dual priest-king who shall lead the Jewish people. My book ***Herodian Messiah*** (Tower Grove Publishing 2010) makes the case for the theory that Yeshua presented himself as the messiah of Levi alluded to in the Dead Sea Scrolls and was the grandson of King Mattathias Antigonus. Please refer to that work for more information on this theory.

21915812R00258

Printed in Poland
by Amazon Fulfillment
Poland Sp. z o.o., Wrocław